Ten Year Stretch

Edited by
Martin Edwards and
Adrian Muller

Poisoned Pen Press

in association with
No Exit Press
and
CrimeFest

The twenty brand new crime stories in this book have been specially commissioned to celebrate the tenth anniversary of CrimeFest, described by the Guardian as "one of the 50 best festivals in the world." Contributors come from around the world and include the legendary Maj Sjöwall who, together with partner Per Wahlöö, was the originator of Nordic noir. The editors are Martin Edwards and Adrian Muller. Martin Edwards is responsible for many award-winning anthologies and Adrian Muller is one of the co-founders of CrimeFest.

Contributors to *Ten Year Stretch* are:

Bill Beverly, Simon Brett, Lee Child, Ann Cleeves, Jeffery Deaver, Martin Edwards, Kate Ellis, Peter Guttridge, Sophie Hannah, John Harvey, Mick Herron, Donna Moore, Caro Ramsay, Ian Rankin, James Sallis, Zoë Sharp, Yrsa Sigurðardóttir, Maj Sjöwall, Michael Stanley, and Andrew Taylor.

First published in association with CrimeFest simultaneously in the UK by No Exit Press, an imprint of Oldcastle Books Ltd, and in the US by Poisoned Pen Press

10 9 8 7 6 5 4 3 2 1

Library of Congress Control Number: 2017963404

ISBN: 9781464210549 Trade Paperback
ISBN: 9781464210556 Ebook

Editors: Martin Edwards and Adrian Muller

Poisoned Pen Press
4014 N. Goldwater Blvd., #201
Scottsdale, AZ 85251
www.poisonedpenpress.com
info@poisonedpenpress.com

Printed in the United States of America

Dedicated to Jane Burfield,
without whose generosity
this project would not have been possible

Contents

Foreword

When my first novel, a not-very-good spy thriller titled *Dead Letter Drop*, was published in 1981, my then publishing contract with WH Allen stipulated the book must be a minimum length of 50,000 words. My finished book was a hair's whisker just over that minimum, clocking in at a skeletal—by today's standards—203 pages.

At the WH Allen Christmas drinks party, the sales director came up to me and asked if I could please write a bigger book next time, as the fatter the book, the better perceived value it was to the consumer—as they were all the same price!

Twenty-five years later my publishing contracts for my Roy Grace and other novels require a minimum of 80,000 words.

When Adrian and Miles asked if I would write the foreword to this terrific anthology, with contributions by the A-list of crime writing, it set me thinking about two questions. First, does size matter? And second, how do we define a short story? Indeed, in today's increasingly short-attention-span world, just how blurred are the boundaries defining fiction?

How short does a short story need to be before it

becomes a novella? And when does a novella become a novel?

Ernest Hemingway is credited with writing the shortest story in all of fiction with his intensely powerful and moving six words: *For sale, baby shoes, never worn*. Another I love is the anonymously attributed: *The last man on earth sat alone in a room. There was a knock on the door.*

The origins of the short story are unclear, but what is certain is that they go back to the earliest roots of storytelling. Aesop's fables, like 'The Tortoise and the Hare', written around 620 BC, are among the first examples. My favourite is the one about the wolf and the lamb:

The wolf, meeting a lamb that had strayed from the fold, resolved not to lay violent hands on him, but to find some plea to justify to the lamb his right to eat him. So he addressed him by saying:

'Lamb, last year you grossly insulted me.'

'Indeed,' bleated the lamb in mournful tone of voice. 'I was not then born.'

'Then,' said the wolf, 'you fed in my pasture.'

'No, sir,' replied the lamb. 'I have not yet tasted grass.'

'OK,' the wolf said. 'You've drunk from my well.'

'No!' protested the lamb. 'I've never drunk water, because up until now my mother's milk is both my food and drink.'

Immediately the wolf seized him and ate him, saying, 'Well! I won't remain hungry, even though you refute all my allegations.'

The tyrant will always find a pretext for his tyranny.

Aesop's vast canon of fables were morality tales. Each one leaves us thinking, amused, shocked, pensive. There are few novelists, past or present, who have not written short stories. I love writing them, but I find them incredibly hard. It may sound an odd thing to say, but in many ways I find it easier to write a novel of 120,000 words than a short story of just 2,000. In a full-length novel you have the luxury to explore characters, set up dramatic scenes, and to put in diversion and even red herrings. In the short story you have, constantly, the memory of those six words of Hemingway around your neck, like an albatross.

Or the elephant in the room, perhaps?

In 1814 the Russian poet, Ivan Andreevich Krylov, wrote a fable—or short story, depending on your definition—called 'The Inquisitive Man'. It was about a man who goes to a museum and notices all kinds of tiny things, but fails to notice an elephant.

The true beauty of short stories is that they enable all of us to explore themes about the human condition in a sharp, succinct way, free of the constraints of the diktats of a novel. Dip into this anthology and pull out the nuggets of characters, situations, life in the raw. You're going to have a rough ride, your eyes jerked wide open, and a good time, for sure!

Peter James
peterjames.com

Introduction

Ten Year Stretch is a special book to celebrate a special occasion. This collection of brand-new stories by leading crime writers marks the tenth anniversary of CrimeFest, a convention in Bristol for everyone who loves the crime genre. During the past decade, CrimeFest has grown steadily, and is now a 'must' for readers and writers alike. The atmosphere is relaxed and convivial, the panels, interviews, and talks invariably of high quality. No wonder the *Guardian* described CrimeFest as one of the fifty best festivals in the world.

The genesis of this book can be traced to the generosity of one woman, an enthusiastic delegate right from CrimeFest's early days. Jane Burfield, a benefactor of the arts in her home country of Canada, approached CrimeFest organisers Myles Allfrey, Donna Moore, and Adrian Muller with the idea of offering sponsorship to mark the convention's ten-year milestone. *Ten Year Stretch* is the result. What better way to promote crime fiction than a collection of fresh works by some of the world's leading practitioners, all of whom have previously attended and who enjoy an especially warm relationship with CrimeFest?

The concept of a celebratory anthology reflecting CrimeFest's international flavour was immediately attractive, and so was the suggestion that profits should go to the Royal National Institute of Blind People, for which CrimeFest has raised substantial funds over the years. The support of two very good publishers, No Exit Press in the UK, and Poisoned Pen Press in the US, was enlisted. I was delighted to be asked to become editor—who wouldn't seize the chance to become the first to read a brand-new story by Lee Child, Jeffery Deaver, Ian Rankin, or...?

The list of illustrious names goes on, as a glance at the contents page reveals. Of course, globally, best-selling authors are much in demand, and have countless calls on their time. But the support that the distinguished contributors have so readily and generously given to this project has been striking. There could be no clearer illustration of the regard in which members of the crime-writing world hold CrimeFest.

Scandinavian crime fiction has enjoyed enormous popularity in recent years, and CrimeFest has welcomed leading exponents of Scandi noir, along with talented authors from right across the globe. Three years ago, Maj Sjöwall, half of the legendary team of Sjöwall and Wahlöö, who were responsible for ten superb and ground-breaking books featuring Martin Beck, was a guest of honour. Maj has—to universal regret—not published a crime novel for more than forty years, but to our delight she agreed to allow publication of one of her short stories, which has been freshly translated into English for the first time.

Plenty of other unpredictable treats are to be found within these pages, as you might imagine with contributors as varied as James Sallis, Yrsa Sigurðardóttir, Michael Stanley, Sophie Hannah, and Simon Brett. There are nods to the traditions of the genre in general, and to the 'locked room mystery' in particular, as well as a glance into the future. Two stories introduce new detective characters who may just return again to solve further cases one day. My belief is that a good crime anthology offers an eclectic mix of stories, something (I hope) for everyone who loves the genre. The contributors have certainly delivered.

I've been lucky enough to take part in CrimeFest conventions right from the outset, and I've never missed one. Like many other people, I have lots of happy memories of time spent at the Marriott Hotel in the second half of May. Not just the programmed events, either. Conversations at the bar, Crime Writers' Association get-togethers, drinks, and meals with a host of delightful authors (yes, and publishers and agents, too!), awards ceremonies, even the occasional award—you name it. The convention has become a hugely popular gathering-place where writers mingle with fans from Thursday afternoon until lunchtime on Sunday. In 2017, it was even the unlikely setting for an impromptu meeting of the Icelandic chapter of the CWA. With CrimeFest, as with a good crime story, you should always expect the unexpected. And you can certainly expect to have fun.

The crime-writing community is a warm and generous one, and Jane's support of *Ten Year Stretch*, which enables the organisers to present a complimentary copy to every delegate at CrimeFest 2018, is a very good illustration of that enduring truth. I'd like to thank all the contributors (and Maj's translator!), as well as the publishers. Most of all I'd like to thank Adrian, Donna, Myles, and other team members—such as Liz Hatherell—whose hard work makes CrimeFest such a wonderfully friendly convention. Here's to the next ten years...

Martin Edwards
martinedwardsbooks.com

The Hired Man

Bill Beverly

Rent was due in four days. My first check would come in five. Neither date was flexible, I'd been assured. My roommates… let's just say the vacancy was because they'd burned the last roommate's shit and beaten him up when he complained. The house was a short walk from the bus lines on Lake and Hennepin, nice old rooms, an attic that smelled of good wood. And four guys to say hi to every day: Bjorn, Rik, Erik, and Henry.

But they were jackals. Four chairs around the table. A calendar in the kitchen with one day circled: *rent due.*

I'd spent my first three weeks and all my money in Minneapolis trying to find work. The fourth week I'd labored at the Northern, scratching up my next month's rent. As for my employer: well, Cook told me not even to ask Manager, Curtisall, for an advance on pay. I'd gone straight to Curtisall anyway. He shook his head. 'That's something you'd have to ask Johnny Bronco.'

'Who is Johnny Bronco?'

'Mr Bronco,' said Curtisall, 'is the friend of the man who owns the Northern.'

'Pardon me, but what the fuck do I care about this friend?'

I'd shown up on time for work every day so far, and I had already been promoted. So I was feeling my oats. But Curtisall shushed me and flashed two L shapes with his thumbs and first fingers.

I said, 'What's that?'

'Guns,' said Curtisall, 'these hands are guns, Ice Cream. They have guns where you come from?'

I guess I was stupid, because Curtisall added, 'You don't ask the Twin Cities mob if you can get your check early. Even one day.' And then he said not to curse in the restaurant. For Minneapolis runs on its manners, Curtisall reminded me.

I was moved up from Bus to Ice Cream my second day—it just wasn't that good a restaurant anymore. On the third day, just before closing, the man in the blue suit came through the dingy white chute of a kitchen to the ice cream counter. I was still learning everything. I read the notes off the wall, recipes and instructions, for every dish, even the things I'd made fifty times already, like banana splits. At the Northern, scoops had to be round and tight. One scoop went in the round dishes, two in the wide, and for two, the instructions said something like, *The scoops should match each other like buttocks, same size, same roundness.* The notes said how much whipped cream went on the sundaes and where the nuts on a banana split went and how much chocolate you put in a chocolate malt. I would have thought it was *all* chocolate.

Suddenly the old man stood beside me. He said, 'You the new Ice Cream?'

'That's me,' I said. Cook. Dishes. Waitress. The bartender was Keep. I'd been Bus and today they had a new Bus, but he was a black kid about seventy-nine pounds, who could barely heft a tub, might have been eleven or twelve. He wasn't gonna make it.

'Ice Cream, you are doing a damn good job,' the old man said, and slapped me on the chest. When I looked down, there was the top inch of a fifty poking out of my shirt pocket.

The only fifty I had.

'Thanks,' I said. 'Good to hear.'

'I might look old,' he said, 'but I know how to swim with the current. You make them just right. That vanilla malted'—I dully recalled making it, twenty minutes ago—'most of these bastards, not enough soda water, they make it too sweet.'

Catching the spirit of the moment now, I said, 'I'll be sure of it.'

'Most of them,' he said, 'they never should have become Ice Cream in the first place. You aren't like them.'

Not like them. Where had I heard that? The week before, when I'd finally got my courage up to go visit Ingrid Ericsson, my college classmate, the day before I dragged myself into the Northern (where the *help wanted* sign had been so long in the window that its red had faded to yellow). I had caught the Lake Street bus over to St Paul, hoping to find Ingrid home—I had left two phone messages and talked to her once, for a feverish half-minute, until she had to break off to go sit down to dinner—and come to find out that the buses weren't cooled, or this one wasn't. By the time I disembarked, I was just a sweaty kid aswim in my blazer and blue tie, and now I was introducing myself to Ingrid's mother, on the front step of the Ericsson house, where Ingrid, unfortunately, was not in. Mrs Ericsson asked me was I Swedish or Norwegian or Danish. None of them, I said, my parents met in Valdosta. She smiled tightly. It was not going well.

The front step was wide and deep, trimmed in marble of bluish-grey, veined with something between green and silver. I took a deep breath and looked up the street. Maybe there are grander streets than Summit Avenue, bigger homes and larger trees, but there was no street anywhere like that in Ocala, Florida, my town. Sure, Ocala had money: we had orange barons and strip club owners and concrete magnates and jai-alai syndicators and mid-level Mafiosi fixing games at the frontons. We had a few old landowners with spreads by the groves, ranches and missions and seven-column plantation mansions. But this boulevard, the dark stolidity, shaded brick and heavy frames and winter-thickened trees with muscular roots—this home, whose address I had memorized long ago from the Student Directory, was the home Ingrid never talked about. She would mention her family's lake house up past Duluth, and the ranch in Wyoming, its thousands of acres: these places birthed *stories*, tales of things she'd seen and snakes that reared and a time she broke her arm. These stories were already sepia-toned as she told them, especially when she reminisced about the hired man named LeeRoy, who was *so* skilled and so funny, and when he'd had a little to drink would do carnival riding tricks atop the horses, feats of strength and dexterity. LeeRoy had died one day, jumped off a horse and just *hit funny*, Ingrid said, and five minutes later his heart beat its last and they buried him in the field that he loved.

Poor LeeRoy, I'd say, and she'd laugh, her eyes rolling back from the yellow Hawaiian weed I splurged on at home and brought up to school for the occasional hour when she would smoke it with me.

'Thousands of acres,' I'd say, rolling another joint. We had never kissed, but we would, given time. In this I had faith. I was putting in the work.

'Thousands,' giggled Ingrid Ericsson.

That poor, funny, deceased hired man. Sometimes it felt like I'd known him too. Maybe, there on the front step, I should have said I had. But instead I told Mrs Ericsson, straight up: 'Your daughter is the reason I came to Minnesota.'

Mrs Ericsson reached out and sampled the damp lapel of my blazer between her fingers. The softly lighted foyer glimmered beyond her, what little beyond her I could see.

'She has plenty of friends, and some boys with high hopes,' she said. 'You aren't like them.'

'What does *that* mean?'

That, Mrs Ericsson did not explain. After barely another minute of discouragement, she excused herself, asking if I knew where the bus stop was. I walked back to Marshall Avenue and caught a bus back across the river.

St Paul was built on these great avenues running east to west, named for men—the Marshalls, the Daytons, the Jeffersons—whose ambition and energy had run east to west, straight and unbroken. In my Minneapolis neighborhood, all the name streets ran north-south, tight one-way strings in a triangle like an autoharp, tuneless, pinched, in alphabetical order, packed with little Nissans and Mazdas. As if here, men would be less grand, nowhere as grand as the scheme. And even the scheme existed to be hijacked, laid waste by lesser men, men like the one I would become in my interview blazer and tie, if I could ever get somebody to call me back.

•••••

On a Sunday, Waitress had a lot to carry, and sometimes there was a party. That day, bridesmaids. When Curtisall stuck in his head and said, 'Ice Cream, go out and bus,' I didn't complain. I took off my rubber gloves. Bus was cleaning up some disaster in the front window. I headed to the party on the upper level.

On the upper level, we could seat four fours, three twos on the back wall, the big roundtable which went twelve seats without crowding, and the four enclosed booths along the right wall with their fringes of strange wooden beads. Smoking wasn't allowed, but on the upper level, everything was smoked. It smelled real up there, like a grandfather's pipe, like cigars.

Sunday's bridesmaids had fanned out wide—over the whole level. Gifts everywhere. I mean, the lucky couple was going to need counter space. All these women would look at home in Ingrid Ericsson's foyer on Summit Avenue. Pink gums, white teeth, hard calves below the hem: rollerblading till the snow fell, cross-country all winter.

They were only a couple years older than me, but I didn't even put on my game face.

I had a gray tub. Filled it twice and came back. I mean, there were fifteen or sixteen of them. I had to step around all of it: the bridesmaids, the chairs, the extra tables they'd shifted over because *Why not?* They'd all arrived in jackets, though it was August, and everything they'd shed had to be hung up on chairbacks here, in their presence—none of it could go on hangers down front, on the rack below the carved sign that read *Since 1913*.

The moment, looking back, had three parts. The first was the bridesmaids' final gift.

The final gift was like some wondrous invention of a century past—a sort of ornamental perpetual motion machine, with ocean-blue marbles scooped up by the tails of a ring of spinning dolphins and flipped to the center, where they rolled out again across a lacquered ocean to the outer rim where the dolphins scooped them again. It made a casino-like clinking and rattling, and the dolphins spun industriously, and who knows what powered it, a battery or a spring or some principle of movement the celebrants had kept from the rest of us, whose motions might by it be someday spared. There were delighted gasps, and I slowed down to watch.

As the bridesmaids vied, taking pictures, the bride-to-be decided that the last traces of luncheon visible along the table would not do. 'Would you,' said the bride-to-be, waving inconveniently below her camera phone, '*take* this?'

I wasn't sure what she meant. But I was mannerly about it. 'Take what, ma'am?'

'This.' She waved the sort of backhand you use to scoot away a gnat.

The *this* was an enormous cut-crystal tray with divots in it, I could only imagine, for five or six dozen devilled eggs. They had not brought it in full of devilled eggs. Instead, the tray had borne their vast white luncheon cake. Coconut frosting, and full of booze—I could smell it from across the room. It complemented the smokiness.

'The tray?' I said. I wasn't sure what to do. I'd only been Bus for nine or ten hours—I hadn't encountered all the permutations. Now all the bridesmaids stared. 'It isn't our tray,' I said.

You didn't want to pick up a crystal tray like this one, not on a good day, much less carry it with your gray battle

Bus tub through a minefield of purses and chairs and gift bags strewn. And a third of a cake on it, uneaten. A cake as big as triplets.

Maybe I wasn't getting it. Maybe my problem was the cake. 'Your Server can put the cake in a box.'

The bride turned on me, and now I saw the face her husband would see forever. To be honest, I quailed.

'You don't want to put a tray like that in the dishwasher,' I added.

'I just wanted you to *move* it,' she steamed, 'if you're not too *stupid*.' And then the second thing happened. Immediately the beaded curtains on one booth smashed all a-clatter as the one person there clambered up and came out.

It was the same old guy—vanilla malted, fifty dollars—in the blue suit. He wobbled out past the beads, the hanging light swinging behind the swinging beads, so that suddenly the room became a tiger-rush of light and shadow. He reached out for me, his eyes going big in their sockets.

But I followed the directions, I thought.

The nearest rim of bridesmaids seemed to crumble away from him. The old man's nostrils whistled once, twice, before I understood what the other hand, the one at his clavicles, meant.

He was choking.

I dropped the bus tub on top of someone's purse. I grabbed him, spun him round, slapped my arms around him and found the lowest ribs with my forearms, joined my hands. The lapels of his jacket were damp, curiously hot. He had an old man's bowl to his belly. But his frame felt so bony, so light.

No time for conversation. I remembered my first aid training, cinched him in, and clenched upwards.

On the very first thrust, a ragged, colorless chunk of something went end-over-end, cleared the bride's coiffure and disappeared into a gift bag. The old man gurgled and drew air.

The bridesmaids went silent.

I let go of the man in the blue suit and asked whether he was all right. He waved his hand, but he didn't reply, didn't even look back. With some dignity, he regained his booth, slipping through the beads and taking his place at the table.

And I just picked up the tub and got as far from that cake as I could.

•••••

I told Curtisall, 'I don't think I can go up there again. I just gave some old guy the Heimlich, and the party, they were freaking out.'

'Some old guy? Johnny Bronco?'

Somehow, in circling to the kitchen with my tub of margarita glasses and cake forks, I'd forgotten that the choking man was Johnny Bronco.

'Stop. Stop, stop,' said Curtisall, who'd been joking about something with Cook, I hadn't quite caught what, but I was the joke now. 'You gave Johnny Bronco a Heimlich manoeuvre? You, like, grabbed him and hugged him? Was he choking?'

'Why do you think I did it?'

'Did he say anything to you?'

'Not a word. He went back in his booth. What kind of name is Johnny Bronco, anyway?'

'It's a *beautiful* name,' Curtisall said.

'*I might look old*,' Cook mimicked the old man. '*But I know how to get through to the youngsters!*'

Cook and Curtisall exchanged a glance.

'You should go home. Right now,' said Curtisall. 'I can do Ice Cream. Just—don't go home. Take twenty dollars and go to the lakes. Take your girl to the lakes.'

He seemed panicked, so I handed him the Bus tub. Stripped off my Ice Cream smock. The twenty he gave me was a ten.

It wasn't even two o'clock. So I went ahead to the lakes. I walked around Lake Calhoun, Lake of the Isles. High school kids throwing a football. Couples were twenty-five, thirty, forty, fifty. I sat for some time, hours, trying to catch the spirit of being twenty-two in Minneapolis, young, single, free, gainfully employed, on my way up to somewhere, something, anywhere. Anything. It was a crisp, bright summer day.

All I could come up with was: I hated Minneapolis. They all knew each other. I hated the connected lakes, all ten thousand of them. I had come five hundred miles to chase a girl who only talked to me because of my dope. I could see the truth, and it wasn't much thornier than that.

There was one thing to do. Get more dope.

'You got a phone call,' said Bjorn, the youngest of my roommates. For the first day or two, I thought Bjorn and I were going to be friends. He had one of those chin beards that climbs up to tickle the lower lip, inflaming it weird and red, like something you'd uncover petting a guinea pig. He had a collection of records he kept in the living room in open crates, displayed. But when I'd studied them, he said, 'Is there something I can help you with?'

'Who called?' I said.

'I don't know.'

'What did they say?'

'Not sure,' said Bjorn. He was sitting at the table circling jobs in the want ads. He already had a job, but he was always getting a new one. All my roommates had jobs. Rik, Erik, and Henry were all entrepreneurs. One was in telecom, the other in sports foods, I forget which.

'These guys, they'll fuck you up if you don't pay on time,' Bjorn had shared with me, those first days, before the looking-at-the-records thing. 'By on time, I mean that day, not midnight. Before dinner.'

'So, by six. Six p.m.?' I'd said.

'If you leave a check in the morning, that would be best,' said Bjorn. But then I learned he'd been as cruel to the last roommate as anyone. He was the one who struck the match.

I slept fine. I'd picked up an irksome sunburn, hanging out at the lakes half the afternoon. The next day was Monday and my shift started at eleven. If you ordered ice cream before eleven, you got whatever Cook could make you. Or maybe Dishes.

Curtisall saw me coming in the door and he slid in beside me and took me to the bar.

'Didn't you listen?'

I said, 'I'm not sure what you mean.' Curtisall was standing, but I took a stool at the bar, put my elbows up. It was a nice bar, the Northern's, the best part of the place, old neons glowing in the corners: Grain Belt. Gluek's. Kato. I couldn't afford a drink there, but it was nice to sit. The bartender didn't report till eleven, either, so if you ordered a Manhattan, you got whatever Cook could make you. Or maybe Dishes.

Curtisall was sniffly. He had a cocaine thing. I didn't judge. It wasn't pretty, being a manager.

'I told you never to come back here.'

'You told me to take my girl to the lakes.'

'That means to never come back. I even gave you twenty dollars.'

'I don't even have a girl,' I said. 'You gave me ten. You're firing me?'

'It's not that,' said Curtisall. 'It's Johnny Bronco. You never should have touched him.'

'I should have let him choke? What about a thank you?'

Curtisall dithered with his hands. He reached over the bar, drew out a glass that was mostly clean, and poured me a long drink of red. 'Thank you,' he said. 'Is that sufficient? College boy? Can we move along now? Here are the undisputed facts. You grabbed a gang lieutenant, Johnny Bronco, by the ass.'

'I grabbed him,' I said, beginning, maybe, to understand. 'I grabbed him *around*, and then, I guess, that's what I did.'

'I don't need the blow-by-blow. Do you understand that a whole crew of starlets saw you humping the guy?'

'I wasn't humping him.'

'There are pictures,' Curtisall said. 'I know what you think. But no one gives a shit what you think.'

I opened my mouth, but he had a point.

'Curtisall, how many bridesmaids are there,' I asked, 'in a typical wedding?'

Curtisall shrugged. 'Maybe four,' he said. 'That wasn't typical.'

'I wasn't humping him.'

'Kid,' Curtisall said, and then he poured himself a red too. We drank in silence, him sniffling and dabbing a little at the finish on the bar top, me thinking: Maybe I am a grown-up now. I'd had my first legal drink a year before, my first whiskey with my ex-father at fifteen, my first tequila sick at twelve. But this silence in the bar felt like a debut of sorts.

Curtisall finished his drink, fumbled the glass into the sink. We both pretended we hadn't heard it break. 'Anyway, you should get the fuck out of here. Because—I hate to spell it out for you—but you embarrassed him. He might need to hurt you.'

'To *hurt* me?' I said, with an unfortunate chirp.

'You embarrassed him,' Curtisall said again.

'So you're not on my side in this. You're firing me. Can I get paid today then?'

'Friday,' said Curtisall.

Four more days. 'What if I'm not around?'

'We mail it to the address on file,' Curtisall said.

'If you were a better manager,' I said, realizing, with one gulp of wine left, that he was conceding me the right to be pissed off, 'you'd front a kid his week of pay when he gets fired. Because he saved a mobster's life.'

'I know, Ice Cream,' Curtisall said. 'I know.'

That was the third part of the moment.

'If I'd trained you better,' Curtisall said, 'you'd know it: back slaps before the abdominal thrusts.'

Now I was rubbing at clouds in the varnish too. 'I went for it.'

'Brave of you.' He stood and tossed my glass to break beside his in the sink. 'Now beat it, kid.'

• • ● • •

At the big post office on Thirty-first, I changed my address. You filled in name and particulars on a small, grey form of incalculable cheapness. So cheap and grimy that it felt impossible that anyone would ever read it. Yet the address change form worked. I'd done it twice already that summer, first when I moved from school to Mom's. My mom and I drove each other nuts for three days, till I got in the Plymouth and didn't stop till I had found a room just across the river from Ingrid Ericsson and given half my money for first month's rent.

Now I rerouted my mail back to my mom's. There wasn't much to reroute. But I'd rather she get the check than my roommates.

I fished out Curtisall's ten-dollar bill and sat in a woody old bar on Lake that had happy hour all afternoon on Mondays: Special Export drafts, a buck apiece. I drank eight, watched TV. The bartender was named Dolores. Other than that, nothing.

I thought about taking the bus over to St Paul, throwing myself on the mercy of Ingrid Ericsson's father—whom I'd never met. But I had no plan to get past that front step. Chasing Ingrid to Minnesota had been my only plan after college, and it wasn't good. I hadn't even wound up in the same city.

Mobsters in Minneapolis. Maybe Curtisall wasn't kidding. I had the fifty-dollar bill I'd earned for following directions. Maybe that could get me on the first bus, take me down 94 to Chicago. But never all the way back to Ocala.

I walked back, a little crooked, a little drunk, to the house on Girard. I sat down on the porch for once—in the shade with four chairs, savoring my buzz and the falling evening. It was quiet. Really quiet.

Inside, tied up in the hall, where apparently he'd been all this time, lay Bjorn, my roommate. I looked at him: he shook his head. He didn't make a sound.

I can't say I minded seeing him trussed in yellow rope. Someone had done it expertly, efficiently—none of this eight-times-around-the-ankle shit you see on TV.

'Hey, Bjorn, what's going on, man?' I said.

His red lip quivered, a warning. He pointed his head at the dining room.

One thing they say about the dead: they all belong. Ashes to ashes. I went in to face the music.

At the table sat my three roommates, quiet too, cuffed together, like three people at a séance, saying strange prayers. Over them stood Johnny Bronco—in a black suit today—casually turning something, which at first I took to be an oversized flashy corkscrew (the bridesmaids had had one with them) but then I recognized as a silver silencer on the tip of a large gray gun.

So this was how it would be. When the killing was all over, they'd say about me: And he was planning to move out that week. He'd even forwarded his mail.

'Hello, Ice Cream,' Johnny Bronco said.

'Hello, Mr Bronco,' I announced. 'Curtisall suggested you might come by.'

Johnny Bronco said, 'We expected you back a couple hours ago.'

'I went out and had a few beers.'

'I understand,' Johnny Bronco said. 'Say, I met your roommates. They've been sitting here waiting with me. And haven't shit themselves, not a one of them. Commendable.'

My roommates glared. Rik had a gash, bleeding over one eye; Erik, a bloody nose. Henry was unmarked.

I shrugged. 'How come Bjorn has to lie in the hallway all by himself?'

'There aren't enough chairs.'

'Right.' And then the courage that burned upon me was like the glory of an afternoon wind. I was twenty-two and ready for anything.

'So, Mr Bronco, you come to shoot me? Because if so, let's get it over with. Minneapolis-style.'

The eyes of my three roommates went left-right-left over the dinner table.

Johnny Bronco's face lit up. 'Shoot my best Ice Cream?' He pointed the gun for the first time. At me. It was shiny and ancient at the same time. 'Kid, there's something you got to get straight. I wasn't choking.'

'It was my first week,' I said. 'I was overzealous.'

'First you're supposed to use,' he said, and dropped his aim, stirring the air with the silencer until the right words bubbled up. 'Back slaps. Back slaps first.'

'They teach it different ways.'

'I don't doubt it,' Johnny Bronco said. 'Back slaps is what you're supposed to use. If you're following the directions.'

'Next time,' I said. 'Let's hope it's never you.'

'Let's fucking hope,' Johnny Bronco said. Then he put away the long, outlandish gun in the pocket of the black suit, which hid it perfectly, silencer and all.

I knew that talking with men for the rest of my life was going to be like this, like taking that first drink with my father. You had to throw it down fast and pretend you liked it, no matter how it tasted. You had to be ready to hurt each other, to be hurt. If you handed off money, do it with a slap. If you smashed one glass, smash the others.

'I'm sorry, Johnny Bronco,' I said. And I was. Not that

I had saved his life, or embarrassed him. But I'd come in understanding nothing. Four years of college hadn't taught me a goddamn thing.

'Ice Cream, forget about it,' he said.

He considered my roommates, and for a moment he eyed Henry, who was still unmarked.

'You little pricks. This kid pay rent to you?'

'*Yeah*,' said Rik. 'Two hundred a month. It's due Friday.'

'Was I talking to you? I'm talking to pretty boy here, with the white collar.'

Henry nodded.

'Well, maybe I might look old, but I get to the point,' said Johnny Bronco. 'You baby fucks, you wet green little baby fucks without a spot on you, you can pay his rent. Work it out between you.'

'Yes, sir,' Henry said.

In the kitchen, the telephone awakened, ringing ring after ring. But I didn't care who it was, or if it was even for me.

Johnny Bronco turned to me. 'Ice Cream. You want to get out of this place?'

I said, 'It depends on what you mean.'

The Last Locked Room

Simon Brett

When I was growing up, I was very close to my grandfather. His name was Dietrich Gartner. I knew he was famous, but I didn't at first know what he was famous for. It was much later I discovered that he had achieved fame in two distinct areas.

The time I am talking about was 1939. My name was then, as it is now, Barnaby Smithson, known later, in my professional career, as Barney. My father, Alec, was in the Navy, always away in other parts of the world on increasingly secret missions. My mother, having never really bought into the notion that charity began at home, was out of the house more and more, manically busy with charitable works. So I spent a greater amount of time in my grandfather's company than many boys of seven would have done.

Dietrich Gartner, though more fluent in the language than many Englishmen, still had a marked German accent. His daughter had shed hers very quickly after marriage, just as she had adjusted her given name Rosa to a more conformable Rosemary. She now lived in England

and consciously suppressed any nostalgia she might have had for her German background. In the same way, she denied that the family was Jewish, an attitude that pained her father, who was proud of his origins. But no, once the family had moved to Brighton, Rosemary Smithson wanted every new person she met to think of her as an ordinary, respectable married Englishwoman. Which was why she called her son Barnaby.

And why she gave Barnaby a very detailed list of things he should never say. He, too, should never admit that his mother's family was Jewish. Had he known that he had been conceived in Hamburg, where his father was on another secret mission, and before his parents were actually married, he would have been forbidden to say that too. Above all, he should never say that his mother was German. Given the prevailing mood of the British people, Rosemary Smithson did not wish to give any ammunition to potential bullies at the boys' prep school where her son, Barnaby, was being processed into an English gentleman.

Unaware of the implications of any of my mother's proscriptions, I was happy to go along with them. In the cause of domestic harmony, I knew better than to argue with her. She was a woman of violent moods, particularly as my father began to be absent for increasingly long periods. I was never allowed to ask what my father actually *did*, but I knew it was something clandestine, and probably dangerous. That knowledge built up in me a fascination with secrecy and duplicity, a fascination which spending so much time with my grandfather did nothing to discourage.

Of one part of Dietrich Gartner's fame I did have an inkling because of the rows of books with his name on the spine, which had pride of place in the sitting room of his mansion flat in Hove. At least, when I say *his* name, I am not being strictly accurate. The name on the books was Richard Treeting. And I still remember the excitement when my grandfather introduced me to my first anagram. 'Richard Treeting,' he explained to me, was made up from the letters of 'Dietrich Gartner.'

I loved the beauty, the simplicity, the pure logic of the construction. It set me on a path of God knows how many hours wasted poring over the grids of crosswords. And led to endless frustration in boring school lessons as I tried to produce a meaningful anagram of my own name, Barnaby Smithson. Compared to the elegance of 'Dietrich Gartner' becoming 'Richard Treeting,' I knew that 'Toby N. Brissanham' didn't really cut the mustard. I felt a level of resentment towards my parents for not having provided me with a more versatile name.

It was some years after my grandfather's death that I found out how apposite his using a pseudonym was. The books he wrote under the name of Richard Treeting were crime novels, specifically in a subgenre very popular in the 1930s. They were 'Locked Room Mysteries,' in which murder victims were found in locations to which the perpetrator had no evident means of entrance or exit.

My grandfather did not push me to read his own books. He reckoned, quite rightly, that they were too grown-up for a seven-year-old. He did, however, encourage me towards Conan Doyle's Sherlock Holmes stories, for which I developed an early and enduring addiction.

He also talked to me about how he wrote his books. 'It is all logic, Barnaby,' he said. 'As with Sherlock Holmes, it is all based on logic. Every impossible puzzle eventually will yield to logic. It is only when there is no logic that everything else is lost.'

In my early teens, needless to say, I lapped up every available Richard Treeting novel, intrigued by the puzzles, trying to understand their logic, but also feeling that the books provided a link to my much-missed grandfather. And I felt proud of his reputation as a master of the Locked Room genre.

It was quite a lot later that I found out the other area of life in which Dietrich Gartner had found fame.

One of the things I loved about my grandfather was that he spoke in quotations. I don't mean that he quoted from other people, but that many of his own utterances were so perfectly observed and perfectly phrased that I remember them to this day. Maybe speaking in his second language—and indeed writing in his second language—made him particularly careful about the way he composed his sentences.

To take an example, I remember an incident from early on in that summer of 1939. I was a day boy at my prep school and frequently, when lessons ended, I would go to my grandfather's flat rather than to our family home. He, I knew, would be there, while my mother's presence, depending on her charity commitments, was less reliable. I had keys to both places, and would let myself in, unannounced, at either of them. At the mansion block in Hove, I would scamper eagerly up the flights of stairs to the third floor, 'one from the top.'

My grandfather always acted surprised, as if he was not expecting me, but his ready supply of bitter milk-free tea and pastries betrayed the preparations he had made for my arrival. He always referred to these delicious confections as *kuchen*. He got them from a specialist shop in Hove, and he always bought enough to give some to Mrs Blaustein, the widow who lived in the flat below his. 'Mrs Blaustein likes her *kuchen*.'

My grandfather's sitting room was wallpapered in dark green. His heavy furniture, dressers, tall chairs and yards of bookshelves, were made of solid, sombre wood. Once there, I always felt as though I was in an impregnable cocoon of safety. In winter, we would snuggle up close to the open fire, blazing in its almost-black stone setting; in summer, we sat in front of the vase of fresh flowers always placed in the empty hearth. My grandfather had no char to keep his home clean and tidy. He did everything domestic himself. Apparently, he had cultivated this independence ever since his wife had died of breast cancer in her early forties. But that had been back in Hamburg, long before I was born. He never spoke of his wife, nor did my mother ever mention her mother. For her it would have been a reference to the past she wanted to expunge from the records. I don't know the reason for my grandfather's reticence on the subject.

After my post-school hunger had been sated, we would then, according to the weather, play word games or go for a walk along the seafront. On our walks, when we reached the promenade, we always turned left, towards Brighton. Sometimes, once we got to the West Pier, we would part, I on towards the Palace Pier and the home I shared with my mother, he back to his flat. When, occasionally, I turned and watched his frail figure making its way through the crowds, I was aware of his age. While he was talking, Dietrich Gartner and I were contemporaries. When I could not hear his voice, he was an old man.

Those walks were precious times for me. My grandfather

made no concession to my age; he talked to me like an adult. And his conversation ranged widely over literature, history, and science. But he never spoke about contemporary politics or the way the international situation was developing. It was not that he did not have an interest in such matters; he just did not talk about them to me.

On our walks, there were sometimes treats. In spite of being filled up with his delicious *kuchen*, I could never resist the offer of a stick of rock, which I would suck avidly, constantly intrigued by how the manufacturers made the word 'Brighton' stay in place all through its length. My grandfather gave me many explanations for this phenomenon, but since most of them involved forest-dwelling trolls, I knew he was teasing me.

That particular afternoon, probably June 1939, as we walked along the prom, we passed a man selling brightly coloured balloons, which he filled with gas from a tank behind his stall. There was an infinitely exciting hiss as each rubber neck was attached and removed. I did not ask, but my grandfather could read the envious look I cast towards the precious objects, and he bought me one. A yellow balloon, I remember, yellow like the sun.

'Do not let it go, Barnaby,' he said. 'Maybe I should tie a loop in the string, then we put it around your wrist, so it will not fly away…?'

'No,' I said. I think my resistance was based on the fact that small children often had reins fixed around their wrists to stop them from straying. And I thought myself far too grown-up to need any such encumbrance. 'I will hold on to it tightly.'

But of course, I didn't. Within minutes, distracted by a small dog growling at its owner, I had loosened my grip, and could only watch as my yellow balloon lifted vertically until, caught in a cross-wind, it made steady, almost stately, progress out to sea.

I turned to my grandfather in dismay. 'Ah,' he said, 'there go our hopes. They are as vulnerable as that balloon. We have just seen the last glimpse we will have of freedom for many years.'

That's what I meant when I said he talked in quotations.

It was not long after that moment on Brighton seafront that my grandfather died. I later found out that the time of death was probably in the small hours. But in those days before mobile phones or excessive consideration of the feelings of the young, no message was sent to my school and it was the end of the day before I knew that something was wrong.

I went, as I so often did, straight to the flat in Hove, in greedy anticipation of black tea and *kuchen*. As I entered the main doors of the block—no security locks to negotiate back in those days—I felt, as always, into my grey flannel shorts pocket for my grandfather's key.

But when I arrived on the third-floor landing, 'one from the top,' I found the closed door blocked by a stout uniformed policeman.

'Can't go in, sonny, I'm afraid,' he said.

'But I'm going to see my grandfather. That's where he lives.'

'Sorry. You can't go in.'

'What's happened?'

'Don't you worry about what's happened, sonny. You go home to your mum.'

I tried further persuasion, but the policeman remained

unmoving, both in bulk and argument. So, I followed his instructions and went home, where I found my mother in deep hysterics being looked after by one of her neighbours, whose expression suggested that she had had one too many such calls for emotional support.

I got little information about the circumstances of Dietrich Gartner's death. Though in a state of deep shock, I sat dry-eyed through his funeral, and hardly heard the reassuring words spoken to me at the post-service reception in the Old Ship Hotel. One word that none of those hushed voices used was 'murder.'

•●⬤●•

Surprisingly, I got more information from school. There was a boy in the class above me called Larkin (nobody possessed a first name at boys' prep schools in those days). He had a habit of singling me out from the rest of my classmates. The way Larkin behaved towards me could not have been described as 'bullying.' 'Taunting' was nearer the mark. He saw me as someone at whose expense he could get cheap laughs. Some of these, though I did not understand the references at the time, were based on what he had somehow intuited was my Jewish heritage.

Larkin was not a boy to get on the wrong side of. For a start, as boys of ten can, he had suddenly had a growth spurt, and stood a head taller than the rest of his class. Even more impressive was the fact that his father worked for the Brighton Borough Police as a Detective Inspector. To me, fed on Sherlock Holmes stories and my grandfather's conversation, that had to be the most glamorous profession in the world.

It was a few days after the funeral. Most of the boys

in my class were playing an improvised game of cricket, using a tennis ball and a dog-eared school hymn book as a bat. I would have been with them, had I not been cornered behind the library by Larkin.

'So, *Smithson*...' He always started like that, elongating the vowels of my surname so that it sounded like something vaguely unpleasant. 'It's not everyone who can say his grandfather was murdered, is it?'

'Are you saying that mine was?' I asked uncertainly.

'Oh, yes,' he replied with great certainty. 'My old man dropped a few hints about it.' When Larkin had started at the school, he had referred to his father as 'Dad,' but he quickly learned to change that. A father who was a Detective Inspector, though impressive to my eyes, did not match up socially to most of the school's line-up of parents.

'Of course, he can't really talk about his work at home—for professional reasons,' Larkin went on rather pompously, 'but occasionally he lets things slip.'

'Oh?' I said, still not sure whether this was another of his long-winded wind-ups.

'Your grandfather lived in a mansion flat in Hove, didn't he?'

'That's right.'

'Where a lot of the Chosen Race live.'

I didn't know what he was talking about, so I made no comment.

'He was killed by a gunshot wound to the head.'

'Really?' I tried not to let the shock show in my voice, but failed.

'The murder weapon hasn't been found.'

I didn't risk another comment.

'The flat was locked, and it's up on the third floor, isn't

it?' I nodded. 'They can't work out how the murderer got in or out of the place.' Larkin corrected himself. 'That is to say: they can't yet work it out. But they will.' He didn't want to cast aspersions on the competence of his worshipped father. 'They've taken a lot of documentation away from the flat.' He was using the long word to make himself sound more authoritative.

'What kind of d-d-documentation?'

It was obvious he didn't know the answer, so he just said, rather grandly, 'I'm afraid I can't reveal that.'

'You promise me you're not making all this up, Larkin?'

'Cross my heart and hope to die.' He paused portentously, then announced, 'My D–, my old man reckons the murder was the work of a Nazi assassin.'

I knew what 'assassin' meant, but it was the first time I had heard the word 'Nazi.'

'That's what he reckons, and of course he knows about these things,' Larkin continued magisterially. 'My old man reckons everything's going to hell in a handcart. He says that there's no logic to what's happening these days.'

I knew that Larkin's father was wrong. As Dietrich Gartner had told me, there was logic to everything. The challenge was to find that logic.

It was not until some time after the war that my mother and I were told that my father was not coming back. Gallant Alec Smithson had helped to defeat Hitler by sacrificing his life in some secret mission for British Naval Intelligence. Whether my mother was ever informed of the exact circumstances of his death, I don't know. I was certainly never told.

The news precipitated my already volatile mother into a full-scale nervous breakdown. By then at a boarding public school (my fees paid for by a grateful nation), I was spared the worst of the initial trauma, but I did inherit from it a woman virtually on permanent suicide watch. During the term times, I was to some extent insulated by rugby or cricket, according to the season, but the emotional strains of the holidays were considerable. If any school sports tours or foreign trips were offered for those times, the name 'Smithson, B.A.' would be the first on the list.

When my mother did die (of natural causes, breast cancer) in her early forties (maybe some hereditary link there from her own mother), I have to confess my predominant reaction was relief.

My initial response to the news of my father's death, however, was one of disappointment. I felt disappointed that I would go through the rest of my life fatherless, but I did not feel grief. I had not seen enough of my father as I was growing up to feel that kind of emotion. Besides, all the grief my thirteen-year-old self could produce was still focused on the loss of my grandfather. Hence the almost manic reading and rereading of novels by Richard Treeting. Maybe I hoped he had hidden some message for me in their pages. But I didn't find it.

●●●●●

I made steady, but unspectacular, progress through my public school. There was some talk of my trying for Oxbridge, but by then the determination to pursue my chosen career was so engrained that my teachers did not argue when I said I wanted instead to go to Hendon Police College. At that time degrees were not thought to be of much benefit to potential police officers. So, in my last term at school I had the honour of captaining the First XI cricket, and then I was out in the real world.

By then, I had come to terms with the bereavements of my life. My father I never thought about, and the death of my mother, soon after I started my training, was, as I said, just a merciful lifting of responsibility. She had been well served by the Navy's pension provisions, so I inherited the Brighton house. This I promptly sold, putting the proceeds into a flat of my own in Muswell Hill.

I still remembered my grandfather, but the anguish of his loss settled down over the years into a mild regret. And I was so absorbed in the career towards which he had inadvertently directed me, that I had little time to think of him.

It was therefore a great surprise, soon after my twenty-first birthday in 1953, to receive a solicitor's letter, informing me that I was the sole beneficiary of the will of Dietrich Gartner. I inherited very much more money than I would have expected, and was able to trade up from the flat to a large family house in Muswell Hill. My grandfather's largesse allowed me a much more varied London social life than most of my contemporaries in the Met.

In time, I met and married Jane, and I think ours would have qualified for the description of 'a happy marriage.' We didn't have children, and I never felt the loss. Looking back from the perspective of retirement, I was something of what would now be called a 'workaholic.' My career was everything to me. Though Jane never complained, there was, at times, a sadness about her. Since she's died—cancer again—I've come to the conclusion that the sadness was probably something to do with our lack of children.

I did well in the Met—rose to the rank of Detective Chief Superintendent and, in the Queen's Birthday Honours in 1991, the year before I retired, was awarded a CBE. More valuable to me, though, was the respect of my colleagues. At my farewell do, the Commissioner described me as 'one of the finest detectives in the force,' and said that I 'would never give up until I had hounded down and arrested the perpetrator of a crime.' And my track record was particularly strong, he announced, 'when it came to the solving of cold cases…'

Then he added a line which was greeted with a huge laugh: '…that is, if Barney's attention could ever be drawn away from his crossword!'

It showed the Commissioner had done his research. My habit of diverting myself from the complexities of the case under investigation by trying to solve the *Times* crossword was notorious throughout Scotland Yard. I knew my colleagues made fun of me about it, but on more than one occasion concentration on an abstract problem had helped me to look with new eyes and achieve a breakthrough on a real one.

I can't say I took well to retirement. My work had been so much the centre of my life that I had few other resources. The false camaraderie of the golf club, which attracted many of my former colleagues, was not for me. And, though I was wealthy enough to travel to any destination I chose, there was nowhere I particularly wanted to go. I was also surprised how much I missed Jane, and I felt an unsettling guilt about how little attention I had given her during my working life.

By November 1992, only six months after I'd retired, I was, quite frankly, bored.

And then my next project became clear to me. Finally,

I had time to reconsider the great unsolved crime of my lifetime. The coldest of cold cases. Perhaps it was the lack of a grandson to whom I could communicate my enthusiasms, as Dietrich Gartner had to me, that made me think again about my grandfather's death.

•●⬤●•

The first thing I did was to reread all of the Richard Treeting Locked Room Mysteries. Maybe, amongst the many 'impossible' murder methods, I would find how the death of Dietrich Gartner had been staged.

But though I enjoyed revisiting the stories, admired their skill, and again felt they brought me closer to my long-dead grandfather, nothing I read got me any nearer to an explanation.

•●⬤●•

One thing the police have always been good at is keeping records. Some got destroyed by fires caused by enemy action during the war, but the Brighton Borough Police's archives for 1939 fortunately remained intact. And—coppers stick together—there was no problem about allowing access to them for a retired officer with my distinguished track record.

The archivist in Hove was very helpful in finding the relevant files. He also very generously gave me permission to photocopy the contents and take the copies with me when I left. I'm not sure that was technically legal, but once again the coppers' old boy network proved its worth.

Though maybe in the future such information will be keyed into computers, what was handed over to me came in a reassuringly old-fashioned manila file. On it, 'Dietrich Gartner' was written in black ink longhand. Across the name had been stamped in faded blue the single word: UNSOLVED.

The papers inside were crisp with age. Some were joined together with old-fashioned treasury tags. Paper clips had rusted and bled brown into the documents they clasped.

The cover page was a standard form about the details of the investigation. It gave me a frisson to see the name of the officer in charge of the case. Detective Inspector Derek Larkin. Must be long dead. I wondered if his proud son was still alive. We'd had no contact since he'd left the prep school we both attended.

The photographic evidence in the file, seen so long after the event it recorded, disturbed me profoundly. The faded monochrome images placed me exactly back in the flat where I had last seen my grandfather. He lay back, in his usual dark wooden chair, close to the fireplace. And, though there was little black blood to be seen from the neat bullet wound on his temple, it pained me to see the reality of Dietrich Gartner dead.

Still, I was trained in viewing horrors and I scrutinised the photographs obsessively, looking for anything that struck a discordant note, any clue that might point me in the direction of a solution.

But I could see nothing, and turned my attention to the documentary evidence.

It was then that I found out, as well as his eminence as Richard Treeting, writer of crime novels in English, my grandfather's other claim to fame. Up until 1933, he had been Herr Professor Dietrich Gartner, a very distinguished academic who headed up the School of European History at Hamburg University. His fall from grace had been predictable and precipitate. It was not long after Hitler's appointment as Chancellor that Jews in many German universities found themselves jobless. Seeing the way the wind was blowing, and under intense emotional blackmail from his daughter, it was then that Dietrich Gartner had left the home of his birth to join her. Once in England, he had never spoken again about his academic achievements. Instead, he started up his new career as Richard Treeting, writer of Locked Room Mysteries.

The researches of Detective Inspector Larkin—or more probably of his juniors in the Brighton Borough Police—had been extensive. As well as this basic biographical sketch, they had found out a lot more about the murder victim. Before being hounded out of his job, the professor had been a vocal critic of the Nazis. He and a fellow don at Hamburg University, Herr Professor Samuel Levisohn, had co-edited a monthly magazine called *Grosse Freiheit*. The title, Larkin's researcher pointed out, had been ironic, referring both to a street in the city's red-light district, but also to the 'great freedom' to which Gartner and Levisohn aspired, in the face of Hitler's bully-boys.

The magazine was, unsurprisingly, closed down in 1933. But there was a suggestion that the two professors might have stayed in touch through the 1930s, and continued to work undercover for the destruction of the Nazi regime.

The likelihood of this was supported by the presence in the file of a newspaper clipping from the *Völkischer Beobachter*, official newspaper of the Third Reich. It was printed in Gothic font and I spoke no German, but one of Larkin's team had been thoughtful enough to provide a translation. Dated May 1939, the report recorded the execution by firing squad of one Samuel Levisohn 'for espionage and crimes against the state.'

The clipping had been found on a table beside the chair in which my grandfather's body lay.

Detective Inspector Larkin's report suggested that the news of his old friend and collaborator's execution might have been sufficient motive for Dietrich Gartner to take his own life, 'were it not for the fact that the circumstances of the death make a verdict of suicide impossible.'

Larkin then went on to detail those circumstances. The bullet which had killed my grandfather came from a Luger Pistole 08, a weapon carried by German soldiers during the First World War. Whether Dietrich Gartner himself possessed such a gun was not known, but it was possible. What made it impossible to find out exactly how the death had occurred was the absence of the murder weapon itself.

And also the absence of evidence as to how the perpetrator managed to enter or exit Dietrich Gartner's flat. The front door was locked on the inside and its key had been found on the table beside the deceased. The block had no fire escape to allow access from outside. All of the sash windows had been locked shut and there was no broken glass or other sign of forced entry.

Perhaps at another time the investigation would have lasted longer, but with the outbreak of war there were more pressing demands on police resources. A clearly frustrated Detective Inspector Larkin concluded the most likely scenario was that Dietrich Gartner had been killed by a Nazi assassin. The victim might have avoided the fate of his former associate, Samuel Levisohn, in Germany, but no one—wherever they hid themselves—could escape the justice of the Third Reich forever.

As to how this conjectural Nazi assassin had effected the crime without leaving any trace, the Inspector could offer no explanation.

The murder was, in fact, the perfect example of a Locked Room Mystery.

•••••

Though many owners had come and gone in the previous fifty-odd years, and the interior décor had been gentrified beyond all recognition, no structural changes had been made to the mansion block in Hove. That November Monday morning, the current occupants, a family with two small children, were very happy for me to look around the flat where I had spent so much of my childhood. They knew nothing of the mysterious death which had taken place there, and I did not mention it. No point in upsetting them unnecessarily. My visit, I claimed, was just an old man's nostalgia trip.

Obviously, although I expressed polite interest in the rest of the flat that I was shown around, my focus was on the sitting room, the scene of the crime. The dimensions were exactly as I remembered them, but white-painted walls made it seem larger. Children's toys scattered across the floor, together with early attempts at primary school art Blu-Tacked here and there, aided the transformation. The old sash windows had been replaced, but with near-identical modern replicas, which must have cost a pretty penny. Maybe some listing restrictions for the block prevented changes to the look of the windows. The replacements had bright brass latches, just like the ones that had all been locked when my grandfather died.

The big change to the room was the fireplace. Gone was the dark stone hearth in front of which I had spent so many happy hours. In its place was an ornate cast-iron structure of Edwardian, or possibly even Victorian, provenance. In front of it stood a vase of fresh flowers.

'Do you use that?' I asked. 'Ever light it?'

The young mother who was showing me round shook her head. 'Oh no, it's just for show. We've got gas-fired central heating. Nice, though, isn't it?'

I conceded that the redundant fireplace was rather splendid.

'Anyway,' she went on, 'there'd not be much point in having an open fire here. You're only allowed to burn smokeless fuel, no logs or anything. And smokeless fuel fires are so…I don't know, somehow soulless. I'm happier with the gas on a day like this, thank you very much.' She shivered theatrically as she looked at the cold rain against the windows.

'So, nobody in the block has an open fire, do they?' I asked, more to make conversation than anything else. I'd the feeling that the room had no secrets to reveal to me. Seeing it had just been an *aide-mémoire*, and I didn't want to outstay my welcome.

'I don't think anyone does,' the woman replied, '…oh, except for Mrs Blaustein in the flat below.'

It seemed incredible to me that Mrs Blaustein, the widow for whom my grandfather had always bought extra *kuchen*, was still alive. Having never met, and only hearing his accounts of her, I had somehow assumed they were contemporaries. Also, when you're seven, you tend to think all old people are the same age. And the word 'widow' implied a level of seniority. But maybe Mrs Blaustein had been very young when she lost her husband.

The lady—she was definitely a lady, not a woman—who opened the door to me was probably in her eighties.

Her grey hair, rigidly fixed in place, suggested a recent visit to the hairdresser. She wore a simple dress in a flowered print. Only her feet, swollen under Velcro-strapped sandals, betrayed her age.

Once I had identified myself, her welcome was immediate. The sitting room she ushered me into almost made me catch my breath—it was so like my grandfather's. It was not just that the two flats had an identical floor plan, hers, too, had the dark green wallpaper and the original stone fireplace. In it, as the mother upstairs had suggested, shone the anaemic glow of smokeless fuel.

While Mrs Blaustein went to the kitchen to prepare her hospitality—black tea and *kuchen* she promised me—I scanned her bookshelves. They were not extensive as my grandfather's, but, in pride of place, I saw the vertical spines of all Richard Treeting's *oeuvre*.

I felt that at last my investigation was making progress.

Unlike a lot of old people, Mrs Blaustein had no desire to talk about herself. She knew that my interest was in the death of my grandfather, and so that was what she concentrated on.

'I was actually away on holiday in Sidmouth when he died.' Her voice still bore a trace of her German origins. 'I was very shocked when I heard the news.'

'The police didn't question you?' I recalled that there had been no mention of her in the file I had scrutinised with such attention.

'No. I did come back to find a letter saying they wished to talk to me.'

'Would that have been from Detective Inspector Larkin?'

'Yes, you are right. I remember the name. But he never followed up the letter. Having not been here at the time,

I was probably not much use as a witness. Anyway, then war was declared and everything went haywire. I was not surprised there was no follow-up.'

'But if the police had questioned you, what would you have told them?'

'About why Dietrich died?'

'Yes.'

'I would have thought it was most likely suicide.'

'Really? Why?'

'He was very depressed.' I had to remind myself that she was talking about the man who had always been so welcoming and cheering for me. 'He was depressed being here in Brighton, that his daughter was so determined to deny her Jewish heritage. That you, his grandson, would never have a *bar mitzvah*. Dietrich often said to me that here in England too, people wanted to destroy Jewish culture. He was afraid the whole world would follow Hitler's example.

'And then, of course, every day he would hear of some new horror from Germany itself. Dietrich could not see any future—or he could not see any future for the kind of world he wanted to live in. It brought him very low; he saw the end coming of everything he had believed in. But the real blow, I think, was the news of the death of a much-beloved colleague.'

'Samuel Levisohn?'

The old woman nodded approvingly. 'You have done your homework—good. Yes, even though he was in England, Dietrich still worked to bring about the collapse of the Third Reich. In those endeavours, Samuel Levisohn was his accomplice—his soul mate, too, I think. The news of his death destroyed all hope in Dietrich. He could see no way forward. I think then he shot himself.' She spoke with the certainty of a truth which she had never doubted for over fifty years.

'I understand the logic of what you're saying…' that word again—my grandfather's favourite—'…but I'm afraid the circumstances in which he was found rule out the possibility of suicide.'

Mrs Blaustein, not having viewed the file that I had and having had to rely only on the gossip of the time, had no idea about the locked doors and windows, or the absence of a weapon. So I spelled out the details to her.

At the end she said, 'It is like one of the Richard Treeting Locked Room Mysteries.' She spoke with approval, and with relish for the puzzle that she had been set.

But sadly, though we discussed the subject at great length over our black tea and *kuchen*, nothing she said brought me any nearer to a solution.

As I left, she made me promise to let her know when I did work it out. She'd said 'when,' not 'if'—a confidence in my abilities, which at that moment I felt to be misplaced.

Then at the front door she held me back for a moment. 'There is something I should give you. Something that might help.'

She disappeared into the sitting room and came back with a notebook, whose fading marbled covers were coming apart at the spine. 'He gave me this. His notebook.'

'Dietrich Gartner's notebook?'

'No,' said Mrs Blaustein. 'Richard Treeting's notebook.'

• • ● • •

It was not till I got back to my study in Muswell Hill that evening that I opened the notebook. There was a ceremonial air to the moment. Now at last the solution to my grandfather's death was within my grasp.

Imagine my disappointment when I found that Richard Treeting, though writing his books in perfect English, wrote his notes for them in German. Even if I could have deciphered the closely written gothic script, I did not have the language skills to make head or tail of his scribblings. And without an understanding of the accompanying text, the hastily sketched diagrams meant nothing either. I had friends who could translate for me, but there was nothing else I could do with the notebook that evening.

I turned restlessly back to the 1939 scene of crime photographs, photocopied from Detective Inspector Larkin's file. I had looked at them so many times I knew every detail by heart, but I thought maybe my recent viewing of the modernised room in Hove might prompt some new perception.

Again, I was disappointed. The photographs looked exactly as they always had done.

I turned to my usual resource in such circumstances, the *Times* crossword, the displacement activity to which the Commissioner had drawn attention at my retirement party. I'd done the journey down to Hove by car, so this was the first chance I'd had to look at the puzzle. Being a Monday, it was a relatively easy challenge, and I quickly filled in the bottom right quadrant.

Then I came across a clue which gave me a moment's pause. 'Mechanical flower and test (10).' Attuned to the compiler's thinking, I knew the solution would be a word that either meant 'mechanical' or 'test.' The 'flower' was part of the answer. I went through a few variations of flowers without too many letters… 'rose,' 'pink,' 'daisy…but didn't get anywhere.

Then suddenly I remembered how much crossword setters like the ambiguity of the word 'flower.' Yes, it could be 'a pretty plant with petals'; equally it could be 'something that flows'... in other words, a 'river.' I had the solution. The 'Indus' was a river, a 'test' was a 'trial,' and another word for 'mechanical' was 'industrial.'

And thinking of 'flowers', in both senses, sent me back to the scene of crime photographs.

It was so obvious, why hadn't I seen it before? The picture was taken in June 1939. In the summer. And there were no flowers in my grandfather's fireplace.

He always put flowers there. So why were there none visible on that occasion?

I snatched up the notebook, and flicked through its pages until I found the relevant diagram. A circle with a long line coming down from it, and at the end of the line the outline of something that was unmistakably a pistol.

It was a Locked Room trick which Richard Treeting had considered using—but had rejected—for one of his books. Dietrich Gartner, though, had used it in real life. To stage a real death.

My grandfather, all hope for the future gone, had sat in his chair by the fireplace. In his hand he had held the Luger Pistole 08. Attached to it was a string which was fed up through the fireplace (from which the flowers that might impede its progress had been removed) to the gas-filled balloon, maybe already floating clear of the roof.

The trigger pulled, the death achieved, the pistol had dropped from the suicide's hand, to be pulled up the chimney into the darkness of the Hove night. Then a crosswind, just as it had to my yellow one years before, would have carried the balloon and its cargo out to sea. As the rubber sac deflated, the Luger Pistole 08 would slowly have sunk into the eternal hiding place of the English Channel.

Finally, I knew I was right. I also knew that I could never prove it.

Just as my grandfather had known that it could never be proved that he had committed suicide. Otherwise, Barnaby Simpson would never have been allowed legally to inherit the money which enabled him to buy his large house in Muswell Hill.

There was a logic to it, you see. Of course there was. My grandfather, thinking of me to the end. I loved Dietrich Gartner. But I think I felt I had more in common with Richard Treeting.

Shorty and the Briefcase

Lee Child

Shorty Malone's legendary week began on Monday, when he got shot in the leg, just barely, in a sanitation department maintenance facility. His squad went in the front door, and another went in the back door, with a vague plan to outflank a guy they knew was concealed somewhere among the parked garbage trucks. Then someone started shooting, and within a split second everyone was shooting. The official report said ninety police rounds were fired that day. No one was killed, not even the concealed guy. The only casualty was Shorty, from an unlucky ricochet. Later reconstructions showed a fellow officer had fired, and his round had taken a gentle deflection off the sidewall of a tire, and then a violent deflection off the chassis rail of a different truck. After that it was badly misshapen and had spent most of its energy. It hit Shorty on the shin bone no worse than a smack with a ball-peen hammer. It broke the skin and cracked the bone. Shorty was immediately hospitalized.

After that it was awkward. It was hard to work up much enthusiasm. Shorty had been in the detective division about a year, so he wasn't a brave rookie anymore, but he wasn't yet a grizzled veteran hero either. He was a nobody. Plus it was technically blue-on-blue. There was even some doubt about whether the concealed guy actually had a gun at all. Plus a rumor it was the wrong guy anyway. Maybe his brother. So the overall feeling was the whole affair would be better forgotten. Which was tough on Shorty. Normally a shot cop would be treated with maximum reverence. Normally Shorty would have been rolling around like a pig in shit. Half a dozen hopeful lowlifes would have started up collections on the Internet. Shorty could have been looking at a decent chunk of change. Maybe even college-fund decent.

But he was ignored. On Tuesday we were all reassigned to new duties. Part of forgetting. Sure, way back in history some mistakes might have been made. But that was then. We've moved on. Now we're making progress. We all started learning the new stuff, and as a result, no one went to visit Shorty in the hospital anymore, except his pal Celia Sandstrom, who was another one-year nobody, except better to look at, unless she was wearing her Kevlar vest. Evidently, she stopped by the hospital frequently, and evidently, she kept old Shorty up-to-date on what was going on. And what wasn't.

We were assigned to Narcotics, as part of their own forgetting. All kinds of previous strategies had come to nothing. It was time to wall them off. Time to move on. Like we had. So that if someone ever mentioned a prior embarrassment, we could all wrinkle our noses and say, 'What, that old thing?' Like your girlfriend, when you tell her she looked good in her sweater yesterday. So their department was starting over, too, the same way ours had, and they swapped us in for their big new redemptive idea, which was to stop following the coke, and start following the money. Which needed manpower. Narcotics was a cash business. Cash was like a river. They wanted to see where it flowed. And how. Some parts they knew. Some parts they didn't understand. They wanted us out there, watching.

Specifically, they wanted us watching a guy delivering a briefcase from Jersey. He made the trip usually two times a week. The assumption was the briefcase was packed with paper money. A wholesale payment, maybe, or a share of the profits. One level of the pyramid scheme kicking up to the next. They said a regular briefcase could hold a million dollars. They said it was a physical transfer because money wasn't electronic until it was in a bank. Which cash wasn't yet. They said there was a clue in the name. They said our job was to evaluate the chances of witnessing a hand-to-hand exchange. Which would be two for the price of one. Plus disruption of a vital link in the chain. It was exciting work. No wonder everyone forgot about Shorty. Except Celia. She must have described the mission, the very same day, because that must have been about when Shorty started thinking.

●●●●●

The guy with the briefcase was an older gentleman. A person of substance. Somehow powdered and expensive. A very senior figure. His very presence a mark of deep respect. With a million bucks in his hand. The briefcase was metal. Some fancy brand. He carried it along the sidewalk, plain as day, all the way to an old-style office building door. He carried it inside. Ten minutes later he came out without it. We saw him do it exactly the same way the report said he always did it.

The office building had a narrow lobby with security. The directory showed twenty tenants. All bland names. A lot of import and export. No doubt a well-developed grapevine. All kinds of early warning systems. No point in asking questions. We wrote it up and sent it in. Our new bosses didn't like it. They pushed back.

They said, 'We need to know which office suite.'

We said, 'We can't get past the desk.'

'Pose as maintenance.'

'They don't do maintenance.'

'Then use your badge.'

'The bad guys would be down the fire escape before the elevator door even opened for us in the lobby. Probably the security guy controls it with a foot pedal.'

'Give him a hundred bucks.'

'The bad guys give him five.'

'Are you proposing to do any work at all?'

We said, 'First day, boss. We're looking for leadership.'

Afterward Celia said Shorty figured we were missing something. He didn't know what. He was on his back with his leg up in traction. Not medically necessary, but the union thought it would make for a better photograph in the newspaper. Shorty was fretting about us, Celia said. He was missing us.

'Shorty who?' we said.

We came in Wednesday morning and as expected found the business with the fancy briefcase already going a little lukewarm. Expectations were being retrospectively downgraded. It was a solid piece of data, another brick in the wall, as intended, nothing more.

Then, even before the coffee was made, it went right back to the top of the agenda. New evidence came in, from a different direction, and it pointed to the same office building. To a specific tenant. They knew for sure the specific guy was sending money out. Now they wanted to square the circle. They wanted to see the same money going in. They wanted eyeballs inside the specific guy's suite. They wanted eyewitness testimony, about the older gentleman maybe placing the briefcase on a table, and the other guy maybe spinning it around and clicking the latches with his thumbs. If we could get close enough to seize the actual cash, well, that would be the icing on the cake.

Afterward Celia said, 'Shorty says obviously that's all impossible.'

We said, 'We don't need the voice of doom drifting down a hospital corridor to tell us that. Of course it's all impossible.'

'So what should we do?'

'Nothing. Maybe they'll move us to Vice. Which wouldn't be the worst thing in the world.'

But the mention of Shorty recalled the previous mention, at the end of Tuesday, which no detective liked to hear, that we were missing something. No one said anything out loud, but I know we all surreptitiously and individually checked everything we could, from the beginning to the end, in the original files, from the handwritten notes.

The guy drove from Jersey, just him alone at the wheel, no driver, in a nice but unspectacular car, through the Lincoln Tunnel, and south, to a parking garage in the West Twenties, which was the nearest to the old-style office building. A small man in a black vest and a bow tie parked his car, while he walked out with the briefcase and set out carrying it on his long march down the sidewalk. His journey invariably ended after a block and a half in the office building lobby, where he was nodded past the desk after respectful but not casual inspection. On every occasion he spent ten or so minutes inside, and on every occasion he came back out empty-handed. Those were the facts. That was what we knew.

Celia pretended to have given the matter no thought at all, but later she said, 'Shorty is sure there's something wrong.'

Which was not what we wanted to hear right then, because the stakes had just been raised even higher. A couple more puzzle pieces had fallen into place. Suddenly the folks upstairs realized they could take out the whole chain at once. It would be the bust of the year. Medals for sure. Votes for the mayor. The whole nine yards. But they needed it immaculate. Every link in the chain had to be rock-solid on the witness stand. Evidence was key.

We argued we couldn't get it. We said instead we should bust the guy on the sidewalk, before he got to the office building, with the money still in the briefcase. Because it was legally justified to assume he was heading for the specific guy in the unknown suite. Where else would he be going? It was as good as eyeballing a transfer. Really the same thing, at an earlier stage. A different snapshot. A previous frame from the same movie.

Nothing was ever more persuasive than having no alternative, so they agreed. We waited in a ready room, for a call from Jersey. The local PD over there was watching the guy's residence. Any occasion he drove out in the direction of the tunnel, they would let us know right away. Traffic was usually bad. We would get plenty of warning. No rush at all.

But the call didn't come. Not on Wednesday. Not on Thursday. It came on Friday. Some apple-cheeked trooper out in the burbs told us the guy was on the move in his nice but unspectacular car, and seemed to be heading for Manhattan. Celia was not in the room with us at that point. She came in a minute later and we told her about the call.

She said, 'Shorty says we're thinking all wrong.'

Which was not what we wanted to hear right then, because we were trying to get all pumped up, ahead of taking a guy down on the sidewalk. But she insisted. She said Shorty had been lying there, with plenty of time to think. We should listen. We were torn. On the one hand, Celia was in the squad. She might be a nobody, but she was ours. Shorty too. On the other hand, the bust of the year was at stake. Medals and votes. Not a thing to screw up by taking the initiative. No one wanted to be the guy who blew it.

Celia said, 'Do we really believe it's legally persuasive, if we take him down on the street with a bag of cash?'

'Kind of,' we said. 'Somewhat. Maybe. Good enough, probably.'

'Would his lawyer be worried?'

'A little bit. Maybe not slitting his wrists.'

'But whatever, it's a huge hassle, right?' she said. 'It's a million bucks in cash. The IRS would get involved. Maybe the Treasury Department. Why take the risk? Why carry that briefcase so openly?'

We said, 'We know the cash is moving from A to B. We know the guy inside is receiving it. How else would he be getting it, except from our guy? No one else goes in and out. And people carry all kinds of things in this city. They carry briefcases full of diamonds, worth much more than this guy.'

'Shorty thinks it's a decoy. He thinks the case is always empty. They're teasing us. They want us to take the guy down. They're begging us. That's their plan. They want us to open the case and find nothing inside. Shorty says we'll look like fools. He says we'll never get another warrant again. Judges will just laugh at us. We'll have to leave those guys alone for years. That way they win.'

We said, 'One guy is paying the other guy money. We know that. That's a real fact. Because it's a chain. A lot of people are depending on us to do our part right. We need the evidence.'

'We can get it,' she said. 'But not on the street. That's not where it is. Shorty says you're right, one guy is paying the other guy money. But not the way we think.'

'Then how?'

'In the parking garage. The guy leaves the cash in the trunk. Maybe in a supermarket bag. The parking attendant takes it out and puts it in the other guy's car. Which is always there because that garage is convenient for the office building. The real handover is out of sight and out of mind. Everyone is distracted by the shiny briefcase.'

No one spoke.

Celia said, 'Shorty says it's a win-win for us. We can check the car real quick, as soon as the guy is out of it, and if after all there's nothing in it, then we can always catch up to the guy in a couple of steps, and take him down anyway, like we're supposed to. Shorty says we have nothing to lose.'

The phone rang again. The Port Authority cops, at the Jersey mouth of the tunnel. The guy had just come through the E-Z Pass.

We got going. We waited in the parking garage.

Nothing to lose.

• • ● • •

Shorty was right. The cash was in a yellow plastic grocery bag in the trunk of the guy's car. As evidence, it was as good as anyone else got, and better than most folks. It contributed mightily to the bust of the year. In front of Celia we felt inhibited about claiming all the credit for ourselves, so mostly we told the truth, and as a result the story got out quickly, about a hero cop shot in the leg on Monday, who then lay in his hospital bed and fought through the agony and by Friday had engineered one of his new department's most spectacular successes, all through brainpower alone. He got a medal for his leg, and another for the parking garage, and then he was in the newspaper, which is what ultimately made him a legend. The union was right about the photograph. It helped a lot.

Moses and the Locked Tent Mystery

Ann Cleeves

My name is Moses Joho. I work at Cheetah, a tented camp in the Ndutu conservation area, close to the Serengeti National Park. We accommodate people who are on safari; they come looking for adventure and for the game that lives on the short-grass plains. I do whatever is needed to look after our visitors, but at night, my job is to keep them secure. When they first arrive, our guests laugh at the idea of security. They have head torches, and solar panels provide power for the lamps that light the path to their tents, so why would they need an African man to guide them? In the morning, I show them tracks made by lion, and the branches ripped off big trees by an old male elephant and they realise that there's a reason for my concern. They see then that I don't just accompany them in the hope of more dollars or Tanzanian shillings in the tip box, but because I want to keep them safe.

Often security in the Serengeti camps and lodges is provided by Maasai, but I am not Maasai. I come from

Pangani on the Indian Ocean, and I miss my family and the salt smell of the sea. I am here because this is where the work is. The wealthy Americans and Europeans come to Tanzania to see lion, cheetah, and leopard and to watch the herds of wildebeest and zebra move across the plains like the shadows of clouds blown by the wind. My dream is to be rich enough to run wildlife tours from my home. It is a beautiful place and I speak English well, so well that I won the English language prize at my high school. So I come here each year between the short rains and the long rains, and every shilling I earn goes into a bank account to make my dream come true.

It is hard work at Cheetah. There are no days off. At the beginning of the season with the other men I build the camp in the space cleared in the scrub close to the lake. We put up the tents with their wooden plank floors, arrange the wiring for the solar panels and the generator, the plumbing for the flush toilets that sit, hidden by a canvas curtain, at the back of every tent. Then we furnish them with grand beds and folding chairs and decorate them with printed fabric and put down woven rugs. Once the visitors begin to arrive, there is no rest. I carry luggage from their vehicles, fetch hot water for the showers, and after dark, I provide security. At the end of each evening, I guide our guests from the large mess to the individual tents. Even when they're safely delivered, I remain on duty, parading the track for an hour or two. I don't resent that time. I like the quiet and the darkness. The stars that I see here are the stars that I see at home. Besides, if I can be of special help, a guest will sometimes give me a few extra dollars, and that all adds to the sum in my bank account.

The night that the Englishwoman died, nothing unusual took place until her body was discovered. She was part of a group that arrived in two Land Cruisers. I recognised the drivers who regularly bring tourists to the camp and who are good men, knowledgeable about the wildlife of the Serengeti. Besides those men who acted as their guides, there were six people in the group: two couples who shared the family name of Brookes and two elderly single ladies. The whole party was British.

It has become my habit to watch each group as it arrives. I like to get a sense of our visitors, even if they only plan to stay for one night. I admit that partly my interest is mercenary—I try to decide how generous each group will be—but partly I watch because I am a curious man. I think it will be important when I guide tourists myself to understand my customers. I have become a good judge of character. I know that the wealthiest people do not always leave the biggest tips. I am always wary of people with loud and confident voices, the ones who claim to have visited Africa many times before. Then there are the guests who expect us to provide the same level of service as the expensive permanent lodges with their elegant restaurants and their swimming pools. They complain if their shower isn't ready at exactly the time that they want it or if the power unexpectedly fails. However difficult the customer, I try to be polite and helpful; it is good practice for when I will be my own boss.

That evening, when we saw the vehicles drive up from the side of the lake, we all went out to greet them. It is important to make a good first impression. I helped the older ladies climb out of the truck and they told me their names: Valerie and Lavinia. Valerie was pale, like an owl appearing in the dusk, thin and nervous with white hair piled onto her head. I never heard her speak again. Lavinia walked with a stick. She grasped the end that had been carved with a buffalo's head, and pointed to her luggage with the other. I lifted her bag carefully onto my shoulder so it wouldn't get dusty, and led her towards her tent. Lavinia had brightly painted nails and wore lipstick to match; she reminded me of a fierce Englishwoman who came to my school to award prizes at speech day. When I set down her bag she gave me a five-dollar bill. I thought she must be a retired lady so I told her it was too much. Perhaps she was reading my thoughts because she said: 'You keep it. I wouldn't dream of retiring. I get bored so easily and how could I afford a trip like this on a pension?'

When I returned to the vehicles, only the four Brookes remained there. I studied them as I walked down the track towards them. I thought they must be a family group, parents, a son and daughter-in-law, perhaps. They were of different generations but seemed comfortable in each other's company. As I got closer, though, I decided that 'comfortable' wasn't a good word to describe them. The older woman seemed restless and decidedly *un*comfortable. They were familiar to each other, but I thought they were not happy.

I was serving drinks at dinner and I watched the family again. It was unusually quiet in the camp that night. There was just one other group—Americans who took dinner early and were almost finished when the Brookes party arrived to eat. The sound of thunder rumbled around Lake Ndutu just as the English people took their seats, and later there was a stab of lightning far brighter than the dim light provided by the solar panels. The family group seemed feverish, excitable, but I have noticed that a storm can affect visitors that way, and I thought nothing of it. The Americans got to their feet and asked to be shown to their tents before the rain came. By the time I returned, the shower had started; water was bouncing off the tarpaulin canopy loud and hard. I didn't expect it to last long. The rains had come early this year but in brief, sharp showers that were soon over.

I listened to the English people as they lingered over coffee, waiting for the rain to stop. The older Brookes were Caroline and Vincent. Vincent was Caroline's husband and eager to please. He must have been married before because the younger pair were his children, not a couple at all. They were called Michael and Alice, and I thought they disliked their stepmother, or they were frightened of her. Caroline reminded me of a hyena, watchful, in charge. She had a strong, square jaw and her eyes were expressionless as they moved round the table. They rested on Vincent.

'Where *have* you brought us, darling? I do think you could have done better than this?'

Vincent blushed and it was Michael who spoke. 'I thought you wanted the authentic African experience, Caroline. That was what you said.'

His sister giggled. She had drunk a lot of wine.

The elderly single ladies sat a little apart. They seemed to be travelling independently. Perhaps the drivers had brought them in to make up the numbers. Like me, Lavinia, the lame one, was listening to the Brookeses' conversation. I could tell she was a curious woman.

The talk moved on to business and I didn't understand much of what was said. I thought Caroline was asking them to agree to some plan. In the end, Michael said:

'Oh, why not? What difference does it make now anyway? We know you already make the decisions.'

Then everyone seemed less on edge. Vincent made a joke and they all laughed, even Caroline. At the same time, the rain began to ease.

Vincent and his children decided to have one more drink, but Caroline and the old ladies were ready for bed. The tents were grouped together, though at a little distance from each other, to form a shape like a crescent moon. Valerie and Lavinia had smaller tents at each end of the crescent, and the others were in the middle. I saw the old ladies in first; by then Caroline had unzipped her tent and was safely inside. The canvas flap was rolled up to let in the air and the entrance was covered by thick netting to keep out insects. There was a faint gleam from the solar light hanging from the roof and through the net I saw Caroline's silhouette. She was standing, raising her hands to her hair, but I saw no other detail.

By the time I returned to the mess, the others had almost finished their drinks. Soon they too were ready to leave. I shone my torch so the beam lit up the path. The rain had made it muddy and I did not want the visitors to slip. The old ladies' tents were in darkness but Caroline must still have been awake, because her light was on. She must have seen my torch because as we approached she shouted out:

'Is that you, Vincent? Why don't you invite Michael and Alice in for a nightcap? There's still a bit left in that bottle of malt and I don't feel ready for sleep after all.'

I knew that they would accept her invitation. Caroline would always get exactly what she wanted. Vincent hurried ahead like a dog anxious to do his owner's bidding and already had the netting unzipped while I was still lighting the path for his children.

'You go away to your bed, old chap,' he called out to

me. 'It's only a few steps to get Mike and Alice to their tents. We'll make sure we get them there safe and sound.'

But security is my job and I wouldn't rest until all was quiet and dark, so I just moved a little way down the track. I could still see Vincent and Caroline's tent and the outlines of the four people inside. By now they were just shadows, but I could picture where they were sitting, on folding canvas chairs around a small wooden table close to the entrance. I had switched off my torch and they could not see me.

I stood, leaning against the trunk of a big acacia tree, lost in thoughts of my own. In my head, I was reckoning the money I already had in my bank account and the cash I still needed to set up my business. I was wondering if my brother, who has a good job with the government in Dar es Salaam, might give me a loan so I wouldn't need to come back to the Cheetah camp again.

Not much later I saw that the party was breaking up. I saw the swaying of Vincent's torch as he walked his children to their tents. I watched carefully and I listened. I hadn't heard a buffalo groaning or an elephant blundering through the scrub. There *were* sounds—the scuffling of small mammals and the buzzing of insects, now that the rain had stopped—but nothing to concern me. However, it is my duty to make sure our guests get safely to their beds and I started swiftly back to the crescent of tents.

I walk quietly on my feet and I must have startled Vincent. He was standing outside Alice's tent when he realised that I was there.

'My God, man,' he said. 'You scared me to death. I told you that we could manage.' He gave a little laugh. 'But better to be safe than sorry, eh? You see me back and then you've done your duty for the night.'

We walked together the short distance back to his tent. I didn't use my torch because I wanted to save the batteries and there was a small moon. The light inside was very faint—there'd been very little direct sunshine during the day to power the solar panels—and I could barely make out the interior. I watched Vincent go in and then I turned away, ready now for my own bed. Almost immediately I was stopped in my tracks by a scream so loud and piercing that I thought it would wake the whole camp. Vincent Brookes was standing at the mouth of the tent, struggling to get out of the netting, trapped there in his confusion.

At the beginning of the season I had placed woven mats on the bare wooden planks for the comfort of our guests. When it is my turn to prepare the tents for new arrivals, I shake the mats outside in the air until the dust flies away. But I wouldn't be shaking this mat again. I shone my torch inside and saw Caroline Brookes lying inside with a wound to her head. Blood had soaked into the fibres and I could tell that the stain would never come out.

The next day I was questioned by a police inspector who wore a shining white shirt and a clipped moustache. He accused me of killing Caroline Brookes.

'All the boys here say that you're saving to start your own business. You decided on a shortcut, huh? You were searching for money and valuable items and Mrs Brookes surprised you.'

'But I showed her to her tent. I knew she was there. It was clear to me then that this Inspector Peter Raphael was a very stupid man.

He tried a different tack. 'You were in charge of the camp security. Why didn't you see anyone? Perhaps you slid away to join your friends for some beer. Or maybe you fell asleep on the job.'

I told him that I'd never fallen asleep on the job, but he'd hit on the question that had already been troubling *me*. How could Caroline Brookes have been killed without my hearing or seeing? I was there all the time. I'd have seen a stranger approaching. Even if one of the old ladies had left their tents I would have noticed. I only turned my back on the Brookeses' tent for a short while when I went to join Vincent as he was taking his children home. It would have taken longer than that to kill a strong woman like Caroline, and I would have heard the attack. There would have been a noise of some kind when she was hit and when she fell to the floor. A louder noise than the scuffle of small animals and the buzzing of insects and that was all I heard.

When I was at the Tanga High School for Boys, there were books in the library that had been donated by an Englishwoman who had once lived in Tanzania with her diplomat husband. This was the same Englishwoman who came once a year to hand out prizes to the best students. The proudest moment of my school life was when I received an award for my skill in the English language. The woman must have enjoyed mysteries because those were the books that she gave to the school and which I borrowed when we were allowed time for 'light reading.'

How I loved those novels! I enjoyed particularly the books written by Mr John Dickson Carr. He wrote stories about impossible murders that took place in locked rooms. I told myself that *this* was a locked tent mystery and I set myself to solve it.

Later that morning Mrs Brookes' body was carried away to Arusha. Police Inspector Peter Raphael had decided that her death was accidental. The woman's shoes would have been slippery with mud from the track. She'd probably fallen when my mind was elsewhere—I was known as a dreamer—and she'd knocked her head against the low table. This was nonsense, of course—I thought again what a stupid man this inspector was—but the theory made everyone happy. Timothy, the camp manager, wanted no fuss or scandal surrounding his establishment. One driver took the Brookes family to Arusha to make suitable arrangements for taking Caroline home and the other drove off with Lavinia and Valerie. I assumed the ladies would make their own way back to the UK.

By the middle of the day the camp was quiet and I began my investigation. First I inspected the inside of the Brookeses' tent to make sure there was no way for a stranger to slip in through the back. But the walls were sewn firmly onto the groundsheet before the wooden planks were placed on top. The killer must have got in through the front, unzipping the netting, and I knew from the way Vincent had become tangled, that this could be a tricky operation in poor light.

Next I looked at the canvas chairs where the family had been sitting. Their muddy shoes had left some marks but most of the footwear prints had dried and it was hard to make them out. I had been up all night and at this point I was tempted to return to my bed to rest. Then I thought of Sherlock Holmes, another of my heroes, and decided he would not have given up so easily. I concentrated on the marks left by the shoes again. I peered under the bed, where there was a little dust. At last, satisfied, I went outside and studied the footprints there. I started by Caroline and Vincent's tent and then looked at the crescent-shaped path, and the long track that led to the mess. I spent all afternoon on my hands and knees and only stopped when the first vehicle arrived in from safari, very tired but pleased with my deductions.

●●●●●

Now my life in Cheetah tented camp continues. I know how the impossible murder has been committed but I have decided I can do nothing with the information. I have no proof, and besides, I know better than to meddle in the affairs of rich Europeans. Everything seems to have returned to normal: I carry water for the showers, greet the visitors, and at night I provide them with security.

The end of the season comes with the rains. We pack up the tents and I make my plans for the future. I've almost forgotten about the locked tent mystery, when I come across the culprit quite by chance. I'm in Kilimanjaro Airport waiting to get a flight to the coast. I have decided to ask my brother in Dar es Salaam for that loan, though I have little hope of success. He is a pompous man and is more likely to give me a lecture than the money I need. Across the busy departure lounge I see the old lady. She's sitting quite still with her stick between her legs, waiting for the flight to Amsterdam. I can't think what she's been doing in the weeks since she left the camp. There's no sign of her friend Valerie. Her lipstick still matches her beautifully painted nails and she wears a silk scarf tied around her neck.

It's the scarf that makes her suddenly familiar, not only as Lavinia, the single woman travelling with the Brookes family, but as Mrs Peacock, the diplomat's wife, who loved Tanzania and donated her books to our school. Mrs Peacock, who awarded me a prize for my skill in the English language.

I sit down beside her. 'How much did the family pay you to kill Caroline Brookes?'

She turns slowly and smiles. 'Moses,' she says, 'how lovely to see you again!'

Despite myself I'm touched that she has remembered my name. While I always make a point of memorising the visitors' names when they arrive at the camp, they seldom make the same effort. She shuts her eyes as if she's a little tired. 'I didn't only do it for the money, you know.' When she opens her eyes again they're bright and birdlike. 'Caroline was a very unpleasant person. I was a pal of Margaret, Vincent's first wife. Before she died she asked me to look after him. She knew he'd be a soft touch. Caroline had already persuaded him to give up control of the family business, and she was after even more. Vincent knew she was bleeding him dry, but he didn't have the strength to stand up to her.' Lavinia shakes her head sadly. 'There are so many weak men in the world.'

In the airport an announcer calls the flight to Mwanza and a lot of people drift away. There's a moment of silence. Lavinia puts a hand on my knee. 'So you worked it all out?'

'The locked tent mystery? Yes.'

'Is that what you call it? How delicious!'

I'm shocked that she seems to be treating this as a game and my voice is stern. 'Is that what you do these days instead of living off your pension? You kill people for money?'

'I very rarely kill. Murder is so vulgar. If Caroline's attitude had been a little different over dinner that night, things might not have taken such a dramatic turn. But I could see there was no other way out for Vincent. My business is in solving problems. Killing is always the last resort.' She pauses and sighs. 'I was a diplomat's wife, you see, and life became very tame when my darling Ian died.'

I am about to tell her that I know she was a diplomat's wife, when she prods my toe with the pointed end of her stick. 'Go on, then. How did I do it?'

'It wasn't just you. Everyone must have been a part of it. Everyone except Caroline.'

'Well, yes.' She nods to concede the point. 'But it was my idea. Mine and Valerie's. Val was Ian's assistant. Indispensable. Then a man was rather beastly to her and she had a nervous breakdown. She works with me now.'

'Were the family coming to Africa anyway?' I hope to get to the point before Lavinia's flight is called.

'Caroline always wanted to do a safari,' Lavinia says. 'There was something of the predator about her. I can see why she'd be attracted. I organised the itinerary and tagged along for the Serengeti leg. Vincent said Val and I were friends of his first wife's and that we'd reduce the cost. That swung it. Like many rich people, Caroline was very mean.'

After another pause, Lavinia continues the story herself. I suspect that she wanted to tell it in her own words from the beginning. 'Vincent and the children bored her. It wasn't hard to persuade her to leave them drinking that night.'

'And when I went back to collect the others from the mess, you killed her,' I said.

She claps her hands. 'Beautifully deduced.'

'It had to be then,' I say. 'I was watching the tent for the rest of the night.'

'I knew you would be.' She smiles. 'I have a spy in the camp. He told me how conscientious you are.'

It occurs to me then that Lavinia would have made a good spy herself and I wonder if she was *more* than a diplomat's wife when she travelled the world. She slides her hand down her stick revealing the buffalo's head at the top. 'This is rather heavy. It did the job very nicely, though it did take a couple of blows to finish her off.'

I feel sick. This woman must have no morals despite her link to the Tanga High School for Boys. But curiosity gets the better of me. 'Then you pretended to be Caroline and called the others in.'

'Well, we couldn't have them accused of murder. You were needed as an alibi.'

I remember the hot night, stillness after the rain. 'You mimicked her voice very well.'

She considers that for a moment. 'It's kind of you to say so, but we hear what we expect to, don't we? And I imagine one well-bred English voice sounds much like another.' She pauses. 'Though I was quite a star in the Amateur Dramatics Society Ian and I formed in Saigon.'

I continue: 'Then when I followed Mr Brookes to his children's tents, you slipped away into your own. I heard a scuffling noise but I thought it was a rat.'

She seems a little put out. 'I have been likened to many things but never to a rat.'

I ignore the comment. 'When Vincent returned to the tent it only took seconds for him to pull the rug with Caroline rolled inside it from under the bed.'

'And I thought I'd been so clever,' Lavinia says. 'How did you work it out?'

'Your shoe marks were inside the tent. You walk with a limp and the left mark was clearer than the right. You didn't seem part of the family so you had no reason to be there.' I pause. 'And outside there were holes in the mud made by your stick.'

She claps her hands again. 'Oh, you clever boy. I could have trained you myself. Now what are we going to do about this? I do hope you're not going to run to the police.'

'It is probably my duty,' I say, 'to tell them that you have confessed to murder.'

She looks at me intently. 'Aren't you the Moses Joho who won the Tanga English language prize in 2006?'

In that moment, I forget about her lack of morals and I love her. I picture Caroline Brookes with her strong hyena jaw and her pitiless eyes. 'Of course,' I say, 'there would be no proof. It would be your word against mine.'

She reaches out and grasps my hand.

We part as very good friends. When Lavinia walks away to take her flight she stops and calls back to me: 'Let's keep in touch. I could use an associate like you.' Then she disappears through the gate.

I go to the Precision Airways desk and cancel my flight to Dar. I don't need to trouble my brother now. Instead, I'll go into Arusha and catch a bus to Pangani. In my pocket is a cheque large enough to buy a good second-hand Land Cruiser. Thanks to the locked tent mystery, I'm already in business.

Blind Date

Jeffrey Deaver

Halfway through dinner, she felt apprehension grow within her like a fever.

Oh, up until then, things had been going great. Sitting in the quasi-fancy restaurant, across from Tim, they'd been laughing, dropping some facts, withholding others, getting to know each other, as they navigated that oh-so-tricky time from first hello to second wine.

Of course, Joannie hadn't been too worried. Sure, they'd met online. But not through a one night-stand site. It was a legitimate service, to meet people with common interests and, possibly spark a friendship, someone who might turn into something more. Hook up wasn't on the front burner, though any time men and women met on a blind date (or 'visually impaired,' Tim's joke on political correctness), that possibility was always present.

But for the first hour or so, through the escargot (they both loved 'garlic butter with snails on the side') and the salad (vinaigrette, their fave), everything had gone smoothly, with little awkwardness.

Joannie Karsten was thirty-four, divorced. The five-foot-two-inch blonde (always cut short) was a marketing manager for a Whole Foods wannabee, with three stores in the Indianapolis area. Tim Evans was thirty-six, never married. When she'd volunteered that she had no children he'd nodded thoughtfully and said, 'I don't either.' A brief moment had passed. 'But I keep getting these notices from around the country, "Paternity Order." What's that mean? You know?'

They'd both laughed.

That was Tim, low-key, funny. He worked for himself, a freelance computer programmer—he tried explaining the code he wrote, but it went right over her head, though she could understand the games he liked to play. They were called first-person shooters. You stalked around some battlefield or distant planet and blew the hell out of bad guys (or good guys, depending on which team you picked). She herself had no interest in computer gaming. But her nephew—her sister's teenager—spent hours playing them. Too violent for her. Tim reassured her, though, that he only killed aliens humanely. Never using a chainsaw or machete.

Another laugh, though she just noted that he sure seemed to play them quite a bit.

At least it was better than getting drunk on beer while watching a game.

Now that she thought about it, he looked a bit like a soldier. Thin waist, muscular shoulders. Trim brown hair. His blue eyes were focused and he had no problem looking directly into hers.

They navigated a few political differences, but neither of them was rabidly red or blue. She went to church occasionally; he did not, but didn't hoist the atheism banner. And on the subject of films and books and NPR programs, they were in close harmony.

But then, just as the main courses arrived, so did the apprehension.

This had nothing to do with Tim. She grew distracted as he was chatting away and cutting a bite of steak. He had, it seemed, asked her a question, but her eyes were on the TV above the bar. The sound was too low to hear but the images were clear and the crawl of type at the bottom of the screen explained that the Roman Numeral Killer had murdered again—a waitress at Callaghan's Road House, which was two miles away from where they sat. The crawl added that the police thought there may be some witnesses in the latest razor-attack murder, but so far the killer was still at large.

'Sorry?' she turned back.

'I was saying, on your Facebook page? Those pictures of the garden, the flowers. Beautiful.'

'Oh, thanks.'

'What kind of camera?'

'My iPhone.'

'You're kidding?'

Tim had explained that he was an amateur photographer and was obsessed with photo gadgets. Then he seemed to think that, on a first date, he shouldn't be using the O-word. And grinned. 'Well, let's just say, I'm not *weirdly* obsessed. But here's a rule: don't order things on eBay late at night after a glass of wine.'

And don't call exes.

Or your mother.

She kept these to herself, though. Family and former relationships were not suitable material for a blind date.

Tim asked, 'Was that Cooper Gardens? I thought I recognized the bridge.'

'Yeah, I live right across the street from the Wilson

Street entrance. I run there every morning. Well, *some* mornings.'

'I live across town but I like to bike there. That last hill—by your house. It's a tough one.'

She nodded absently. Her mind was elsewhere, thinking about the girl's murder. The cold, still, dark-green body bag. The detective's face was somber. His silent words would be about urging people to be careful, she guessed.

'You okay?' Tim asked.

This brought her around. 'Sorry. Just, that story. It's terrible.' She indicated the screen.

'The killer.' He closed his eyes momentarily. 'That's the third, right?'

She nodded and said she thought so. 'And, you know, none of the murders were very far away.'

'Young white professionals,' he said. 'The first one was a nurse. Tonight...' He glanced at the screen. 'A waitress. Both women. But there was a man, too, wasn't there?'

Joannie frowned. 'I think so. Right. A grad student.'

'Nothing sexual?'

'No, they're saying he just likes to kill for the thrills of it.'

'And cuts those numbers in their foreheads. Roman numerals. What's that all about?' Tim's eyes were now on the screen, too. Some talking heads were saying something—surely speculating on motive or the psychology behind serial killers. The crawl said, 'Who's at risk?'

Me? she wondered.

Then she forced herself back—mentally—to the table.

But the damage had been done.

The odds were that she wasn't in any danger, of course. But Joannie Karsten was the queen of paranoia. She was meticulous in every aspect of her life. Always prepared, she planned ahead of time to avoid any risk or problems. Like having her house checked for termites and rot monthly. She carried plenty of property, health, and liability insurance (even for Bosco). In her shoulder bag she kept hand wipes and spare footwear and even a spare driver's license, in case she lost her wallet. At work her reports were always prepared early, and she triple-checked them for typos.

On the street she was always aware of her surroundings and sized people up carefully. (Okay, she'd Googled Tim Evans and checked him out carefully before the date, though she stopped short of a criminal background check. Because how to explain *that* if the subject came up later?)

And all this serial killer talk—what could she do to be safer?

And she had to be safe. She couldn't afford to have anything happen to her. Kim—her mother—was on disability; Joannie's father had lived a high life and, when the heart attack finally got him, the resulting insurance proceeds went mostly to pay off debts. Joannie helped out with the woman's rent and getting her to and from PT twice a week, as well as paying some of the medical bills. She was the go-to babysitter for her nephews. And, of course, Bosco needed her, too.

Then she forced away her concerns, almost smiling to herself at the thought that a Jack Russell terrier was a reason for her to be on particular guard.

Girl, you definitely need to get out more.

The news story changed to a game. Tim launched into an account of a disastrous bachelor party he'd put together for a co-worker. And the waiter asked if they'd like dessert.

Her concerns didn't vanish, but she was able to turn her attention back to the man across from her and laugh at one of his silly jokes.

•●●●•

The bananas Foster—the flambé dish that was showy and always tasted damn good—was spectacular.

She and Tim dug with relish into the syrupy dessert and found they had sweets in common too…and that they both were lucky that they liked to exercise. Biking was his thing. She liked to run. They almost simultaneously commented on how unfair it was that so few calories were burned by a workout. Her comment was: 'This morning I ran half a bagel, dry, with a teaspoon of jelly.'

They both laughed once more.

Joannie reflected how good it was to be out with someone and feel no awkwardness. No pressure. He really was a very nice man. And, she had to admit, a good-looking one, too. Of course, he might never call her. That happened, even on the best of blind dates. But instinctively she had a sense that she'd hear from Tim Evans again.

The conversation continued to meander, pleasantly, for a time, over coffee. The restaurant began to empty. It was Friday night, but this part of town was populated more with families than professionals and folks were heading home to bed. Joannie, too, was tired and she knew the time had come to leave. Never overstay a good thing.

He insisted on picking up the check—wouldn't even let her leave the tip. She said, impulsively, 'Well, next time's on me.' And he responded with what was clearly genuine enthusiasm, 'That's a deal.' She felt a thud, a pleasant one, looking into his eyes.

She rose, picked up her large bag and slung it over her shoulder.

Joannie wondered what would happen next—if Tim would suggest driving her home. He'd driven. But there was a protocol for the blind dates. You arrived separately, you left separately. Even if things went perfectly, this was the way it worked. You needed to make your companion comfortable. Tim played by the rules perfectly. When she said she'd better grab a cab back home, he offered her a ride. But when she demurred, saying, 'Oh, no, it's late,' he nodded and didn't take it any further.

A gentleman for offering, a gentleman for not pushing after she refused.

In front of the restaurant, he flagged a cab for her.

The old Toyota pulled up. As she turned back to Tim, to thank him again, she glanced through the window of the restaurant and frowned to see that the news was back on, and the anchor was running the clip once more of the police detective talking about the Roman Numeral Killer.

'Hey,' Tim said, 'you all right?'

He'd been saying something once more, something she'd missed.

'Yeah, sorry.' They hugged and kissed cheeks—lingering for just a moment. A first date is generally a three-second hug, and this approached five.

Which was fine by her.

Joannie sat in the backseat of the cab and told the driver her address. The vehicle pulled away from the curb. She turned back to wave but Tim was already gone.

The car clattered along the streets. Yep, a very nice night. If only it hadn't been tainted by thoughts of the killings. It was crazy to think she had anything to worry about.

The Paranoia Queen.

The city was huge, the population high, and there was no reason at all to think that she'd be in danger.

The cab was careening down a deserted street, going

just a bit faster than she would have liked. She glanced toward the speedometer and noted the driver was looking at her in the rearview mirror. She met his eyes and he looked back to the road. He must've realized he'd been concentrating on her and not the speed, and he slowed up.

He seemed nice enough. Nothing about his appearance was troubling. His hair was perfectly trimmed and sprayed. His face clean-shaven. Fingernails cut very short and clean. He wore a suit and tie. It was spring but there'd been a few beautiful sunny days, balmy, filled with soft breezes. She spent every minute she could spare outside; he clearly didn't. He was quite pale. He struck her as one of those people who come to your house to spread the Gospel. A little too squeaky clean, but harmless.

Chill, girl. All's good.

The drive from the restaurant to her house was about twenty minutes—all surface roads; there was no highway connecting her neighborhood to the chic little enclave of boutiques and dining spots where she and Tim had eaten. A number of routes would have taken her home, some slightly faster than others, but the driver seemed to be taking a slightly longer route.

'Having a good night?' he asked. His voice was high.

'Yeah. You?'

He gave a laugh. 'I always seem to have good nights. It's easy when you enjoy your line of work. Do you?'

'Uhm, less.'

A glance in the mirror showed that he was looking her way once more.

'Have you been a resident of this area long?'

Who said I lived here? Joannie thought. *Maybe I'm visiting.*

Then told herself once more to relax. He was a clean-cut momma's boy, who liked to talk.

She said, 'A while.'

Another laugh. 'I love it here. I know it pretty well. Of course, that's a requirement for my job. I've lived here all my life. Are you going to the May Day parade?'

A popular ritual in this suburb. Nothing to do with Communist workers, the fete was about flowers and gardening.

That he'd mentioned it, though, gave the event a slightly ominous pagan tilt, a fertility rite.

'I don't know. I'll probably be working.'

'I'm going. I get there early to get a good spot.'

Now she glanced up again and found him examining her once more. Closely.

She felt a trickle of fear and looked away.

They were now in a very deserted area. The houses were set back from the road and there were large patches of empty fields. Joannie oriented herself. 'Could you turn here. Left.'

'On Madison?'

'Yeah. That's right.'

'You sure you want to go that way?'

Joannie didn't want to antagonize him. 'If you don't mind.'

'It's just that there's construction. Those plates in the road. You know those steel plates? It's not so good for my car. I wrote the commissioner about the problem, but he never wrote me back. It was rude, don't you think?'

'I suppose.'

'So do you mind if we go a little farther on this road? I'll have you home in no time.'

Her palms were sweating. Why was he looking at her so closely?

'Okay,' she said softly.

'Yes, indeed, you'll be home in no time,' he whispered and sped up, his eyes flicking between her face and the road.

•●⬤●•

Joannie Karsten strolled slowly up the concrete walk to her house. It was a small single-family two-story Colonial, with a detached garage.

She was calm now, reflecting wryly on how uneasy she'd been under the gaze of the cab driver.

Silly to think she'd been in danger. No risk, no threat. That damn paranoia.

He'd just been a clean-cut, if odd and quirky, young man.

Joannie unlocked her front door and stepped into the alcove, decorated with antique pictures of farmland—a hobby of hers, collecting, as she called it 'bad but comforting art.' A few photos of her family, too. An ornate mirror. She tossed her keys into a bowl and dropped to her knees to greet Bosco. At eight, he wasn't as lively as he once had been, but still he bounded up and down, licking her face. She fed him in the kitchen and then she climbed the stairs to her bedroom—done up in frilly pink-and-blue floral décor. She stripped off her date clothes. Into the shower.

It was late, close to eleven, but she wasn't ready for bed yet. She was still exhilarated after the blind date. Dressing in jeans and a red ISU sweatshirt, stepping into slippers, she headed downstairs once more. She let Bosco into the fenced backyard and poured a glass of Sauvignon Blanc. The night was cool but clear and dry and she decided to sit on her front porch. You could hear bullfrogs and the wind singing through the trees of her front yard and the park across the street. Sometimes she spotted eager bats pirouetting through the dark sky.

As she dropped into the swing, chained to the porch ceiling, she noted something odd. There was a dark car parked in front of the house next door. It hadn't been there when she'd arrived. She rose and stepped to the edge of the porch to get a better look. No, it wasn't the neighbors' Nissan. And it was strange there'd be a car parked in that spot anyway, since the family was away. She wondered—

A creak behind her.

She gasped, turning.

'Ah, there you are,' the man's voice said.

'I—'

It was Tim.

'You…you scared me.'

'Sorry.'

It would be his car.

He was looking around her yard and at the front door of her house.

'How did you…?' She was going to ask how he knew where she lived, but then remembered he'd gotten that information at dinner– referring to the pictures she'd posted on Facebook. She'd mentioned she was right across from one of the entrances to Cooper Gardens. Later, she'd mentioned that she lived in a two-story Colonial that was green, but that she was thinking of painting it white. On a blind date, she wouldn't normally give away that kind of personal information but she'd been distracted, gazing at the TV.

Police are continuing to investigate the case of the Roman Numeral Killer…

'I tracked you down.'

Silence for a moment. She glanced past him briefly. He was standing between her and the door.

'I was worried,' he said.

In the distance a dog barked, nearby the bullfrogs croaked. But otherwise it was quiet. Nobody on the sidewalks. And all the lights on the neighboring houses were out.

Not a soul around.

'Worried?' she asked.

'Your face. Just before you got into the cab, you were looking back in the restaurant. It was like you'd seen a ghost.'

'Oh, well. It was nothing. Just that story about the killer.'

'The Roman Numeral Killer?'

'Yeah.'

'Is that what it was?' he asked in a soft voice.

Here, on the walk, with only a dim front-porch light—behind him, turning him into a silhouette—he seemed so much bigger than at the restaurant.

She said, her voice trembling 'Sorry you came all this way.'

'I tried to call. But your phone was off.'

Had he really tried? She wasn't so sure.

Neither moved for a long moment. The faraway dog barked once more. Another bullfrog joined the chorus. And Joannie Karsten believed she could hear, as well as feel, her heart pounding faster and faster.

• • ● • •

The Monroe, Indiana, Police Department didn't generally see a lot of high-profile crime.

It was mostly DUIs and domestics, carjackings, and the occasional armed robbery. Oh, and the always-popular weed, meth, crack, blow, horse…

'Drugs don't pay attention to ZIP Codes,' read the MPD poster, the brainchild of some public affairs wonk in the police department. It would have been laughable if it wasn't so goddamn true.

But lately the Detective Division had had to expand—unwillingly and largely unprepared—into the serial killer investigation department.

Thanks to the guy slicing throats with a razor and carving Roman numerals into the corpses' foreheads.

The lead investigator was a stocky, thirty-eight-year-old detective named Judd Bell, from whose name you might suspect roots in Georgia or Alabama, but in fact was a taciturn Maine native, and Indiana was about as far south as he'd ever been, when you excluded the Disney outing with the family.

Bell was contentedly asleep in a comfy Sleep Number bed (he 58, the wife 89) when he was awakened by the blare of his work mobile.

Fumbling for it, he picked the unit up and, to avoid waking Betsy, headed into the hallway. He stepped carefully over the minefield of two black labs, whose sprawled posture in sleep and coloring made them a dangerous booby trap.

'Who?'

'Ebbet. Didn't I come up?'

'Don't have my glasses. Middle of the night. What?'

'It's four a.m.'

'Fine. What?'

'Got another one, Detective.'

'Roman numeral?'

''Fraid so.'

'Where?'

'Near Cooper Gardens.'

There hadn't been any killings in that part of town. Bell had the not-so-funny thought: *Well, our boy's expanding his market.*

'Throat cut again?'

'Yep. Ear to ear.'

He sighed. 'All right. I'll meet you at the station. Crime scene and coroner?'

'On the way.'

Bell disconnected and returned to the bedroom, threading his way over the canine obstacle course, to kiss his wife and tell her he'd be heading to work early and wouldn't be back till late.

The bedroom windows faced east.

The pink curtains were spread wide and the dawn sun poured into the spacious, airy room and fell upon skin like a warm caress.

Joannie Karsten opened her eyes and looked at the face close to hers.

Tim Evans was awake, too. Had been for a few minutes, it seemed. He smiled. She did as well.

Good. It had been good. She recalled being on the porch last night, her heart pounding in anticipation of what was coming next...a culmination of the attraction—the undeniable heat—that had arisen at the restaurant.

No, Tim hadn't come to see if she was upset, worried outside the restaurant.

That was crazy. Nope, he was here because he wanted her.

Well, guess what? She wanted him, too.

They'd kissed hard, embracing, to the soundtrack of the

bullfrogs and the wind easing through the spring leaves. Then they'd made their way upstairs.

Strewing clothes on the floor, they'd fallen into bed.

Sometimes, rarely, it all comes together, and two people fall so easily into patterns of touching, tasting, smelling, as if each was composed of incomplete genes and only by joining could their hearts become whole.

Now, Tim asked, 'Are you…?' As men will do at times like this.

She leaned up and kissed his cheek. And touched a finger to his lips.

'Brunch?' He fluffed pillows and eased into a sitting position, pulling the comforter up to his chest.

'Perfect.'

He picked up his iPhone. 'I'll check OpenTable.' He logged on and frowned.

'Everything all right?' Joannie asked. She reached to the floor and pulled on her t-shirt. Enjoyed it when he snuck a peak.

'My home page is local news. There was another murder last night.'

'What?' she gasped. 'The Roman Numeral Killer?'

He nodded. 'It was near *here*. Just the other side of the park.'

'No! Who was it?' she asked this with breathless urgency.

'A cab driver. The police think maybe it was a fare.'

'Do they?'

And Joannie Karsten reminded herself: Careful. Act interested but not too interested.

Thinking: Of *course* it was a fare.

A fare who'd grown ever more concerned that the *Book of Mormon* driver kept looking her way in the rearview mirror. Leading Joannie to believe that, despite the unlikelihood, maybe he was one of the witnesses to the earlier killings that the police had been talking about.

Witnesses…That was why she'd been so worried at dinner—not that she'd be the victim, but that the police were apparently making some strides in finding out that she was the Roman Numeral Killer.

Who's at risk?

Me?

She eased a bit closer to Tim, enjoying the comfort of the sunlight, the comfort of his flesh against her. She asked if the police had any leads.

'Nothing so far.'

She'd been careful. She thought again about last evening. Replaying the last minutes of the driver's life. Having him take her to the other side of the park, a mile from her house, nowhere near witnesses.

'Stop here, please.'

'Here?'

'Please.'

The driver had turned his scrubbed face toward her in the mirror. 'The park? You want to walk through the park after dark?'

'If you wouldn't mind.'

He had done so and on the pretense of handing him the money, she'd slipped the razor against his throat and screamed, 'Do you know me? Have you ever seen me?'

'What, what? Lady! Please. No. I was just making talk. I was…I didn't mean nothing.'

'Answer my question. Have you ever seen me before?'

'No, I don't who you are. My God!'

She'd believed him.

But she'd already made up her mind.

Swish…And then leapt back, away from the enthusiastic spray.

His screams became choking, the choking silence.

She'd already shut her phone off, to avoid GPS tracking, thinking that things might develop this way. Then she'd taken the Sani-Wipes from her purse and wiped everything she'd touched. Which was very little; she was always cautious that way. Then she'd replaced her shoes with the men's boots she carried in her bag, and climbed out of the cab with a tissue. She'd pulled open the driver's door—just to confuse the police a bit more—and walked in a circle around the car, leaving plenty of bootprints. Then she disappeared into the park, walking on the grass. She changed her shoes halfway through.

So, the driver hadn't been a threat, hadn't been a witness to one of the earlier killings.

Just a clean-cut, if odd and quirky, young man.

Though one who had committed an unpardonable offense. He'd made her uneasy. Made her feel bad. Made her worry.

And those offenses, for Joannie Karsten, were punishable by death.

It had taken her years to have the confidence to accept this urge, which had dogged her all her life. Years ago, teenage Joannie had been alone with her father—a serial philanderer and drunk—when he'd dropped to the living room floor with a ferocious heart attack. As he'd crawled toward the phone, screaming for her to help him, Joannie had risen from the lounger where she was watching *The Brady Bunch*. She lifted the cordless handset away and sat down once more, sipping her cherry Slurpee and watching him with detached interest until he died.

She wondered how it would feel.

Wonderful. It felt wonderful.

But she'd kept a lid on her passion to repeat the

sensation…until about a year ago and she knew she had to give in.

First, the sadistic nurse at her mother's rehab center—a woman who was continually rude to Mom and who left her waiting in a freezing hallway on more than one occasion. Then the grad student making money as a dog-walker. He'd kicked Bosco when the dog was pulling on the lead, thinking Joannie hadn't seen. And two days ago: '*Hi I'm Your Helpful Server, Lois*,' at Callaghan's Road House, who hadn't given Joannie any service at all, and then shouted at her for not leaving a tip.

Swish, swish, swish…The sound was largely imaginary—a razor through the veins and cartilage of the throat is almost silent—certainly compared with the screams of the victim, and the ensuing gurgling. Which was, to her ears, delightful, if loud and messy.

Tim rose from the bed and found his shorts. Pulled them on. 'What's Roman numeral four?'

He didn't know?

'Hmm,' she said thoughtfully. 'I'm not sure. IV, I think.'

'Wonder why the killer leaves those?'

'Something in his sick mind. In his past probably. That's what they always say on TV. Those true crime shows.'

The real answer, though, was that there was no reason whatsoever.

When she'd decided to kill the nurse, and had waited for the woman's shift to end, she'd sat in her car near the hospital reading a magazine she'd brought with her. There was one article she found interesting. It was about the fall of the Roman Empire. The writer suggested that one of the problems that civilization experienced was that the numbering system had no zero. This limited scientific and economic development. *Hmm. Fascinating.*

So, an hour later, after watching the nurse spasm then twitch to stillness, she'd decided on a good approach to deflect suspicion. The public, as well as police, she guessed, would much rather have a psycho killer with an obsession with *Game of Thrones* or the Roman Empire than a petite blonde who killed because somebody pissed her off.

So she'd carved the *I* on the woman's forehead.

Of course, the cops didn't get it. And thought it was the first-person pronoun, I, not the numeral.

She'd laughed at that, having a glass of white wine afterward, with her dog at her feet, watching the news. And so with Brad the dog-walker, she'd gone with a *II*.

The cops got it then, or thought they did.

And the Roman Numeral Killer was born.

'Where do you want to eat?' she asked.

'Oh, no preference,' Tim said. 'Whatever you want.'

She thought for a moment. 'I'm in the mood for sushi.'

He barked a laugh. 'For brunch?'

'Why not?'

'I was thinking eggs Benedict. I always like to have breakfast things in the morning.'

She reflected, *well, he* did *say whatever I want*. But she said, 'That sounds great.'

'You sure?'

'Absolutely.'

'Okay. I'll jump in the shower.'

After he stepped into the bathroom, she rose and pulled on her jeans and slippers, then headed downstairs to feed Bosco and let him out.

Tim began singing.

Hmm. She'd heard about that, singing in the shower. But had never known anybody who actually did it. Seemed a bit odd.

But Joannie reminded herself to relax. Tim was a nice guy, he was good in bed, he had a responsible job. She could do a lot worse.

And as for any foibles? Only breakfast food for brunch, ignorance of Roman numerals, hours playing video games? Any others…?

Oh, she could put up with them.

And if not…well, she'd cross that bridge when she came to it.

Strangers in a Pub

Martin Edwards

What am I getting myself into?

Jefferson surveyed the dingy saloon bar with a jaundiced eye. Ever since Maddy had run off with her personal trainer, he'd looked at most things with a jaundiced eye, but this pub might have been designed to tease out his prejudices. Who ever believed that things could only get better? The country was going to the dogs.

The Case is Altered would, in times gone by, have been called a workingman's pub, but Jefferson saw no sign of a darts board, or a snooker table, or any working men, come to that. Two-thirty in the afternoon, and a bunch of shaven-headed bikers were pummelling the fruit machines while excitable commentators rhapsodised about the baseball game on the huge plasma TV screen. Jefferson didn't share the fashionable enthusiasm for La Liga or Serie A, but at least the Continentals knew their football. A proper sport.

So many pubs had closed these past few years, places with low beams and inglenooks, where you could get a decent pint of bitter to wash down your bangers and mash without needing to take out a second mortgage. It didn't seem right that this dump on the corner of a Mancunian mean street had survived. But that was life. The undeserving got away with murder; Jefferson had seen it a million times. He chose a seat at the table nearest the door. All the better for a quick getaway.

To say he was having second thoughts about this job was an understatement. The phone call had come out of the blue. He'd have rung off at once if he'd not been startled to find a fellow human being at the other end of the line. Usually it was a recorded message urging him to claim compensation for losses he'd never suffered, or a cold caller wanting him to replace his windows with environmentally friendly replacements. He'd still not got the hang of his smartphone, and he kept pressing the wrong thing whenever he didn't want to be disturbed. It was far too sensitive to his touch. He preferred phones that were as unresponsive as Maddy.

So he listened to what the bloke had to say. His name was Binks, and he spoke in a whisper, as if terrified of being overheard. Jefferson, he said, came highly recommended. He wanted a diligent ex-copper to follow his wife, and see if she was playing away. Maximum discretion and maximum haste were what he needed, because he was a partner in a national firm of estate agents that was planning to float on the London Stock Exchange, and he wanted to get the divorce papers in before she got wind of his true worth. Before Jefferson could kill the call, Binks mentioned what he was willing to pay.

For a simple job, it was money for old rope. So much money, that it would be rude not to express cautious interest. Binks wanted to meet Jefferson in a pub well away from his office in central Manchester. Somewhere neither of them would be recognised. He'd bring the down payment, plus a photo of his wife and some background information.

Only then did Jefferson ask who had recommended him. 'Chap called Gus Illingworth,' Binks said. 'I sold him his new house.'

Everything fell into place. Gus was having a laugh. He'd never liked Jefferson. Probably this was Illingworth's way of getting his own back because Binks' commission had been a rip-off. No wonder he could afford to throw his cash around.

But Binks rang off before Jefferson could say he'd changed his mind.

It still wasn't too late to back out. He'd arrived half an hour early, to give himself thinking time. Actually, fifteen minutes in these miserable surroundings would be plenty. If Binks didn't turn up before...

The door swung open, and in walked a very short, very fat man wearing an expensive grey suit and a Rolex. He was clutching a leather briefcase. His gaze fell on Jefferson, and his porcine eyes widened. Wiping a line of sweat off his brow with a silk handkerchief, he plopped down onto the other chair at Jefferson's table.

'The early bird catches the worm, eh?'

When he wasn't whispering, Binks' voice was unexpectedly squeaky. He put down his briefcase, and offered a damp hand. Jefferson shook it with malicious vigour.

'Can I get you a drink?'

Jefferson nodded. 'Pint of best.'

Binks plodded towards the bar, placing his order with a pimply purple-haired girl whose face was festooned with more rings than a shower curtain. A week before leaving him, Maddy had announced she'd had her nipple pierced, and a silver ring fitted. Jefferson was sure she'd done it as much to annoy him as to fascinate the gym trainer. Same with that ankle tattoo of a butterfly. A butterfly, for God's sake! A praying mantis would've been nearer the mark.

Jefferson actually thought about doing a runner while Binks' sizeable back was turned, but the lure of a pint was too much. He'd listen to what the man had to say, then make his excuses and leave. Unless the job was an absolute doddle, that was.

Binks returned with the drinks. His was a gin and tonic, and he raised his glass with a nervous theatricality.

'Here's to…business.'

Jefferson took a gulp of his beer. Scarcely *best*, but just about drinkable.

Binks cleared his throat. 'I'll be honest.'

Jefferson frowned. In his experience, this phrase invariably prefaced something dishonest or unpleasant.

'I was expecting a younger man.'

Jefferson's left hand was resting on the little table. His fingers were knobbly and misshapen. He'd have stuck the hand back in his pocket, but he hated seeming defensive.

'I've got arthritis in my finger joints. Not in my brain.'

'I suppose…you're very experienced?'

Jefferson wasn't in the mood for an in-depth debate about his CV. 'I was on the job for more than ten years. They made me an Inspector, before I jacked it in. Since then, I've freelanced. A bit of this, a bit of that. Working on contracts, you know.'

'Contracts, yes, of course.' Binks seemed impressed, almost overawed. 'Sorry, sorry. Just need to do my…due diligence.'

'Uh-huh.'

Binks coloured. 'I suppose I'd better give you some

details about the lady in question. I thought it'd help if I brought a photograph.'

It was on the tip of Jefferson's tongue to say that was exactly what they'd agreed. But he kept quiet as the fat man fumbled with his briefcase before bringing out an A4 envelope. He laid it down on the table, and gave a quick glance around. Once satisfied that nobody was paying them any attention, he slid out a photograph, and a folded sheet of paper.

The woman in the picture was slim, with blond hair. Fifties, Jefferson guessed, though with women, you never could tell. Her coat was open, revealing a white, well-filled blouse and black jeans. The shot was taken somewhere in the countryside, and she was gesticulating angrily at whoever was holding the camera.

'Fucking do-gooder,' Binks said.

Jefferson grunted. 'That right?'

'Hard left, more like. Bleeding heart, any road.' Binks swallowed the rest of his drink. 'Can't be doing with 'em.'

Mrs Binks sounded like Maddy. The menopause had heralded a metamorphosis. She'd turned into a different woman.

'Know how you feel.'

'You're a man of the world.' Binks breathed out noisily. 'Business is business, and she's costing me a fortune. It just can't go on, you know what I mean?'

'I do that.'

Binks handed him the sheet of paper. 'Here's the information you need. Anything more, let me know.'

Decision time had arrived, and Jefferson tucked the photo and paper into his jacket pocket. Maybe it would be a laugh, becoming a detective all over again. He was pretty much at a loose end, and there was a limit to the amount of daytime television he could tolerate without taking a hammer to the TV screen. Besides, the cash wouldn't hurt.

Binks closed his eyes for a moment. 'How long then, before—the job's done?'

'Shouldn't take long. I'll let you know no later than this time next week. Maybe sooner.'

'Thanks. Hell of a weight off my mind, I can promise you.' Binks sighed. 'I was told you didn't mess about.'

Not like Gus Illingworth to be free and easy with his compliments. Well, well, you lived and learned.

'Oh.' Binks gave a sickly smile. 'I almost forgot.'

He bent over again and pulled out of his briefcase a thick package sealed with brown tape. He thrust it into Jefferson's hand.

'You'll find it's all here. As we agreed. Half now, half… afterwards.' Binks looked around again. Still nobody was taking an interest. Something exciting was going on in the baseball game, if the commentators were to be believed, though the audience seemed catatonic. 'I'd best make myself scarce. I'll wait to hear from you.'

He scurried out of the pub as fast as his little legs could carry him. Jefferson weighed the package. It was surprisingly heavy. Surely Binks hadn't padded it with rubbish? What would be the point of that?

As he finished his pint, the door opened again, and a squat man in his forties bustled in. His gaze fell on Jefferson.

'Jeff Hope?' His voice, barely a whisper, seemed oddly familiar.

Jefferson narrowed his eyes. 'Who wants him?'

'We spoke on the phone. I was recommended to you by Gus Illingworth.'

'Your name isn't…?'

'Please.' The whisper became urgent. 'I said on the phone, I need maximum discretion.'

Jefferson gritted his teeth. It was an *oh shit* moment.

• ● ⬤ ● •

'Tell you the truth, I've been having second thoughts about the whole thing. She reckons I'm paranoid, but she's started dolling herself up all the time. Very tasty, but it's not like her. After years of marriage, a man knows.'

Jefferson grunted noncommittally.

'Let me get you another pint, then we can get down to brass tacks. I've got her photo in my pocket, by the way. I've written the address and phone number on the back.'

As he headed for the counter, Jefferson made his way to the gents, taking his package with him. Once locked inside the solitary cubicle, he tore the tape off, and put his hand inside. He pulled out three thick bundles of fifty-pound notes, and stared at them for fully sixty seconds before replacing them.

When he was sure there was nobody around, he unlocked the door, and re-entered the bar. He could see Binks—for Binks it must surely be—returning to the table near the entrance. Another chap strode straight past him. He was in his late thirties, dark-haired, tattooed, and muscular. Possibly ex-military. He was looking this way and that. Presumably in search of the fat little bloke who had just handed Jefferson fifteen thousand pounds.

• ● ⬤ ● •

When in doubt, think it out. The only sensible option was to make himself scarce. He didn't fancy an acrimonious encounter with the muscular newcomer, and following a supposedly errant wife had never held much appeal in the first place.

He spotted a back way out of the pub, and within moments he was outside, and relieved to find his car still in one piece. He put his foot down, and before long he had the chance to park in a deserted rural lay-by, and check that he wasn't hallucinating.

No, the money was real, all right.

Half now, half later.

So what might the fat little bloke pay thirty thousand quid for?

Jefferson took another look at the photograph of the fair-haired woman. It was rather blurred, certainly not posed. Her expression made clear that she was very cross about something, though cross in quite a classy way. Her coat looked expensive. A Barbour, he supposed. And those were probably Timberland boots.

A bleeding heart, maybe, but Jefferson couldn't help liking the look of her. *Well-preserved* was the phrase people used, wasn't it? But that made a woman sound like a monument in the care of English Heritage. She was definitely fit.

He unfolded the sheet of paper that the man-who-wasn't-Binks had given him. It bore a name, Heather Chase, her e-mail address and landline phone number, and an address in north Cheshire.

What clues could he glean from the photograph? He could make out three or four shapes, people right in the background. A couple seemed to be holding makeshift placards, but he couldn't read what was written on them. Was this a picture of some kind of low-grade protest march? If Heather Chase was a do-gooder, it would make sense. That's what they loved, protesting. Being *against* something.

But whatever mischief she caused, Jefferson had no intention of killing her. And he was sure that was what he'd been paid to do. No wonder not-Binks had been so impressed by his casual mention of contracts in the Middle East.

Different sort of contracts, obviously.

The easy option was simply to do nothing, pocket the money, walk away, and forget about it. One thing he'd learned, there was often a lot to be said for masterly inertia. Or he could make a rare foray onto the moral high ground, and go to his nearest police station, and explain everything that had happened. But would anything much be done about it, even if he talked to someone he'd worked with and who'd managed to survive the cost-cutting culls and the lure of early retirement on an enhanced pension? Nothing specific had been said by not-Binks. The money wouldn't be easy to explain away, but even so. In these days of strained police resources, and lazy ex-colleagues quick to rely on lack of manpower as an excuse for doing nothing, there was a better-than-even chance that his allegation would be filed in the too-difficult pile, and left to moulder for a while, possibly forever.

Meanwhile, what would happen to Heather Chase? On a fleeting glance, the muscular bloke didn't impress as an easy-come-easy-go fatalist ready to write-off the loss of fifteen grand as simply one of those things. He'd want his money, and presumably he was willing to earn it.

Even if there were too many bleeding hearts in this world, Jefferson didn't want Heather Chase to bleed.

He reached for his mobile, and dialled Binks' number.

'Yes?' The whisper was even hoarser than usual.

'Jeff Hope. Sorry I couldn't...'

'Sorry? *You're* sorry?'

'What happened?'

'That...animal thought I was going to pay him to do something...criminal.'

'You talked, then?'

'I wouldn't call it a conversation. I've just arrived at A&E. He hit me in the face. I think my nose is broken, and I'll be black and blue in the morning.'

'He asked who you were planning to meet, I suppose? You gave him my name?'

'*Of course* I fucking gave him your name. You think I want to wind up on a mortuary slab? This is bad enough, it's…'

'Don't talk anymore,' Jefferson advised. 'It'll only make the pain worse. You need peace and quiet and a lie down. At least it's not on a mortuary slab. Good luck with the medics.'

He rang off, and asked himself what he should do next.

Forty minutes later, he was sitting in his car, parked on a grass verge halfway down a wooded lane. Winding down his car window, he glimpsed through the trees a sizeable villa in mellow brick, probably built as a country retreat by some Victorian cotton merchant. He could smell the leaves, and the money. Heather Chase certainly wasn't short of a few bob.

There was a video entryphone system by the iron gates. He put the photograph in his pocket, and pressed the button.

'Who is it?'

A woman's voice came from the speaker, pleasant rather than guarded.

'My name's Hope. I'd like a word with you, if I may.'

'If you're wondering if I've had a car accident that isn't my fault, the answer is that it's always my fault. According to my ex-husband. Bye now, thanks for calling.'

At least she administered a brush-off in style.

'I only want to help you look after yourself.'

'If it's about a stair lift, I'm still fully mobile. And my home security is working just fine, as you'll find out for yourself if you try to open the gate.'

He mastered his exasperation. *Put yourself in her shoes, Jefferson.* Probably he'd not expressed himself too well.

'Please don't cut me off. I'm not here to sell you owt.'

'They all say that.'

'Sorry, but this is a matter of life and death.' He started to gabble, fearing that she'd decide he was deranged, and cut him off. 'You've made a bad enemy. Short, fat bloke with money to burn. He's taken a serious dislike to you, and you need to protect yourself.'

A pause.

'You're not talking about Vinny Padgett?'

The name rang a bell, but only in the distance.

'I don't actually know what he's called. But he gave me a picture of you.' Jefferson waved the photograph so that she could see it through the video camera.

A very long pause.

'Oh, my God.'

'So can you spare me ten minutes, please?'

'Who are you? Really?'

'I used to be a police officer. Now I'm...' Jefferson hesitated. *Caretaker* didn't sound good. *Security consultant* was misleading and borderline intimidatory. Maybe go for something with a touch of romance. 'A private investigator.'

Her tone acquired a flinty edge. 'And he's hired you to investigate me?'

'Not exactly. Not at all, in fact. I don't work for him; I didn't know his name until you mentioned it. It's simply that our paths crossed…and I thought you should know what he's up to.'

'All right.' The iron gates began to open up in front of his eyes. 'Would you like a cup of tea? Herbal? Camomile?'

'English Breakfast, if it's all the same to you.'

The bay window of Heather Chase's sitting room looked out over a rosebed and circular, leaf-strewn front lawn. Her taste in interior design was a bit much for Jefferson, all throws and rugs and cushions in lurid colours. There was a faint musky scent in the air, and he was reminded of the souks of the Emirates. Not that he'd enjoyed his three months out in the Middle East; he always felt too hot and too thirsty, the ultimate fish out of water.

A scattering of books lay on occasional tables. One was about yoga, another celebrated eminent eco-warriors. At least she made a decent pot of English Breakfast. In person, she didn't seem like a harridan. Medium height, slim and elegant in a pink t-shirt and white trousers. Her feet were bare, and so were her fingers. A touch of puzzlement clouded her brown eyes, but for a few moments she set about putting him—and herself?—at ease, commenting on the unpredictability of the weather, and asking if he'd come far.

'Yorkshire.'

He wasn't much of a one for small talk, never had been. Maddy used to complain that he was an absolute pain in the bum at parties. Not that he minded; party-going ranked just ahead of trips to the dentist in his league table of unpleasant experiences.

She leaned forward in her chair, as if she'd decided the time had come to get down to business. 'All right, then. What's all this about Vinny Padgett?'

He'd Googled the name on his smartphone while walking down her gravelled drive. Much as he detested new technology, and the way it had created a generation of earphone-wearing zombies, it had its uses.

Vinny Padgett owned a business called Padgett Prime Properties. He was a speculative developer who had bought a slice of North Cheshire's countryside five miles away from here. But there were rumours that he'd done some sort of deal with a fracking company which wanted to test-drill in the area. He'd told the local press that this was a conspiracy theory, dreamed up by a tiny group of diehards determined to block progress. These people called themselves Green and Pleasant, and their spokesperson was Heather Chase. Padgett argued that he was performing a social service by building much-needed houses, and that the not-in-my-backyard brigade should focus on the common good. The report quoted Heather as saying that a gated community of six-bedroomed executive mansions wouldn't help first-time buyers, and that the site should only be used for social housing. But what she feared most was the coming of the frackers. The argument had become increasingly vitriolic. There was talk about High Court injunctions and people lying down in front of JCBs.

'Am I right in thinking you and your pals stand between him and a small fortune?'

'Probably not that small,' she said. 'No wonder he's getting desperate. I hear his business is up to its neck in debt. To keep it afloat, he's had to do some very murky deals.'

'What would happen if you fell under one of his lorries?'

She looked him in the eye. 'It's not about me. The fight would continue.'

'But you're the driving force behind Green and Pleasant?'

'We're certainly not a one-woman band. I can assure you, we're not in the least hierarchical.'

'This isn't the time for modesty,' he snapped. 'Or diplomacy. Be honest, Mrs Chase. If you were out of the way, would Padgett be likely to get his way?'

'It's Ms Chase,' she retorted. 'My ex-husband was called Stott. Rotten name, I ditched it the moment he told me he'd got his secretary pregnant. As for Padgett, well, perhaps. But...'

'There's no gentle way to put this,' Jefferson said. 'Padgett wants you dead.'

Her eyes widened. 'He doesn't like me, certainly, and the feeling's mutual, I can...'

'It's not about dislike,' Jefferson said. 'Earlier today, he tried to hire me to kill you.'

'What?' She put a hand to her mouth.

'It was a misunderstanding. If he runs his business the way he recruits his hitmen, no wonder he's in trouble. I didn't understand what he was talking about. I turned up in this pub to meet a new client, but I was early, and bumped into Padgett instead.'

'My God!'

'Before I knew what was happening, he'd handed me your photo, address, and a load of dosh. It wasn't until after he'd left that I put two and two together. Especially when the bloke I was supposed to meet turned up, swiftly followed by a guy who looked like someone out of *American Sniper*.'

The room wasn't cold, but Heather Chase shivered as Jefferson told the rest of his story.

'So Padgett went off thinking he'd hired a contract killer to murder me?'

'That's about the size of it.'

'If there's anything in what you say…'

'I'm not in the habit of making things up,' he snapped.

'Then we must go to the police.'

'And tell them what?'

'Well, that he's willing to pay to…'

'I wasn't wired, you know. It'd be his word against mine.'

'But the photograph, the money…'

'Who's to say I haven't been blackmailing him? I might even be the cause of his business misfortunes. Or maybe you've paid me, to discredit him. On the Internet, you're quoted as saying that you'll go to any lengths to stop Padgett Prime Properties. Any lengths. You repeated that.'

'I didn't mean it like that!'

'No? Well, perhaps he didn't mean to have me kill you. What you said is down in black and white. It's evidence, and police love evidence. Trust me, I used to love it myself back in the day, when I was on the job.'

She gave a heavy sigh. 'And now?'

'Now I go by gut feel.'

Heather Chase's eyes strayed to his stomach, and he felt uncomfortably aware that there was more of it than was healthy.

'Is that right?'

'Instinct, I mean.' He glared at the book about eco-warriors. 'You'd probably call it prejudice. But I'll tell you this for nowt. I've got a prejudice against people being killed for no good reason.'

She closed her eyes, and leaned back in her chair. 'So what do you suggest?'

•••••

At first, none of his suggestions found favour, and the idea of sheltering in a hotel under an assumed name she rejected out of hand.

'How long would that go on for?' She threw out her arms in a theatrical gesture. 'I don't mean to offend you, but how can I be sure you're not in cahoots with Padgett, or somebody else who simply wants me out of the way?'

He gave her a withering look. 'I wouldn't like to be on the receiving end if you did try to offend me. Why would I lie to you? I didn't have to come here, y'know. I could have left you to take your chances. Maybe...'

'I'm sorry, I'm sorry.' She raised her hands in mock surrender. 'It's not fair to question your good faith. But I can't just hide away like a scaredy-cat.'

He blinked. Maddy hadn't been the sort who ever said sorry. Fair enough, neither was he. He sucked in a breath.

'You need to understand, Mrs...Ms Chase. You're at risk. Would you rather talk to the police instead of me? If so, fine. It's a free country, and that is what they're there for.'

She shook her head. 'I don't have much faith in the police, at least not when it comes to taking on a pillar of the establishment like Padgett. The things I've seen on protest marches and demos…'

'I need to talk to Padgett,' he interrupted. Much more guff about protest marches and demos, and he'd wash his hands of her. 'Give him his money back, but make it clear that I've spoken to you, and that you won't press charges as long as he calls off his hired thug.'

'You'll be wired up?' she asked. 'I suppose you need to record him. Make sure you get a few incriminating statements.'

'No time for that,' he said.

'Why on earth not?' She had this irritating habit of questioning everything she was told.

With exaggerated patience, as if lecturing a particularly recalcitrant apprentice, he said, 'This man, the one whose money I was given, he didn't strike me as the patient type. He's made a nuisance of himself already with Binks. My bet is that he won't rest until he's picked up the money he was expecting. And maybe done something to earn it.'

'He doesn't have my name. Padgett gave the information to you.'

'So he'll want to see Padgett. Who lives where?'

'In a rather grotesque house in the next village. We've picketed it more than once.'

'Have you, indeed? And what's grotesque about it?'

'It's a converted water tower. Ironic for a man who famously overdoes the gin-drinking, don't you think?'

In the end, she insisted on accompanying Jefferson to Tower House. He didn't like it, but he didn't have time to sit around arguing if he was to reach Padgett before the would-be assassin did. Reluctantly, she promised to stay in the car, and out of sight, while Jefferson went to talk to the property developer. Her presence, he was sure, could only complicate a conversation that promised to be tricky enough.

'Are you sure about giving him back the money?' she asked. 'He'll only misuse it.'

'Not mine to keep, though, is it?' He felt a slight pang as he spoke. Even in this inflationary age, you could do a fair bit with fifteen grand.

Soon they arrived in the small village where Padgett lived, an affluent place, all thatched roofs and driveways cluttered with luxury cars. The brick water tower had a telephone mast on its roof, and was visible long before they passed a sign telling them that the village welcomed careful drivers. Padgett's house, Heather explained, was reached via a bumpy, twisting lane.

'You can't see until you round the last bend,' Heather said, 'but there's a huge modern extension built onto the original tower. All concrete and glass. An excrescence, as far as I'm concerned, though it's won awards for imaginative design.'

'Yeah, well,' he said. 'Awards, huh? Enough said.'

She scanned the road ahead. 'Here it is. Next left.'

They turned down a narrow lane, and Jefferson braked as they reached a passing place. Trees masked the tower, but he supposed it was about a hundred yards away. 'You keep your head down. I'll go and have a natter with his lordship.'

Signs of strain were showing on Heather Chase's face, but she sounded calm. 'If I could reason with him…'

He clicked his tongue in reproach. 'Fellers who are willing to pay huge amounts of cash to kill women who irritate them aren't usually receptive to reason. Don't you move a muscle.'

'Good luck,' she whispered as he opened the car door.

•••••

Jefferson heard the voices before he could see their owners. Two men were shouting at each other. He couldn't catch the drift, but it didn't sound as if they were enjoying each other's company. Reaching a bend in the lane, he poked his head forward cautiously, and took in the scene.

Two cars were parked next to each other at the foot of the tower. One was a sleek white Mercedes, the other a rusty Vauxhall. Jefferson had been beaten to it. He looked up, and saw that the top of the tower had been transformed into a roof garden, ringed by a glass balustrade. Padgett and the muscular man Jefferson had spotted in The Case is Altered were facing each other. Their words were indistinguishable, but the fat man had his arms outstretched, as if in supplication. The other man was waving a gun, and his body language suggested that he was in the mood to use it.

As Jefferson watched, Padgett made a grab for the gun. A shot was fired, but to Jefferson's astonishment, it was the ex-military type who sank to the ground. The fat man had found the strength from somewhere to knock his adversary off balance. In the rough-and-tumble, the contract killer had shot himself.

Padgett disappeared from sight. Jefferson reached for his mobile, meaning to dial 999, but instantly thought better of it. Padgett was losing the plot. He'd shot and possibly killed one man, and Jefferson had fifteen thousand pounds that belonged to him. In a state of shock, the fat man might do anything.

'What's happened?' Heather Chase's voice came from behind him. 'I heard a shot.'

'I told you to stay in the car!' Jefferson hissed. 'Get away from here!'

A muffled cry of anguish froze the reply on Heather's lips. Something had happened inside the tower house.

For a moment, nothing stirred. Jefferson thought he'd never known such silence. Then he felt the woman clutch his sleeve, heard her soft, urgent voice.

'Please! This isn't your concern. Don't risk your life.'

He turned to face her. 'Of course it's my concern. If I hadn't blundered in...'

'But...'

'Don't argue!' He caught her hand, and squeezed it. 'Wait here. I'm going inside.'

He edged forward. The garden, small for such an extravagant property, was bordered by a low wall. The gate was open, and as he drew nearer, he saw that the main door to the house was also ajar. The killer, he supposed, had arrived here in a frenzy of rage. Probably out of his mind on some drug or other; that was surely the only way Padgett could have got the better of him.

Through the front door he glimpsed a large entrance hall, by the look of it a gleaming showpiece. Would the fact that the owner had killed someone here depress or add to its value? It would take an estate agent like poor old Binks to answer that.

'Mr Padgett?'

His voice was scratchy with tension, causing him a pang of dismay. Like any other serving police officer, he'd confronted his fair share of desperate people, some of them armed with knives or blunt instruments. Had he grown soft during his years out of the force?

There wasn't a sound to be heard. Nothing for it, then, but to take a look-see. He squared his shoulders. It was almost as if he needed to prove something to himself. But what could that be? He had nothing to prove; it didn't make sense.

He crossed the threshold. No sign of Padgett. The hall was roomy and open, and he could see a spiral staircase at the far end. That must go up the tower itself.

A couple more paces, and he could see the staircase more clearly. As well as the huddled form lying below the bottom step.

Vinny Padgett had fallen down the staircase. An attempt at suicide, or deliberate? Was he dead, had he fractured his neck or his spine or both? Jefferson couldn't guess. The man's body was motionless, that was all he knew.

He must call Heather Chase; they must summon an ambulance and the police. He turned round, and almost collided with her. Determined not to do as he'd asked, she'd come up right behind him. And so she'd seen Padgett's broken body. Her pretty face was stricken with horror, and tears were trickling down her cheeks.

'So, what about the money?' she asked that evening.

They were having a bite to eat in the conservatory of a pub restaurant five minutes' drive from the old water tower. The Drum and Monkey was barely thirty miles from The Case is Altered, but it belonged to a different world. Its clientele mostly comprised well-heeled couples in designer leisurewear, and the walls were lined with shelves of old books. Jefferson was tucking into a beef and ale pie, while Heather had chosen the ricotta gnocchi. When they were looking at the menu, she'd announced that she was a vegetarian, had been since her teens. Somehow, Jefferson wasn't surprised.

After the police had taken their statements, she'd invited him back to her house, and they'd agreed to have a drink and a chat before Jefferson went on his way. Once she'd changed into a summer frock, they'd decided they might as well have a meal together. There was, after all, a lot to talk about.

The paramedics had arrived in quick time, and done their utmost, but Padgett died just as they were setting off for the hospital. The assassin was already dead. Heather had insisted on taking charge of the explanation of how she and Jefferson had come to arrive at Padgett's house at just the moment of the fatal confrontation between him and his mysterious assailant. It had been, she told a sympathetic middle-aged constable who obviously fancied her, like watching something out of a Hollywood blockbuster. She'd said that she wanted to talk to Padgett about her fears that he was cooking up some cosy scam with the fracking company. It was the truth, if far from the whole truth, and it seemed to satisfy the constable. Jefferson she described as a friend who happened to have called on her today, and who had agreed to accompany her in case Padgett became aggressive. Before the police arrived, they'd agreed it was best to keep the story simple. The truth, but definitely not the whole truth.

The next question was where they stood with Binks. Thankfully, it seemed he wasn't going to cause any trouble. Jefferson had called him, and given him a highly edited account of what had happened to the man who had attacked him in The Case is Altered.

'All a bit messy, but at least he won't be troubling you again.'

'Thank heaven for that.' The estate agent couldn't disguise his relief.

'What an absolute nightmare. Yes, a nightmare, that's what it's been. Still...'

'Yes?'

'Something like that, well, it shakes you up. When I got back from A&E, Moira was shocked to see me in such a state. One way or another, we got talking. I put my cards on the table, and so did she. Yes, there was someone, but she's given him the heave-ho. She and I are going to give our marriage another try.'

'Right,' Jefferson said. 'All's well that ends well, I suppose.'

'Funny old world, eh?'

'You said it.'

So that only left Heather Chase, and of course the fifteen thousand pounds. The package of cash was locked in his glove compartment. He only hoped that car thieves weren't operating in the vicinity. It looked too affluent to be a risky area, but you never knew in life, you never knew.

'The money?' he asked, playing for time. 'Well, I meant to give it back to Padgett. I suppose his estate will have some claim on it.'

'His estate?' Heather Chase was scornful. 'He was twice divorced, and didn't have kids. He's probably left his worldly goods to some right-wing pressure group. If I were you, I'd hold on to the cash. Every last penny of it.'

'I didn't earn it,' Jefferson said.

'Nonsense. You probably saved my life, and you've certainly saved that estate agent's marriage. You said before that you didn't know what to do with yourself. Spend it on fun stuff. Or on setting up a little business or something. Anything but giving it to Padgett's heirs.'

He frowned. 'I'm not much of a businessman.'

She grinned. 'I helped my husband with bookkeeping

when we were first married. I'm no capitalist, but I know my way around a balance sheet. I'll give you a hand, if you swear that Padgett's estate won't get a penny of the cash.'

'I dunno. I'm not even sure what sort of business I'd be any good at.'

'You told me you were a private investigator.'

'Yeah, well. Poetic licence.'

'Why not give it a go?' Her eyes were shining; perhaps it was the wine. 'Be your own boss. Make the most of your professional experience.'

'You're kidding me.'

She looked at him thoughtfully. 'Jefferson Hope…I'm sure I've heard the name before. In a book?'

He sighed. 'Blame my old man. Hope is a character in a Sherlock Holmes story.'

'There you are, then. What could be more fitting? I can see it in neon lights now. *Jefferson Hope, private eye*.'

'Only one snag,' he said. 'I wasn't named after a detective, but a murderer.'

She raised her eyebrows. 'Seriously?'

'Seriously.' He swallowed the last of his pie, and belched. 'Is it any wonder I'm a tormented soul?'

As she threw her head back and laughed, he considered her.

What am I getting myself into?

Crime Scene

Kate Ellis

'*Comment vous appellez-vous*, Madame?' Barney Tollemache's French was rusty but he always believed in trying.

His expensive fountain pen hovered over the title page. He'd bought the pen when he'd received his first contract and he regarded it as a talisman. Everybody needs luck. Especially in his line of work.

'You already know my name.'

His eyes had been focused on the book so he hadn't been paying much attention to the woman standing in front of him, the last in the queue to have her copy of his hardback signed.

He looked up at her. After a day spent murdering the French language, her English voice aroused his interest. She was in her early thirties, around his own age, with blond hair and a short black skirt which left little to the imagination. Her long scarlet fingernails reminded him of the talons of an elegant bird of prey whose nest was lined with old copies of Vogue. He experienced a faint bat squeak of recognition but the more he studied her, the more convinced he was that he'd never seen her before. He would have remembered.

'Sorry. You'll have to remind me. My memory's...' he said with an apologetic grin. He went through a rapid mental list of all the females he'd encountered over the two years since his novel was published, but there'd been so many festivals, so many libraries, so many book-signings, that it wasn't humanly possible to recall everyone. Especially for someone like Barney, who'd always been terrible with faces.

'You really don't remember me?'

'You'll have to give me a clue.'

He suddenly had the awful thought that he might have slept with this woman, that she might have been one of his literary festival one-night stands. To forget about such intimacy seemed bad manners at best, sordid at worst. But these things happened—especially after the amount of drink he usually put away at such events. And he needed a drink now, so he glanced at his watch, wondering how soon he could get away.

She was smiling now, teasing, enjoying his discomfort. 'I'll give you a clue. It was a very long time ago.'

'Before I was published?'

'Long before.'

'At Oxford?' he said hopefully. His university days had been equally alcohol-soaked and his memories were consequently hazy.

'Before that.'

'School? Bilson Hall?'

Her smile widened. He'd got it right. If only he could remember her name.

'Of course. I remember now,' he lied. 'Sorry it took so long to muster my brain cells into action.' He beamed his most appealing smile at her, the smile that guaranteed forgiveness of any sin—and he'd committed quite a few in his time.

'That's okay. Aren't you going to sign my book?'

He looked at the book and realised it was an English edition, whereas most copies he'd signed that day had been French translations. 'Remind me how you spell your name again?' He looked at her expectantly, pleased with himself for thinking up this ploy.

'S U Z Y. Suzy with a Z.' She leaned forward and he felt an unexpected thrill of desire pass through his body.

'Of course. How could I forget?' he said. But he had forgotten and he was still no wiser.

He began to write. 'For Suzy. Once seen, never forgotten.'

'Would you like love or best wishes?'

'Just your signature will do.'

He signed it with a flourish and when he handed it back to her their fingers touched. Then he looked round and realised the other authors on his panel had departed and they were now alone apart from a thin girl who was refilling bottles of water in the far corner.

'What brings you to Paris?' he asked.

'Same as you. Work. Enjoying the festival?'

Barney shrugged. 'It keeps my French publisher happy.'

'Fancy a drink?' said Suzy, her voice full of promise.

'Why not?' With the prospect of a large red wine dangled before him, he hurried to pack up his things, hoping the bar wouldn't be too crowded.

'I wasn't thinking of here,' she said as though she'd read his mind. 'My apartment's not far away and I bought a case of rather nice Beaujolais when I was down that way last year.'

'Your place it is, then.' He suddenly felt reckless, like a boy released from school at the end of term. He was stuck there in a strange city without any of the usual drinking buddies he met at British festivals and here was an attractive woman about to ply him with decent wine. Things were looking up.

The convention hotel was on the banks of the Seine overlooking the Île de la Cité. Barney could see the towers of Notre Dame from his third-floor window but the demands of his French publisher and the punishing schedule of panels and book-signings meant he hadn't been able to get out and explore the city as much as he would have liked. But now he was eager to seize his chance.

Suzy assured him her apartment was nearby, although they seemed to walk for ages through the narrow, picturesque streets of the Marais, so different from Haussmann's imposing boulevards. After a while they found themselves in a large square surrounded by fine arcaded buildings with a fountain in the centre of a formal garden where children played on the manicured grass watched by their elegant mothers. When he asked Suzy where they were she told him it was the Place des Vosges. The name was familiar and he knew he must have been there before as a student when he'd spent a weekend sampling the cheapest alcohol the city had to offer—not that he remembered much about it. He stopped to take in the scene, until Suzy took his arm and led him off down a side street into a maze of ancient buildings. Eventually she stopped by an old wooden front door with an iron grille set into the top and a row of neat bell pushes at the side.

'This is me.'

She pushed the door and it opened smoothly to reveal a stone-flagged hallway. A stone stairway with intricate wrought-iron banisters snaked to the upper floors of the building. The walls were whitewashed and the flaking paint looked as though it was meant to be that way. French shabby chic. But Barney's mind was on the wine—and any other treats that might be on offer. He followed her up the stairs to the top floor.

'A Parisian garret,' he said as he stepped into the small apartment in the eaves. The walls sloped but the white walls and the light flooding in from the tall windows gave it a feeling of space. 'Yours?'

'Yes. I'm working in Paris for a couple of years.'

She made for the kitchen and he followed. He needed that wine; he could almost taste it. He stood in the doorway of the tiny room, little more than a cupboard, and watched her extract the cork from the bottle. There was a sensuous quality about the movement but he was focused on the red liquid cascading into the glass rather than the prospect of any sexual delights to come. When she passed him his drink, he caught the ghost of her perfume—something heady he didn't recognise.

'Cheers,' he raised the glass.

'*Santé*,' she replied, her eyes fixed expectantly on his face.

He drained the glass like a thirsty man in a desert and she smiled when he held his glass out for a refill.

'Let's sit down.' She made her way to the sofa, and when she sat, she patted the space beside her. Before accepting the invitation he picked up the bottle and placed it on the tiled coffee table with exaggerated care. The wine was starting to affect him, which was unusual because he'd always been able to hold his liquor; he'd had years of practice. But now the room was swimming in and out of focus. He put down his glass. Perhaps the life of a crime writer was catching up with him at last.

'Sorry,' he said, concentrating on getting the slurred words out. 'I haven't had anything to eat since lunch.'

'Drinking on an empty stomach doesn't agree with me either,' she said sympathetically. He was aware of her fingers stroking his hair. 'Why don't you lie down for a bit? I'll rustle up something to eat.'

Barney murmured his thanks and closed his eyes. The world was still spinning and when he sat back, he felt himself drifting into sleep. The convention had exhausted him so, a doze would do him good, he thought.

He felt bad, as though a thousand builders with lump hammers were hard at work in his head. He opened his eyes and immediately closed them again because the light streaming in from the window hurt him. A minute later he tried again, looking at the room through half-open eyelids until he summoned the courage to lever himself upright. This had never happened before and he was seized by panic. What if there was something seriously wrong with him?

Once he was in a sitting position he looked round, confused at first. Then he remembered. He'd been having a drink with a woman called Suzy when he'd fallen asleep. He looked at his watch. Seven-thirty. He must have been out for a couple of hours. He remembered the bottle of wine and glass on the coffee table but they weren't there now, so she must have tidied up and left him to sleep it off. The heavy silence told him she was no longer in the apartment. Perhaps she'd gone out to buy something for dinner—or more wine, he thought hopefully as he tried to stand up. He felt shaky and collapsed onto the sofa again, but on the third attempt he managed to struggle to his feet.

He needed a pee so he staggered towards a closed door he hoped led to the bathroom, undoing his zip on the way. He opened the door and the bright white tiles told him he was in the right place. The bathroom was spacious and he headed straight for the toilet, closing his eyes as he relieved himself. He immediately felt better—until he turned his head and caught a glimpse of red against the clinical white.

She was sprawled in the bath, eyes closed as if in sleep. The blood on her blouse stood out, red against the whiteness of the crisp cotton. It formed a heart-shaped patch on her chest and he knew she was dead. He tore his eyes away from her and saw a knife on the bathroom floor; a sharp kitchen knife with a white handle covered in blood. Then he caught a glimpse of himself in the mirror and saw blood on his own shirt, splashed on the front and creeping up the cuffs.

He stood staring at the body, paralysed with fear. He should call the police. It was the only thing to do. The private eye in his book wouldn't have bothered; he would have solved the crime with no official help. But this was real life, not fiction. Although...there was something horribly familiar about the scenario.

It took him a few moments to recognise the similarity to the opening scene from his novel; the blood-soaked girl in the bath; the detective passing out and not knowing how she got there.

When he stumbled into the main room to fetch his phone from his jacket pocket, he found his battery was dead.

•••••

He had second thoughts about the police and got out of there fast after wiping the place clean of fingerprints with a tea towel, hoping nobody had seen him. If he alerted the authorities, he'd be subjected to hour upon hour of awkward questions, and he knew nothing, apart from the fact that he hadn't killed her. *Had he?* He'd lost a couple of hours and that blank in his memory made him uneasy. As did the resemblance to the murder in his book.

He hurried back to the hotel, his jacket concealing the blood on his shirt. It was the gala dinner that night and he needed a shower before he ventured down. His head felt better, but he wondered whether it would be wise to drink. Maybe he should stick to orange juice that evening—although the prospect of such abstinence horrified him.

He didn't know how he got through the evening—picking at his food, chatting with his French publisher and translator and greeting his fellow writers with his usual bonhomie while all the time trying to banish the vision of the dead woman in the bath from his mind. Had he really been so drunk that he couldn't remember what happened? He hadn't had that much, so surely it wasn't possible. But he had seen what he had seen.

He excused himself early and returned to his room. He'd put the shirt into a plastic bag and he knew it would be wise to get rid of it, so the next morning he rose early and caught the Metro to the Gare du Nord, where he dumped the bag into a bin. He'd wiped it clean of fingerprints before going out—he was a crime writer so he knew about these things—and he'd been careful to place it into another bag and pull it out protected by a handkerchief at the crucial time. After it was done he returned to the hotel in a daze. He made his living by writing about murder but he'd never before encountered its reality.

At breakfast he found that morning's newspaper on a neighbouring seat and he trawled through it, using his schoolboy French to translate the headlines. But nowhere did it mention that a woman's body had been found in a Marais apartment.

She hadn't been found yet. And he was returning to Manchester in three days' time.

The temptation to go back to the apartment was great, especially when he remembered that she'd been in possession of a book signed by him. He knew enough about police investigations to know that, if it was known that they'd had any contact, he'd have to be traced, interviewed, and eliminated from inquiries. The brand-new book, signed at the convention, would be a clue.

He told himself there was no way they could link him to Suzy's death just because he'd signed a book for her. But what if he'd been seen leaving the hotel with her? What if they'd been caught on CCTV? Although he'd once heard that the French weren't as obsessed with surveillance cameras as the British, who were said to be the most watched people in Europe. If he kept calm he'd be home soon and all would be well.

The day before he was due to leave for England his French publisher took him for lunch in a good restaurant where he consumed a bottle of Burgundy with no ill effects and walked back to the hotel feeling mellow. If there were going to be repercussions from the incident in the Marais, he would surely have heard by now. Perhaps the similarity to the murder in his book was just a coincidence. Perhaps she had been killed by a lover who came in, found him there asleep, jumped to conclusions, and killed her in a fit of jealous rage. The French were reputed to be very forgiving about crimes of passion.

He returned to his room intending to shower and pack before that evening's session in the bar, and as he helped himself to a bottle of water from the minibar, he noticed a large brown envelope lying by the door as though someone had pushed it underneath. Curiosity made him tear it open and his heart hammered as the photographs slithered onto the bed. He stared at the coloured images and felt sick. She was lying there in the bath, her chest a mass of crusted blood. The photographs had been taken from different angles, like crime-scene pictures, some close-ups and others taking in the whole bathroom. There were others, too—Barney slumped on the sofa with his eyes closed, a bloody knife clasped in his hand.

Then there was the accompanying note, written in neat capitals on deckle-edged note paper:

DO AS YOU'RE TOLD OR THESE GO TO THE POLICE.

Barney was so preoccupied with his problem he hardly noticed time passing as he journeyed back on Eurostar. Could he have killed Suzy without remembering a thing? He wasn't a violent man and he had absolutely no recollection of it. Besides, why would he kill her? The pictures were hidden at the bottom of his case and he couldn't wait to destroy them; a symbolic act because he knew they were only copies.

The sender of the letter had ordered him to do as he was told but there'd been no more communication. Perhaps it was some sort of frame-up. But who had taken the pictures?

Once back at the flat in the centre of Manchester he'd bought with the publisher's extremely generous advance for his first novel, he ripped up the photographs and pushed them into the waste disposal. He needed to resume work on the manuscript he'd abandoned to go to Paris. It was a second draft, an untamed mess of a plot that needed sorting out. But when he sat at his desk staring at the words on the paper, his mind refused to focus.

His debut novel, *In My Flesh*, had taken the world of crime fiction by storm, been awarded the CWA Gold Dagger, and had made his name and his fortune. The book had been translated into forty languages, a film had been made of it with a major Hollywood star in the leading role, and his agent frequently fielded requests for TV interviews and festival appearances. *In My Flesh* had changed his life, but since then he'd found it difficult to produce anything as noteworthy. His agent had assured him that 'second novel syndrome' was common. But that didn't stop the sleepless nights and the increasing feeling of hopelessness.

Over the next days he found it hard to concentrate on work. Instead he found himself trawling the Internet for reports of a body found in a Paris apartment. But there was nothing. Perhaps she hadn't been discovered yet, he thought. Perhaps she wouldn't be found until the neighbours noticed an unpleasant smell. The thought disgusted him but it was the most likely explanation. Surely somebody, her colleagues perhaps, would notice her absence, but then he realised she hadn't told him what she did or where she worked. He knew nothing about her, apart from the fact they'd been at school together.

He had some old photo albums stuffed in the back of the sleek, pale wood sideboard in the living room. He wasn't normally the sentimental type, but he'd felt a need to have something from his past in the sterile modern flat in the glass tower. After a brief search he pulled out an album filled with pictures from his childhood. Then there were the school photographs, teenagers lined up in rows wearing smart uniforms and forced smiles. The name of the school 'Bilson Hall' was printed at the bottom of the cardboard frame in embossed gold letters along with a date—2004. He turned it over and saw a list of names printed on the back, row by row and left to right—but none of them was Suzy. There was, however, a Susannah listed, but when he studied the photograph he saw that the corresponding girl was black. He remembered she'd been deputy head girl and had gone on to medical school. She definitely wasn't his Suzy...and neither, on close inspection, were any of the others.

Perhaps she'd been away that day but he hadn't kept in touch with anyone from school, so there was nobody he could ask. When he'd gone to Oxford, he'd discarded his old friends like a butterfly shedding a chrysalis.

Then three days later the second letter arrived.

The postmark on the envelope was unreadable and Barney held it for a while before slitting it open with the dagger given him by a fan which now served as a paper knife. His hands shook as he unfolded the note written on the same thick deckle-edged paper as the one that had accompanied the pictures. Although the bloody image of the dead woman still disturbed his sleep, his memories of the Paris incident were beginning to fade. But the words on the paper brought them flooding back, raw and fresh:

DEAR MURDERER,
MEET ME IN THE READING ROOM.
CENTRAL LIBRARY.
3 P.M. TUESDAY.
TELL NO ONE.

It was Tuesday already so he didn't have much time to brood on it. He spent the morning trying to edit his manuscript but the increasingly meaningless words swam in front of his eyes. His flat was open plan and from where he was sitting he could see a bottle of wine squatting on the kitchen worktop. He needed a drink. Dutch courage. Giving silent thanks to the inventor of the screw top, he opened the bottle, pouring the ruby liquid into a large glass. If he was going to face his nemesis that afternoon, he needed to take the edge off his fear.

Creeping into the Central Library's magnificent circular reading room, he barely noticed the huge dome above his head and the elaborate clock in the centre. He'd always loved the room, a temple to reading created by a proud industrial city, but now the place seemed tainted by this new association with his Paris experience. He looked round, scanning the faces. His letter-writer had to be there somewhere.

None of the people there appeared to be the type who'd

send those photographs, although he was sure blackmailers came in all shapes and sizes. And was it blackmail? There had been no mention of money in the first note delivered to his hotel room, just 'do as you're told or these go to the police,' But what was he supposed to do?

He sat down at a table and waited, his eyes fixed on the entrance. Nobody had reacted when he'd walked in, so he was as sure as he could be that his letter-writer hadn't yet arrived. He looked at his watch. Five minutes to go.

At three o'clock on the dot, a man appeared in the doorway and looked around. He was thin, almost emaciated, with a long face and, even though his mousy hair was thinning, he was a similar age to Barney, he guessed. And there was certainly something familiar about him, although he couldn't place what it was.

The man was circling the room, studying faces. Barney picked up a newspaper and hid himself behind it, although this meant he couldn't keep an eye on the newcomer. He was aware of someone sitting down on the chair next to him and he sneaked a glance at his new neighbour. It was him.

As the man leaned towards him the sense of familiarity increased. Then he spoke, in hushed library tones.

'Hello, Barney. Long time no see.'

Barney put the paper down and twisted round to face him, his heart beating fast. 'You'll have to remind me.'

'School days. Sixth form at Bilson Hall. Luke Vardey. Remember?'

Barney stared at him. He remembered all right. They'd been best mates, sharing each other's hopes, dreams, and secrets until they'd gone their separate ways—although Luke had changed a lot in the intervening years, almost beyond recognition.

'So…er, what have you been doing with yourself since school?' Barney asked, feeling a sudden nag of guilt that he'd made no effort to keep in touch. Luke had gone through a bad time when he was eighteen. He'd suffered some sort of breakdown and failed his A-levels, while Barney had swept off to Oxford without giving his old friend a second thought.

'This and that,' Luke whispered. 'You got my letter?'

Barney saw desperation in Luke's eyes—and suddenly felt afraid.

'What do you want?'

Luke opened the shabby old briefcase he was carrying and drew out some photographs, copies of the ones Barney had received in Paris.

'How did you get these?' Barney pushed them away. He didn't want to be reminded.

'Never mind how I got them. If you don't do as you're told, they go to the police.'

'You want money?'

'It'll do, for starters.'

'What do you mean?'

Luke hesitated for a moment. 'I'll be in touch,' he said before picking up his briefcase and hurrying away.

It was obvious that Luke had endured hard times since leaving school and Barney supposed that when he'd heard about his literary success he must have decided to try his luck. Although this didn't explain how he came to have the photographs.

After leaving Oxford, Barney had taken a series of dead-end jobs while he struggled to establish a career in writing.

He'd failed at first, receiving rejection after rejection, until he'd found an old synopsis amongst a load of old school books in his parents' loft and set about transforming it into *In My Flesh,* which rapidly became a best seller. He'd been lucky and as he'd moved on with his life, he'd put Luke out of his mind. Now he had the uneasy feeling that maybe he owed him something. Perhaps paying him to keep quiet about Suzy's murder would be the right thing to do.

A few days later he received another letter, suggesting a meeting at Luke's address, naming the time and place. What he had to say to Barney needed to be said in private.

Luke lived in a large Victorian house in a run-down area favoured by students. Barney's nose wrinkled as he passed the wheelie bins lined up for collection in the once prosperous tree-lined road that had plummeted down the social ladder over the course of the twentieth century. There was a row of plastic buzzers beside the front door, some broken and mended with peeling tape, and Barney was struck by the contrast to Suzy's Marais apartment building.

As Luke led the way up the uncarpeted staircase, Barney could smell drains and stale cooking. The bedsit was a small, seedy room with a tiny kitchenette at one end and an unmade bed at the other. There was an old gas fire and the wallpaper was peeling. The only thing of interest, as far as Barney could see, was an old-fashioned typewriter on a desk in the large bay window.

'This Suzy...did you know her?' Barney asked as he took in his surroundings.

'She was a friend of mine,' Luke answered. 'She helped me.'

'So you were in Paris when I was?'

'What if I was? It's you we're talking about.'

'I didn't kill Suzy.'

'You were holding the knife. Your prints were all over it. And there was blood all over your shirt.' He made for the kitchen and rooted in a cupboard. Barney immediately recognised the carrier bag he produced. It was the one he'd dumped in the bin at the Gare du Nord.

'How the hell…?'

There was a look of triumph on Luke's face. 'For a crime writer you're not very good at this sort of thing, are you?'

'How much do you want?'

'This isn't about money. It's about truth.'

The seed of suspicion that had been growing in Barney's mind suddenly sprung to life. 'It was you who killed Suzy? You stabbed her while I was asleep and left her body in the bath like in my book?'

'What makes you think you didn't kill her? I don't expect you remember much about that afternoon.'

'I think I was drugged. It's the only explanation.'

'Or drunk. You drink too much, Barney. You didn't know what you were doing.'

'How do you know all this? Were you following me?' Barney felt himself sweating with panic. Luke was right. He didn't know what he did that afternoon. He might be a killer. Then he noticed Luke's hands shaking as he fidgeted with the hem of his shirt.

'I'll offer you a deal. I'll destroy all the photos, provided you tell the truth.'

'I don't know the truth. I can't remember what happened.'

'I'm not talking about Suzy now. I want you to tell the truth about *In My Flesh*. The idea was mine. I wrote that synopsis and the first two chapters in the sixth form—I gave you a copy, remember? Asked your opinion about it. I kept a copy, so I can prove you're a fraud.'

There was a heavy silence while Barney took it in.

'I want you to call your agent and tell her,' Luke continued. 'Then you'll make a public announcement—tell the world the story was mine.'

'Did you kill Suzy because of this?'

Luke shook his head. 'I didn't kill her. You did. And I want half the royalties you've earned so far from my idea because I need to get out of this shithole. If you haven't announced it by the end of this week, the pictures go to the police.'

Barney gaped at him, his fists clenched. What Luke said was true. His inability to write wasn't due to second novel syndrome; it was because he hadn't produced the idea for the first. He'd put Luke's detailed synopsis into decent English, tweaking it so that the narrative flowed and the tension built. But the story hadn't been his, and he couldn't see how he was going to create the follow-up. His mind didn't work that way. Maybe he had no choice but to give in and do as Luke asked.

But what else did he have in his life? *In My Flesh* had brought him everything he'd longed for—fame, money, security, a purpose. And what was to stop Luke from demanding the remaining half of his royalties, using the threat of being named as Suzy's murderer to wield power over him for the rest of his life?

Barney had a sudden bitter vision of the life he'd built on the lie vanishing, of being forced to hand over everything until he and Luke eventually swapped their lives. He saw a vegetable knife amongst a heap of apple peelings on the stained table a couple of feet away and, on impulse, he grabbed it and lunged at Luke, thrusting the blade in once, twice—just as he must have thrust it into Suzy's body that day.

He'd heard it said that murder is easier the second time around, but it didn't feel that way as he stared down with horror at the thin, shabby man lying lifeless at his feet. He felt as though he was in the middle of a nightmare but this was real and he knew he needed to eliminate all evidence that they'd ever had any contact. There was no sign of a computer in the flat and Barney was grateful for Luke's old-fashioned habit of communicating by letter. But then Luke had always been different.

After wiping everything he might have touched, Barney crept back down the stairs, listening for telltale noises in the silent house. When he reached the front door he covered his hand with his sleeve before touching the handle.

Then he heard the scrape of a key in the lock so he sprang back, but there was nowhere to hide. The door swung open and he saw a blond woman standing in the doorway, staring at him in astonishment.

It's not often people return from the dead.

Susan Vardey was the chief witness for the prosecution and she admitted to the court in hushed tones that she'd persuaded her brother, Luke, to claim what was rightfully his by blackmailing the man who'd stolen his idea all those years ago. She lived in Paris and when she'd read that the defendant was to attend the crime convention, she'd thought up the idea of drugging him and staging the murder scene in the bathroom—she'd worked in the theatre for years—and her brother had taken the photos.

Luke had been duped by Barney Tollemache, an

arrogant boy she'd never liked when he'd visited their home. She'd been in the year below the boys, but she'd been plain then with mousy hair and braces on her teeth, so it was no wonder Tollemache hadn't recognised the girl he'd ignored. Luke had suffered problems for years and Susan had wanted justice for him—but now she realised her deception had been wrong. She'd thought it would force Tollemache to tell the truth. How could she have foreseen his violent reaction?

After Luke's funeral she postponed her return to Paris to clear out his Manchester flat. It was a filthy dump and the thought of him living out his last sad years there depressed her. Poor Luke had had nothing, not even a computer. He'd lived in his own narrow world of fantasy. But he'd been her brother and she'd loved him.

As she slid his sparse possessions into black plastic sacks, she came across five fat manuscripts, all typed on the little manual typewriter on the desk in the window. Five novels.

She placed them carefully into the suitcase she'd brought with her. With all the publicity about Tollemache's deception, she was certain there'd be a lot of interest. It was the least she could do for Luke.

Normal Rules Do Not Apply

Peter Guttridge

'Nobody wants to see a boob frowning,' Bridget Frost bellowed.

I looked down at my friend, the former Bitch of the Broadsheets, now a TV celebrity of sorts. And at what the *Daily Mail* would call her 'ample assets.' They didn't seem to be frowning. I glanced at the crowd of people around us. Until this crime festival in this labyrinthine hotel in Cathedral Gardens in Bristol, I hadn't seen her for ten years. However, age didn't seem to have withered her nor affected the loudness of her voice one iota.

Aside from my embarrassment, there was a potential Walls of Jericho situation here. As of old, I imagined traffic on other continents screeching to a halt. The floor actually shuddered, as did we all. About twenty of us, waiting now for an irritating length of time for the lift doors to open. We were all trying to get to the Saturday 2.30 p.m. panel featuring U.S. global-best-seller Randall Spear.

'Botox boobs?' I said. 'I thought Botox was for crow's-feet, lined foreheads, and stuff.'

'And armpits.'

'Armpits.'

'Yeah, have you never seen how wrinkled your armpits can be?

'To be honest, I don't look at my armpits much. Plus I've got hair in them.'

Bridget snorted. An interesting sound.

'Armpit hair is the latest trend on Instagram among women. According to the *Daily Mail*—so it must be true—a quarter of millennial women have hairy armpits.'

'Okay—but going back to what you were saying…'

'Botox has taken over from implants for boobs. Painless, scar-free, immediate. Lasts between four and six months.'

'How's it work?'

'I should know that, how? And care, why?'

A skinny American woman with knitting needles sticking out of her shoulder bag (best not to ask) was standing behind Bridget. She chipped in:

'It weakens the pectoralis minor muscles beneath the breasts which means that the major muscles above have to do more work. It gives your breasts a lift. And you don't get crepey cleavage. In fact, it knocks years off your cleavage. It works especially well with a large embonpoint.' She looked at me. 'Tits to you.'

Well, tits to you too, I thought but didn't say. I'm a writer, for goodness sake, I know what an 'embonpoint' is. More or less. I looked at her bag again. She had so many knitting needles sticking out, it looked like Robin Hood's quiver of arrows. She indicated her own flat chest. 'Not that I have that problem.'

What were the chances of two women with a clearly intimate knowledge of Botox boobs meeting at a lift door in a hotel in Bristol hosting a crime fiction festival? Well, quite high, given that in the crime-writing fraternity normal rules about what was…well, normal, did not always apply.

There was momentary silence filled by a tall, bald, stoop-shouldered Canadian saying loudly to his much shorter wife:

'It's a *de facto* monopsony.'

He spoke loudly, I knew, because he was hard of hearing. But all I could think of was reaching over and brushing the flakes of dandruff off his shoulders. I've always assumed that dandruff on a bald man can only mean God really has it in for him. This guy looked like he'd been standing too near a log fire where the ash had drifted and settled on him.

'Obviously,' his wife said, quietly but fiercely.

'What?' he said, stooping more. I saw that her height and (maliciously?) low voice were probably the reasons he was stoop-shouldered. Relationships, eh?

'I said *obviously* it's a *de facto* monopsony.'

Bridget swung round to face them.

'What the *defuckto* are you talking about?'

'Monopsony—it's an economics thing,' the gangly Canadian said. 'Where a single buyer has a choice of the same product from a number of suppliers. So the convention bookshop has a problem because crime fiction buyers have a range of suppliers to go to and if they are volume buyers, then obviously, they are going to be looking at price—'

I saw Bridget give him a withering look but, foolishly, I paid no heed.

'Yes,' I piped up. 'It's from the Greek "mono" and–'

'It's *all* Greek to me,' Bridget snapped.

'One bit is actually Latin,' I said. 'It means—'

She squared off to me. I'd like to say I towered over her,

which, theoretically, given I'm six-foot, four, I did. But at this moment think of me as Nick Pisa (Leaning Tower of) rather than my actual daft name, Nick Madrid.

'Why can't you guys speak normal English?' Bridget said. 'Why do crime authors feel they have to come over as bright and high-falutin'—I've read the crap you write.'

There was a collective gasp and not a little tutting (there were 'cosy crime' fans among us). There was also nervous laughter, not least from me, but then Bridget always has made me nervous.

'You're not a fan of the genre?' asked the American woman with knitting needles sticking out of her shoulder bag.

'*Genre*—see, there you go again,' Bridget harrumphed. 'What's wrong with using an English word? Like *rubbish*, for instance. Are you a fan of this *rubbish*, Bridget? I mean it almost becomes a rhetorical question then, doesn't it? Why would I want to read made-up stuff with all the real stuff going on in the world that you just couldn't make up?'

'But of course you've read Nick's stuff,' the Canadian said. 'True crime—and featuring you, after all.'

'Best not to go there,' I said quickly.

Bridget Frost, the Life Force embodied in one feisty, promiscuous, hard-drinking, vulgar, loud-mouthed, loving, irresistible woman, with whom I had stumbled over various crimes in the course of our friendship. Stumbled over far too frequently, frankly, but, hey, I've got six books out of them.

I've been promoting the books at crime fiction festivals around the world with some success and a lot of pleasure for the past ten years. Every year, here at Bristol CrimeFest. Although, prior to this, Bridget has never accompanied me to any other festival, even though she loomed large in the books (and my life).

The truth is I hadn't seen Bridget for almost ten years, because she finally got round to reading the first of my books based on our adventures. She wasn't happy.

'We could walk up the four floors,' I said as the lift doors remained closed and there was no movement on the floor indicator above.

As if I'd said abracadabra, the lift door slid open. And there was a collective gasp as we all looked at the spread-eagled body of Randall Spear, on the floor of the lift, a knitting needle sticking out of his throat and an enormous pool of blood soaking into the carpet around him.

Not a totally collective gasp. Bridget sniffed. Then tottered away (in her usual unfeasibly high heels), muttering (loudly): 'So that event isn't happening. Let's go back to the bar.'

And the woman with the knitting needles said: 'That looks like my number three!'

•●⬤●•

'Who would want to murder Randall Spear?' I said as we settled at a table on the terrace so she could smoke one of many cigarettes.

'You've obviously not been to bed with him,' Bridget said, blowing smoke in my face.

True. Hang on.

'Bridget?'

She just looked at me. Well, I suppose we had been here two days.

Bridget's shoulders suddenly slumped.

'What is it?' I said.

'I can't believe you would describe me like that in your books. What have I ever done but given you love and affection?'

'I'm sorry,' I said meekly. 'Are you okay?'

'I'm managing,' she said, her voice breaking.

'Bridget,' I said, putting my arm around her, 'it must have really got to you.'

'Another triple vodka and a bowl of pistachios, handsome,' Bridget said, as the barman walked by. Emphasising the request by nipping his bum.

'Really got to you,' I muttered.

The barman returned with her drink. He smiled; she smiled; I paid. Life, as I know it. When the barman had gone, she said: 'Saying I have no dress sense—how fucking dare you?' Given it was through gritted teeth, the volume was impressive. She saw my look. 'And don't think that coming over all meek is going to make any difference.'

Coming over all meek? I *am* meek. That's a good thing… isn't it? But actually my expression was bemusement. I'd been worrying about describing her promiscuity, drunkenness, and vulgarity and she was more concerned about a throwaway remark about something she was wearing.

'What was Randall Spear like?' I said, attempting to shift the subject.

'That's a bit personal, isn't it?' she said, looking over my shoulder to see if someone more interesting was around. 'The usual disappointment,' she added absently.

'I didn't actually mean that, I meant what kind of person was he?'

'I would know that how?' she said.

'Well, you must have had a conversation with him. How did you meet him?'

'In the underground car park. He helped me with my luggage.'

'Did you know who he was?'

More smoke in the face.

'I still don't know who he is. Then I saw him later out here. He was with that enthusiastic man full of conspiracy theories. Who in turn was sharing a water bottle with a Cockney geezer who writes Westerns—the bottle was full of gin and tonic.'

'How did you know it was gin and tonic?'

She looked at me.

'Good gin too. Twelve quid for a glass of Sauvignon Blanc in this place? No wonder people bring their own.'

'And Randall was with them?'

'There was a gang of people. He left when that very tall man who is played by a midget in films…'

'I think you mean his character is played by a midge—Bridget, we don't use that word these days.'

'You just did.'

'I meant horizontally challenged,' I said.

Bridget smirked.

'I think you mean vertically challenged. But let's agree on "that short Scientologist," shall we?'

'And you mean Lee Child. Any of the organisers?'

As I said this, the CrimeFest team—Adrian, Myles, Donna, and Liz—came onto the terrace and fanned out. Individually, they went up to each group of crime writers and readers in turn.

'Tell Bridget who Randall Spear is,' I said as Adrian, the organiser with the shaved head, came over to us. 'It's her first time at a crime festival.'

'*Was*,' he said. 'And it's a convention not a festival.'

'He's Dutch,' I said to Bridget by way of introduction. Both looked at me bemused. 'You know…so a stickler for accuracy,' I added weakly.

'Why is it called CrimeFest if it's a convention?' Bridget said. Adrian frowned but ignored the question.

'Anyway, I just want to reassure you that events will continue as soon as possible but when they do, people will have to use the lifts at the back of the hotel as police have cordoned off the lifts at the front as a crime scene. But in the meantime we all have to stay in the bar. They're going to want to interview everyone who had any dealings with him.'

'That'll take hours,' Bridget said. 'Are the drinks on the house?'

'We're working on that,' Myles said as the other three CrimeFest folk joined us.

'Tell Bridget who Randall Spear was.'

'I thought I saw you with him,' Donna said cautiously.

'So?' Bridget said airily.

'Randall Spear wasn't his real name,' Adrian said. 'Though that's the name his books are marketed under. Probably the most successful crime writer in the world, though it has never been clear whether he was one man or an army of writers all writing under the same brand. And, of course, nobody could be sure he was a *he* at all.'

'Bloody gender fluidity,' Bridget muttered.

'I just meant he might be a woman writing as a man,' Adrian said.

'Theories abound,' Liz chipped in. 'He'd hidden behind anonymity for years. No photographs, no interviews until he turned up here. This would have been his first interview. At least we know now he wasn't Stephen King writing under another name.'

'Or a literary author slumming it, as John Banville says he does,' I added.

'I always thought that rather than a posse of writers, he

was two writers,' Myles said. 'Relatively common in crime and mystery fiction.'

'So why didn't both of them come, like Michael Stanley?' I said.

Bridget looked puzzled. 'I met Michael Stanley. I'm pretty sure he's one person.'

'You met Michael not Stanley.'

'How many Lee Childs are there?' Bridget said. I recognised that predatory glint in her eye.

'Is that a metaphysical question?' Adrian said.

'He's married,' I said.

'There's nothing metaphorical about it,' Bridget said.

'Metaphysical,' I murmured.

'Let's just keep it at physical, shall we?'

'So when did Randall Spear arrive?' I said, trying to get the investigation back on track.

'Yesterday midday,' Liz said. She turned to Bridget. 'I liked you on *Countdown*.'

Countdown was a long-running UK afternoon show involving two contestants making words out of random letters and adding up long strings of numbers. It was news to me that Bridget had been on it.

'I don't know why they took such offence,' Bridget sniffed.

'Unprecedented number of complaints,' Myles said.

'For what?' I said.

Bridget shrugged.

'It was probably the first time either "fisting" or "rimming" had appeared on the *Countdown* board,' Myles said. 'And certainly never in the same show.'

'It was the sums that let me down,' Bridget said. 'They've never been my strong point and when they confiscated my calculator just before the game started, I knew I wasn't going to win.'

'Your maths were very entertaining,' Myles said drily. 'And that randy comedian Russell Brand in Dictionary Corner was equally entertained by your word choices.'

'That could have been interesting after the show but I was fourth on his list and I wasn't having that,' Bridget said. 'Which, mind you, was a step up from sixteenth in the queue he proposed after I was part of the audience on *Big Brother's Little Brother* years ago.'

None of us could think of an answer to that. I knew something of Bridget's various TV appearances. She had told me on the phone, when she agreed to come to Bristol to do an event with me about our adventures, that she'd surfed the zeitgeist of reality television as if it had been created for her. (Well, okay, her actual words were: 'I decided that if all those D-list morons could make it work for them, so could I.')

She'd explained that she'd toyed with *X Factor* but decided she couldn't figure out an angle. She had the 'winning would mean the world to me' stuff down pat (she'd already used it in four other shows) but the problem was that she had a perfectly pleasant singing voice. So she couldn't steal the show as one of the self-deluded idiots who sound like cats in a sack or drone on as if their medication has kicked in big-time, but nor could she hope to win because her voice wasn't fantastic. And the last thing Bridget would ever admit to being was average.

She'd been trying to reach a tipping point where she could move into the celebrity versions of reality shows. She was eager to go into the Australian jungle for *I'm a Celebrity...Get Me Out of Here* and even to eat a kangaroo's testicles if that's what it took.

Alas the opportunity never arose on screen, even though she had done something not altogether dissimilar in private with some Antipodean guy who'd claimed to be a TV producer and had promised her a shot on the show in return for a sexual favour. She was livid when she realised he'd conned her, but with age had come cunning, and she went through the procedure with him again. This time, however, he ended up in hospital. Percy would never be pointed at the porcelain in quite the same way again.

'Did Spear arrive alone?' I said, trying to get the investigation back on track.

'We've told all this to the police, you know,' Myles said.

'Of course he arrived alone,' Bridget said. 'I told you I met him in the car park.'

'Oh, the police will definitely want to talk to you,' Adrian said. 'How long were you with him alone?'

'Bit longer than usual but not by much,' Bridget said.

'He meant in the car park, Bridget,' I said quickly as the four of them exchanged glances. Well, they had read my books and now they were meeting her in the flesh.

'Men are a constant disappointment,' Bridget continued. 'As you ladies will know if you've ever wasted your time getting up close and personal with Nick here. But at least with him it hardly takes any time.'

'Me with Nick?' the women said in horrified unison. Which hurt really.

'Can we get on with solving this crime?' I said, trying not to harrumph. Bridget looked at me. Okay, so I'd harrumphed. 'When you're ready,' I said quickly.

'Why did he break cover here?' Bridget said.

Adrian shrugged. 'He just e-mailed out of the blue. Said he was going to be over in the UK and could he come. Then he turned up.'

'He got off to a flying start with the ladies,' Donna said. 'I suppose he had a kind of roguish charm.' She nudged me. 'Shame he wasn't around long enough for you to learn a trick or two, Nick.'

'I have charms for those who have eyes to see,' I said.

'I do need new specs,' she said.

'I did see him engrossed in conversation with Viz, that Found poet turned crime writer,' I said. To protect Bridget's feelings, I didn't add that I'd seen them head off to the lifts with their arms around each other's waists.

'Just the word *poet* makes me want to vomit,' Bridget said sharply. I remembered she rates poets about as highly as paedophiles, serial killers, and former boyfriends. 'Is she the one who bills herself as a class warrior? I can't decide whether to admire or pity someone in their forties who still bangs on about class war and the evils of capitalism.' Bridget wasn't one to keep up with politics so probably didn't even know about the current Labour leader and his shadow chancellor. 'So what is a Found poet anyway?'

'She does cut-up poetry,' I said. 'She takes random lines from newspapers then shuffles them until she gets something.'

'Something that makes sense?' Bridget said.

'Depends what you mean by sense,' Myles muttered.

'She performs with another poet with a disability but nobody likes to ask what his disability is,' I said.

'Well, he can't write poetry,' Liz chipped in. 'Does that count?'

'Does she knit?' Bridget said. We all shrugged.

'What about the knitting needle lady?' I said.

'Margot?' Adrian said. 'She's being interviewed now. Can't see how she would do something like that.' His phone rang. He listened and nodded then ended the call. 'They've found a name tag under the body. It might be open and shut.'

They all went off, leaving Bridget and me alone. We went back into the bar and surveyed the scene. It was packed and the noise level made even Bridget sound timid. Over there was a gang of hard-boiled writers, men in their thirties and forties, one of them wearing shades despite the gloom, drinking beer out of bottles. They were regulars here, but some of them never went to panels, preferring to stay in the bar, sometimes late into the night. A couple of them, I believe, had learned to exist without any sleep at all for the length of the weekend.

There were excitable groups of men and women in their twenties chattering together—a mix of writers, editors, and PRs. There would be a certain amount of pairing off later. And some broken hearts and marriages when texts sent to arrange an intimate late-night rendezvous with a new acquaintance went in error to the wife or husband back home.

There was a small gaggle of committee members of the Crime Writers Association. (The CWA had just recently decided to drop the apostrophe from *Writers'*. That apostrophe, only introduced by a syntactical purist some fifteen years after the association was founded, had been the bane of sub-editors in the national and local press for decades and now troubled the work-experience tykes who produce those newspapers these days.)

A temporary guardrail had been put along the space between the bar and the corridor beyond it. A policeman stood there, currently bending to speak to a tiny, elegant woman wearing what looked like enormous ear muffs or headphones.

Over in the far corner I could see a bunch of familiar, friendly faces from America, a mix of readers and writers, all of them into cosy crime. I led Bridget over there, figuring they would know about Margot, the knitting needle lady.

An energetic woman with neat clothes and hair was saying: 'My bookmark is currently in a cat quilter novel but I'm afraid it will be a DNF book.'

Bridget glanced my way as we hovered behind their chairs.

'Did Not Finish,' I murmured.

'The two cat characters are a ragdoll and a savannah. Excellent casting but I'm not sure the author actually knows cats. I mean she puts clothes on the cats so they can model them—which is fine—except that she does it in front of strangers. I can't see cats being comfortable with that. In addition, it's proselytising. If I want to be "saved" I know where my local church is.'

The woman next to her, hugging a bag of books, said: 'I'm reading a book about Graycie, the killer parrot. It's called *Winging It* and it's very funny. And next up is one about Diesel, the Maine Coon.'

Bridget started to move away. I put my hand on her arm—very lightly—and leaned in. 'This is pet noir—the latest thing.'

'The latest thing is my need for another exorbitantly priced drink,' Bridget said, shrugging my hand off and manoeuvring back to the bar.

'Hello ladies,' I said. 'I wonder if you knew whether Margot was okay?'

A white-haired older woman in a tracksuit looked up at me. She had a sweet face.

'You should ask her friend, Diane. They're the knitting bee here this weekend.'

'And where might I find her?'

She shrugged.

'Follow the clews of wool.'

I laughed.

'Were you at the craft-based mysteries panel this morning?' the sweet woman said. 'Diane was on the panel.'

I shook my head.

'What kind of crafts?' I asked.

'Knitting, miniatures, and cheese.'

'Cheese?'

She nodded.

'Lots of cheese recipes,' she said. 'Rather than B and G.'

It took me a second to get that one.

'And miniature what?' I said.

'Houses.'

'Oh, you mean like dolls' houses? So are these just small crimes?'

She gave me a quick smile in response to the 'small crimes' but I noticed it didn't reach her eyes.

'She doesn't like to call them dolls' houses because she doesn't much like dolls or people in them—though she does put miniature dirty dishes in the sinks of her houses, as if people do live there.'

As I was digesting that, I thought I should introduce myself.

'I'm Nick, by the way,' I said.

'I know who you are,' she said. 'Even without your name tag. Your reputation precedes you.'

I decided not to follow that up—I've been bitten that way before. Especially as her sweet face was suddenly not looking quite so sweet.

'Well, I'll go in search of Diane,' I said, waving goodbye to the group, most of whom had ignored me anyway.

Bridget was at the bar with two drinks in front of her, a man either side of her. That figured. I started to go by but she gestured at me to come over.

'This guy has written this novel which, if I've got it right, is the conscious evolution of the staid three-act horror narrative.'

I looked at him and nodded. He looked normal enough—but then so do most serial killers.

'It's a savage indictment of the corporate mentality,' he hissed. 'A challenging, twisted book that assails the underpinnings of modern society and does so much more than spit in your face.'

So much for normal. I turned to the other man. Ditto, normal looking.

'I was just saying that I write crime reviews for one of the nationals, though I've got a book deal,' he said. He showed a lot of teeth beneath a curled lip as he talked, which reminded me of some ancient TV series about a talking horse called Mr Ed. 'I just had a falling out with a sub-editor. You may not understand this, but I know Bridget will. He made so many mistakes. And worst of all. Dumbest, deafest, shittiest of all, he removed the unstressed "a" so that the stress that should have fallen on "dosh" is lost and my piece ends on an unstressed syllable.'

He looked at me fiercely.

'Terrible,' I agreed, singing to myself a bit of the theme song from *Mr Ed* ('a horse is a horse, of course, of course' if you must know). He nodded vigorously.

'When you're winding up a piece of prose, metre is crucial. Couldn't he hear? Couldn't he hear that it's wrong? It's not fucking rocket science. It's fucking pre-GCSE scansion. I have written 350 crime reviews and I have never ended on an unstressed syllable.' He took a swig of his beer. 'Fuck, fuck, fuck, fuck.'

Bridget picked up both her glasses and leaned in to whisper in my ear: 'Can we go back to Planet Earth, please?'

I smiled cheesily at the two men, saying: 'Really got to go now.'

I steered Bridget away.

'This is Planet Earth,' I said. 'Haven't you noticed how the world has gone bonkers since we last saw each other?'

We went back outside and Bridget handed me one of the wineglasses, which was unusually unselfish of her. I wondered briefly what she was after. But she just lit another cigarette, so I looked on my laptop and saw that every person and their dog had been tweeting from the festival about Randall Spear's death. I imagined the press would be arriving in force any time now.

Usually, the crimes Bridget and I had got involved with had been away from the police, but here the police were on the spot so there was nothing for us to investigate. Even so…

I Googled Randall Spear. Wikipedia had no photo, of course, and scant biographical details. Internal evidence from his novels apparently suggested he was familiar with Nebraska thirty years ago. He'd looked to be in his forties when I'd caught sight of him—I'm pushing fifty, which these days is about the only exercise I get, aside from a less rigorous yoga than I used to do, a couple of times a week.

Each of his novels were set in different parts of America so it was hard to pin down where he lived. His novels were gruesome—more Thomas Harris than Michael Connelly—but he definitely nailed the psychopathic mind and, globally, readers responded to that. Personally, I didn't think there was a posse of writers behind the brand because the consistency of the darkness of vision and gruesomeness seemed to suggest a single viewpoint, or at most, two people who were very close. All of it sick, of course.

'A knitting needle—is that a weapon of deliberation?' I said.

'He's off,' said Bridget, from behind her phone as she was busy tilting her head this way and that to take selfies.

'I mean if you were going to commit an impulsive act wouldn't you be a bit more…savage? This was so precise, from what we could see—straight into the throat below the Adam's apple.'

'I didn't see,' Bridget said, showing me the screen of her phone. 'Which is best?'

I looked at the images of Bridget she paraded before me.

'They're all great. So this was planned. And, assuming Margot didn't do it, was that part opportune for the killer, nicking the needle from her quiver?'

Bridget was still fiddling with her phone.

'Well, here's a thing,' she said. 'Randall Spear has just tweeted that the announcement of his death is fake news.'

Back in the bar, there was a hubbub among all the Twitterers. The hapless policeman on the makeshift barrier at the bar had to confirm that, yes, there was a dead body in the lift but, no, he couldn't confirm that person's identity.

'He's supposed to be a writer, for goodness sake,' someone was grumbling. 'Why couldn't he quote Mark Twain about the news of his death being greatly exaggerated? "Fake news"—hate that expression.'

'You go to the trouble of killing someone and you don't get the right person,' said some woman with a strong Birmingham accent. 'That's a bummer.'

Viz, the Found poet she was talking to, nodded her

head in vehement agreement, which made all the metal piercings in her face and ears sway and jingle.

I saw the coven of quilters and cosy crime aficionados all atwitter—in the old-fashioned sense of the word—on the other side of the room. The sweet-faced, white-haired woman looked quite put out.

'So the guy was an imposter,' I said to Bridget.

'If you mean he pretended how good he was in bed beforehand, I don't fall for that anymore.'

'I meant not really Randall Spear at all.'

'Any of them?' Bridget said.

That was a point. If I was wrong and there was actually a Randall Spear posse, maybe the victim was one of them officially or unofficially masquerading as him.

'Bridget, is there anything about him that struck you as odd?—no, I don't mean anything sexual.'

'Not really. Though I did think he was from Birmingham when I met him in the car park.'

'He had a Brummie accent?'

'I thought so. It was only when I realised I was wrong I let things go further.'

'You mean you wouldn't sleep with a Brummie because of the accent?'

'Would you?'

I thought of the woman in the bar with the Birmingham accent I'd heard a few minutes earlier. I'd never seen her before but she wasn't wearing a name tag so I hadn't known who she was. She was a bit of a looker with her Louise Brooks bob and ripped jeans.

'Well…'

'Oh, yeah, of course,' Bridget interrupted, 'you're so desperate you'd sleep with anyone.'

Ordinarily I would have protested, especially as these

days I rarely got up to any shenanigans, but I was thinking about the Brummie woman in the bar and who she was with. All kinds of conspiracy theories were forming in my head.

'Nick, what is it?' Bridget said.

'I'm thinking,' I said.

'Thank God. I thought from your expression—well, let's just say you're still a bit young for incontinence pads.'

'I think I've got it,' I said. I saw Bridget start to speak. 'No cheap comments.'

'I don't do cheap,' she sniffed.

'Let's suppose he was from Birmingham.'

Bridget grimaced. 'I don't want to hear that.'

'He conned everybody—nothing easier when you're pretending to be somebody no one has ever seen or met.'

'But why?'

'For the fun of it. The prestige. The sex.'

Bridget grimaced again.

'But supposing he's married or has a partner and she finds out about it and follows him here?'

'I heard a Birmingham voice in the bar a minute ago,' Bridget said slowly.

'Exactly.'

'I knew that city wasn't to be trusted.'

I let that go.

'That woman in the bar was with the Found poet.'

'Where's she from?'

'Richmond-upon-Thames. Her daddy was a banker,' I said.

'Fucking figures. But you said you'd seen her with the Spear character. You think wife and poet were in cahoots?'

'Works for me,' I said, looking over to the policeman. 'Come on.'

'Nick, it's a bit thin,' Bridget said as we headed towards the copper.

'Wafer thin,' I agreed as Adrian led in two plainclothes and two uniformed policemen and looked round the bar.

'They've figured it out, too,' I said. 'Must be the name tag Adrian said they'd found.' I looked to where the Birmingham woman and Viz were, and gestured Bridget to move aside so we weren't in the policemen's path. As I did so, I tried to catch Adrian's eye and point out where the culprits were.

Bridget and I ended up beside the cosy crime ladies as my gestures to Adrian and the police got increasingly large. They saw me, the lead plainclothes policeman frowned, and they all headed towards me.

'They're over there,' I said to Adrian as the policemen barged past me and surrounded the sweet faced, white-haired lady sitting in her chair behind me.

'Matilda March, would you come with us please,' the lead policeman said.

'Method, means, and opportunity,' Matilda said, smiling, well, sweetly. 'I stole the knitting needle from Margot's bag when I was standing behind her waiting to go to the craft event; I was staying on the same floor as that man; and I seized the opportunity as we both got into the lift.'

'But why?' I blurted, earning a scowl from the policemen.

She stood, holding her wrists out in front of her as if expecting to be cuffed.

'I told you—I don't like B and G in crime novels. It's abhorrent to me. And his were full of it.'

B and G: blood and gore.

'You stabbed somebody in the throat and left him

bleeding to death because you didn't like the blood and gore in his novels?' I said.

'You look puzzled,' she said as the police began to lead her away.

'No, no. If it makes sense to you, it makes sense to me.' I turned to Bridget. 'Right?'

She shrugged and watched Matilda March leave the bar.

'My starting point is that you're all fucking nuts, so normal rules do not apply,' she finally said. She looked around. 'Now where's that Lee Child?'

Ask Tom St Clare

Sophie Hannah

Tom St Clare is a pathological liar.

Normal, occasional liars—a category that would include most of us, perhaps—use deceit to make our lives run more smoothly, to avoid trouble or spare loved ones' feelings. We generally only do it when we think there's a chance it will work. Pathological liars are different. They lie even when there is no chance of fooling anybody, and when it will cost them everything.

Why do they do it? Does anyone yearn to be described as the least trustworthy, most startlingly sociopathic person all their acquaintances have ever known?

Don't ask me. Ask Tom St Clare.

'He's been missing for six days. I've heard nothing,' I explained, pressing the phone against my ear harder than I needed to, gripping it so tight in my hand that my arm ached. 'I'm worried something awful's happened. Look, when I say "missing"…his friends or family might know where he is—maybe it's just me who thinks he's disappeared off the face of the Earth. We were texting each other all day long for months, then suddenly, silence! He's not replied to my last three messages, he's not at work...I keep getting his auto-reply, which tells me nothing!'

'Okay,' said the calm voice on the other end of the line—calmer than mine, thank goodness. Someone needed to think straight here. 'So you've been dating this guy for, what, three months?'

'Yes. I've put all the relevant information in a draft e-mail, which I'll send you. His e-mail, mobile number, address, work address, family's names, addresses, workplaces. Literally, everything I know is in this e-mail—what he's told me, anyway. For all I know, he's made up his entire life story! Still...hopefully it'll give you some leads.'

I couldn't believe I'd just said, 'leads.' I even more couldn't believe that I was on the point of employing a private detective. What else could I do? Going slowly crazy didn't appeal to me. The police wouldn't have cared. His auto-reply message had said, 'I'll be away from the office for the next fortnight, unable to access e-mails.' Any policeman—anyone not paid to indulge me—would have said, 'He doesn't have to tell you where he's gone, does he?' No, he didn't. That didn't make me any less desperate to find out.

This detective—randomly selected from Google search results—was no Sherlock Holmes. He sounded not remotely intrigued by the mysterious disappearance of my boyfriend. He sounded, rather, keen to get me off the phone. He explained with a yawn in his voice that I had to pay up front—six-hundred-fifty pounds plus VAT—and that he couldn't do anything that was in contravention of the law: he couldn't tap phones, hack into e-mails, break into homes.

I did my best to conceal my frustration. 'Why the hell not?' I nearly screamed. I had been misled by books and movies in which maverick heroes break every rule that stands in their way.

I asked the yawning detective if he thought he could help me. 'No idea,' he said cheerfully. I asked if he could ensure that no one would ever find out I'd hired him. Oh, yes, he assured me—he could certainly do that.

There was no progress of any kind in the week that followed. I was frantic—cursing myself for not having demanded regular updates. After a week of silence, I e-mailed the yawning detective, asking for news. He replied within minutes. I was delighted, until I read his message: 'His colleagues reckon he'll be out of the office for the next two weeks or so. His PA, Donna Crompton, might know more. Have you tried ringing her?'

I felt like punching the wall. The e-mail told me nothing that the auto-reply hadn't. It had even mentioned Donna Crompton as the person to contact in his absence.

And two weeks 'or so' was bad news. I'd been thinking, 'He'll be back at work after a fortnight. I can find him then, if not before.'

So disappointed I could hardly breathe, I bashed out an angry e-mail: 'No, I haven't rung his PA. Have you? Have you rung his family/friends? Please send details of what you've done so far. Have you tried his flat? The mail sits on a big table in the communal hall area. Get in there (maybe follow someone else in?) and you'll see if he's been picking up letters, or if there's a big pile waiting.'

As I typed, I thought: I shouldn't have to tell him this.

He's a detective, for Christ's sake. All right, so he's not fictional and can't break the law or work magic, but he could at least have the right attitude: 'I will not rest until I uncover the truth'. His motto seemed to be the opposite: 'I will rest until I don't uncover the truth.'

After four more days of silence, I rang him. 'I told you,' he said impatiently. 'He's off work for a bit. Why don't you wait and see if he turns up in a few weeks?'

'Can you check hospitals?' I asked, seething.

'Not really,' came the bored reply. 'I mean, if I knew he was in hospital and which one, I could ring them, but I can hardly phone every hospital on the off-chance, can I?'

I was about to start wailing in frustration when a banging on my window startled me. I turned, and...no, it couldn't be.

My heart hammered as I stared like an idiot. Either my missing boyfriend had reappeared, or else someone with his face was looking in at me. Smiling apologetically.

There was no doubt. It was him: Jonathan.

'Sorry,' he said. I could hear him clearly through the glass. 'I got cold feet. The good news is...they've warmed up again.' There was a bunch of roses in his hand.

I turned away from him, let him see the phone at my ear. So he wasn't dead, wasn't in a coma, wasn't lying unconscious in hospital. Why hadn't he texted me? In the time it took him to get here, he could have sent a hundred texts—could have spared me half an hour of panicking about worst-case scenarios.

I decided he could wait until I'd finished on the phone.

'Look, if this guy wants to contact you, he'll get in touch, won't he?' asked my suspiciously rubbish detective with a chuckle.

Suspiciously rubbish. As in, actually laughing at me,

his paying client. Yet, until that moment, I had not been suspicious, only crushingly disillusioned.

Jonathan banged on the window again. I ignored him.

Still on the phone, I opened my laptop and typed the detective's name and the word 'scam' into the search box. Dozens of results appeared: 'Do not trust Tom St Clare, aka Thomas Brankin. He is NOT a detective. He's an unemployed ex-chartered surveyor who can't hold down a job because he lies to everyone he meets. He'll leech your money, find out nothing, and taunt you for as long as you let him. THIS MAN DESTROYS LIVES.'

•●●●•

Tom St Clare is a pathological liar. I am an ordinary liar who deceives only when it makes sense to do so. I have not told my fake detective that Jonathan came back, or tried to. At least three times a day, I ring and bombard him with insane, obsessive questions (Have you tried this retro vinyl shop? That pub? That bookshop? The bike repair warehouse? Jonathan might have popped in/walked past/bought something/had a puncture). I disguise my caller ID, so Tom can't avoid me. He's starting to sound scared of me. Good.

I could forgive the lying. I can't forgive his abject failure, when I urgently needed him to solve a mystery. No mercy for that. Especially since, as it turns out, he is a fictional detective.

Blue and Sentimental

John Harvey

For Anna and Lucy

Kiley hadn't been to the Vortex in years. A celebration of Stan Tracey's seventy-fifth birthday, December 2001. Bobby Wellins joining the pianist on tenor sax, the two of them twisting and turning through 'In Walked Bud' before surprising everyone with a Latin version of 'My Way' which, for the duration of its playing and some time after, erased all thoughts of Frank Sinatra from memory. Now both Tracey and Wellins were dead and the Vortex had moved across East London, from Stoke Newington to Dalston. A corner building with a bar downstairs and the club room above, which was where Kiley was sitting now, staring out across Gillett Square, waiting for the music to begin.

The call had come around noon the previous day, just as he was leaving the flat, his mind set on a crispy pork *banh mi* sandwich from the Vietnamese place across the street from the Forum. The 02 Forum, as it was now less fortunately called, Kiley old enough to wish for things to be left, mostly, as they were.

'Am I speaking to Jack Kiley?'

He'd assured her that she was.

'You find people who've gone missing?'

'Once in a while.'

'That doesn't sound too encouraging.'

'I'm sorry.'

There was a silence in which he guessed she was making up her mind. If he moved the phone closer, he could hear the faint rasp of her breathing.

'Can you meet me?' she said eventually.

'That depends.'

'Tomorrow? Tomorrow afternoon? Somewhere around four? Four-thirty?'

'Yes, I think so.'

'You know the Vortex? It's just off…'

'… Kingsland High Street. Yes, I know.'

'I'll see you there.'

She rang off before he could ask her name.

Out in the square a group of elderly black men were sitting quietly playing dominoes, oblivious to the cries of small children and the bump and clatter of skateboarders negotiating a succession of mostly successful pirouettes and arabesques.

Behind Kiley, the musicians who had been arriving, haphazardly, for the past ten minutes or so, stood chatting, shrugging off their coats, freeing instruments from their cases, starting to tune up. On stage, the drummer finished angling the last of his cymbals correctly and played an exploratory paradiddle on the snare. With the concentration of someone threading a needle, one of the saxophone players fitted a new reed into place.

Gradually, the composition of the ensemble took shape: rhythm section at the back, piano off to one side; three trumpets; two, no, three trombones; the saxophones, five strong, down at the front of the stage, one—the baritone player—leaning back against the side wall.

The leader stepped forward, called a number from the band's book, signalled with his hand: four bars from the piano, then four more and the sound of fifteen musicians filled the room.

Smiling, Kiley eased back in his chair.

The repertoire mixed original compositions with new arrangements of the tried and tested; after an extended workout on 'Take the A Train,' Kiley got up and made his way to the bar.

Only one woman sat alone amongst a scattering of couples and a dozen or more single men; smartly yet casually dressed, dark hair swept back, Kiley wondered if she might be the person he was meeting, but when he passed close by her table she gave no sign, and by the time he'd paid for his beer she'd been joined by a stylishly bearded thirty-something energetically apologising for being late.

Back at his seat by the window, Kiley saw that a woman wearing a bottle green apron over a brightly patterned floor-length dress had stationed herself behind the domino players and was busily cutting hair, a short but steadily lengthening line of clients waiting their turn. A quartet of youths crisscrossed the square on scooters, revving noisily, while on stage the band strolled its way into the interval number, a slow rolling blues that climaxed all of ten minutes later, electric guitar ringing out over a volley of brass.

As the applause faded, the musicians began to set their instruments aside, the taller of the two tenor players unclipping her saxophone from its sling before crossing the room.

'Jack Kiley? I'm Leah Temple.'

Kiley reached out his hand. He'd noticed her before, one of four women in the band: piano, trumpet, tenor, and alto saxophones. Tall, auburn hair tied loosely back, she had a way of holding her instrument off to one side when she played; long fingers, large hands. The right or wrong side of forty-five.

'Let's go and talk downstairs,' she said.

The bar was deserted, not yet open for the evening. Leah pulled a stool down from one of the tables and angled it back against the window, waiting for him to do the same. Eyes that had shone green in the lights, he could now see, close up, were flecked with grey.

'So what do you think?'

'The music?'

'Uh-huh.'

'I like it. You're good. All of you. But then you don't need me to tell you that.'

She smiled. 'Not bad for a rehearsal band. Afternoons like this, about the only time we can get together. Most of the guys have got regular gigs, pit bands in the West End, sessions. Some of them even get paid for playing jazz.'

'You?'

'Once in a while.'

For a moment she looked out into the square. Several of the other musicians were standing outside, sharing a joke, smoking.

'Look, the reason I rang you…' She left it hanging, fidgeted a hand back through her hair. 'I'm sorry, I'm feeling really stupid about this.'

'Don't be.'

'I just feel I'm…I don't know…making a fuss about nothing.'

'Nothing?'

'Yes.'

'You don't strike me as the type.'

She smoothed her hands down her jeans, deciding. 'It's my partner.'

'Who's missing?'

'Yes. I mean, I think so. Maybe.'

'How long since you saw him?'

'Her.'

'How long since you saw her?'

'Ten days now. Eleven, more or less. That doesn't seem long, I know.'

'It depends.'

'I had this gig at Ronnie's. Upstairs. No big deal. Ellen was going to meet me there but she never showed. I didn't think too much of it at the time. It wasn't exactly unusual. But then, when I didn't hear from her, and she didn't answer her phone, reply to my texts, that's when I began to get worried.'

'You're not living together, you and Ellen?'

'It's complicated.'

Kiley smiled. 'It usually is.' How long had he and Kate Keenan been not living together, living together, barely speaking?

'She's got a place in Camberwell. I went round there, of course. No sign. No one else in the building had seen her going in or out. Not for days.'

'You've got a key?'

Leah shook her head. 'There never seemed a lot of point. If we were together, it was usually round mine.'

'How about where she works?'

'Freelance. There's a shared work space in Southwark where she rents a desk. She's not been there, either.'

One of the musicians knocked on the window and gestured upstairs.

'I can explain more later,' Leah said, 'if that's okay? If you don't think I'm wasting your time.'

'As long as we can eat while we talk. All that music, gives me an appetite.'

The second set was mostly originals, only a driving version of 'Rockin' in Rhythm' reminding Kiley of an Ellington LP, long mislaid, he'd bought for next to nothing in the early seventies—worth a small fortune now, thanks to vinyl becoming newly fashionable.

Just before the finale, the bandleader called Leah front and centre. 'We'd like to feature Leah Temple on a slower number from the Count Basie repertoire, first recorded on the 6th June, 1938, with Herschel Evans on tenor. "Blue and Sentimental."'

Kiley didn't know Evans from Adam, but to his barely tutored ears, Leah sounded a lot like Lester Young.

• ● ⬤ ● •

Session over, Leah guided them to a Turkish ocakbasi restaurant just off the high road, where she recommended the mixed kebab with a side order of grilled aubergine and peppers. She wasn't wrong.

'So,' Kiley said, 'tell me more.'

Leah skewered a piece of lamb with her fork and dipped it into the chili sauce at the edge of her plate. 'We met just over a year ago. A&E, where I work.'

Kiley's face showed surprise.

'What? You think I make a living from music?' She laughed. 'Chance'd be a fine thing.'

'So you're what? A doctor? Nurse?'

'Nurse practitioner.'

Kiley nodded as if he understood the distinction.

'Ellen was brought in with quite serious injuries. Cuts, abrasions. What turned out to be a dislocated shoulder. She'd had an accident on her bike on the way home. Some idiot opening his car door without looking. Usual story. Ellen swerved to avoid it and got sideswiped by a lorry. Could have been a lot worse.' She smiled, remembering. 'She was in quite a bit of pain. A little out of herself after the gas and air. Even so I thought we had some connection. It wasn't until she came back in again a week later, pretending she'd lost her way to the orthopaedic clinic, that I realised I'd been right.'

'And the rest was what? Plain sailing?'

'Hardly. I was just coming out of a relationship, not sure if I wanted to get involved again so soon.'

'On the rebound.'

'Exactly.'

'And Ellen?'

'Married for twenty-five years. Two kids, one just finishing university, one starting.'

'You said complicated.'

'Ellen had never been in a gay relationship before, never even thought about it.' She grinned. 'Well, maybe she'd thought about it.' The grin broadened into a fully fledged smile. 'The real thing, she said, was a revelation.'

'To her husband as well, I daresay?'

Leah leaned back a little in her chair. 'I kept trying to get her to tell him, Derek, come clean. When finally she did, all too predictably, he went crazy, screaming and shouting, calling her all the names under the sun. Told her if she didn't get out of his sight he wouldn't be held responsible for what he might do. She came to me, which, of course, he must've known she would. By the following day, he'd changed the locks, put her stuff out in boxes on the drive.'

'Still, she didn't move in?'

'Not permanently, no. My place is pretty small. We'd have had to get somewhere together. But Ellen said she needed somewhere of her own, time to sort things out. Twenty-five years, it's a lot to walk away from. And now Derek's stopped threatening to beat her black and blue, he's been moving heaven and earth trying to persuade her to move back in. Texts, phone calls, e-mails. Says he'll forgive her. Forgive her, mind! Wants them to give it a second chance. At one point he even started waiting for her after work, following her home.'

'Stalking, sounds like,' Kiley said. 'She could have gone to the police, got a protection order. Domestic violence.'

'She didn't want to do that. Thought it might make him angry all over again. It was a risk she didn't want to take.'

'She was frightened of him, then? Physically, I mean?'

'Yes. Yes, I think so.'

'He'd hit her before?'

'No. At least, not as far as I know. And, besides, it wasn't just that. There were the kids to consider. Not that they're kids any longer. Boys. Not even that. Eighteen and twenty-one. Both taking their father's side, apparently. The older one won't speak to her at all.'

'All that pressure, must have been hard for her to withstand.'

Leah nodded. 'I know. Pressure from me, too.'

'How d'you mean?'

'I've got this chance to go to New Zealand. In a year's time. Hospital in Wellington. Promotion. More responsibility. I want Ellen to come with me.'

'And she's what? Not keen? Uncertain?'

'I think she likes the idea of spending time in New Zealand well enough…'

'It's just spending it with you she's not so keen on.'

Leah laughed. 'Maybe. The thing is, it should be pretty straightforward. New Zealand's a lot more liberal than many places. As long as I've got the skill set they're short of, and healthcare's one, I can get a visa easily enough and Ellen can get one as my partner. We don't even have to be legally married, but we do need to have proof we've lived together in a stable relationship for at least one year.'

'Which doesn't exactly leave a lot of time.'

'Tell me.'

'And if she doesn't agree to go, all that means, you'd go ahead anyway? Go on your own?'

'If I had to, yes.'

'She knows that?'

'I think so.'

Kiley broke off a piece of pita bread and used it to wipe up what remained of the sauce. 'Faced with all that, I just might do a runner myself. Give myself a little more time and space to think, at least.'

'If it were just that, then fine. I'd understand. But not to go off without a word. Leaving me worried silly.'

'You've spoken to the husband? Derek, is it?'

'I've tried. All I get's a stream of abuse. And when I went round a couple of days ago, he slammed the door in my face.'

Kiley eased away his plate. 'You know, if you're right and she's really gone missing, the police have got a lot better resources than me.'

Leah shook her head. 'One step at a time, eh?'

'Okay. I'll need a photograph. Addresses. Anything else

you think might help. And we ought to take a look inside that flat. Camberwell, you said?'

'Like I told you, I haven't got a key.'

Kiley grinned.

•●⬤●•

At the end of his first month in the Met, walking the beat in North London, the netherland of Colindale, a wily old sergeant, close to retiring, had taken Kiley aside and tutored him in the art of gaining access to whatever, within reason, had been locked against intrusion. From petty cash boxes to shuttered windows and burglar-proof doors. The technology had changed but the methods were the same.

The entrance to the building was a cinch. Ellen's bike was safely chained up in the shared space beneath the first flight of stairs. In a matter of minutes they were inside the top-floor flat and Leah was reaching round for the light.

Bed-sitting room, bathroom, kitchen. Single bed, neatly made; two-seater settee; swivel chair; a folding table that doubled as desk; concertina file to one side, angle lamp to the other; a shelf unit Kiley recognised as coming from IKEA; a three-high chest of drawers; clothes hanging from a long metal rail on wheels. Inkjet printer, retro-styled radio, small screen TV. Half a dozen photographs Blu-Tacked to the wall: Ellen and Leah on what looked like Brighton Pier; Leah on stage somewhere soloing on saxophone, bell of her instrument close up to the microphone, eyes tightly closed; a young man, Kiley presumed to be Ellen's oldest son, flourishing his certificate on graduation day; the other boy, sandy-haired, smiling a little shyly at the camera, and then, younger, twelve or thirteen, standing close by his mother, the pair of them happy, laughing, sea and sky behind.

In the kitchen the sink and draining board were empty; everything washed, dried, put away. Towel folded over the radiator in the bathroom; shampoo, conditioner, and moisturiser in a line. Whenever, wherever, Ellen had gone, she had not done so in a hurry.

'Your place as squared away as this?'

'You're kidding, right?'

'Notice anything out of the ordinary?'

'Not so far.'

'How about clothes? Anything missing?'

'I'll check.'

It didn't take long. Ellen's padded down jacket was no longer to be seen; denim skirt, one pair of jeans, assorted tops—Leah couldn't remember which—underwear, tights, socks; one—no, two pairs of shoes. Enough for a week away, two at most. The pull-along case usually kept beneath the bed was no longer there; nor the makeup bag Leah knew Ellen liked to take for overnights, weekends. Her passport, however, was still in the concertina file, under P.

'Any idea where she might go, this country, if she fancied some time away? Anyone else she might go and see. Old friends? Family?'

'No one I haven't already been in touch with, no. As for places… Dorset, maybe? The Jurassic Coast, is that what it's called? Lyme Regis, round there.'

'Somewhere you've been together?'

Leah shook her head. 'She talked about it, that's all. Wanting to go. Ever since that film. Meryl Streep? We saw it on TV.'

Kiley took a last look round the room. 'You think

someone else could have been here, taken just the right things, left it just how Ellen would have done herself?'

Leah hesitated. 'Someone who knew her well, yes.'

'Her husband, he have a key?'

'Not as far as I know.'

Back on the street, Leah stopped him, her hand on his sleeve.

'When Ellen finally plucked up courage to tell Derek about us, he pushed her back against the kitchen wall and held her there with his arm across her neck. So tight she could hardly breath. The bruise was still there, more than a week later.'

Kiley wasn't sure what to expect when he rang the bell at 25 Forester Road a little after seven-thirty the following morning. The car, a grey Audi Saloon, was still in the drive and the dew still on the grass. A light showed faintly through the glass above the door. It had taken him no more than twenty minutes, Kentish Town to Finchley Central, five stops on the Northern Line. Now all he needed was for Derek Carpenter to still be at home.

He heard approaching footsteps, then the key turning in the lock, the bolt sliding across.

'Yes?'

The question was testy, just short of belligerent, the door open no more than halfway. Carpenter was medium height, stockily built, fiftyish, fair hair growing thin; dark trousers, striped tie, toast crumbs littering the blue of his shirt.

'Jack Kiley. I wonder if I might have a word?'

'A word about what?'

'Your wife, Ellen.'

'What about her?'

'She seems to have disappeared.'

The door opened a little wider. 'Who the hell are you?'

Kiley gave him his card. *Investigations. Private and Confidential.*

'What is this? Some kind of joke?'

'It's just a simple matter of wanting to get in touch with her. Make sure she's all right.'

'Why shouldn't she be?'

'I thought you might know the reason for that.'

Carpenter tore Kiley's card in half and let the pieces fall. 'I'd like you to leave.'

'Maybe not quite yet.'

Carpenter swung the door closed but Kiley's foot was quicker, wedging it open with the sole of his shoe.

'Five minutes, Mr Carpenter. That's all I ask.'

After a few moments' deliberation, Carpenter relinquished his hold and took a pace back into the hall; Kiley moved his foot away and Carpenter slammed the door shut and thrust the bolt into place.

Tugging at the collar of his overcoat, a man came out of the house next door, cast a glance in Kiley's direction, and hurried past and up the street towards the tube. Out of sight a dog was barking, impatient to be off on its morning walk.

Kiley crossed the street and took a seat on the low wall opposite. Seven forty-five. Two cars went past, one closely following the other, big four-by-fours, young mums ferrying the kids to school. An upstairs light in the Carpenter house went on then off. A trio of youths slouched grudgingly by, hands in pockets, shoulders hunched, the tinny sound from their headphones just audible as they went past.

Ten minutes more and the door to number twenty-five opened and, careful not to look in Kiley's direction, Carpenter stepped swiftly out, and into his car. Another moment—seat belt, ignition—and the Audi swung out of the drive and away, small plumes of greyish smoke rising behind it in the air.

•●⬤●•

Back home, Kiley made coffee, switched on the computer, and set to work. Hospitals, hostels; a contact at the National Crime Agency's Missing Persons Bureau charged with unidentified body identification. More coffee and then a slow trawl through hotels and bed-and-breakfast places within a twenty-five-mile radius of Lyme Regis. Nothing. His back was beginning to ache and the air in the room was dry. He'd twice earlier called the place in Southwark where Ellen rented workspace and got the engaged tone both times. He picked up a sandwich in Pret, a flat white from Bean About Town and took it to the Thameslink train going south to the river.

The building was a converted warehouse, its guts torn out and refitted: rows of open-plan desks, cubicles, pods for private meetings. Natalie Joseph's office was on the second floor, a view out across Tooley Street towards Tower Bridge and the Thames.

Glancing at his card, she smiled. 'If you're looking to rent a space, Mr Kiley, I'm afraid, just at the moment, there's rather a long waiting list.'

She was late-thirties, small-featured, blue-eyed, fair hair cut short. A look Kate had once told him was made fashionable by Jean Seberg in a film by Godard. Funny how the mind can cling to the inconsequential.

'Is there anything else I can do for you, Mr Kiley?'

He slid a photograph across the desk.

'Ellen Carpenter. Yes. Her partner called asking about her. She seemed worried. I told her, the last time Ellen was here was… Wait, I can check…' Her fingers moved fast along the keyboard. 'See, here…' She swivelled the screen round so that he could see. 'Over two weeks ago. Friday.'

'And there's been no contact since then?'

'None.'

There was something else, though. He could see it in her eyes.

'Anything you could tell me that might help to find her would…'

'I don't know, it might be nothing. And I don't like to…well, gossip, I suppose.'

Kiley smiled encouragingly.

'That last day she was here. Ellen. I just happened to be looking out onto the street as she was leaving. She was just fitting her pannier onto her bike when this man came up and they started arguing. I couldn't hear what they were saying, but you could see he was getting really worked up and angry, and at one stage he pushed her up against the wall, shouting. There was some sort of kerfuffle, Ellen dropped her helmet and he booted it out into the road and stormed off. Another cyclist retrieved it and gave it back. She was still standing there some minutes later, recovering, I suppose. I thought I might try and talk to her about it, the next time she came in. But like I say…'

'This man,' Kiley said, 'fifties, stocky, going a little bald? Most likely wearing a suit?'

'That sounds like a lot of people round here. But, yes, it could have been.'

'Thanks.'

She held his hand just a moment longer than strictly necessary. 'If you do ever find yourself in need of desk space, I think you'll find our rates very reasonable.'

'I'll bear it in mind.'

•●⬤●•

The Audi was parked on the second level, a block away from where Derek Carpenter worked. Kiley leaned back against one the columns and checked the messages on his phone: a friend encouraging him to join his local walking football team; his insurance company trying to convince him of the need for extra cover in these uncertain times; a selection of attractive young Ukrainian women, all good English speakers, seeking marriage; and an invitation from Kate to join her at the Almeida to see a newly translated version of Ibsen's *Ghosts*. He thought he might give the walking football a second thought.

Carpenter exited from the lift, paused to light a cigarette, then headed towards his car.

'What the fuck?'

'Good to see you, too.'

'How did you…how'd you know I'd be here?'

'I'm a detective, remember?'

'And I've got nothing to say to you, remember that?'

He made to brush past Kiley and reach his car door but Kiley had his feet firmly planted and wasn't budging.

'Your wife, Ellen, she's still missing.'

'Yes, well, she went missing a long time ago. Her decision, her choice, not mine.'

'And you were seen threatening her the day before she disappeared.'

'Bollocks.'

'On the street in Southwark, near where she works. You pushed her up against the wall and were this close to hitting her. There are witnesses. CCTV as well, I daresay, if I search around.'

Carpenter's shoulders drooped as the bluster drained out of him.

'What d'you say,' Kiley said, 'we go and get a drink?'

•●⬤●•

The pub was busy with after-work drinkers, outside and in; smokers blocking the pavement, spilling out into the street. The majority men, white men between twenty-five and fifty; a sprinkling of women drinking and smoking hard to keep up and laughing too loud at jokes that were often at their own expense.

Kiley found space on the upper floor, a corner table wedged between a grimy window looking out onto a blank wall and the secondary toilet door.

'I didn't realise anything was up,' Carpenter said, 'until she texted me, her, that…woman…'

'Leah.'

'Yes, Leah. And I thought, bloody great, she's coming to her senses at last, keeping her distance. But then, just today, Andrew phoned. Rang me at work. He never calls at work. Wanted to know had I heard from his mum. Seems they've been in touch pretty regular since he went down to Bristol…'

'Bristol?'

'Uni. Classical Studies. Don't ask me why.' Carpenter lifted his glass, didn't drink. 'Like I say, they kept in touch. Facebook, Twitter. He hadn't heard from her in—what?—getting on for a couple of weeks. Wanted to know had I heard anything? Was she ill or something? Told him I'd be the last one to know.'

'But that's not true, is it?'

'How d'you mean?'

'From what I hear, you've been keeping pretty close tabs.'

'Want to stop her making any more of a fool of herself, that's all.'

'Fool?'

'This…' Carpenter made a face like his beer had gone abruptly sour. 'This pathetic…I don't know…cry for attention, whatever it is.'

'The relationship with Leah, you think that's what it is?'

'What else? Hanging round with that…She's not gay, for Christ's sake, Ellen. She's no more fucking gay than I am. If she was, twenty-five years of fucking marriage, don't you think I'd know?'

Several heads turned in their direction and the toilet door banged.

'The argument that Friday,' Kiley said, wanting to bring things back on track, 'what was that about?'

Carpenter drank, wiped his mouth with finger and thumb. 'I'd been…what was the expression you used?… keeping tabs on her. Following her, I suppose. And she said if I stopped, kept right away, then she'd agree to meeting, sitting down somewhere, just the two of us, civilised, talking things over. Everything. And I agreed. Agreed and kept waiting for her to get in touch and say okay, you know, a date and everything, and she never did. So I went round there, when I pretty much knew she'd be leaving work and said how about it, this meeting you promised? And she said she wasn't ready, things were happening, I don't know, some new stuff she had to consider, and I said, well when the fuck are you going to be ready? And she said she didn't know, I'd have to be patient, and that's when it kicked off. I lost my temper and for a minute, just for a minute, it all got nasty.'

'You pushed her up against the wall.'

'I pushed her up against the wall and it was all I could do to stop myself taking a swing at her. But I kicked that stupid fucking helmet of hers out into the road instead and got away from there as fast as I could.'

He took another drink, a quick swallow, and looked toward his own reflection in the grime of the window.

'I didn't hit her, if that's what you're thinking. I've never hit her. Never would.'

He set down his glass and Kiley could see his hand was trembling.

'I just fucking miss her. All the fucking time. And, no, I don't know where she is and I wish I did.'

He met Leah on the Heath, close to the hospital where she worked. A pale November morning from which the mist had never quite cleared. The occasional leaf still falling, the rest turning to mulch underfoot.

'I talked to Ellen's husband,' Kiley said. 'I could be wrong, but whatever might have happened to Ellen, I don't think he's responsible. And I don't think he knows where she is. But, like I say, I could be wrong.'

They sat awhile on a bench in the lee of the hill, walked, then sat again.

'When I don't think something awful's happened to her,' Leah said, 'I keep getting this picture of her lying ill somewhere, some room, just four walls and a bed and no one to help or hold her hand or...'

She stopped, her breath like grey smoke upon the air.

'I remember the first time I touched her, Ellen, other than—you know—professionally. Just my fingers brushing her arm at first, like it could almost have been accidental. Then, when she didn't move away, running my hand along the muscle where it rises from the shoulder up into the neck. All the while thinking she's going to tell me to stop, ask me what did I think I was doing. But she just stood there, her face turning slowly towards me, and beneath my fingers I could feel her starting to tremble.'

She looked away, as if not wanting Kiley to see her face.

'What I felt then, those first weeks, first months, it was something I thought I'd never feel again.'

'And Ellen?'

'I think it was the same for her. More so, even. As if—what was it she said?—as if her body had been sleeping. And now…I just don't…I just don't understand.'

Kiley didn't know how to respond, what to say. He knew that people responded, some people, in terrible ways when faced with choices they felt unable to make, situations from which they could see no escape. He knew they opened up their arms, took pills, threw themselves in front of trains, climbed up to some high place and stepped free. He knew people who had assumed new identities, slept rough, become travellers, cut themselves off from their past lives so completely they forgot who they were, who they had once been. He knew Ellen could be any one of those. Or none.

'I ought to be getting back,' Leah said, rising to her feet.

'I'll walk down with you.'

'No need.'

He watched until only a hint of her auburn hair stood out amongst the withering grey and then not even that.

•••••

In Bristol it was raining. Nothing spectacular, just that fine English rain that laced across your face and, without you noticing, seeped into your soul. Kiley took a cab from Temple Meads Station to the edge of College Green. A first-year student, Andrew Carpenter's accommodation was in a row of terraced houses converted into flats. When he heard Kiley wanted to talk to him about his mother, the blood drained from his face and he steadied himself against the iron railing alongside the door.

'It's okay,' Kiley said, 'I've no reason to suspect anything's happened to her. No reason at all.'

'Wait then. We can't talk here.'

He re-emerged minutes later with an anorak thrown over his shoulders, hood pulled up.

'Coffee, yeah?'

'Fine.'

The place was busy with students earnestly staring at their laptops, women feeding their babies while they sipped chai lattes; there was a vacant table upstairs, looking down over a dampened garden.

'My dad sent you, that's what you said.'

'Not exactly.'

'Then what…?'

'He told me where you were, what you were studying. That you were worried about your mother.'

'He had no right…'

'But you are worried?'

'Yes, yes, of course I am. She's always, you know, since I've been down here, kept in touch. Just a text or something. And now…' His mouth puckered sharply as if he had just tasted something bitter and unpleasant. 'It's that woman, isn't it?'

'Leah?'

'Yeah, her. She doesn't want her to have anything to do with us, does she? Not any of us. As if we didn't bloody exist.'

'I don't think that's true.'

'Don't you?'

'No.'

Andrew looked back at him defiantly, disbelieving, then down at his hands, fingernails broken and bitten to the quick.

'What I think Leah wants from your mother is to know where she stands. It's as simple as that. I don't think that means turning her back on you at all. I think she realises how important you are to her, you and your brother.'

'What about my dad?'

'That's something they have to work out for themselves, him and your mum.'

Andrew stared down at his almost empty cup and then out through the window at the darkening, sodden earth, the false shine of stonework in the rain. *What was he,* Kiley thought? *Eighteen? Nineteen? What had he been like himself at that age? Ignorant. Cocksure. If he couldn't be a professional footballer, then he was going to join the police.* His parents—unimaginative, solid, dependable; his father in the same job since he was seventeen; roast on Sundays, cold meat Mondays, what was still remaining into the mincer for shepherd's pie on Tuesdays; two weeks holiday every summer, Filey, North Yorks coast, bracing, blow the cobwebs away, get ready for another year. If his parents, either of them, had as much as strayed, never mind left home, walked out, walked away, fallen in love…

'There's a photo,' he said, 'in your mother's flat, on the wall. The two of you. By the sea somewhere; it looks like...'

'Cape Cornwall. Summer before last. We went down there, just mum and I. Sort of treat for doing well in my exams. AS-levels. She used to go there when she was a girl, she said. Her parents. Not been back since.'

'Looks as if you were both having a nice time.'

'We were.'

He looked away and Kiley knew Andrew didn't want him to see the tears in his eyes.

•●⬤●•

She was staying in St Just, a small grey town a short distance inland and just a few miles from Land's End. This far out of season there were few visitors and those who were there were easy to find. Ellen Carpenter had taken a late breakfast in a small café-cum-book store—poached eggs and bacon on granary toast—lingering over a latté while leafing through that week's *Cornishman*. Small of stature, greying hair; a face that had once been pretty and had grown into something more attractive, eyes that were intelligent and alive. Kiley waited until she was upstairs amongst the second-hand books.

'Ellen?'

The paperback she'd been looking at slipped through her fingers to the floor.

'It's okay. No need to be alarmed.'

'Who are you?'

Kiley explained, needing to gain her confidence, quell her fear.

There were two seats in the far room and they sat there surrounded by history, biography, people's lives.

'You think I'm running away, don't you? And I suppose I am. It's cowardly, I know. But whatever I decide to do—and I know I must…make a decision, I mean—it's going to result in someone getting hurt. Someone I love.'

'People adjust.'

'Do they?'

'I think so, usually. Yes.'

'So do I. Rationally, I suppose. But people aren't rational, are they? Not everyone. Not all the time.'

'You're thinking about your husband?'

She gave the sleeve of her cardigan a little tug. 'Derek's a prisoner to his own feelings. Instincts, I suppose. Faced with something he can't quite understand, can't control, he strikes out. Oh, afterwards he's sorry, even if he can't bring himself to say so. But that doesn't stop it happening again. Just the mention of Leah, if I do try to talk about what's happening, try to explain…Well, he feels threatened, I expect you can understand, another woman especially. And if I had to tell him I was going—we were going—to New Zealand. Moving there…'

'Maybe if you had someone else there with you when you told him? Then he might not react so…well, violently.'

'Maybe, supposing that's what I decide to do.' She rose quickly to her feet. 'I'm going down to look at the ocean. Come with me if you like.'

They climbed the steep short path over the headland to the tall chimney stack at the head of the cape, remnant of the mine that had operated there from the last years of the nineteenth century, extracting tin and copper from under the sea, and sat on a bench seat, looking out over the rocks, the water lashing from both directions, throwing up spray. Powerful. Angry.

'I'm trying not to—and I know being on my own like this doesn't help—but I keep thinking about those dreadful things you read about in the paper. Men who've been rejected. And it is always men. Sometimes there are children involved, sometimes not. Rejected, anyway. And they sit on it, brood, send themselves into I-don't-know-what...dark places, until suddenly, one day, they can't keep it down anymore and it's, "If I can't have you, no one else will." And they set homes ablaze and they stab and they kill.'

'And that's what's frightening you? Keeping you here?'

'Of course it's bloody frightening me.'

'Yet you must know, those cases, they're awful, but they're rare.'

'And they still happen.'

'Yes, of course. But not—'

'Not what? Not to me?'

'It's unlikely.'

'Unlikely! Is that the best you can do?'

They walked back around the side of the headland, with views across a broad bay towards what remained of a derelict mine, close by the shore.

'You know,' Ellen said, 'along with whatever metals they used to take out of the ground, they used to process arsenic. Great for pesticides, apparently. Not only that. Back in Victorian times, women used to use it as a cosmetic. Dr Simms' Arsenic Complexion Wafers. Guaranteed to result in clear and blooming skin. Drank it, even.'

'No idea, presumably, that they were taking poison?'

'No, but they did. It said so, there on the bottle. Dr Fowler's Solution. Caution: Poison.'

'Then, why…?'

'Because they thought the way they looked was important, perhaps more important than anything else. And because, like people today who read *Smoking Kills* on a cigarette packet and light up all the same, they think it won't happen to them. So they're prepared to take the risk.'

'And you're not?'

'Would I take arsenic to improve my ageing complexion?' Ellen laughed. 'I think perhaps not. Would I go back to smoking Marlboro Lights, like I did when I was twenty-one? Not now. No way. But does that make me a coward or just sensible? Risk-averse, is that the term?'

'I dare say.'

'It's not just the as-you-say remote possibility of being the victim of uncontrollable anger that's preventing me from making up my mind, it's everything. Do I want to relocate halfway across the world and leave behind everything I've spent the best part of fifty years putting together? My two boys, my sons. Anthony, he'd be okay, but Andrew…'

'There's always Skype,' Kiley said. 'Or so I'm told.'

Ellen stopped on the cliff edge. 'It's different for Leah. She doesn't have children. And she knows what she wants. She wants to go to New Zealand. And she wants me. If I don't agree to go with her, it means I don't love her. At least, not enough. That's what she'll think. And she'll go without me if she has to, I realise that. She's been after a job down there for ages and the chance may not come again. She's not going to throw it away now.'

A gull flew close overhead and wheeled off across the bay.

'It sounds to me,' Kiley said, 'as if you've made up your mind.'

'Does it?' Ellen's laughter caught on the wind. 'Then you better tell me what it is.'

•●⬤●•

Sunday afternoon. The band was on stage and the skateboarders were in the square. Kiley was back in his usual seat. As the drummer battled it out with the ensemble in an arrangement of "Skin Deep," Kiley saw Ellen making her way down past the men playing dominoes, a steady walk, not looking round, the walk of someone who knew where she was going and why.

Number over, the drummer stood to acknowledge the applause, flicked sweat from his brow.

'Now,' the bandleader was saying, 'it's my pleasure once again to bring to the microphone, on tenor saxophone, Leah Temple.'

As the music started, Kiley turned to see Ellen walk into the room, step forward, stop and listen, the expression on her face not giving anything away. "Blue and Sentimental." Leah was lost to everything but the moment, the sound that rose and fell around her as she played, her eyes tightly closed.

How Many Cats Have You Killed?

Mick Herron

I saw a snake once, near the railway track in Oxford. This must have been thirty years ago. I didn't get a clear view; just saw a section of its length, wrapped round a fencepost. The rest was hidden in long grass. It was moving, very slowly, and was inches thick: definitely not indigenous. God knows where it came from—abandoned pet? Escapee from a circus? I didn't want to get closer (it was a few yards away), so I just stood and watched and eventually it slithered from view.

This really happened. I didn't report it, though I should have done: I remember thinking, *who's going to believe me?* I was a student at the time, or an unemployed graduate; definitely layabout territory, so I didn't think turning up at a police station and explaining I'd just seen a really huge snake would meet anything but scorn. So, anyway. That's a short story for you; the real kind, which has nothing up its sleeve, and no twist in the tail. It's just something that happened once, that's all. I saw a snake that had no right to be there. And none of us are ever going to know what that was about.

I remembered this for the first time in decades the other day, because somebody asked me how many cats I'd killed.

•●●●•

Okay, rewind. There was a train of thought there, and a perfectly logical one, too. I'm a novelist. Like just about everybody else in this hotel right now, I'm a crime novelist; I invent dark stories, and people die. Occasionally, too, pets die, and this is one of the issues we novelists like to raise in the bar at places like CrimeFest—how many animals have you done away with? 'How many cats have you killed?' we ask each other, and laugh about it; and then we get asked the same question in public forums, and God help us if we show amusement at that point, because one thing readers are hot on—are *very* hot on—is animal cruelty. You can slaughter prostitutes, tabloid journalists, politicians, and bankers (the more the merrier, frankly), but if you've put away a moggy in a book, you're beyond the pale. That's a no-go area. And the whole 'it's only a story' get-out doesn't help either. Case in point: in my book *Dead Lions*, there's an opening passage in which I describe Slough House, the location for most of my recent novels, by writing something like: 'Let's imagine a cat got in,' and then following the passage of that imaginary cat through the building. It was a way of introducing characters; their individual responses to the intruder giving the reader an insight into what they're like, and I had fun with it up to and including the point at which the cat reaches the final room, whereupon it's tossed out of the window and hit by a passing car. So okay, technically a cat dies. But you know, even within the realms of fiction, it was an imaginary cat. Not merely a fictional animal, a *pretend* fictional animal. And still this drew gasps of dismay from an audience once. (Americans, if you're interested. I don't mean anything by that, but it happened in America. Just saying.)

But anyway, why this question 'How many cats have you killed?' drew the snake to mind was this: it occurred to me while delivering my well-rehearsed answer that I never use real experiences in my books. I'll happily describe the adventures of an imaginary cat, but I never talk about the snake. Avoiding truth, I make stuff up instead. Which isn't a bad approach for a novelist, I've always said, but the bad news I got this morning has left me with second thoughts. So I've decided to use my contribution to this anthology celebrating CrimeFest's tenth anniversary (Happy Birthday, guys!) as a platform from which to make an honest statement about my real life. Hence my mention of the snake, which has been waiting years to appear in a piece of fiction, and my now addressing—candidly, for once—the question that all crime writers get asked (the one about killing cats), and the other one that all espionage writers face: 'Have you ever been a spy?'

Cards on the table, then. How many cats have I killed? None. Not one. Not a solitary kitten.

And have I ever been a spy?

Yes. Yes, I have.

Still am, in fact.

•●⬤●•

But not for my own country. I'd better make that clear from the outset. I mean, I'm as patriotic as the next novelist, but let's face it, the pay is just *stupid*. Besides, I don't actually know anything that would be of use to MI5: I get pretty much all my information from Radio 4, and I imagine it's got that covered. No, let's just say that the country I work for is not the one you might expect; is not commonly understood to be hostile to our own; and has a far bigger budget for covert activities than Wikipedia, for a start, is aware of. I'm not giving any more clues, except to say that it's the size of Wales (but isn't Wales, obviously. That would be ridiculous).

Anyway, it all started shortly after *Slow Horses*—my first spy novel proper—was published, and in a manner embarrassingly familiar to anyone versed in the rules of tradecraft. There I was, sitting on a park bench reading a newspaper, like you do, when two bowler-hatted men came and sat either side of me. The first—who looked a lot like Trevor Howard, if that helps—said, very politely, 'I wonder if you'd care to come along with us, sir?' except, the way he said it made it clear I had little choice in the matter. (That was what the second man was for. He looked a lot like Dwayne Johnson.) I was somewhat nervous, obviously, but also curious, as well as outnumbered, I got into their car and, after being driven a very long way, almost exactly the amount of time it would take to drive to, say, Cardiff (but not Cardiff), found myself delivered to an underground complex beneath a rugby stadium. And there my life as a spy began.

Because, as it turns out—and this was explained to me in great detail—almost all spy novelists are, in fact, spies. And how they get to be spies happens in exactly the way it had just happened to me: they publish a spy novel, which attracts the attention of MI5 (apparently, spooks do a lot of reading), which then recruits them on account of the crafty brilliance displayed in their book. Put like that, it sounds like a reasonable process, a no-brainer even, though I'll admit I was quite surprised to begin with. But it seems it's a widespread practice across the crime-writing industry. Did you know, for example, that most cosy-crime writers are in fact undercover taxidermists or cupcake designers or whatever? True fact. But anyway, most espionage novelists are real-life secret agents, which no doubt gives them a chuckle when they're asked, at conferences and in interviews, 'Have you ever been a spy?' (Though that remains a ridiculous question, and the fact that the honest answer should almost always be 'yes' doesn't make asking it any more sensible. I mean, the answer's going to be 'no' regardless, right? Either because it's the truth or, especially, because it isn't. QED.)

All of this was interesting, of course, but got more so when the Trevor Howard lookalike laid out his proposition. His name, by the way—not his real name; just a code name—was Daffyd. Now that I've come to write this down, incidentally, I'm struck by how Welsh it sounds, but that's just a coincidence. Anyway, the job I was being offered was to spy on all these other spy novelists, in order to determine who among their number might prove susceptible to blackmail on account of leading a deviant and unsavoury personal life. Even given that the answer to this was clearly 'all of them,' natural loyalty to my fellow authors left me aghast at the notion of such treachery, until it was explained that I would receive a salary. But there remained one obvious question, i.e., what would happen when MI5 tried to recruit me, as per its usual practice? At this, Daffyd hummed and hawed a bit, and looked embarrassed, and finally explained that, in an exact antithesis of his own approach, MI5 tends to focus on spy novelists whose output is both plausible and clever.

Which I thought harsh at the time, but as it turned out, MI5 has never displayed the slightest interest in my work, so he may have had a point.

•●⬤●•

And thus, as I say, began my life as a spy. I've continued to write novels, of course, and the salary I receive from the Secret Service has allowed me to give up my day job. The Service has also managed to suborn various juries to ensure that certain titles of mine appear on awards shortlists, and to solicit, via generous 'presents,' favourable reviews from the more notoriously corrupt critics, resulting in the kind of attention which produces invitations to attend crime-writing conferences and speak at public events alongside other crime writers and, more often than not, spy novelists. When this happens I'm as affable and sociable as possible, joining in with the usual post-event celebrations; trotting along to whichever pub or bar my fellow authors aren't currently banned from; merrily matching them drink for drink, despite my own inclination towards temperance and moderation; and then, once they've passed out, searching their hotel rooms, bugging their laptops and cloning their phones. Money for old rope, really.

Daffyd is proud of me. Pretty much every communication that every spook novelist has with MI5 now goes straight into his Service's database, TAFF, which sounds Welsh but stands for Telecommunications Appertaining to Fiction-writing Faction, so is normal. The dossiers he has on my fellow spy novelists are such that not one among them has been able to withstand the pressure to become a double agent; indeed, Daffyd has such confidence in this fifth column that he's even drawn up plans for a hostile takeover of MI5 itself. When Daffodil Day arrives (a code name that was assigned by a random word generator, and has no special significance), MI5 will find its entire network of novelists well and truly scuppered, and all down to a midlist scribbler whose work 'doesn't meet our current requirements,' as one early reader put it. So I think I can safely say I've made a lasting impact on my genre.

Or at least, that was how things stood until this morning, and the event which triggered this output.

I was fast asleep here in the Bristol Royal Marriott when I was woken by the buzzing of my Service-supplied state-of-the-art de-encryption device-slash-satellite-transponder handset, which is cunningly packaged to look like a severely retro mobile phone. It was Daffyd, with bad news.

'Boyo,' he said—short for 'Bosanquet', my middle name; I generally keep this quiet, but Daffyd found out—'Boyo, you're in big trouble.'

Because, it turns out, MI5 isn't entirely stupid. It had not escaped its attention that its network had become compromised, and in its search for the novelist responsible had narrowed the field of suspects down to the contingent of crime writers currently attending this year's CrimeFest—a particularly large number, due to the rumours of an open bar to celebrate the festival's anniversary. And having done so, it would not rest until it had identified the individual who had done such damage, whereupon it would—with that same arrogant cruelty that, as Daffyd pointed out, has characterised the English nation's treatment of those it regards as subversives ever since its persecution of, random example, the Druids—terminate him/her (i.e., me) with extreme prejudice.

Not thc gentlest of alarm calls, I think you'll agree.

My first response was to announce my immediate retirement. If I simply curtailed all activities, I reasoned, MI5 would be unable to track any further subversive movement and would conclude that the operation had ceased. My brilliant undercover career peacefully brought to an end, Daffyd and I would make our good-byes and have no further contact. The game would be over.

'And what will you do then, Boyo?' he asked.

'Well,' I said, 'I'll continue my writing career without your behind-the-scenes support.'

He chuckled, and wished me good luck with that ('Good luck with that' were, in fact, his exact words), but suggested that it might not be enough. 'I'm not sure, Boyo, that they'll give up that easily,' he said. 'I mean, you've nobbled some of their star names. J N , for example. You nobbled J N !'

'I did,' I agreed. 'I did nobble J N .'

'J N , man!'

'J N ,' I said.

I could hear him shaking his head on the other end of the de-encryption device-slash-satellite-transponder handset. 'J N ,' he repeated softly. Then he said, 'Well, they're not going to take that lying down, Boyo. They're going to want to kill you really badly. Really, *really* badly. That chap who turned up in those suitcases? In those *three* suitcases? That's how badly they're going to want to kill you.'

Three was certainly a terrible number of suitcases to be found in. I sat up. 'What should I do, Daffyd?'

'Well, Boyo,' he said. 'What you need to do is supply them with an alternative culprit.'

'I see.'

'And ideally,' he went on, 'one not in a position to deny anything.'

•••••

He was right, of course. The only thing that will persuade MI5 to give up its search is if it thinks it's found what it's looking for. All I need do, then, is to identify among the crowds of crime writers attending this year's anniversary CrimeFest a credible villain; that is, one who's been to all the right conventions, who's appeared on a lot of platforms alongside writers of spy fiction, who's spoken at a lot of events, and who might plausibly fit the bill as a treacherous, back-stabbing, amoral, soulless snake in the grass.

Moreover, I have the means to hand, too. When first kitted out as an undercover operative, I was supplied with the usual tools of the trade: the de-encryption device-slash-satellite-transponder handset; the exploding leek (other vegetables available); and, crucially, the travel-size vial of poison, which is not untraceable exactly, but, as its symptoms exactly match those of extreme drunkenness, crippling nausea, and the mother of all hangovers, is unlikely to arouse comment if used in the crime-writing community. The fact that this hangover ultimately results in unstoppable haemorrhaging and painful death is more attention-grabbing, of course, but if the crime community can't cope with the occasional body in its midst, then it really ought to think about a rebrand.

So here's the plan. I'll wait until the bar downstairs is full—mid-afternoon should do it—and make a circuit of the room, vial up my sleeve, stopping to chat to the many good friends I'll encounter along the way. Then, when the opportunity arises, I'll squeeze a few drops of poison into the unguarded glass of a random novelist, who by this time tomorrow will be enjoying the best reviews of his or her career, all of them including the words 'sorely missed.' The serial corrupting of MI5's agents in the spy-writing community will cease forthwith, and those in charge of the mole-hunt will therefore assume that our late (sorely missed) friend was the creature responsible. By which time, having put aside my own undercover career, I will be focusing on producing more of those novels that have made me an all-but-constant fixture on Amazon's list of the top ninety-seven thousand bestselling writers of (British) (Male) (Spy) thrillers.

There's an argument, of course, that announcing this intention in an anthology which could easily attract tens of readers might not be the wisest course of action, but to that, I'd point out that a confession made in a short story collection is of dubious evidential value. I mean, every word a crime novelist writes has to be treated with caution, yes? We're people who discuss in public how many cats we've killed, when the truth is, hardly any of us have killed very many at all. (Single figures, I expect. Low double, max.) So I doubt there'll be serious comeback; and even if there is, well, I'll still have a nearly full vial of poison left.

Almost time to go, then. I'll finish this then attend a panel or two—because I could do with a nap after being woken early—and then hit the bar. I hope it's not a particular friend who ends up carrying the can for my covert activities, but those are the breaks, and anyway, as a proud member of the Crime Writers' Association, I can state with near certainty that most of my fellow members would jump at the opportunity of laying down their lives for a colleague in difficulty. Besides, unstoppable haemorrhaging and painful death notwithstanding, I'm the one with the real problem.

I no longer have a salary.

Daylight Robbery

Donna Moore

'You told me your father was dead.'

Graeme just mumbled something incomprehensible and flapped the pages of his newspaper. Polly spread a thin layer of supposed-to-taste-like-butter on her toast and reached for the own-brand, reduced-sugar jam that Graeme insisted she buy because he didn't eat jam. His body was a temple. A cliché-ridden, jamless, joyless temple. She stuck her knife into the jar, then glanced up. His face was still hidden behind the reactionary rag he insisted on reading. All she could see was the latest '*Are Immigrants Giving British Taxpayers Cancer?*' banner headline. Polly upended the jar, tipped a thick covering of jam over her toast and added a heaped teaspoon of sugar. 'You told me your father was dead. I've thought that for the last twenty-one years. And now you just announce out of the blue that he's coming to live with us?' She took a bite of toast. 'What are we going to do? Stick his coffin in the gazebo and hope the smell doesn't annoy the neighbours?'

'Don't be facetious, Polly, it doesn't suit you.' Graeme folded the paper into a precise square and tucked it into the briefcase at the side of the dining room table, where they sat having breakfast. 'And, for God's sake, what are you doing putting all that jam on there?'

'I can't believe that you told me he was dead. And why does he suddenly have to come and live with us?'

'I don't want to talk about it.'

'Well, you bloody well *have* to.' Polly threw the remainder of the slice of toast she was eating across the room. It landed—jam side down, of course—on her spotless wooden floor. 'Graeme, this isn't one of your normal sins of omission. You've not forgotten to tell me that you're going to be home late from work, or that you're going to watch the football down the pub and you've forgotten we were going out for a meal, or that you've already decided we're going to Tenerife on holiday.' She bit back the '*or that you're having an affair with Denise in Sales*' that threatened to burst out. 'This is something much more significant. You told me before we married that both your parents were dead. Our child has been brought up thinking he has no paternal grandparents. There are no photos of your father anywhere in the house and you never even mention his name. And now you tell me that not only is he alive and well and living in Glasgow, but also that he's going to be coming down here and moving in with us for a few months. What do you expect me to do? Roll over and accept it without a word?' As she usually did. 'Well, it's not bloody happening.'

Graeme pressed a napkin to his lips and ran a hand through his thinning hair. 'Okay, okay.' He sighed. 'Look, the reason I told you he was dead is that he's a complete waster. There aren't any photos of him because he spent most of his time in and out of jail.'

'In and out of…*jail?* And you want him to come *here*?'

'He's not a murderer or anything, he's not violent. Just a useless wanker of a petty criminal—and not very good at it, is all. Burglary, breaking and entering...that sort of thing.'

'And what about your mother? Is she alive too? Maybe running a brothel in Ayrshire or something?'

'No. She's...'

Polly stared at him as he lapsed into silence. 'You *have* to be kidding me. She's alive too?'

'Look...it's complicated. They're useless. Always were. I got out as soon as I could, came down to England, and made a life for myself. One that didn't include them.'

Polly sometimes didn't understand her husband. And she was beginning to wonder if she even *knew* him. 'And now?'

'Now he's ill. Needs a bit of looking after. He got my Uncle Reg to help track me down and sent me this letter.' Graeme pulled the letter out of his pocket.

'What happened?'

Graeme shrugged. 'He was out on bail and had a heart attack in the pub. Bloody typical. When the case went to court he was tried in his absence by some soft, bleeding-heart judge who let him off on the proviso that he got help and got out of the area for a while.'

'And your mum?'

Graeme shrugged. 'Apparently, she finally got fed up of his behaviour, and, while he was in hospital, she stuffed all his belongings into a dustbin bag, took it to the hospital and buggered off.'

'That's a bit cold, isn't it? The man had just had a heart attack.'

Graeme looked at her blankly. 'She should have done it years before, as far as I'm concerned.'

'What did he do, anyway?'

Graeme sighed. 'He broke into someone's house and was caught when they came home and found him fast asleep on the sofa with a half-eaten cheese sandwich next to him, having racked up a two-hundred-seventy-five-pound telephone bill calling a psychic hotline.'

Polly laughed. 'You'd have thought he'd have seen that one coming.'

Graeme stood up and put his jacket on. 'It's not funny, Polly. If the neighbours get to hear about this, we'll be the laughing stock. We're going to have to have a serious think about how we handle this. We'll have to keep him indoors, get him well as quickly as possible, and get him back up the road to Glasgow.'

The alarm bells started ringing. 'And who, exactly, is going to play Florence Nightingale to your old lag of a father?'

'Old lag? What do you think this is—an episode of *Prisoner Cell Block H?*'

'Don't duck the question, Graeme. Who's going to look after him?'

Graeme picked up his briefcase. 'Well, you, of course. It's not like you have anything better to do, is it? I'll be home late. We've got a board meeting. Michaelson is getting us all together for some blue-sky thinking.' And with that, he let himself out of the front door. She watched him as he got into the top-of-the-range Mondeo he'd bought without consulting her and backed carefully out of the drive.

It was true, she *didn't* have anything better to do. She'd been thinking of getting a hobby—scuba diving, maybe, or starting a course at the local college—creative writing; she'd always wanted to do that. What she *hadn't* anticipated doing was babysitting a convict.

●●●●●

Polly stood outside the entrance to the station, biting her nails, her eyes flicking to her watch and back to the gate. The train from Glasgow had just pulled in and people were starting to come through the gates. She held up the cardboard sign with her father-in-law's name on it and scanned the faces. She didn't know what to expect—it was like a game of Russian roulette with people. She knew it certainly wasn't going to be the dapper, well-dressed man with grey hair, but please, please, *please* don't let it be the thug with the spider's web tattoo halfway up his face. What did a convict look like, anyway? Was he going to look like the characters in all those black-and-white films she watched on Film Four while Graeme was at work? Maybe something like Edward G Robinson. Or Robert Mitchum in *Night of the Hunter*. Maybe she should start looking for tattooed knuckles.

She put a hand to her mouth to stifle a sob. Oh, why had she agreed that he could stay with them? She'd need to keep her jewellery box locked away. Her hands flew from her mouth to her ears and she fumbled as she tried to take out the gold-and-diamond studs Graeme had bought her for their twentieth wedding anniversary. Better not leave temptation in the old crook's way. And what if he was violent? What if all that time in the slammer had turned him into a nonce? What if he'd brought a skank with him? Wait, that wasn't right, a skank was something else...a shank. That was it. She dropped her earring on the floor. A cheery-looking rotund man wearing a pair of high-waisted navy slacks and a bright yellow polo shirt stooped down to pick it up. The top of his bald head was shiny and liver-spotted under the strands of white hair. He stood back up again with a grunt.

'Jeez-o, I shouldnae have done that.' He beamed at her and stuck out a hand. 'Awright, hen? You'll be Polly, I take it?'

'Oh.' She was taken aback. No scars, no teardrop-shaped tattoos on his cheeks. No chib mark from mouth to ear. 'You're Mr Fulton?'

'Aye, hen. You sound surprised. What were you expecting? A suit wi' wee arrows on and a bag marked "swag"?' Her face obviously gave her away as the smile went down a few notches in wattage. 'Aye. That son of mine been singing ma' praises, has he? Well, I can't blame him, right enough.'

'I—' Polly felt flustered and tongue-tied. Why couldn't Graeme have done his own bloody dirty work and come to pick up his father?

'Nae worries, hen. Ah'm just kidding ye. And in the name of Christ, don't call me Mr Fulton. It's Colin. Col to ma' pals. Mr Fulton makes me sound like a screw.' He must have registered the confusion on her face. 'A prison officer, hen.'

Polly wasn't sure what to say. She'd never come across anyone quite like him before. She'd come to the station fully prepared to find a scarred, morose, knife-wielding thug, and instead she was faced with a man who wouldn't look out of place in a Father Christmas suit. Even in mid-July. But he was a criminal, and he was coming to stay. She sighed. And sighed again when he picked up a dustbin bag that she hadn't spotted before. 'Is that your luggage?'

'Aye. The wife took the Samsonite. Left me with the fancy stuff. Fancy a pint, hen?' Colin nodded his head towards the bar in the station.

'A pint?' Polly looked at her watch. 'Of *beer*?' She mentally added another black mark to Colin's tally. *Alcoholic*. 'Oh, I don't think so. It's only eleven in the morning. Besides, I promised Graeme we'd be back before midday. And…well, you're just out of hospital after a heart attack. Surely you shouldn't be drinking?'

'Aye, mibbes you're right, hen. The doc said I should give up the drinking and the smokes. I've got a new addiction now, anyway.' He registered the look of horror on Polly's face. 'Calm your jets, hen. Pear drops.' He shook the bag at her and popped one into his mouth. 'And where is the fruit of ma loins anyway? Couldn't be bothered to come and meet his old da?'

Polly wasn't quite sure how to answer that one. She looked this harmless-looking elderly gent in the eye. 'Something like that, yes.'

Polly hated driving. It made her shoulders tense. Graeme always told her off for leaving the seat all the way forward. She clenched her hands on the steering wheel, nose almost touching the windscreen, and carefully put the car into gear. As they drove along in silence, she could sense his eyes on her and felt strangely uncomfortable in her faded blue skirt and the bobbly pink jumper that was three sizes too big and twenty years too old. She wanted to take a hand off the wheel to smooth down her mousy brown hair. She should really get her roots done.

'You look a bit stressed, hen.'

'Really? I have no idea why that would be.'

'Those tension lines have been there a wee bit longer than you've known about me.'

She glanced round at him but he had turned away and was looking out of the window at the dull, flat countryside which bordered the road. Fields of carrots, potatoes, and wheat, interspersed with occasional ploughed fields of rich, dark earth. 'Beautiful,' he murmured.

Polly swerved. 'I'm sorry?'

Colin pointed towards the sleek, white blades of a small cluster of wind turbines scything through the sky. 'The wind farm. I love to see them.'

'Oh. Right.' She lapsed into silence again and he turned away once more, as if disappointed. 'Graeme hates them. Says they're ugly and a blight on the countryside. He stands at the living room window and glowers at them.'

'And you? What do you think, hen?'

She shrugged. 'I like them. They're...graceful. I wish they came in other colours, though.' She flicked her eyes his way, briefly, before turning back to the straight road. 'You know—wouldn't it be lovely if they were bright red, turquoise, purple, daffodil yellow? Like a town I once saw in a documentary about Madagascar. I tried to get Graeme to go on holiday there a couple of years ago, but…'

'He preferred Margate?'

Polly sighed. 'Something like that, yes.' She pulled off the main road into a neat housing estate. The houses looked new and there was hardly anyone around. Despite that, Polly dutifully indicated as she turned down various streets named after waterfowl—Grebe Way, Gull Crescent, Heron Place—finally turning into Cormorant Avenue and pulling the car into a gravel driveway.

'Very nice, hen. No grass. No good for burgling, what with the crunch of gravel under your feet. And those spiky bushes under the front windows.' She looked at him, mouth open in horror. 'Ah'm kidding, hen.'

He followed Polly to the boot of the car but she waved him away. 'You've just had a heart attack—I'm sure heavy lifting isn't allowed.' She lifted the black bin bag out of the boot. As she did so, the bag caught on the boot's latch and split open. Trousers, jumpers, underpants, socks, and a pair of trainers came tumbling out. 'Oh, I'm so sorry Mr Ful–Colin.'

'Nae problem, hen. No idea how that could have happened—I double bagged it tae.'

'Didn't you...couldn't you...?'

'Nick a suitcase?'

She felt herself reddening. 'I didn't mean that. I meant... couldn't you...*borrow* one or something?'

He was about to answer when the front door of the house opened. 'For Christ's sake, Polly, get that damned mess cleared off the drive and bring it in here before the neighbours see.'

Colin nudged Polly and gestured with his head towards Graeme. 'He talking about me, or ma' stuff?'

Graeme stomped out of the house and snatched the bin bag from his wife's hand. 'Christ's sake, it's not as though I asked you to do anything difficult, is it, Polly?'

Polly stood aside to let Colin go into the house in front of her. He was careful to wipe his feet ostentatiously on the welcome mat, which said 'Come In' in bright red letters. He raised an eyebrow at Polly. 'What does it say on the other side? "Fuck Off?"'

Polly sat at the dressing table in front of the mirror. She adjusted the table lamp until the light shone more clearly onto her face, reflecting off her cheeks—shiny from scrubbing with exfoliator—and seeming to deepen the lines around her eyes. She was only forty-four—how could she have such deep lines? It wasn't as though they were laughter lines—God knows she had little enough to laugh about. She picked up the tube of moisturiser and started to spread some on her face, dabbing her cheeks, nose, chin, before carefully patting it outwards. Mind you, she'd had a few giggly moments since Colin had come to stay, which had surprised her rather. She still didn't want him there but he wasn't the monster Graeme had painted him as. Nor had he stolen anything. Not yet, anyway. She'd been checking every morning but, so far, all their valuables seemed intact. She'd even tried that trick with the hair, to see if he'd opened any doors and put a bit of thread under some of the Lladro figures Graeme loved, but they hadn't been moved at all.

'He's all right, really, isn't he, Graeme?'

'Who?' Graeme sat on the bed, undoing his tie.

'Who do you think? Your dad, of course.'

Graeme snorted. 'All right? All he's done since he got here is sit on his useless arse and read the *Racing Post*. Are you coming to bed? You know I can't sleep with the light on and I need to be sharp tomorrow.' He puffed out his chest self-importantly. 'Michaelson's out meeting his art dealer about some painting he's gone gaga over and he's asked me to whip the sales team into shape.'

The unwanted image of Graeme in chaps, carrying a cat-o'-nine tails and bending Denise over his desk came to Polly's mind. She tried to banish it. 'I'm thinking of getting my hair cut and coloured.' She fingered the lank mousy tresses, surveying the split ends.

'Why? It's not as though anyone ever sees you.'

Because you never take me anywhere, she felt like saying. 'I just thought I'd treat myself, is all.'

'Well, as long as you can afford it from the housekeeping budget.'

She looked at him in the mirror. He was taking off the diamond-studded cufflinks she'd bought him last Christmas—bought with money she'd saved from the admittedly generous housekeeping budget he made a great show of giving her every month. The same Christmas he'd bought *her* a new lawnmower. Yes, she had *plenty* of money saved out of the housekeeping budget. She'd get him a pair of socks next Christmas. From the pound shop. She pulled her hair back off her face and turned her head from side to side. Blond? Maybe red. Shoulder-length? Or should she be really brave and go for short and spiky?

• • ● • •

'A *job* interview?' Raspberry jam dripped off Polly's knife onto the kitchen table. She scooped it up with a finger and licked it off. She looked over at Graeme, who just grunted.

Colin took a bite of his toast, chewed slowly, and swallowed. 'Aye, hen. Ah thought it was time I paid my way around here.'

Graeme grunted again. Polly kicked him under the table. 'That's great. Isn't it, Graeme?' Another grunt. 'But are you sure you're up to it, Col? You're not long out of hospital.'

'Aye, hen. The advert said it was just light work. Look.' He pulled the job advert that he'd cut from the local paper out of his pocket and read it to her. "Men aged between 40 and 60 wanted urgently for light manual labour. £25 an hour paid, plus expenses. Please meet on corner of Market Street and Hazel Lane at 10 a.m. on 26th July. Transport will be arranged. Please come ready to work: jeans, fluorescent-yellow working jacket, hard hat, and industrial face mask." I popped into B&Q and got myself kitted out.'

Polly was dubious. 'Twenty-five pounds an hour for light manual labour? That sounds a bit too good to be true. What do you think, Graeme?'

Graeme stood up and picked up his briefcase. 'Just let him get on with it, Polly.' He looked over at his father, who was spreading butter on his fourth slice of toast. 'It'll be the first honest day's work the old bastard's ever done. And. for God's sake. stop calling him "Col" as though he's your new best friend.'

'Graeme!' Polly stood up as her husband stomped out of the house, slamming the door behind him. She turned to her father-in-law. 'I'm so sorry, Col. I don't know what's got into him.'

Colin turned away and looked out of the window at his son, who pulled the Mondeo out of the driveway with a screech. 'He's right, hen. I've not been very good about honest work. But I'm trying to make up for that now. Can't blame the lad if he needs a bit more proof.'

Polly joined him over at the window. 'But there's no need for him to be such an...arsehole.' She felt weird saying it, but it was the only word that suited her husband's behaviour.

'Maybe it's in the genes. I've been an arsehole all my life.'

'I'll take you down there and do a bit of shopping. I might even go to B&Q and get myself one of those jackets and hats and join you.'

• • ● • •

Polly dropped Colin off on the corner where he was meeting his new employers, just outside the bank.

'Good luck!'

She parked at Sainsbury's, just across the road, and rummaged in her bag looking for her notebook and pen to write out a shopping list. Graeme didn't like her to go into the supermarket without a plan, just in case she came home with something frivolous. She hesitated and then wrote 'something frivolous' at the end of the list.

She glanced over towards the bank. Colin had been joined by around thirty other men in fluorescent-yellow donkey jackets and jeans, all milling around outside the bank. Some were carrying their face masks and hats; most were already wearing them. Passersby were looking curiously at the motley crew as they passed. It looked like some sort of weird living art installation.

Polly was about to get out of the car and head to the supermarket when she heard a shout. A man—dressed in fluorescent-yellow jacket, jeans, hard hat, and mask—was running out of the bank, a large sports bag in his hand. He dodged in and out of the crowd of identically dressed men, chased by two security guards who looked increasingly confused.

Polly started the car. The man with the sports bag rounded a corner and Polly pulled out of the car park and drove off in the same direction, leaving the chaos behind her. As she turned into the quiet street, she saw the man throw the bag into the back of a silver BMW, jump into the front seat and drive off. She followed him, her heart pounding. Fuzzy black spots started appearing in front of her eyes. She should stop and call the police, but if she did that, she would lose the car. She could take the plate number down but it would probably turn out to be fake—she watched enough crime dramas on TV to know that was a dead certainty. The only thing she could do was follow.

Luckily, the man was driving carefully and slowly. Another thing she had learned from TV—no doubt he didn't want to risk getting caught. She followed him out of town and across the fen roads. The traffic was becoming lighter, but luckily, the terrain was so flat that she could stay quite far back without losing him.

Polly wondered once more whether the sensible thing would have been to call the police. And what would Colin be thinking? Two cars ahead, the BMW was slowing down. It turned into a driveway. Polly speeded up and was just in time to see the BMW disappearing through a tall iron gate between high stone walls. The gates closed behind the car. As she passed, Polly caught a glimpse of an imposing and ostentatious front porch—all pillars and lions. The kind of porch that indicated an interior reminiscent of a 1980s cruise ship. Polly speeded up and drove on for a mile before pulling into the side of the road to call the police. As she took her phone out of her bag she discovered a missed call from Colin. She listened to the message.

'Ah'm at the polis station. The one near the park. You're ma one phone call, hen. The nice young polisman that's just brought me a cuppa says you can come and pick me up. Bring a file wi' a cake in it.' She could hear someone mumbling in the background and then Colin again. 'He says I'm a cheeky auld bastard. Ah'm gonnae report him for police brutality for making ma tea too hot.'

She clicked the phone off and stuffed it back in her bag. She would tell the police when she went to pick up Colin.

Polly had never been inside a police station before. A group of disconsolate-looking men wearing fluorescent jackets and hard hats sat on the waiting room chairs. They looked collectively like a rather uninspiring group of strippers. She hoped they didn't suddenly break into 'You Can Leave Your Hat On.' She walked straight up to the counter and said to the man behind the desk, 'Polly—Hippolyta—Fulton. I'm here to collect my father-in-law—Colin Fulton.'

'Here I am, hen.' Polly turned round to see Colin standing behind her, workman's jacket and mask in hand.

'Oh, my God—are you okay? Have you been arrested? What have you been charged with? Do you need a brief? Are they going to send you to the big house?'

Colin exchanged a look with the policeman on the desk. 'You any idea what she's on about, Officer?'

'Not a clue, sir.'

'I was just helping the polis wi' their enquiries, as they say on *Crimewatch*.' Colin took Polly firmly by the arm and led her towards the door. 'C'mon, hen, let's get out of here and go and get some scran. By the way...*Hippolyta*?'

Polly could feel the blush always occasioned by the revelation of her full name. 'Unfortunately, yes. My parents were hippies. And probably smoking something. They saw fit to blight my childhood and make my life utter hell at school by naming me after a Greek goddess. She was—'

'Aye, I know who she was. Queen of the Amazons. She had superhuman strength.'

Polly looked at him. 'That's right. How do you know that? Are you a fan of the Greek myths?'

Colin spluttered. 'Naw, hen. DC comics. She was Wonder Woman's maw.'

As he led her outside she took her arm away and turned back. 'I need to tell the police I saw him.'

'Who?'

'The bank robber. I followed him. I know where he lives.'

Colin stared at her for a moment before taking her firmly by the arm and leading her down the steps outside the police station. 'Is that right, hen? Well, let's just cool our jets on that one a wee bit, shall we? I've got a wee score to settle wi' that arse.'

• • ● • •

'And why, exactly, are we here?'

Colin's eyes were fixed on the tall gates. 'Just a wee scouting mission, hen. Gie's yer mobile.'

'My…You're not…?'

Colin sighed. 'Naw, hen. I'm not gonnae call to get ma horoscope. I want to find out who lives here.'

Polly passed her phone across. After a few seconds, Colin let out a shrill whistle. 'Well, well, well.'

Polly tried to see over his shoulder. 'What is it? Who does the place belong to?'

Colin turned to her, grinning. 'Have you never been invited for dinner at the boss's house?'

'Mr Michaelson?' Polly blinked. 'Oh, no. Graeme's been a couple of times, but he says I'm too dull, so he made excuses for me. I've met him, of course, but Graeme always rushes me away before I can say something stupid. Why? Why are you asking about Mr Michaelson?' Colin tilted his head towards the house and raised his eyebrows. 'Mr Michaelson? Mr Michaelson lives *here*? Oh! Then we should really tell the police that the robber's hiding out here and Mr Michaelson might be in danger. Graeme would never forgive me if his boss came to harm and I could have stopped…' She broke off. Colin was slowly shaking his head, the grin still on his face. 'You mean…?'

'Aye, hen. That's exactly what I mean. And that makes this a whole load easier for us.'

'But what…? But why don't we just go to the police and tell them?'

'Because, hen, then we'd never see hide nor hair of *this*.' He took a piece of paper out of his pocket and smoothed it out. 'I picked this up at the polis station; the bank were quick off the mark. They're offering a hundred thousand pounds reward for the return of that money. They must have lost a packet. Now, let's go home. We need to get into that house and see what we can find before we go to the polis. And I've got a plan for getting us in.'

Polly clutched her knees and rocked backwards and forwards as Colin paced the living room. 'Are you sure this is going to work, Col?'

'Like a dream. Now, remember, leave all the talking to me, hen, okay?'

Polly nodded, then opened her mouth to say something else. She was stopped by the crunching of tyres on gravel and looked at Colin. He nodded and they both rolled the balaclavas down over their faces and pulled on gloves.

Polly was quite enjoying the sight of Graeme spread-eagled on the bed, trying to free his ankles and wrists from their bonds. She smiled to herself beneath the balaclava. That would serve him right for insisting she wore Spanx to keep what he called her 'ugly rolls of flab' in check. Now they were keeping *him* in check. He had been bellowing and blustering for the last ten minutes to no avail, his face red and sweating underneath the blindfold—her sleep mask with the cat's eyes on it.

Colin spoke for the first time since they had…well, Polly supposed that, technically, they had…kidnapped Graeme. 'Now then, Mr Man. Why don't you just stay quiet on that cock-a-doodie bed?' His accent was American and his words were…strange. Colin turned to her and shrugged and she could see a movement in the balaclava where his eyebrows would be. However, his words had the effect of quietening Graeme down.

'Now,' Colin drawled, 'we're going to put this little ol' newspaper on your belly while we take a couple of snaps of you, you dirty birdie.' He flung the newspaper down on top of Graeme where the headline screamed: *Time to scrap pointless Human Rights Act!* just underneath the date.

As Colin took photos with Graeme's phone, Graeme opened his mouth once more. 'I don't know what you two thugs think you're doing, but I swear I will…I will—' Polly didn't give him a chance to finish. She stopped his mouth with the dirty socks he had thrown on the floor the night before.

As she pulled the door closed behind them as they left the bedroom, she whispered to Colin, '*Misery*?'

'Aye, hen. Great film.'

Colin nudged her in the ribs as she pressed the buzzer on the gate. 'Look distraught,' he said, out of the corner of his mouth.

'I *am* bloody distraught. I've just kidnapped my husband, tied him up, possibly choked him with a pair of sweaty socks and I'm now trying to break into a bank robber's house.'

'We're not breaking in. He's going to *let* us in.'

'Same difference. Anyway, what look is it that *you're* going for?'

Colin tilted his head to one side and opened his eyes wide. 'I'm going for harmless old codger, first stages of dementia. What do you think?'

Polly snorted. 'You look like you're suffering from irritable bowel syndrome to me.'

'Aye, that, too.'

The box on the side of the gate sprang into life. 'Yes?'

'Mr Michaelson? It's Polly. Polly Fulton. Graeme's wife. Something terrible's happened. Can we come in?'

Polly couldn't believe how easy it had been. She was now sitting in one of Michaelson's slippery black leather armchairs and holding the largest glass of gin she had ever seen. She was quite impressed with her performance. She'd even managed to conjure up a few tears from somewhere as she told Michaelson how they'd been overpowered by a gang of thugs and forced to come here with the phone pictures as proof.

'But what did they want? Why did they want you to come here?' Michaelson was—*understandably*, Polly thought—confused. They hadn't quite thought that one out themselves, having concentrated on getting into the house. She looked at Colin, who was playing his part almost too well, gazing round vacantly at the walls full of art.

'I need a pish,' he said.

'Oh, errrr…right. There's a bathroom at the far end of the hall, just by the stairs.' Michaelson waved a hand and Colin shuffled off. 'Will he be all right on his own?

'Oh, yes. He'll be fine, I'm sure.'

'So…did they mention a ransom?'

'Errrr…what?'

'This gang. Did they say they wanted money?'

'Oh! Yes. Um…they said they knew that Graeme worked for you, and that you were rich and could afford to pay for Graeme's safe return. And…yes…that's what they wanted. Money.'

Michaelson laughed, hollowly. 'Yeah, well. They were wrong.'

'Wrong? What do you mean?'

Michaelson shook his head. 'Business isn't great at the moment.'

'But…they only want…ten thousand pounds.' She plucked the figure from thin air. It had a realistic ring to it, she thought.

'Ten thousand?' He gestured towards the garden. 'I couldn't afford to pay a ransom for one of the koi carp at the moment.'

Polly stared back at him. The man had over a million pounds tucked into a sports bag somewhere in this house and he couldn't afford a measly ten thousand to get her husband away from the clutches of a dreadful gang of thugs? In other circumstances, she'd have been quite indignant on Graeme's behalf.

Michaelson looked at her. 'I was actually thinking of giving Graeme the old heave-ho.'

'The…but after all those extra hours he puts in? How loyal he is to the company?'

'Extra hours? He's strictly a nine-to-five man. What extra hours?'

Ah. Denise. It would serve Graeme right if he *did* choke on his own sock.

A groan from the doorway made them both turn. Colin was standing there, clutching his coat to his stomach. 'We need to go, hen. Ma IBS is playing me up something awful.' He turned to Michaelson. 'Sorry, Mr…Matthews. I'm sorry; I've made an awfy mess in that bathroom. It's the stress of ma' beloved son being taken hostage.'

Michaelson sprang up. 'Oh, my God. I've just had that room re-grouted.' He dashed off down the corridor.

'C'mon, hen, let's go.'

'But your stomach. Don't you want to wait…?'

Colin lifted the corner of his jacket. Tucked underneath was a sports bag.

Polly looked glumly down at the pile of cash on the living room floor. 'I just can't believe you did that. We were supposed to go in there and find proof that he had taken the money. Now what?' Colin looked at her, sheepishly. 'We have my husband tied to a bed upstairs—which, by the way, he has wee'd all over. I will *never* get that out. We have a bank robber who will soon discover that his money is missing and can only have been stolen by us. And we'll soon have the police after us for stealing…stolen goods.'

'Just like Bonnie and Clyde, eh, hen?'

Polly picked up a packet of notes and threw it at him. 'Bonnie and Clyde were *shot*, you idiot. Graeme was right; you *are* useless.' His head dropped. 'Oh, I'm sorry, Colin; I didn't mean it. But…what *are* we going to do?'

Colin stood up and moved over to the window, slapping the notes she had thrown at him against his palm. The wind turbines turned slowly over the other side of the neat and tidy estate. 'Did you know, there's no extradition treaty with Madagascar, hen?'

The Snapperoody

Caro Ramsay

Yesterday was a great day. It was her birthday. I had to be polite and wear a frock, but it was okay. SHE got a Tiny Tears and a vanity case and had to kiss Auntie Nell. I had to kiss Auntie Nell, too; well, I tried to escape first but she caught me a smacker. I told her the bristles of her moustache hurt. It was sore. I got a sore ear for being cheeky.

My first for the day.

SHE was showing off in the front room, twirling in front of the aunties in a lemon ballerina dress and angora jacket. The aunties were impressed. Auntie Chrissie said she was an angel. Auntie May said all she needed was a halo. I said all she needed was a Christmas tree up her arse.

Sore ear number two.

I did enquire, sometime after the ritual singing of 'Happy Birthday,' the lighting of the candles, and the cutting of the pink cake, why SHE got new things and I didn't.

'Because you're the youngest.'

It's the same reply, every time.

'But I'm the tallest.'

'You're still the youngest.'

'But…' there was a pause, I sensed another sore ear coming and left it at that.

But the bestest, bestest thing of all, was her Big Present. The Diana Flash Camera. Working on the inheritance theory, I crept into her room, like a thief in the night, and claimed the Box Brownie. I wasn't going to wait. I hung it round my neck, tucked under the collar of my jumper, putting a special napkin over it for birthday-cake-eating purposes. I do like eating with my mouth open because it annoys them and they all go hysterical when food falls out.

As we are having a day out tomorrow, I spend the evening practising. I decide to be George of the Famous Five. Kimmy Kim is Tim, but our fat old Staffie is much more smelly and much less obedient. She darts around, posing for photographs, snapping at the camera as it snaps her. Kimmy Kim and I have fun together. Then SHE, I suppose SHE would be Anne, the pathetic girlie one in the Famous Five, comes out and tells us to Stop The Carry On.

I stand with the camera flat against my stomach, and pirouette on my good leg. I pretend to be a submarine, periscoping to the world. SHE is standing in view. If I had a decent torpedo, I could fire and SHE would be blown away into a million pieces.

Which wouldn't be enough.

SHE takes the lens off her Diana Flash and explains to me, in simple words, that her camera takes proper photographs. My inherited camera, the Box Brownie, can only take snaps. It is a camera for children.

I tell her that Kimmy Kim and I have no interest in photographs and immediately christen our camera 'the Snapperoody.'

So today the Snapperoody and I are going on a great adventure, an awfully great adventure as the Famous Five would have it. They are all going to Millport in the car, going on the ferry. I am allowed to tag along if I am well enough. I have a secret plan, of course.

Kimmy Kim was not allowed to join us, so I will be numbered in the adventure. Kim has been confined to barracks for chewing the fridge so I ate her doggy chocs ensuring I will throw up in the back of the car. True enough, just as we go down the Haylie Brae at Largs, I am violently sick, up it all comes, a brown stinky sludgy mess. I manage to get some of it on SHE.

I get a slap on the leg for not using the sick bag, but I claim I didn't have enough warning.

I feel rather proud as people walk away to avoid the smell on the ferry.

As we walk from the slip to Millport, I refuse to answer to anything but George. I lag behind, of course, as they forget.

SHE explains to THEM about George of the Famous Five and that she was a girl pretending to be a boy. She explains it is a 'little girl's story.' She thinks she is grown up. SHE tells them I read too much. THEY say I have an overactive imagination.

I think they might be laughing at me. THEY are walking well in the front of me, thinking I can't hear, but I notice everything.

Once we are on the beach near the Crocodile Rock, THEY put down a travelling rug and slip off their socks and shoes. Mum starts to unpack the peanut butter sandwiches and I show her the worm I have been carrying around in my pocket for a while. Then, SHE says 'that is not a grown-up thing,' and the worm flies from my hand, accidentally hitting her in the face. I explain it was an accident, but I still get a slap on the ear 'for frightening your sister.' I try the 'as she is older' defence but age is no defence against worms, it seems.

So I walk away and sit down, stretching my leg. I feel the tension. I have to change, before they change me.

So I change.

I decide to change into a wild dog of Africa, a bit like Kimmy Kim, but taller and with a brain. As a wild dog, I am alert to all that is around me. My nose finds scents on the breeze. All my senses are keen to the sound of nature. I am also keen to the sound of Dad asking if anybody wants an ice cream.

He must be in a good mood, we are getting 99s.

I watch him carefully, my cunning eyes narrowed, my ears pricked, as he breaks a flake in half. I tell him, that I know from my rods, that a half is two equal parts of one. So why is SHE getting the bigger half? Indeed, is there such a thing as a bigger half?

He says it is a grown-up thing and bites the larger of the two bits of chocolate, making the long bit shorter now. Then he bites the other, the only person getting chocolate is him. My good foot starts to tap in anger now. I point out the error of his ways, so SHE ends up with both bits of flake and I get a slap and another sore ear. I guess that's a grown-up thing, as well.

Children must be seen and not heard. Wild dogs of Africa, ditto.

Still, I can escape. I put a peanut butter piece and three happy-face biscuits in my pocket. I am wearing my brown

Sloppy Joe and bush hat so I can merge in the crowd on the beach. I disappear. I walk invisible. I am the adventurer.

I don't tell THEM where I am going. I circle round THEM, watching carefully. Dad is making a paddle steamer out of sand, measuring the funnels with a straw. SHE is collecting seashells to make portholes on the boat. Mum, who must be obeyed, is rubbing sticky stuff into all and sundry, and saying 'don't come crying to me if you get sunburned.' They are playing happy families.

I am not playing.

Because we are not a happy family.

The sun starts to climb in the sky, and the air gets hot. I may die from dehydration, but that never bothers George, so it won't bother me. George would have lashings and lashings of ginger beer. I've tried it, but it gives me the dry boke.

I slip away. I have my piece of peanut butter. I have my Snapperoody. I have a mission in life. I am off to snap a crocodile.

I scramble over the rocks quickly, but my leg is heavy and it gets caught on the jaggy bits. I keep having to pull it clear. I keep having to stop and rest. I stand up and periscope, surveying the scene, viewing the horizon. I am still the wild dog of Africa. I am alert to all danger and all beasties with nasty stings. I pan round, eyes and ears alert, all-sensing, twitching, hearing and seeing all that there is.

The crocodile slides into view.

A big grey rock with a bright red smile and white teeth.

From here, one eye looked a bit skelly…or maybe it was the other. Or is that the same thing?

I scramble down from my viewpoint, holding the Snapperoody high in case my leg should give way and I fall. I walk right up to Mr Crocodile. He is very big. With a very big smile.

'That's a nice camera,' says the man emerging from the other side of the rock.

I don't answer. It isn't a question.

I hold the Snapperoody to my stomach. I stare hard down the lens, trying to line up the picture.

'A Box Brownie, I see.'

So I figure he's not blind.

I am too busy periscoping to answer. I watch him, watching me, through the camera. And soon the man is walking towards me. He is now watching me, watching him, watching me. And he is in the way of my picture.

The crocodile is big and fierce from this angle. George would be proud of me, and Dick and Julian would make me an honorary boy.

I ask the man to get out of the way. He shrugs his shoulders. He still walks towards me. I ask him to go away. The man says I shouldn't know language like that, as I am a nice girl. He asks me if I like chocolate. I tell him I am busy. That really gets me annoyed and I snap the crocodile anyway. I walk around, here and there, unsteady on my leg, avoiding this man who persistently gets in my way. He's talking but I'm not listening. I have Kimmy Kim, so I don't want to see some puppies, thank you, and I have a peanut butter piece in my pocket, so I don't want sweeties from you.

I walk up the beach and sit on a rock; my leg is really sore now. I pick the dog hair from my jammy dodgers and start to eat, beginning to wish I had lashings of ginger beer. It is very hot now. I keep the crocodile in view.

He is not watching me now.

I am watching him.

He says something to another girl, pulling his hat down over his face, then points the little girl in the direction of her mum and dad. The man offers to take a photograph. The family poses in front of the crocodile. Thanks are said. The man walks away.

But I am not fooled.

The bloody cavalry appears along the beach. My wild dog of Africa senses tell me SHE is there, her slim arms and legs spinning in the air, she is looking for me. SHE dances along the sand, turning cartwheels with the grace of a gazelle. Her long brown hair blowing behind her in the gentle breeze as she makes her way up to the crocodile.

I watch her as the man talks to her.

She nods her head. She points along the beach, points along the direction I have come from. She points to her leg, indicating my calliper. A horizontal hand indicating my height.

He points along the beach, away from the rocks. Away from everybody.

I watch as she nods her head again. His hand comes out of his pocket. His face is hidden by sunglasses now. He takes one last look behind him, nobody is paying any attention.

They walk away together. His hand is on her back, guiding her to where he has told her I am.

I watch, finishing my biscuit, stretching my bad leg and walk slowly after them.

Snapperoody is at the ready. The wild dog of Africa has seen its prey. The hunter and the hunted...and the hunter.

I have a bad leg. I may have an overactive imagination. I can be George, a submarine, or the wild dog of Africa.

The one thing I am not—is stupid.

Inside the Box

Ian Rankin

'Bloody hell, I thought you were dead!'

The hand stretched out towards John Rebus and he gripped it, returning the firm shake.

'As good as, Jerry.' Rebus gave a thin smile. He was at the bar in the Police Club on York Place. 'Get you one?'

'Gin and slim.' Jerry Calder made a show of patting his stomach.

'You've lost a bit of weight,' Rebus agreed.

Calder looked Rebus up and down. 'Same goes—you're not ill, are you?'

'Funny how often people ask that.' Rebus took a sip from his pint glass. The barman had heard the order and was placing the drink in front of Calder. Rebus paid the man. They were in the downstairs room. No natural light. Trestle tables topped with paper tablecloths. Bowls of nibbles rapidly depleting. A DJ had set up his rig in the far corner but wasn't due to start till the top of the hour. Rebus would be gone by then. He'd only popped in for one.

This week's retiree was Babs Elliot. She'd risen to the 'giddy depths'—as she'd put it to Rebus himself not five minutes back—of Detective Constable, back in Rebus' St Leonard's days. A good twenty years his junior but on her way out while she still had 'a vestige of life left in me.' Husband worked at HMP Saughton, and Babs was minded to pick up a bit of work—part-time; as mindless as possible.

'Job's gone to shit, John,' she'd confided in a stage whisper.

'I keep hearing that,' Rebus had obliged, not bothering to add: *but I still miss it like hell.*

Babs was at the centre of the room, receiving new arrivals with a peck on the cheek or a more fulsome hug. Some people had brought gifts and cards, and Rebus wished he'd done the same. He'd dropped by on a whim, reminded by a text from DI Siobhan Clarke, who'd followed up just after he'd crossed the threshold with another message to say something had come up and she might not make it.

There were plenty of faces he knew in the room, and others he didn't. The youngsters looked idealistic and full of zest. They liked the job. Liked it, too, when their elders retired—more chance of that sought-after promotion.

'I feel like Methuselah,' Jerry Calder muttered, scanning the room.

'What does that make me?' Rebus asked him. 'Methuselah's grandpa?'

'You're still here, though, that's what counts.' Calder had finished his drink and was gesturing across the bar for another round.

'I've still half a pint here,' Rebus complained.

'Time was, you drank quicker.'

'I did a lot of things quicker, Jerry. Just not necessarily *better*.'

Calder gave a snort and rubbed a finger across the bridge

of his nose. 'I didn't see you at Rab Merrilees's funeral.'

Rebus shrugged. 'I couldn't make it. Heard it was a decent turnout, though.'

'Better than the old shitbag deserved. Mini sausage rolls at the reception after. *Mini!* Stone-cold they were, too.'

'It's what he would have wanted.'

'No word of a lie there—mean old sod that he was. Not that I'm one to speak ill of the dead.'

'Indeed not.'

'Know what music he wanted as the coffin was lowered?'

'Surprise me.'

'"The Sash"!'

Rebus couldn't help but laugh.

'*The* bloody Sash,' Calder confirmed. 'Talk about old school. Sevco scarf draped over the coffin, too. Wouldn't have surprised me if an Orange Marching Band had come parading down the aisle.'

Rab Merrilees had been one of those coppers—ruddy-cheeked Protestants raised on stories of the Old Firm and Ulster. Only a handful of years older than Rebus, but a generation apart. Rebus had served in Northern Ireland in the Army, had witnessed firsthand how those old stories twisted young men's minds. He could see Merrilees now—a barn-door of a man in a uniform just too small for him. Handy with a truncheon and his fists when it kicked off on a Saturday night. Nothing Big Rab liked better than to wade in, hauling brawlers out of High Street howffs and dispensing some pavement justice in the halcyon days before CCTV and camera-phones.

'He saved your skin once, didn't he?' Calder was remembering.

'I was off duty. One for the road when some bawbag

clocked me and decided to arrange a meeting between a bar stool and my head. Big Rab happened to be passing.' Rebus toasted the memory before taking a slug from the fresh glass.

'You heard what happened on his deathbed?' Calder leaned in a little closer. 'He was in hospital. Third or fourth heart attack. Few of the old boys paid him a visit. The inevitable came up…' Calder's voice drifted away. It took Rebus a moment to recollect which 'inevitable' he might be meaning.

'Garrison's the Jeweller's?' He watched Calder nod.

A shop on Rose Street. Someone had got in through the ceiling, having broken into the empty flat upstairs. Safe emptied, thousands missing. Mostly necklaces and earrings, a few high-end watches, a wedge of cash. Not many names in the frame when it came to getting into a safe. The second house they'd tried, firm questioning back at the station had led to an admission. The stuff was stashed in the culprit's kid's wardrobe. But there'd been nothing there. The wife was suspected of moving it, but swore blind she had done nothing of the sort. Then a few weeks later, Big Rab had been spotted on a weekend jaunt in his shiny new BMW. Nice car, just slightly out of his league. People remembered he'd been present at the initial arrest. People seemed to think he had lingered after everyone else had left. Those same people knew he had a bit of form—prisoners turning up for processing lacking the funds they swore had been on them when they'd been cuffed. Blind eyes turned. Whispers and winks.

'He owned up?' Rebus guessed, raising an eyebrow.

'Not exactly.' Calder's smile was wry. He moved to let new arrivals get to the bar. Rebus had no option but to follow him to one of the tables, where Calder was already getting comfortable, sweeping a handful of crisps into his mouth.

'Go on, then,' Rebus prompted him.

'Well, Jazz Helmsley—you know Jazz? He was in Drylaw for a while but works at the airport now?'

Rebus shook his head.

'You sure?' Calder persisted. 'Sandy hair and freckles? Used to play rugby?'

'I swear, Jerry, I'm going to be in my box before you finish this bloody story.'

Calder ignored the glower Rebus was giving him. In fact, he smiled.

'Funny you should say that, John, actually.'

'Why?'

'Because when Jazz asked Big Rab if he'd lifted all that stuff, Rab told him: "You're not thinking inside the box, son."'

'You mean outside the box,' Rebus corrected him.

Calder offered a shrug. '*Inside* is the way Jazz told it to me. He probed a bit but Big Rab wasn't giving any more than that.'

Rebus considered. 'What do you think he meant?'

'You know Rab, John—bloody joker at the best of times. Number of people in this room he played a trick on. Phoning, pretending to be somebody-or-other's boss. Handcuffing Bert Jackson to the steering wheel when he fell asleep in his patrol car…'

'That, I remember,' Rebus said. 'Bert woke to an emergency call and had to try driving with the cuffs still on.' The two men shared a chuckle.

'Funny thing is, of course,' Calder said, lifting his glass, 'a box is exactly where Rab ended up. He's buried out near the Hearts ground.'

'You don't think…?'

'Taking it with him, you mean?' Calder thought for a moment then shrugged. 'Not possible, is it? The undertakers would have it. But, that car apart, I never heard tell of him living the high life. Though his widow didn't look too unhappy at the funeral.'

'He left her provided for, then?'

'Or she was just glad to see the back of him. Your shout.' Calder slid his empty glass towards Rebus.

'This'll be the last one for me,' Rebus warned him.

'Getting out before the disco—can't say I blame you. I'm staying for the buffet, though. Babs has promised sausage rolls—full-size and piping hot…'

•●⬤●•

Rebus's dog Brillo kept staring up at him.

'I know,' Rebus said. 'Longer walk than usual. Try not to get used to it.'

They had passed through the cemetery gates and were heading for what Rebus always thought of as the 'arrivals section.' The grave wasn't hard to find. The polished black headstone was brand new, its gold lettering unweathered. Most of the floral tributes were beginning to wilt. Rebus crouched in front of them and focused on something placed in their midst. A child's plastic toy. He recognised it as Doctor Who's Tardis and knew at once why it was there. Merrilees, the old beat cop, had secured his own fiefdom once upon a time—a police box towards the foot of the Canongate. Such boxes had been a feature of policing back in the day. You could boil a kettle, settle back and eat your sandwiches, and then pee in the tiny sink. Big Rab, always the joker, would go further, however. He would watch through the tiny window as tourists traipsed past on their way to Holyrood Palace, then would drop a few coins on the stone floor of the interior, chuckling to himself as the tourists stopped and checked the ground around them, wondering if they had a hole in a pocket, baffled by the lack of any money on either pavement or roadway. Rebus lifted the Tardis and examined it. There was no note to say who had left it, but he didn't suppose that mattered. What *did* matter were the words that had started to dance around the inside of his head: *thinking inside the box*.

'Aye, maybe,' he muttered to himself. Brillo was looking to him for instructions. 'Walk's not quite finished yet,' Rebus obliged, rising to his full height.

So: Fountainbridge to the Grassmarket and then along the Cowgate and Holyrood Road, dog and owner both panting with the effort. Cutting up Gentle's Entry to the Canongate, with a pause to look in the window of the secondhand record shop. There was a pub hard by the old police box with a bowl of water placed at its door. Brillo slaked his thirst while Rebus studied the battle-scarred box with its faded blue paint. He had noted a trend in the city for these old boxes to be reconditioned and used to sell coffee and hot food, their cramped interiors just about able to accommodate a single barista and some rudimentary catering equipment. This particular box, however, had yet to undergo any kind of gentrification. It was securely locked, glass panels boarded over, and festooned with graffiti and ragged flyers for music venues. Rebus studied as much of the exterior as he could, even picking away at some of the flyers, but he found no clues. Nor did giving the door a good shove do anything other than remind him he was not a young man anymore.

'They don't like it when you tear off their adverts,' a

voice called. Rebus turned towards the pub doorway. A young man was standing there, lighting a cigarette. He bent down to give Brillo a rub behind the ears.

'You work here?' Rebus gestured towards the pub.

'Behind the bar,' the man explained. 'That thing's an eyesore, but what can you do?'

'Any idea who owns it?'

The barman stood up and stared at him. 'Thinking of buying?'

'It's not yours, is it?'

He snorted. 'Wouldn't mind it for my back garden, though, if I had a back garden. My son's daft on *Doctor Who*.'

'Never really saw the appeal,' Rebus said. 'If I want to meet alien life forms, I'll walk down the Cowgate at closing time.' An open-top tour bus crawled past, offering commentary on the nearby Scottish Parliament. 'Get many MSPs in?'

'The odd one or two. So what's your interest?' The barman nodded past him to the police box.

'Old pal of mine used to walk this beat. We just buried him. He used to rest up inside.'

'Memory lane, eh?'

Rebus patted the box's door. 'I just fancied a keek at the interior.'

'I can maybe help with that.' The barman took one last draw on his depleted cigarette. 'And dogs are almost as welcome as paying customers…'

So Rebus followed him inside.

•●⬤●•

'What did you buy?' The woman standing in front of Rebus gestured towards the carrier bag on the seat next to him.

'A Nazareth LP. Had to do something while I waited.'

'Probably one reason I don't come down this way very often—I spend too much at Unknown Pleasures.'

Her name was Camille Riordan, just a hint of Ireland left in her accent. She was in her mid-thirties, dressed in a leather biker jacket. Shoulder-length dark hair with streaks of silver. Upon entering, she had waved a greeting towards the barman.

'Nice mutt, by the way,' she added. Brillo was lying on the pub's wooden floor, tired out by the day's exertions.

'Can I buy you a drink?' Rebus asked. She shook her head but settled on a low stool at Rebus's table.

'But you can tell me the story again.'

As he went through it, she watched him so intently he began to feel like a specimen in her laboratory.

'So you were a cop?' she commented when he finished. 'And that's all there is to this? An old pal gone, a pilgrimage to his wee man-cave?'

Rebus offered a shrug. 'Your business,' he stated, 'is buying these boxes and opening them as going concerns. Makes me wonder why this one's been left to rot.'

'It was a job lot. Most turn a profit. A few don't. The footfall here isn't all that great. Tourists tend to arrive by coach and anyone heading to the palace or the parliament knows there are cafés inside both.' She gave a shrug of her own. 'We might try it eventually as a taco stand, see if we can grab the lunchtime trade.'

'Great,' the barman said, coming to clear Rebus's empty glass. 'As if this place wasn't dead enough…'

Riordan gave a smile that could have passed for apologetic. Then she lifted a jangling keychain from her shoulder bag, waving it at Rebus. 'So shall we go finish your little quest?' Rebus was about to speak but she got in first. 'Not that I believe that's all there is to it.' Her eyes narrowed slightly. 'And that means you're going to have to promise me something.'

'What?'

'The real story. Sometime. Whenever you're ready…'

Rebus nodded slowly and they headed out on to the pavement. The first key she tried was the right one. She pushed open the door and peered inside. 'No skeletons, anyway,' she concluded, moving to one side so Rebus could squeeze past. He motioned for her to take Brillo's lead and then headed in. The interior was bare. Even the tap from the sink had been stripped out. No clutter; just dust and grime. There were a few scraps of paper on the floor and Rebus scooped them up. They were tattered remnants of old flyers, probably blown in from outside through the gap at the bottom of the door. There was a flue to let fresh air in—and the smell of cigarette- and pipe-smoke out. Rebus inserted his hand but could feel nothing other than cobwebs. Riordan was smiling in the doorway, hunch confirmed.

'Once a detective,' Rebus said with a wink. But he was stumped. He stood in the small space and shuffled three hundred and sixty degrees. Then studied the floor again. And ran his fingers around the underside of the corner sink. If he'd had a screwdriver, he might have been tempted to open the electrical socket. Instead, he wiggled its casing. The screws were brown with rust. Not enough room in there for a pocket-watch, never mind anything bigger.

Exasperated, he raised his eyes to the ceiling. The light bulb had long gone and the cream-coloured paintwork was peeling. But he could make out scratches. He took out his mobile phone and switched on its torch function, angling it upwards, standing on tiptoe to get a better view.

'Is that writing?' Riordan was asking.

'Looks like.'

'A dirty limerick?'

'An address,' Rebus said. Scored into the paint in blue ink. Blue: the colour of preference for coppers of the old school…

Back home, Rebus phoned Jerry Calder and asked for Merrilees's address.

'What for?'

'I was going to send condolences to the widow.'

'I can probably get it for you. All I remember is, it's on the main road as you drive into Balerno.'

Rebus looked at the address he had written on the back of one of the police box flyers. 'How about before that?'

'Eh?'

'Where did he live before Balerno?'

'This is about the Jeweller's, isn't it? I saw that wee twinkle in your eye.'

'Maybe I was just emotional, Jerry.'

'Aye, and maybe I'm the tooth fairy.' Calder paused. 'There'll be a finder's fee, I dare say?'

'I'll have to think about that.'

'Well, he was in Balerno the best part of twenty years and before then I think it was the mean streets of Uphall.'

'So if I said the words Mountcastle Terrace to you…?'

'Mountcastle Terrace out by Willowbrae?'

'That's the only one I know.'

'And it's connected to Big Rab?'

'Maybe a relative lives there...'

'How did you come by it anyway?'

'Thinking inside the box, Jerry,' Rebus said, ending the call.

•••••

Having fed himself and Brillo, he decided to take the Saab out to Mountcastle Terrace. It was part of a drab housing scheme between Holyrood Park and the coast. Dogs barked from behind fences, and he was glad he'd left Brillo sleeping at home. The house he approached looked identical to its neighbours. A handkerchief-sized garden; door needing a new coat of paint. The curtains were partially open and there were lights on within. Seeing no doorbell, he knocked with a fist, taking a step back and waiting. When the door was yanked open, he could smell cooking fat and hear a television. A stocky man in a faded t-shirt demanded to know what he wanted.

'Might be a daft question, but does the name Rab or Robert Merrilees mean anything to you?'

'Diddly-squat, pal.' The door began to close. Rebus leaned forward, pressing his hand against it, maintaining eye contact.

'You sure about that? He was a copper.'

'Means hee-haw to me.'

'Is there anyone else inside you could ask?'

'Look, we only moved here six months back. He an old tenant? Owes back rent or something? Whoever was here before us, all they left was the smell. I'm going to shut this door now, and if you try and stop me, it won't be words we'll be having.'

Rebus considered for a moment, then dropped his hand and watched the door slowly close.

'Worth a try,' he told himself, remembering all the times on the job when he'd had to knock on doors. Dozens if not hundreds of them, usually leading nowhere. Back on the pavement, he studied the houses on either side. One was just that little bit neater than the other. Doormat on the step. Windows cleaned within memory. So he walked up to it and rang the bell. A stooped woman in her seventies answered, but only after she'd slid the security chain in place. Rebus smiled through the four-inch gap.

'Sorry to bother you,' he said. 'But do you know the name Merrilees? Rab or Robert Merrilees?'

'He passed away,' she said, her face instantly sad at the memory. 'I saw his obituary. You get to that point, don't you, where they're the first thing you check in the newspaper?'

'I know what you mean.'

'I couldn't get to his funeral. I had a doctor's appointment that day and they're like gold-dust.'

Rebus kept smiling and nodding. 'How did you know him, Mrs…?'

'I'm Elspeth Tanner. People used to tease me, you know.'

'Tease you?'

'Elsie Tanner—from *Coronation Street*. Not that I've ever been anything like that little madam.'

'Mrs Tanner, how did you know Big Rab?'

'He changed the light bulb in my living room. Nice big strapping man, he was. Helped with the Christmas tree, too.'

'So you met him…?'

'Through Alison, of course. Alison from next door.'

'He used to visit her? Were they related?'

Mrs Tanner's eyes sparkled and she lowered her voice a little. 'He was her *gentleman friend.*'

'Oh.' Rebus paused while this sank in.

'He was married and everything—Alison told me. He'd leave his wife if he could—that's what he told her. But he'd made his bed and must lie in it.'

'Two beds, actually, when you think of it.'

Mrs Tanner gave a little squeal of laughter, hiding her mouth behind her hand. 'I couldn't condone his behaviour, but he was always considerate—and Alison didn't seem to mind. He brought her flowers and things.'

'Anything a bit more extravagant? Maybe earrings or a necklace?'

'Perhaps once or twice—Christmas and her birthday.'

'No more than that?'

Mrs Tanner started to frown. 'Why all these questions? What business is it of yours?'

'I'm an old friend of Rab's. I was sorting out some of his stuff and found Alison's address.'

The wariness eased from Mrs Tanner's face. 'I see,' she said. 'Did he leave her anything in his will? Difficult without his poor wife finding out.'

'Difficult, yes.' Rebus paused. 'So is Alison still with us?'

'She's in a home. Has been for a year or so. I used to try to visit but it's two buses, sometimes three.'

'Do you know if Rab still saw her?'

'He broke it off three Christmases past.' Mrs Tanner grew thoughtful. 'Actually, I think it was Alison who persuaded him. Soon after, she had an "episode," and it got so she couldn't look after herself. Maybe she knew it was coming. We sometimes sense these things, don't we?'

Her eyes brightened. 'If he'd maybe left a note for her… something that would cheer her up?'

'I didn't find anything.' Rebus winced at the lie.

'You could look again. I doubt she knows he's dead. Will you break it to her?'

'Do you think I should?'

Mrs Tanner was nodding. 'Wait there,' she said. 'I'll go find the address…'

• • ● • •

Alison Hardy's care home was in Morningside. It looked to Rebus as if a couple of large semi-detached houses had been knocked through to create it. He'd decided to walk there—it was only quarter of an hour from his flat—in the weak sunshine of the following morning. He tied Brillo to the iron railings outside and gave him a pat.

'Five or ten minutes tops,' he promised.

The door was being opened as he approached it. A uniformed woman stood there. 'We allow dogs,' she said. 'The clients quite like it.'

'Well, if you're sure…'

So, tail wagging in delight at his inclusion, Brillo accompanied his owner indoors. Rebus had expected to smell cheap talc and strong disinfectant, but was met with neither. The place was brightly lit and freshly decorated.

'You'll be Mr Rebus,' the woman was saying. 'It was me you spoke to earlier.'

'Thanks for letting me visit.'

'We're not a prison, Mr Rebus. Guests are welcome day and night. But as I said, I'm in two minds about breaking the news to Alison. She's not had an episode for a while, and it'd be best if nothing brought on another one.'

'Has she ever mentioned Mr Merrilees to you?'

The woman—he recalled now her name was Semple—shook her head. 'But you say he was married and their affair was just that, so…'

Rebus nodded slowly. Some secrets had to be kept. 'Well, maybe I'll just say hello, then, and pass on her neighbour's regards.'

Semple led the way without another word, down a wide carpeted corridor towards the last door before the fire escape. The door was ajar but she knocked anyway before putting her head inside.

'Someone to see you, Alison. He's a friend of your old neighbour, Elspeth. Is it all right if he comes in?'

Without waiting for an answer, she led the way. Alison Hardy sat in a chair with a tartan rug around her lower body. She had been flicking through a magazine and peered at Rebus from above her half-moon spectacles.

'Elspeth never comes,' she commented. Her hair was fine and silver, her face gaunt. A breeze could have toppled her. Rebus tried not to think about her trysts with Big Rab Merrilees.

'Can I fetch you tea or anything?' Semple was asking. Rebus shook his head and watched her withdraw. She hadn't quite shut the door, so he did it for her.

'Lovely dog,' Alison Hardy said. Brillo was still on the lead so Rebus neared the woman's chair. Brillo obliged by lifting his front paws onto the travel rug, so that Hardy's slender hands could rub at his ears.

'He's called Brillo,' Rebus informed her.

'I never had a pet. Goldfish and budgies when I was a bairn, but nothing since.'

Rebus extended the lead a little so he could sit down on the chair opposite. 'Elspeth's sorry she doesn't come as much as she'd like.'

'It's the buses, isn't it? She'd spend half of every visit complaining about them.'

Rebus smiled an acknowledgment. He wasn't sure what he'd been expecting. Maybe someone bedbound, or with a wandering mind. The woman he was facing didn't even seem that old—not more than a handful of years older than him.

'My name's John, by the way,' he said. 'I was a policeman for a long time.' She focused a little more deeply on him. 'I knew Rab Merrilees back then.'

She gave a twitch of her mouth. 'I saw in the paper that he'd died. I thought about the funeral, but with his wife and everything…'

'I visited his old police box on the Canongate. Did you ever go there?'

'Maybe once.'

'He scratched your address on the paintwork—did you know about that?'

'No.'

'Any notion why he'd do something like that?'

'Maybe to lead someone to my door, John. And here you are.' She pursed her lips and peered at him.

'You know, don't you?' he eventually broke the silence to ask.

She took a deep breath. 'All I know is, Rab reckoned one day someone would turn up.'

'Would you care to take a guess *why* they'd turn up, Alison?'

Her face broke into a smile. 'You want the bookshelf over there.' She gestured over Rebus's shoulder. He turned to look. The shelves by the window contained mostly ornaments rescued from Hardy's old home. But there were also a dozen or so paperbacks. He rose to his feet and approached the unit.

'The Muriel Spark novel,' she directed him. 'It's what I was reading at the time.'

Rebus lifted it down and looked at it. *Loitering With Intent.*

'Inside the back cover,' he heard Hardy say.

A small white envelope. Still sealed, no writing on it.

'Rab said someone nosy might come asking questions, and if they did I was to give them this.'

Rebus put the book back on the shelf and carried the envelope to the chair.

'Do you know what's in it?' he inquired. She shook her head. 'Never tempted to take a look?'

'I knew Rab had done some things during his life. It was *him* I was interested in, not them.'

'What do you *think* is in it?'

'The answer to a question you've not been brave enough to ask.'

'So I have your blessing to open it?'

She nodded slowly and watched him get to work.

Back in his living room, once he'd fed Brillo, he stood by the window, staring out at the street. Eventually he took the sheet of notepaper from his pocket and unfolded it, reading it for the fourth or fifth time.

I got rid of the lot and spent the cash. What else was I going to do? I'm not the mug here.

One final practical joke on the world. A wild goose chase around the city. And Rebus the mug who'd fallen for it. He twisted his mouth and managed a pained smile, then took out his phone and called Camille Riordan.

'You wanted the story,' he said. 'So here it is.'

When he finished, he heard laughter on the line, then her voice. 'Why didn't you say?'

Rebus's eyes narrowed. 'Say what?'

'If you'd given me Merrilees's name, I might have saved you the trouble.'

'How do you mean?'

'All the police boxes—the job lot. We bought them from someone called Robert Merrilees. I'd no idea he'd been a cop—he was just a name on a purchase agreement. They'd have cost him a few thousand back in the day but they cost us a good bit more.'

'How long had he owned them?'

'Long enough.'

'That's what he did with the proceeds then? He bought half a city's worth of redundant Tardises?'

'And made sure his widow's sitting pretty as a result, I dare say.'

Rebus remembered Jerry Calder's words: *Widow didn't look too unhappy at the funeral…*

'Which means,' Riordan continued, 'he was doing the same two things as you, John.'

'What's that?'

'Thinking inside the box *and* out.' And she started to laugh again.

Freezer Burn

James Sallis

Within a week of thawing Daddy out, we knew something was wrong.

He claims, seems in fact fully to believe, that before going cold he was a freelance assassin; furthermore, that he must get back to work. 'I was good at it,' he tells us. 'The best.'

When what he actually did was sell vacuum cleaners, mops, and squeegee things at Cooper Housewares.

It doesn't matter what you decide to be, he's told us since we were kids, a doctor, car salesman, janitor, just be the best at what you do—one of a dozen or so endlessly recycled platitudes.

Dr Paley said he's seen this sort of thing before, as side effects from major trauma. That it's probably temporary. We should be supportive, he told us, give it time. Research online uncovers article after article suggesting that such behavior, in fact, may be backwash from cryogenics and not uncommon at all, 'long dreams' inherent to the process itself.

So, in support as Dr Paley counseled, we agreed to

drive Daddy to a meeting with his new client. How he contacted that client, or was contacted by him, we had no idea, and Daddy refused (we understand, of course, he said) to violate client confidentiality or his own trade secrets.

The new client turned out to be not he but she. 'You must be Paolo,' she said, rising from a spotless porch glider and taking a step towards us as we came up the walk. Paolo is not Daddy's name. The house was in what we hereabouts call Whomville, modestly small from out here, no doubt folded into the hillside and continuing below ground and six or eight times its apparent size. I heard the soft whir of a servicer inside, approaching the door.

'Single malt, if I recall correctly. And for your friends?'

'Matilda, let me introduce my son—'

Immediately, I asked for the next waltz.

'—and daughter,' who, as ever in unfamiliar circumstances, at age twenty-eight, smiled with the simple beauty and innocence of a four-year-old.

'And they are in the business as well?'

'No, no. But kind enough to drive me here. Perhaps they might wait inside as we confer?'

'Certainly. Gertrude will see to it.' Gertrude being the soft-voiced server. It set down a tray with whiskey bottle and two crystal glasses, then turned and stood alongside the door to usher us in.

I have no knowledge of what was said out on that porch but afterwards, as we drove away, Daddy crackled with energy, insisting that we stop for what he called a trucker's breakfast, then, as we remounted, announcing that a road trip loomed in our future. That very afternoon, in fact.

'Road trip!' Susanna's excitement ducked us into the next lane—unoccupied, fortunately. She must have forgotten the last such outing, which left us stranded carless and moneyless in suburban badlands, limping home on the kindness of a stranger or two.

Back at the house we readied ourselves for the voyage. Took on cargo of energy bars, bottled water, extra clothing, blankets, good toilet paper, all-purpose paper towels, matches, extra gasoline, a folding shovel.

'So I gotta know,' Susanna said as we bumped and bottomed-out down a back road, at Daddy's insistence, to the freeway. 'Now you're working for the like of Old-money Matilda back there?'

'Power to the people.' That was me.

'Eat the rich,' she added.

'Matilda is undercover. Deep. One of us.'

Susanna: 'Of course.'

'In this business, few things are as they appear.'

'Like dead salesmen,' I said.

'*My cover*. And a good one.'

'Which one? Dead, or salesman?'

'Jesus,' Susanna said and, as if on cue, to our right sprouted a one-room church. Outside it sat one of those rental LED digital signs complete with wheels and trailer hitch.

COME IN AND HELP US HONE
THE SWORD OF TRUTH

Susanna was driving. Daddy looked over from the passenger seat and winked. 'I like it.'

'I give up. No scraps or remnants of sanity remain.'

'Chill, Sis,' I told her. 'Be cool. It's the journey, not the destination.'

'To know where we are, we must know where we're not.'

'As merrily we roll along—'

'Stitching up time—'

Then for a time, we all grew quiet. Past windshield and windows the road unrolled like recalls of memory: familiar as it passed beneath, empty of surprise or anticipation, a slow unfolding.

Until Daddy, looking in the rear view, asked how long that vehicle had been behind us.

'Which one?' Sis said. 'The van?'

'Yes.'

'Well, I've not been keeping count but that has to be maybe the twenty-third white van since we pulled out of the driveway.'

'Of all the cards being dealt,' Daddy said, 'I had to wind up with you jokers. Not one but two smart-asses.'

'Strong genes,' I said.

'Some are born to greatness—'

'—others get twisted to fit.'

'Shoes too large.'

'Shoes too small.'

'Walk this way…'

Half a mile further along, the van fell back and took the exit to Logosland, the philosophy playground. Best idea for entertainment since someone built a replica of Noah's Ark and went bankrupt the first year. Then again, there's The Thing in Texas. Been around forever and still draws. Billboards for a hundred miles, you get there and there's not much to see, proving yet again that anticipation's, like, ninety percent of life.

'They'll be passing us on to another vehicle,' Daddy said. 'Keep an eye out.'

'Copy that,' Susanna said.

'Ten-four.'

'Wilco.'

Following Daddy's directions, through fields with center-pivot irrigation rollers stretching to the horizon and town after town reminiscent of miniature golf courses, we pulled into Willford around four that afternoon. Bright white clouds clustered like fish eggs over the mountains as we came in from the west and descended into town, birthplace of Harry the Horn, whoever the hell that was, Pop. 16,082. Susanna and I took turns counting churches (eleven), filling stations (nine), and schools (three). Criss-cross of business streets downtown, houses mostly single-story from fifty, sixty years back, ranch style, cookie-cutter suburban, modest professional, predominantly dark gray, off-white, shades of beige.

'You guys hungry?' Daddy said.

Billie's Sunrise had five cars outside and twenty or more people inside, ranging from older guys who looked like they sprouted right there on the stools at the counter, to clusters of youngsters with fancy sneakers and an armory of handhelds. Ancient photographs curled on the walls. Each booth had a selector box for the jukebox that, our server with purple hair informed us, hadn't worked forever.

We ordered bagels and coffee and, as we ate, Daddy told us about the time he went undercover in a bagel kitchen on New York's Lower East Side. 'As kettleman,' he said. 'Hundred boxes a night, sixty-four bagels to the box. Took some fancy smoke and mirrors, getting me into that union.'

Bagels date back at least four centuries, he said. Christians baked their bread, Polish Jews took to boiling theirs. The name's probably from German's *beugel*, for ring or bracelet. By the 1700s, given as gifts, sold on street corners by children, they'd become a staple, and traveled with immigrant Poles to the new land, where in 1907 the first union got established. Three years later there were over seventy bakeries in the New York area, with Local #338 in strict control of what were essentially closed shops. Bakers and apprentices worked in teams of four, two making the rolls, one baking, the kettleman boiling.

'So. Plenty more where that came from, all of it fascinating. Meanwhile, you two wait here, I'll be back shortly.' Daddy smiled at the server, who'd stepped up to fill our cups for the third time. 'Miss Long will take care of you, I'm sure. And order whatever else you'd like, of course.'

Daddy was gone an hour and spare change. Miss Long attended us just as he said. Brought us sandwiches pre-cut into quarters with glasses of milk, like we were little kids with our feet hanging off the seats. If she'd had the chance, she probably would have tucked us in for a nap. Luckily the café didn't have cupcakes. Near the end, two cops came in and took seats at the counter—regulars, from how they were greeted. Their coffee'd scarcely been poured and the skinny one had his first forkful of pie on the way to his mouth when their radios went off. They were up and away in moments. As they reached their car, two police cruisers and a fire truck sailed past behind them, heading out of town, then an ambulance.

Moments later, sirens fading and flashers passing from sight outside, Daddy slid into the booth across from us. 'Everybody good?'

'That policeman didn't get to eat his pie,' Susanna said.

'Duty calls. Has a way of doing that. More pie in his future, likely.'

Smiling, Miss Long brought Daddy fresh coffee in a

new cup. He sat back in the booth and drank, looking content.

'Nothing like a good day's work. Nothing.' He glanced over to where Miss Long was chatting with a customer at the counter. 'Either of you have cash money?'

Susanna asked what he wanted and he said a twenty would do. Carried it over and gave it to Miss Long. Then he came back and stood by the booth. 'Time to go home,' he said. 'I'll be in the car.'

We paid the check and thanked Miss Long and when we got to the car Daddy was stretched out on the backseat, sound asleep.

'What are we going to do?' Susanna asked.

We talked about that all the way home.

Caught on Camera

Zoë Sharp

Traffic was murder. Olivia sat simmering inside her vehicle, one of a stationary herd on the A40 eastbound. Part of the usual vast migration into London on a Monday morning. All going nowhere.

She clenched her fingers around the rim of the steering wheel, a useless gesture when the car was in self-drive anyway, but it gave her some small illusion of control where none existed.

'Time?' she snapped.

The in-dash unit responded promptly, although to Olivia's ears its soothing female tones sounded ever so slightly smug. 'The time is 08:18 and 26 seconds. The distance remaining to your destination is 4.9 miles. Your current speed is 0.0 mph. At your current speed you will be unable to reach your destination by 09:00.'

'Yeah, thanks for that,' Olivia muttered. 'Now tell me something I *don't* know.'

'I'm sorry, I don't understand that question. Can you repeat it?'

'No.' And before the computer could query *that*, she added quickly, 'Mute audio.'

In her head, Olivia was already practising the excuses she was going to have to make for committing the cardinal sin of being late on her first day in a new job. But that's just how they came across—as excuses.

'How could you be so *stupid*?' She should have known it was going to be bad. They'd been digging up this section between West Acton and the White City toll plaza for months. One snarl-up after another.

It was all supposed to have got better after they privatised the major arterial routes into the capital. Olivia had only made sporadic visits into the city from her family home in Northolt while she'd studied for her degree at Oxford, but she couldn't say she'd noticed much of an improvement.

And now it was going to make her woefully late for her first day on the job. Not just her first day, but her first *job*. First proper job since the mandatory community tasks to build enough citizen points to attend uni in the first place, anyway.

The car in front restarted, travelled another two yards, and stopped again. The hope that had begun to bloom in Olivia's chest stopped with it.

Still, at least she could see the squat grey concrete structure of the toll plaza up ahead. There were only three lanes open, according to the in-dash monitor, which probably accounted for the delay as vehicles jockeyed for position.

Left to its own devices, the auto self-drive would feed everyone through the plaza in no time, but as soon as people with high-end models hit their priority overrides to jump the queue, you were back to chaos again. They were also the only ones who could afford the annual passes, which had their own express lane. Everyone else—Olivia included—had to buy the shorter duration tickets. Her parents had celebrated her graduation by chipping in towards her first month's pass.

But it was the far left-hand lane—the cash lane—that always caused the most problems. The amount varied according to pressure of traffic and time of day, so you could never be quite sure in advance how much. Half the time people failed to bring the right money, or simply didn't have enough for the toll. In fact, Olivia could see a young man standing by the cash window now, arguing with the woman behind the glass. His body language was pleading.

Olivia was too far away to hear anything of the exchange, but his thin arms windmilled. There were nervous stains on the back of his hooded sweatshirt.

The young man stepped back, shoulders slumping, and for a moment Olivia thought the argument was over. Then he reached inside the unzipped sweatshirt and when she could see his hands again, he was holding a gun.

Olivia's mouth fell open, the spit on her tongue evaporating instantly. She scrabbled for her handbag, fumbled inside. When she glanced up again, the young man was still by the toll booth, still brandishing the gun unsteadily at the woman inside. She'd ducked out of sight.

With a growl of frustration, Olivia tipped the contents of the bag out onto the passenger seat. It landed in a haphazard sprawl of keys, hairbrush, makeup oddments, documents, but no smartphone. Then she remembered. When she arrived this morning she was due to be issued with her official kit, including communications. With that in mind, she'd left her own phone at home on the hall table. No point in carrying both.

That thought jogged another. At her final interview they'd shown her the Taser stunner she'd be using. It was twice as old, and probably twice the size and weight, of the one her dad bought her just before she went to uni.

She'd decided there and then to bend the rules and carry her own. She had it with her now, in the glove box. It was fully charged.

She leaned across, flipped open the glove box lid and pulled out the Taser. It wasn't a top of the range model, but not far off, made of black composite and shaped like a conventional pistol. She swallowed. Her dad had insisted that she practise with the stunner, but that was back when he first presented it to her. She'd certainly never had to use it in anger.

Another glance. The young man was still by the toll booth window, still waving the gun. The similarity between the size and shape of the weapon to the one in Olivia's hands was not lost on her. But she knew without a doubt that his was a real gun.

She hesitated. *Should I get involved? Or sit tight and leave it to the professionals?*

'Time?' she demanded again.

'The time is 09:01 and 13 seconds. The distance remaining to—'

'Mute audio.'

The deciding factor.

Olivia had been a fully fledged graduate detective in the New London Police Service for one whole minute.

Pushing out her chin, she opened the car door and stepped out onto the road. The engine cut off automatically as she exited the vehicle. The driver alongside barely gave her a second glance as she strode forward between the lines of cars. She kept the Taser down by her side so it was hidden in the folds of her long skirt.

The gunman was shrieking at the crouching cashier as Olivia approached, so he didn't notice until she was a little more than five yards from him. Then he spun round, the fear leaping in his eyes.

'Stay back!' He was close to screaming. The barrel of the gun arced wildly in Olivia's direction. Had he pulled the trigger it was unlikely he would hit her, but she had no intention of relying on that.

She took a deep breath, resisting the urge to raise her hands. The stunner was still hidden from view by her side. Its maximum range was fifteen feet. She knew she needed to be nearer to be sure.

'Look, all I want to do is get to work,' she said, pushing out a smile, aiming for reasonable with maybe just a hint of irritation. 'It's my first day, and I'm already late. You want money? Okay. I don't have very much, but I can give you some money. Let's get this over with and then we can all be on our way.'

The would-be robber hesitated, glancing back at the toll booth. The cashier was still down out of sight, and the slots in the window meant he could neither shoot at her nor reach the cash drawer, lying tantalisingly open inside. He hammered both fists against the bulletproof glass in frustration, hurling abuse.

Olivia edged a step closer. She could see he was barely out of his teens, his cheeks and chin heavily blotched with acne. His hair clung to his scalp in unwashed clumps.

He was scared, too— maybe even more scared than she was. Fear forced the sweat out of him like tar on a summer hot stretch of road. It sheened on his face and leached through the armpits of the thin sweatshirt.

The gun was a Smith & Wesson Model 14 revolver, practically a museum piece. What her dad would have referred to as a 'thirty-eight special.' It looked dark and solid in the boy's hands.

She swallowed.

Now or never.

She slid forward another foot, trying to gauge the distance, keeping her right hand hidden. In her left she held out a few crumpled banknotes. The euros favoured by the black economy rather than new sterling. Not enough for the fix his body so obviously craved but, she hoped, folded over enough to seem enticing, nonetheless.

And once he caught sight of it, the boy couldn't drag his eyes away. Muscle memory brought him closer by another couple of steps, closing the gap between them until an instinctive wariness overruled.

Come on, come on, Olivia willed. *Just another couple of feet…*

He must have sensed something of her own anxiety. The boy's eyes twitched constantly overhead, checking for the first sign of the Tactical Response Unit that was undoubtedly en route. He began to back up, swinging the revolver up as he did so.

'Look,' Olivia said, watching him scurry out of range, 'I'm going to put the money down right here, and you can come and get it, okay? But be quick, because otherwise you'll miss your chance.'

She caught the agony of indecision on the boy's face before she stooped to scatter the euros onto the cracked tarmac at her feet. As she straightened and took a couple of small steps in reverse, the wind was already plucking at the curled notes.

That was too much for him. With an inarticulate cry, the boy dived for the cash just as the next gust sent it skittering out of reach. He pounced again, barely six feet away from her now.

Olivia brought the Taser up level and into full view, gripping it in both hands. She pointed the muzzle at the centre of the boy's chest, just like her dad taught her.

Oh God, what do I say? For a split-second her mind went totally blank.

'Police!' she barked then. 'Don't move!'

At least, it *should* have been a bark, but came out closer to a yelp—more lapdog than attack dog.

The boy had just pounced on one of the errant notes, but his head snapped up, and the triumph on his face shattered into terror.

'No, no, *no*!' He paddled backwards, robbed of both coordination and coherence.

He lifted his right hand. Olivia had time to register the grime caked into his skin, the fingernails bitten past the quick. He scrambled another couple of feet farther away from her, gaining distance all the time. The window of opportunity wasn't so much closing as being slammed shut.

'Please, don't shoot me. It's not—'

A distant part of Olivia's brain heard the words, but could not compute their meaning. Her eyes were locked on the gun in the boy's hands. It seemed to have grown suddenly huge, like a cartoon version, and it was swinging directly towards her.

She shut her eyes and pulled the trigger.

With a disappointingly modest snap, the explosive air cartridge at the end of the Taser's barrel discharged. It sent the pair of tight-packed electrodes fizzing outwards at just over 130 feet a second. The probes followed fractionally divergent trajectories, widening to their optimum spread. Hair-fine wires spun out in their wake, making a faint whirring noise as they rapidly uncoiled.

Despite Olivia's haphazard aim, both darts lanced into the front of the boy's grubby sweatshirt. She opened her eyes just in time to watch the glimmer of surprise cross his face before the fifty-thousand-volt charge hit him.

The initial burst lasted eight seconds, by which time he was on the ground and twisted into a tight foetal ball. His limbs juddered and twitched. The gun dropped from fingers distorted into the arthritis-ravaged claws of an old man. He was ageing and shrinking before her eyes.

Sick to her stomach, Olivia realised that she had no idea how to make it stop. Her dad hadn't included that particular piece of information in his briefings. After she'd fired, she was supposed to simply put the Taser down and run away, leaving her would-be attacker wracked by uncontrollable spasms. The device would continue to fire short bursts into his system, enough to keep him down, until she had made her escape.

The worst thing was the noise it made. A sort of gleeful crackling, like one of those blue neon tubes in old-fashioned butchers' shops. The kind used to electrocute flies.

In desperation, Olivia ejected the cartridge as though it was spent. As soon as it was separated from the power pack in the main body of the Taser, the voltage chopped off, and the terrible noise ceased.

The boy continued to jitter and shake for what seemed like a long time afterwards. Olivia toed the Smith & Wesson out of his reach and waited. Her hands were shaking, but she slotted a new cartridge onto the end of the Taser and kept him covered, just in case.

The drama over, she was aware of other sights and sounds returning to her consciousness. The cashier stuck her head up but refused to leave the safety of her toll booth.

A few people from the closest cars called congratulations to her, although she noted none had ventured earlier out to help. But she would bet they'd all taken vids on their dash-cams or phones that would already be up on the Internet.

Overhead, above the constant buzzing of the surveillance drones, she heard a chopping thunder approaching through the low cloud to the southeast. The boy had recovered enough to hear it, too. He pushed himself up into a sitting position, glancing fearfully at the sky like a fat rabbit in hawk country.

'You a copper or something?' he demanded then.

She nodded.

'Privvy or State?'

'State,' she said, and caught something in his face, no doubt surprise at the way she'd fumbled the whole thing.

The noise above them rose through loud into uncomfortable. The boy's panic seemed to grow with it. As fast as they'd opened their car doors and windows, the onlookers retreated, shutting them again. She missed the boy's next words, had to duck her head for him to repeat them.

'I said, arrest me,' he shouted. 'State can still do that, can't they—even here?'

The helicopter dropped suddenly out of the cloud, a black Westland with the English Constabulary plc logo on the body. Olivia stared up at it, shielding her eyes against the dust. The side door was open and the first of the TRU team was poised in the aperture. He was holding one of the new BAE sniper rifles with the butt pulled up hard into his shoulder, ready.

'Please!' the boy yelled. 'Do it now. Before they land.'

Confused, Olivia launched into the revised standard caution. It was one of the first things they taught you, but she'd known it by heart since she was a child, in any case. 'You have the right to remain silent…'

While she spoke, the helicopter circled once as the pilot recce'd for a fast landing site. The downdraught blasted grit from the construction works into Olivia's hair and eyes.

By the time she'd finished the boy's rights, the pilot had threaded the craft between the earth-moving machinery and the overhead wires and touched down less than a hundred yards away.

The six-man squad, in bulky body armour and bristling with tech, debussed with smooth precision and came pounding across the tarmac towards them.

'Thanks,' the boy said, more quietly now, as the whine of the rotors died away.

'What for?' Olivia said, stung by his obvious relief. 'You're still under arrest, you know.'

'Yeah,' he said, sullen, jerking his head towards the men now surrounding them, 'but if you'd left me to that lot, I'd be dead.'

Detective (Grade 1) Damien Wheeler checked out his reflection in the mirrored back wall of the lift as it clanked its way down from the fourth floor and was thoroughly satisfied by what he saw. He smoothed down his tie and made sure that, when he thrust his hands into his trouser pockets, his jacket opened just far enough to reveal the shoulder holster underneath. Pity that all it held was a Taser.

It was one of Wheeler's great regrets that he'd come into the service too late to be allowed a real gun. The prospect of carrying had been one of the attractions of applying for police training college in the first place. But, by the time he'd qualified, public disquiet over the number of civilian casualties had grown into uproar, and the brief experiment of wholesale arming of the British police was over.

Anyway, there was no police training college anymore.

Just a boot camp for the front-line bobbies—cannon fodder most of them, who would have been squaddies if there was still a defence budget. That and university degrees for the wannabe detectives.

Despite his comparative youth—only just turned thirty—Wheeler thought of himself as last of the old school. A *real* policeman. Came up the hard way and proud of it. He'd made it to Detective Sergeant before the reorganisation, when they'd got rid of the old system of ranks. Somehow, DG1 didn't have the same ring to it at all.

He ducked his head, like a boxer, and practised his ice-cool cop stare. He was pleased with that look. It suited him. Went with the square jaw and cobalt-blue eyes. He just hoped it would have more effect on the new girl than the waste-of-time trainee he'd ended up with. It had taken three days of being at his most charming before he discovered she was a lesbian. Bitch. He bet that was why the lieutenant had foisted her off on to him in the first place.

He still couldn't get used to calling former Detective Inspector Job 'Lieutenant'—just too damn American for his taste. Still, if Job couldn't be bothered to go down to reception to meet the new girl in person, why shouldn't Wheeler have a crack at her?

And at least it showed that even the mighty Lieutenant Job could throw his toys out of his pram occasionally. Wheeler had been secretly pleased when Job's trainee hadn't arrived dead on 09:00. By 10:30 he was struggling to contain his glee—hadn't been able to resist a quick dig.

'I'm sure Ms Milton will provide a perfectly reasonable explanation,' was all Job had said, but Wheeler was sure he was seething, underneath. He must have been. After all, the old man outranked him. He'd had first pick and

Olivia Milton was his choice, and she'd screwed up on her first day.

And then the call had come in. Bloody Milton had not only managed to foil an armed robbery on her way in, but had disarmed and arrested the perpetrator, single-handed. Unbelievable. The captain had already been up to congratulate Job, like the lieutenant had anything to do with it. The bastard always came up smelling of roses.

The lift finally wheezed to a stop at ground-floor level and let out a half-hearted bing-bong as the doors lurched open. Wheeler stepped out, running a hand over his styled blond hair. He pushed through the doors to the reception area to find a couple of gorillas from English Custodial Services plc were just signing for the new prisoner.

The Milton girl was standing facing away from the door, but even from that angle what he saw made Wheeler suck in his six-pack a little more, and set a predatory gleam in his eye.

She was tall, with long red hair tied at the nape of her neck by a velvet ribbon. From the back, her figure was classic hourglass, emphasised by the long skirt she wore, which flared out from a narrow waist. Now, *that* was more like it.

Wheeler sauntered over.

'Miss Milton, is it?' he asked casually. 'Or should I say, newly minted Detective (Grade 3) Milton?'

The girl turned, nodded, and he found his eyes naturally drawn to the slightly bulging third button of her cream blouse. After a second he caught himself enough to thrust out a hand.

'Damien Wheeler—DG1 Wheeler, to be precise,' he said, giving her his best smooth smile and manly handshake. It was slightly disconcerting to come across a woman whose eyes were on a level with his own. Hers were hazel where he'd been hoping for green, but you couldn't have everything. 'Lieutenant Job asked me to take you up to the office, show you the ropes. If you're all done?'

The wary look on the girl's face lifted. 'Oh, yes. Fine.'

She flashed a quick smile to the ECS guys, who lit up like all their Christmases had come at once. To Wheeler's surprise, the smile also extended to the junkie trash she'd just brought in. 'This is where I leave you,' she told him. 'Mike and Tony here will sort you out with the details of the rehab centre. When your solicitor arrives, she should be able to arrange a deal if you agree to enter the programme voluntarily.'

The kid smiled back at her, grateful and more than a touch adoring. Wheeler hastily led her away, hurrying to open the door out of reception for her. A bit of old-world gallantry always went down well.

She moved through ahead of him and made straight for the stairs, ignoring the waiting lift. He had no option but to follow her lead.

'Bit of exercise—good idea,' he said, hearty, trying to make the best of it. 'Thought you might have had enough of that for one day, eh?'

She didn't respond, and he saved his breath until they were on the second floor landing.

'You're quite something, you know,' he said then, pausing to treat her to his coolly assessing stare. The one that had them melting in his hand. 'Bringing that kid in by yourself takes some guts. Not to mention getting on first-name terms with the boys from ECS so fast. Piece of advice for you though, Olivia—it is Olivia, isn't it?'

She nodded, frowning. Sweet, really.

'Don't try to mother all the lame ducks you bring in. Caring is the last thing you need to do, or you'll burn out inside five years.' He looked her up and down. 'Not that you'll be here that long.'

She bridled at that. 'Are you implying I'm not serious about my career?'

He flashed her another smile, his amusement genuine.

'Not at all, babe. Quite the opposite, in fact. Bright girl like you? I think you'll be here twelve months, tops. Get some experience at the sharp end. Then you'll have had enough of slumming it with us at State and you'll jump ship to the Privvies, just like all the rest.'

The girl looked about to speak, but remained silent. Confirmation if ever he heard it. You could always spot the ambitious ones. Still, no reason not to make hay while the sun shone. He moved closer, touched her arm.

'Hey, don't sweat it. Not everybody has what it takes to stick with a pretty thankless job—underfunded, understaffed—when they could be swanning around as a company cop with all the latest investigative toys to play with, and their own armed backup squad on call twenty-four/seven.'

'If you think it's so great with the private force, why are *you* still here?' she demanded.

He straightened his jacket, shot a cuff. 'Not everyone can afford to be a shareholder and pay for their justice,' he said, aiming for quiet dignity and not quite hitting it. 'State—it's a tough job, but somebody's got to do it.'

•••••

In other words, Olivia considered, *you aren't good enough to be taken on by the private sector.*

She pegged the type as soon as she laid eyes on Wheeler. It was a relief when he introduced himself and she realised he wasn't the one she'd be working for directly. Olivia hoped she hadn't made her reaction too obvious, but good God, the man was an octopus in rank aftershave and a cheap tan suit.

Okay, he was good-looking, in a way, but something slightly artificial stopped him short of being actually attractive. The upside-down-triangle physique was impressive enough, but by the time they'd climbed to the fourth floor, he was breathless. All show and no go.

Still, her course tutors had warned her she might face resentment from those State coppers who didn't have the ability or the drive to make the switch. Olivia supposed that even this smarmy approach was better than outright hostility.

And besides, he'd been almost spot-on in his assessment. She'd been planning on a year—two at the most—to add some extra shine to her degree, then looking for an opportunity with all the perks he'd mentioned. Who wouldn't?

Wheeler led her into the untidy, open-plan office and introduced her to his own trainee, a demure-looking Asian girl. The girl gave her a sympathetic smile and, as soon as Wheeler's back was turned, rolled her eyes and made a fast hand gesture that confirmed Olivia's initial impression.

Even the captain put in an appearance. Boydell was a short, stubby little Welshman, with fat-fingered hands and a rounded face. He also had the most penetrating gaze Olivia had ever come across. She could still remember it boring into her during the preliminary interview. Trying to get inside her skull and probably unravelling her motives all too successfully.

Captain Boydell shook her hand vigorously, welcomed her to the team, and left with a cheerful throwaway remark that she should be ready to give interviews to the press at 15:30.

'Interviews, sir?' she repeated faintly

Boydell paused in the doorway. 'You're quite the heroine of the hour, Detective Milton. You don't think I'm going to pass up a golden PR opportunity like this when it's dropped in my lap, do you?'

Olivia watched him leave with the first stirrings of apprehension. An inkling that maybe her best course of action this morning might have been to stay in her car.

What, and let that TRU sniper shoot the kid? It might have been her conscience talking.

'Well, Ms Milton, you've certainly made quite an impression on your first day,' said a measured voice behind her.

She turned to find a sombre man regarding her without the faintest trace of approval, no discernible inflection in his voice. Distantly, she heard Wheeler introducing Lieutenant Job, and her heart sank a little farther.

'Yes, sir.'

Job continued his brooding stare for a moment longer. He was old—fifty at least—and what hair he had was clipped short and grey. Who stayed balding these days when they no longer needed to? Suddenly, even Wheeler's obvious charms began to seem preferable.

'Do you mean "yes, sir" that was your original intention, or "yes, sir" that was merely an added bonus?'

Olivia opened her mouth, then shut it again and glared at him. He was playing word games with her. Whichever option she chose, she was damned.

'Well, sir,' she said at last, sweetly. 'I thought I'd start as I meant to go on.'

'Hm.' Job's expression didn't alter, she was sure of that, but something flickered in his stone-grey eyes. 'That's what I was afraid of.'

He glanced at Wheeler, who'd been lounging on the

corner of a desk. 'If you wouldn't mind taking Ms Milton to collect her equipment.' It was assembled as a question, delivered as an order.

Wheeler straightened at once. 'My pleasure, boss.'

His manner didn't soften any when he was dealing with any of his underlings, Olivia noted with slight relief that didn't last.

'And after that, Ms Milton, I'll see you in the review suite,' he said. 'Then you can give me a full account of your actions this morning.'

As he moved away Wheeler's voice murmured in her ear. 'Cheer up, babe. People hardly *ever* die during interrogation any more...'

● ● ● ● ●

'Again, Ms Milton,' Job ordered. 'Take me through it again, from the beginning, and don't leave anything out.'

'I've already told you,' Olivia said wearily. She'd done well in the Interview and Interrogation module of the course, but having a good theoretical knowledge of the techniques being used against her was, she discovered, little defence.

'Well, tell me again.'

Job sat back in the moulded plastic chair on the other side of the scuffed 3D projector grid and took a sip of his coffee. Olivia's own cup stood untouched by her elbow, cold now, the recyclable cup starting to go soggy at the base.

Apart from the deactivated table-top grid, four chairs, and the standard recorder, the room was bare. Grubby and unforgiving. Above Job, the diodes in two of the cheap LED spotlights were burning out. Their flickering threw his face into sinister, unforgiving shadow.

Doggedly, she went back over her story, forcing herself to stick rigidly to the facts, not to add inconsequential details. Occasionally, Job scribbled one-word notes on paper rather than directly into his tablet. He used a pen—a real ink pen—and who used those anymore? Olivia couldn't read his writing.

'So,' he said when she'd petered out, 'what have you learned from this, Ms Milton?'

'Learned, sir?'

'If you were put into exactly the same situation tomorrow morning, what would you do?'

'Probably the same again,' she said without hesitation.

'Hm, would you, indeed?'

He did pick up his tablet then, dabbed the screen to fire up the projector. It was an old unit, the cooling fans squeaking, and when the holographic image appeared on the grid between them, it flickered as badly as the lights.

The Privvies had whole rooms given over to reconstruction and review, Olivia knew, not just this crappy miniaturised display. There, you could move among life-size figures rendered from footage from the security drones that buzzed constantly overhead. It brought new meaning to the words 'caught in the act.'

The pictures from the toll plaza were incomplete in the camera blind spots and these processors weren't adequate to supply the missing pixels. Still, she could recognise the scene easily enough. The time display showed it was moments before the boy—she now knew his name was Trevor—approached the cashier.

Job let it run until the gun came into view, then froze the image, which shivered as though an earthquake had struck. He nodded to the time marker.

'08:59,' he said in that cold, clear voice she was coming to dislike. 'The drones' recognition software has just alerted the Tactical Response Unit. The cashier has worked for the company for five years. She's fully trained and knows that all she has to do is keep her head down for eleven minutes, maximum, and it will all be over. Clear so far?'

'Yes, sir.'

He glanced at her, his expression unreadable. At some point, she noted, his nose had been broken. Not badly, just enough to slightly thicken the bridge.

He thumbed the tablet and they watched events unfold in silence. Another few minutes crawled past while Trevor hammered and threatened at the booth window. Then another figure appeared—her own.

Olivia shifted in her seat, trying not to squirm. It was plain even to her own eyes that she had been terrified, her body movements jerkily stiff. It was embarrassingly obvious, too, that she was clumsily trying to hide something in her right hand. In her left she held out the money, as if trying to coax a wily horse with lumps of sugar.

Job froze the image again, just, it seemed to Olivia, when she was at her most ungainly. 'What were you thinking at this point, Ms Milton?'

Olivia shrugged. 'I don't know…that I needed to stop him before he injured the cashier, I suppose. Why, what should I have been thinking?'

The last bit came out snappier than she had intended, if his brief stillness was anything to go by.

'Any number of questions spring to mind. Where did the boy come from? You've said you didn't see him actually arrive. So, did he walk? Get out of a car? Off the back of a motorcycle? The vital question is, is he alone, or does he have accomplices who may be armed, also?'

He tapped a finger as if on the head of her 3D image and she flinched, like he'd just stuck a pin into a voodoo doll.

'At this point you are fixated on your one main target, Ms Milton. You are blind to your surroundings and have completely disregarded any other possible sources of danger—to yourself or the public.'

The tableau moved on again, while her blush scaled her cheeks and neck. It wouldn't have been so bad if he'd been wrong…

He didn't comment through her brief exchange with Trevor, and the boy's grab for the money. Olivia watched herself bring the Taser up, holding the weapon out in front of her as if she was afraid of it. Afraid of what it might do. *Pathetic, really.*

At the time she'd been so certain that the boy had aimed his gun at her, that he'd been about to pull the trigger. Now she saw that he'd been trying to surrender it.

And she'd shot him anyway.

Job stopped the replay again. The projector juddered in protest. 'If one of the legal scavengers decides to take this on, you may face charges for excessive force. Just as, before the firearm ban, you'd now be held on a manslaughter charge at the very least.' He leaned closer, studying the weapon in her hand. 'That's a nice piece, but carry the standard-issue Taser in future.'

'I'm told they're not as good. Less range and power.'

'That might be so, but they are also instantly recognisable, and impossible to mistake for anything else.'

'I see,' she murmured, but her voice must have told him that she didn't.

He sighed. 'You have a lot to learn, Ms Milton, but you have a great deal of potential, and if you're prepared to stay for long enough, I can train you. But it's not something you can pick up in six months or a year, and then move on. Not if you truly want to fulfill all that promise.'

Her blush had been subsiding. Now it bloomed upwards again.

Job ignored her discomfort. He remotely collapsed the scene and opened another in its place. Still the toll plaza, but cleaner imagery from a higher perspective.

Initially, Olivia struggled to work out where the camera had been positioned. Then it swept around as though the scene itself was rotating, and she realised it could only come from inside the TRU helicopter.

The view pitched and steadied. For the first time, Olivia noticed a tiny set of cross hairs overlaying the picture.

Down on the ground she saw herself standing over the boy, aiming the weapon at his writhing body. The hologram zoomed onto her face. For a split second the cross hairs centred on her forehead as she stood there, gaping up directly into the lens. Then, as Olivia watched, she saw herself lift a hand to shelter her eyes against the debris from the rotor wash. As she did so, the outline of the Taser she clutched became more clearly defined.

A cold prickle ran across her skin as the hairs struggled to rise. She knew now exactly where that camera had been mounted. When she looked through the ghosted scene to Job, she found him watching her reaction, unsmiling.

He nodded. 'Yes, it was a close one, wasn't it? Just be thankful, Ms Milton, that the TRU sniper hesitated long enough to recognise your non-standard-issue Taser for what it was. And also that he was your average hot-blooded heterosexual male with an understandable disinclination towards killing a pretty girl, despite his undoubtedly thorough training.' He rose, buttoned his jacket and looked down at her. 'Tomorrow, you might not be so lucky.'

Road Trip

Yrsa Sigurðardóttir

The car began to slide sideways on the icy road, slowly and somewhat gracefully. Signý tightened her grip on the steering wheel and the peeling, dried-up leather pinched her palms. The car was old and in way too bad a shape to be making this journey. But it was what was on offer. The influx of tourists had hiked prices up enough to make renting a car a non-option. The newspaper Signý and her companion Eiríkur worked for was so in debt she had not even raised this idea. Instead she had offered her beat-up car, failing on purpose to mention the bald tires that had now completely lost their grip on the road.

'Shit, shit, shit.' Signý's voice sounded needy, her tone summing up the situation quite nicely. The car was headed off the road and there was absolutely nothing she could do about it.

'Brake! Brake!' The level of urgency in Eiríkur's screech just about matched the level of stupidity in his command. Signý wasn't surprised. He was the archetypical hipster, rode a bike wherever he and his manicured beard were headed and he probably didn't even have a driver's license.

He had no way of knowing that stepping on the brake would only make the situation worse.

Signý tried forcing the car back onto the road but the tires refused to follow the steering wheel's lead. She hurriedly changed down a gear in an effort to slow the car's progress, but it was too late. They were off the tarmac, crossing the hard shoulder at a neat forty-five-degree angle and suddenly tipping over onto the incline leading into the trench beside the road. There the car came to an abrupt halt and the motor went quiet, the snow that filled the trench having done nothing to soften the blow. Eiríkur's large camera bags on the back seat flew into Signý's seat. It hurt, but to a lesser degree than the harsh catch of the seat belt. It was certainly better than face-planting into the windshield but Signý would not be surprised if it left her with bruising across her torso. A zombie beauty pageant sash of sorts.

'Fuck.' Eiríkur let go of the ceiling-handle and rubbed his chest. He then removed his earbuds and the vague, muffled tones of an ancient Fleetwood Mac song filled the car. 'Fuck, fuck, fuck.' He stared out the front window while cursing and turned his angry gaze to Signý. 'Why didn't you brake?'

She met him with a death gaze of her own. 'Don't. Just don't.'

Never one for confrontation, Eiríkur turned back to the view in front of them. Snow, snow, and more snow. The field stretching before them was a sea of white, as were the snow-covered mountains rising into the dark evening sky at its far end. The only colour which broke the monotony was the brown wooden poles of a raggedy fence lining the field a few feet from the car. Eiríkur let out a tired sigh. He fetched the stupid iPod he had been listening to from his pocket and turned the music off. The car went silent. 'Do you think we can push it back onto the road?'

Signý thought about making a snide comment comparing the weight of a bicycle to an automobile but decided against it. They had enough problems without adding a sour mood to the mix. 'No. I don't think we can. The incline is too steep. We have to phone for help. Get someone with an SUV to pull us out.'

'From where? We haven't passed any farmhouses or seen any cars since we left the main road.'

It was true, they were in the middle of nowhere. The place they were headed to had been chosen to house the boy they were going to interview for exactly that reason. It was isolated. Signý pointed ahead. 'Phone the farmer. We aren't that far off.'

'Why should I phone? I'm only the photographer.' Eiríkur reached to loosen his seat belt with one hand while supporting himself with the other in anticipation of falling forward. 'You phone. You're the reporter.'

Signý thought she could make out a pout under his beard. Considering the circumstances, it was understandable. She did not want to make the call any more than he did. The last call to the farmer had not gone too well. It had been around two hours ago when they stopped for gas in Akureyri. The purpose of the call had been to confirm their impending arrival, but instead it had turned into the farmer berating them. He was opposed to the interview and made it clear in no uncertain terms. She had barely got a word in edgewise. Apparently their visit had upset the boy, made him agitated, and put him on edge. Her saying that the boy had agreed to the interview did not calm the man. Neither did her argument that the boy was eighteen now and able to make his own decisions. She could hear yelling in the background that only emphasised the man's point and undermined hers. But there had been no conclusion; the phone call had ended rather abruptly with the man telling her he had to go and that they should turn back. A call now, asking him to pull them out of a ditch, was not one she was very eager to make.

But a minuscule part of life was set aside for doing things one was enthusiastic about. 'Fair enough. I'll do it.' Signý followed Eiríkur's lead and braced herself before unfastening her seat belt. She felt the pressure on her ribs subside as she became free of its unforgiving grip. She managed to manoeuvre herself into a position that allowed her free use of her arms and took her phone out of her coat pocket.

The farmer's phone number was at the top of her recent calls. She had not made any others since they left early this morning. Her husband was angry at her for making the trip and she hadn't felt like talking to him. Still didn't. That call could wait until tonight, after the interview. She did not need to hear him repeat how unsafe the car was for winter driving outside the city, especially now that he had been proven right.

Signý phoned the farmer. She felt Eiríkur's eyes on her but did not acknowledge his presence while she listened to the ringtone repeat itself over and over. She hung up when a recording began and tried again. The same. She decided against a third time. 'He's not answering.'

'Do you think he left? Took the boy with him to avoid the interview?'

'How should I know?' Signý stared at the lit screen of her phone. Then she looked up and shook her head. The movement nearly made her lose her grip and fall forward. 'No. They're still there. Where would they go?'

'Then why isn't he answering?'

'Again. How should I know? Maybe there are cows to milk. Eggs to collect. Livestock to feed. It's a farm. They have stuff to do.' The words had a reassuring effect on them both. Of course both the man and the boy were still at the farm. The farmer did not strike her as the type to leave without at least letting them know that their trip would be in vain.

Eiríkur was apparently in agreement. 'So what then? We wait and call back later? Or walk?'

'Walk. Waiting isn't really an option.' Signý started the car and the snow covering the hood lit up momentarily. It then went dark again when the engine shut off and the headlights followed. 'We'll freeze if we wait. The heater won't work if the car won't.'

'How far is it to the farm?'

Signý braced herself once more so that she could navigate the screen on her phone. Google Maps had the answer to Eiríkur's question. As soon as she accessed 4G, her phone reminded her that she had gone over her data limit. Anger at the photographer swelled anew inside her bruised ribcage. Why couldn't he have a smartphone like everybody else? Why did she have to rack up charges because he mistakenly believed it was cool to carry around an old Nokia 3210? Fucking hipster. She swallowed her annoyance. 'It's about a fifteen-minute walk. We were almost there.' His shoes caught her eye and the anger at his lifestyle choices subsided. He was wearing the trademark footwear of his kind: lace-up Timberland boots. Perfect for walking along the icy road. Much more so than her meant-for-the-pavement-but-really-good-looking shoes. His roomy, mustard-yellow parka with the fur-lined hood was also perfect for the occasion.

'So what are we waiting for?' Eiríkur zipped up his coat.

When Signý did not do the same, it dawned on him. 'You want me to go alone?'

'Yes. One of us has to wait here in case a snowplough arrives. If they see an abandoned car, they'll have it towed away. I can't afford to pay for that.'

'How about I wait and you go?'

'You don't have a licence.'

'So? It's not as if there's any need for driving.'

'There will be if the snow-plough pulls the car up on to the road.' Signý hadn't a clue whether snow-ploughs offered this sort of service. It didn't really matter as the imaginary snowplough in question wasn't going to pass by. It was late, almost dinnertime, and already pitch black. No one was going to pay overtime to clear a road as little used as this one. 'You go. The farmer will be fine. He's sure to have a car big enough to help out and equipped for winter. No one can live here and not have one.'

'Won't you freeze?'

'No. You should be back in twenty minutes. I'll be fine.'

Eiríkur nodded. 'Okay, then. But if he starts arguing about the interview I'm going to tell him to save the speeches for you. I'll tell him how it is. I'm just the photographer.'

'Sure. Whatever.' Signý felt her anger increase. Eiríkur might be the photographer but this interview was just as important to him as to her. There was talk of downsizing at the paper and neither of them would be on the to-go list if they repeated the click-fest that the interview with the boy's mother had turned out to be. Anyone could write the article that was most-read that week. Few could repeat it the week that followed. Eiríkur should be happy she chose him to come with her. His job was on the line too.

Eiríkur opened the door and got out. It took a lot of

wrangling, the incline made all movements awkward and clumsy. Once out, he bent down, stuck his head back into the car and waved goodbye. 'Sure you will be okay?'

'I'll be fine. Just get the farmer to come immediately. Don't let him make you wait while he finishes some farming stuff. I don't want to sit here for an hour or more. Then I won't be okay. Got it?'

He nodded and closed the door, swinging it with force to counteract gravity. Signý watched him clamber up the steep incline and walk away, the mustard-yellow parka quickly disappearing from the limited view she had of the road. As soon as she saw nothing but her desolate surroundings she began to feel the oppressive silence. She regretted not asking him to leave his stupid iPod behind. Even corny old hipster music was preferable to listening to the silence of the deserted environment.

It was a still evening. No howling wind, no falling snow, no birds, no horses. No nothing. Just her, the car, the snow, and the silence. She looked at her phone and contemplated phoning her husband but decided against it. What would she say when he asked if everything was okay? She did not want to lie and she did not want to explain her circumstances either. It sucked to have to admit that he was right; she could brush off the incident more easily once she had something to tell him about the interview. He was just as curious as the online readers. Everyone wanted to hear the boy's side of the story after what the mother had to say. Signý corrected her own thoughts. Everyone wanted to know what the boy had to say regardless of his mother's sudden willingness to talk. He was, after all, a curiosity of the driving-by-a-car-accident type. A boy people were interested in from a safe distance. No wonder, he was the country's youngest murderer and crazed to boot. As if that hook wasn't enough, interest was further fuelled by the fact that the coverage at the time of the murder had been very limited. Everyone knew the story but its details were mostly based on conjecture and rumours. The records were locked away, not in the public domain as was the case for most murder cases that had gone to trial.

The boy had only been ten years old and hence under the age of criminal responsibility, so the case never went to court. His guilt was established by the police, based on his mother's description of events and a confession that was made after intense interrogation. His sentencing, if that term applied, was decided by the child welfare system. Its ruling: ship the boy to a faraway farm and keep him there until further notice. The idea was probably that no one need keep out of harm's way if the harm itself is well secluded. But was the boy dangerous? Was he even a murderer? Not according to his mother. To be more precise, not according to his mother now. Signý had spoken to a contact from the police in preparation for the interview and he maintained that the mother's testimony had been very clear. Her son killed his stepfather. Stabbed him many times. So many times that the dead man's stab wounds had stab wounds.

But now the mother had experienced a change of heart. During the interview, the gaunt woman had told Signý that she had been the one to kill her then-husband. Her son had merely had a panicked reaction to the bloody event, picked up the knife she had previously used to kill and stabbed away. Considering the abuse the boy had experienced at his stepfather's hand, as well as what he had witnessed him doing to his mother, his actions were understandable. Well, almost.

What was less understandable was the mother's decision to let her son take the hit for her actions. During the interview Signý had repeatedly asked her to explain herself but the woman never fully managed to do so convincingly. She spoke of being in shock. Emphasised having been a victim for so long that she was easily led by the police. She even suggested having been in the midst of a psychotic episode. None of this explained why she had said nothing for eight years while her son gathered dust in a remote valley. Nor did it throw any light on why she had decided to step forward now.

But Signý thought she knew why the woman had thrown her son under the bus and was now making amends. She had even run her theory by the woman, who had at first stared at her, mouth agape, before becoming flustered and looking away. Signý got the feeling she had hit the nail on the head and was still pretty sure of herself.

It was obvious, really. The mother, a borderline simpleton either from birth or as a result of head trauma from her husband's beatings, had believed that the boy would not be punished because of his age. That they would walk away, free to resume their lives. When that did not transpire she would have waited a bit, hoping that her son would soon be set free. It was easy to imagine that once one or two years had passed she would have decided to wait one more and so on and so forth. But now that he was eighteen and there were no signs of his freedom on the horizon, she had to face the facts. If her son was to have any semblance of a life she had to step up. So she phoned the paper asking for a tell-all interview. Enter Signý. Enter Eiríkur the hipster photographer.

Despite everything—the argument with her husband this morning, the long annoying ride and the accident with the car—Signý felt upbeat. She couldn't wait to hear what the boy had to say. Did he remember what had really happened? Had he let his youth pass in a lighthouse-keeperish environment out of love and his misguided protective feelings towards his mother? Or had he been brainwashed into thinking that he actually killed his stepfather? If so, what did the realisation of having been wrongly accused feel like? What would he have to say regarding his mother's actions? Did he hate her or had he found it in his heart to muster up some sort of understanding? The interview had all the markings of a success.

Signý smiled. She looked at her phone to see how much time had passed since Eiríkur left. Her smile evaporated. Not long at all. Not even ten minutes. She bent down a bit to look out over the field and the mountains lining the valley. No sign of life. Just cold, white snow that softened all outlines and obliterated the jagged edges of the mountain's rock face. Signý shivered a bit, and was reminded of the temperature outside. It would not take long for the car to cool down to the same level. She tried starting the engine in the hope she could put the heat back on. She watched the snow in front of her light up while the engine churned. But it lasted only a moment before the car went silent and the snow back to normal.

She tried again a few times. Every five minutes or so. She wasn't stupid, she knew the result would be the same each time, but it gave her something to do. There was no sign of Eiríkur, something she did not worry much about until he had been gone for half an hour. She did a simple calculation in her head. It was a ten-minute walk to the farm, five minutes to explain the situation and five minutes to get into the farmer's car and drive back to her.

Altogether, twenty minutes. So where the hell was Eiríkur? She did a recalculation. A ten-minute walk to the farm, five minutes establishing that no one was home, ten minutes walking back to her. Altogether, twenty-five minutes. It came out to the same thing: where the hell was Eiríkur?

The car was now as cold as the air outside. Colder. Signý knew from experience that confined cold was worse than cold in the open. The same degrees were more powerful in a closed space. It defied the little physics she had learned at school but it was true nonetheless. Despite this, she stayed inside the car, watching the short-lived puffs her breath made when she exhaled. It was better inside than outdoors. There was something menacing about the solitude it offered. The lack of life and abundance of nothingness.

Despite not wanting to appear anxious or afraid, Signý called Eiríkur. The ring tone was different from that of the farmer's mobile but the end result was the same. No one answered. She tried not to read too much into it. Eiríkur often turned down the volume on his phone and it would not be the first time she was unable to reach him. She tried to see the bright side. Now she was annoyed and annoyance was a much preferable feeling to being on edge.

Her phone beeped in her hands, the familiar sound announcing the arrival of a text message. Her cold fingers immediately went for the screen and to her surprise it was not from Eiríkur but from her husband. The text was brief: *Did you see this?* It was followed by a link that she copied into her browser. Fuck the roaming charges. She recognised the beginning of the URL; it was a rival newspaper. The article reference was a long number so she had no idea what the subject matter was or why her husband thought she would be interested.

The page opened to a headline reading: *Do not be fooled.* Underneath it was a picture of a familiar woman, the boy's mother whom she had interviewed last week. It was not of the same quality as the photos Eiríkur had taken which had accompanied Signý's interview. Instead it was a bit fuzzy and seemed to have been snapped without the woman's knowledge. She was exiting a building that Signý recognised as the hospital in Reykjavík. She was just as gaunt as Signý remembered, her rather cheap and worn parka not managing to hide her thin frame.

Signý had forgotten all about the cold and her missing photographer. She scrolled down and read the accompanying article. She read the paragraphs in a similar way as one would drink to quench a desert thirst, in gulps. The piece began with a slap to her professional face and only got worse. And worse. When she was done, Signý closed her eyes and tried her damnedest to calm down. She had made a total fool of herself and could more likely than not kiss her new-found job security good-bye. As could Eiríkur, just by association. She was actually surprised that she had not got another text message, one from her editor telling her not to show up for work again. She had brought shame down on the publication and that shame would be meted out to the editor in equal measure to her. That was not something he was likely to forgive easily.

The article was an exposé of her interview with the woman. It was based upon groundwork Signý should have done after conducting it. But her enthusiasm over the piece had blinded her inner journalist. It had wrapped a blindfold over her eyes and plugged her ears, her alertness doused as if by a hefty dose of alcohol. Under ordinary circumstances she would have done more, spoken to more people and checked for any mistakes. Excitement to share the interview with readers had got the better of her. If she was fully honest, it was more excitement over being praised and becoming popular with her bosses.

Signý did not know if she would have spoken to the woman's sister if she had operated with less haste. At the moment she believed she would have, but it was hard to say. Hindsight is always twenty-twenty, while glaucoma seems to rule the present. But after reading what the sister had to say, one thing was clear. It would have changed everything. According to this woman, who looked super sour in the photo that accompanied the piece, her sister had made everything up. She had not killed her husband or otherwise harmed him. It was her son. Just like she had dutifully told the police at the time. The only reason she was making this nonsense up now was because she was dying. She was in the terminal stages of lung cancer with only a few months to live. The sister had gone on to say that she had this firsthand. The boy's mother had told her of her intention to give him his freedom as her parting gift, hoping to make up for not having protected him as a child when he was molested, beaten, and broken by his stepfather. She would take the blame and die as a pariah. The woman who let her child take the blame for her actions.

Terminal cancer. The face reminiscent of a skull should have told Signý that something wasn't right. She had put it down to smoking but hadn't thought anything about the fact that the woman had not lit up once during the three-hour interview. Looking back Signý remembered ashtrays in the small grubby apartment. One on the sofa table, one on the windowsill in the kitchen, one in the hallway. There had even been one in the bathroom. All empty. It should have told her something. Even asking whether she had given up smoking might have caused the woman to give something away, enough to make Signý's journalist radar sense there was something off. But she had not cared about the woman. Not at all, really. Definitely not enough to enquire about her smoking habits. She had merely put up with her company to get the story.

Signý picked up her phone again and closed the browser. She did not want to see the article next time she needed to access the Internet. In fact she never wanted to see it again. Never to be reminded of the jibes that the other journalist had managed to pepper the text with. The one that stung the most was when he quoted his interviewee saying that only a simpleton would not have seen through her sister's made-up story. This was followed by very indignant words about trash journalism and using vulnerable people as click-bait. Signý was certain that the reporter had put those words into the woman's mouth. Just to be mean. Professional success was known to cause envy and a strong urge to take the winner down. She was not inoculated against it herself. She would probably have done the same had the tables been turned.

Signý tried not to think about the readers' comments she had stupidly viewed. Such comments were never positive. Mercifully the article had not been up for long so there weren't many. In her mind she could see them growing in number by the minute, becoming increasingly negative as each commentator tried to outdo the indignation of those who had come before him. Those she had seen called her unprofessional and stupid, by midnight she would be called much worse. Evil, heartless, and as ignorant as dirt. If she was lucky. Worse name-calling often occurred in the comments section. Usually the worst of them were removed but she had the feeling the rival paper would let them fester for a while. They might even add some of their own to fuel the fire. After all, she was the one tied to the stake in its midst and she worked for the competition.

If the new article had only been an interview with the sister, Signý might have been able to sit out the backlash and slowly float to the top again. Given ample time. But the rival journalist had gone the extra mile. He had interviewed a psychologist and asked the man to envisage what the original article could do to the boy. The specialist had not been shy when it came to pouring out his thoughts and none of them were good. He believed that the boy's mental state was likely to suffer from such irresponsible reporting. In his view it did not matter what was true; whatever recovery the boy had made during his time at the farm had probably been jeopardised. Hopefully only temporarily, but possibly for good. It was the psychologist's opinion that no matter how many people came forward saying that his mother made this up, the boy would still have doubts. The damage done could therefore not be erased. The boy's doubts could develop into anger, and anger for someone with his mental issues was really bad news for everyone around him. Seriously bad news. His words had probably been dumbed down to make for easier reading. No one liked to read quotes full of medical or psychological jargon. Layman's terms were more effective.

The psychologist's statement echoed in Signý's mind. She recalled the yelling in the background when she spoke to the farmer. His strong insistence that they stay away took on another meaning. A more serious, menacing meaning.

Signý tried Eiríkur's number again. As before, there was no answer. But unlike previous attempts, it wasn't simply annoying but a reason for serious worry.

The darkness outside seemed to have intensified. The mountains in the distance were barely discernible from the black sky. The moon was new and the pinprick lighting provided by the stars overhead had nothing to say. Signý realised that if someone decided to creep up on her she wouldn't make him out until he was almost beside the car.

Jesus Christ. Jesus Christ. Signý tried to gather her thoughts but couldn't. Any thought process leading up to what she should do if something had happened to Eiríkur seemed unable to get past the original thought of him being attacked. Her mind immediately jumped from that thought to one where she was the next victim. And from there to the cop's description of the shredded body of the boy's stepfather. The stab wounds having stab wounds and how it must have hurt. She tried to stop imagining how it would feel to have a knife stabbed into the soft part of her abdomen, under the ribs. But she could not. Her mind refused to let go.

She phoned Eiríkur again. Still no answer. When the ringing died out she sat in the silence, staring out the window, wondering if she should phone the police. The nearest station was over an hour and a half away. But that was probably a shorter wait than sitting around hoping someone would pass by. This section of the road led nowhere. Only the farm. The farm and the boy.

The silence had become more intense, like the darkness. Signý realised that this was something she could actually use to her benefit. She might not see a possible attacker crossing the field or coming at her, but unless this person could fly, she would hear the crunching of snow underneath his shoes. She lowered her window until the glass reached under her ear. Her previous theory about it being colder inside the car than outside proved to be wrong. Her ear and forehead felt the brunt of the increased chill but she forced herself to grin and bear it. She would phone the police, count down until their arrival. Her ear would probably suffer frostbite before that happened but there was no way she was covering it up. She needed to hear everything.

Before phoning the police she tried one last call to Eiríkur. It would look good if her phone was confiscated. After two rings she realised that the tone was somehow different. An odd echo followed each ring. She had phoned often enough to know Eiríkur's ringtone by heart. Or by ear. And it had no echo. She listened more carefully, covering the cold ear exposed to the elements. The ringtone went back to normal. She removed her hand and the tone changed again. Taking the phone from her ear she realised she was hearing a separate ring coming from outside the car.

Slowly she turned her head in the direction she believed the sound came from. It wasn't from the field. It came from the road. She tried lifting herself up a bit to get a better view but couldn't see far because of the incline. She had no choice but to get out of the vehicle in the hope of seeing what the hell was going on. It was cumbersome and turned out to make very little difference. The visibility was crap due to the darkness. Yet she did not get back in or close the door. Instead she stood holding on to it so as not to slip while she stretched her head to see even further. And she did. Someone was walking down the road. Towards the car. Towards her. She couldn't make out more than a dark outline but with every step the figure became more discernible. What should she do? She hadn't planned for anything happening so soon. She had yet to formulate any sort of plan. Should she lock herself in the car? Run?

Where to?

Frozen to the spot, Signý stared at the figure that was slowly approaching. It resembled a shadow, one that had pulled free from its maker and ventured alone into the world. Mesmerised, she realised that she was losing any head start she had if she needed to run, but her feet refused to move. The dark outline of the figure was becoming clearer and she thought she could make out one of its hands lifted upwards, held high into the air. It was waving. Her breathing became calmer. Who waves at someone they intend to harm? Obviously no one. Maybe it was the farmer, maybe Eiríkur. The hand gesture indicated someone friendly at least.

A couple more steps and she could now see a hint of colour and clothing. A mustard-yellow. Eiríkur's coat. Signý breathed a sigh of relief. It was swiftly replaced by anger at the man for not answering his phone. The only reasonable explanation for it was his headphones. He must have plugged his ears to listen to the stupid iPod that he had brought along. What was he thinking?

Signý stood by the car for another minute until she was certain that it was him. When there was no mistaking the large yellow parka she got back in and shut the door after her. How dare he cause her this unnecessary distress. Fuming, she gripped the steering wheel but soon her anger at Eiríkur subsided and in its place came the realisation that they were still in a predicament. The farmer had obviously not been at home or unwilling to help since Eiríkur had returned alone. The phone call to the police could not be put off. She began to mentally prepare for the speech they were certain to give her about winter driving safety and the state of her car. If there was a fine for driving with bald tires she was sure to get one. This would be added to her additional roaming charges and possibly the cost of repairs. And all for nothing. There would be no interview and quite possibly there would be no job when she returned. Her husband would have a field day.

The sound of snow crunched underneath the soles of Eiríkur's Timberland boots became discernible. Signý welcomed it; the monotony of the silent surroundings had done little to relieve her misery. Despite this she decided to close the window; her ear had started to throb with pain from the severe cold. She was again shrouded in silence and despair set back in. She was about to become unemployed and unemployable, to boot. She pushed the thought away for now. Soon she would have Eiríkur to share her depressive mood with; he would be just as badly affected by the news of the new article as she was. He would probably emphasise over and over that he was 'just the photographer' and hold on to the hope that his part in the fiasco would be overlooked. But she would make sure to smash that hope and had already decided to tell him that as the photographer he should have noticed the woman's frail appearance. He was the one who should have questioned her health and alerted Signý. He had taken countless photos of people and should have recognised the signs. It was imperative that he be as miserable as her while they waited for help. She needed a partner in this fiasco. Misery divided by two felt only half as bad as experiencing it all on your own.

Lost in thought, Signý was distracted from Eiríkur's impending arrival. Her heart nearly jumped out of her chest when he knocked on her window. She lost her balance in the slanted car, knocking her forearm on the hard and unforgiving steering wheel. Fucking fool. Why didn't he just get in the car? Signý turned to the window and stared at the mustard-coloured parka almost touching the glass. It was dirty. Covered in dark streaks. And ripped. What the hell had happened to Eiríkur? Perhaps he had an explanation for his delay after all. Possibly one involving him falling into a ditch in the darkness. Too bad about the parka then. It was a ridiculously expensive one. Not one easily replaced when living on unemployment benefits.

She rolled down the window. 'What the hell happened? Get in.' Eiríkur didn't reply. She could not see his face from her position so she could not see if he still had the earbuds in. Perhaps he had suffered a concussion and was delirious. Did one lose hearing under such circumstances?

Signý's eyes focused on the damaged coat and she involuntarily shifted in her seat, away from the window. The dark spots weren't mud. Mud wasn't red. The ripped material did not look as if it had been damaged by a fall. The edges were not jagged but straight and smooth, as if cut. 'Eiríkur? What happened?' Still no reply. Carefully Signý moved back towards the window so that she could angle her head upwards and look him in the face.

'Eiríkur?' Her eyes did not reach to his face. Instead they fixated on his left hand, or what he was holding to be exact. A knife. A fancy large butcher's knife with a black handle. And a dirty blade. The only thought she managed to muster was that Eiríkur wasn't left-handed. Why was he holding a knife in his left hand?

Slowly Signý looked upwards. Her eyes passed over the damaged parka, all the way up to the hood and the face it partially hid. There was no beard. The face was not Eiríkur's. It was younger. Much younger. She realised she had seen it before. An even younger version of these features. It was the boy. A grown-up version of the boy she had seen in a framed picture hanging on the wall of his mother's apartment. Signý swallowed a huge lump that threatened to suffocate her otherwise.

The boy grinned, his teeth crooked and lips thin. He raised his left hand, bringing the knife aloft while he opened the car door with his right hand. 'I didn't want to be photographed.' His features became grim, the lopsided and awful smile disappearing as if wiped off. 'And I don't want to do the interview anymore either.'

Neither did Signý.

But it was too late. She would do no more interviews. Not ever. Signý realised she was about to find out what a knife feels like instead. Plunged into the soft area of the abdomen, just under the ribs.

And just about everywhere else.

Long Time, No See

Maj Sjöwall, translated by Catherine Edwards

Despite the fresh snow lashing at her face and the slush on the pavement, which was seeping in through the cracks in her left shoe, Blomman was in an excellent mood.

As soon as she had woken up, she'd had a sneaking feeling that this cold, grey January day was going to bring her luck; a feeling which grew stronger later in the morning, when she went through the rubbish bins on Ringvägen and found such a rich harvest of cans and empty bottles that she could fill both her large plastic carrier bags to the brim.

At Metro in the Ringen shopping centre, she was able to cash in the receipt from the can recycling machine for eighteen kronor, and in the alcohol shop on Götgatan, two shiny ten-kronor and four one-kronor coins rattled down into the coin slot of the bottle bank.

Blomman laid out the change on the counter and then gathered it up into a small package, stuffing it into the roomy pockets of her overcoat as she looked around the brightly lit shop.

'It's nice here,' she thought, 'especially with so many people, like now, in the Friday lunch rush, and with the shining rows of bottles and glass cabinets all along the wall.'

She stood still for a long while, looking at the expensive fine wines and champagne bottles which passed solemnly by on the display cabinet's rotating shelves.

Together with the twelve kronor she already had in her pocket, she now had enough to buy a half-bottle of dessert wine and still have seven kronor left, but after six days sober, her need for alcohol had lessened rather than increased, though the latter would have been more natural. She thought age had something to do with it. Being drunk was more fun when you were young; now you almost got more of a kick from being sober. Often you'd drink just because the alcohol was there, or to keep yourself warm in the cold. Besides, there was plenty of time to change her mind before the shop closed.

She adjusted the strap on her shoulder bag and went back out into the sleet. Her left sock was soaking wet and her toes were freezing. Blomman decided to do something about that and, since she was feeling exuberant, she was sure it was going to go well.

With squelching but rapid steps, she crossed the street and went into Åhléns department store. The sock department was on the ground floor and she wandered around there for a while, until she was convinced that the shelves in front of her were unguarded, and quickly yanked down a pair of thick knee-high socks, putting them in her bag.

It was dangerous to shoplift when you looked poor and unkempt. As soon as she went into a shop, the assistants stiffened and seemed to assume that she was in there to steal. She knew that from experience. So she rarely shoplifted, and only did it when she was absolutely certain that no one could see her.

On the way out, she stopped here and there and pinched one or two more things as she tried to establish whether she was, after all, being watched. Then, calmly, she went out through the doors and continued across the street, without anyone stopping her.

Her toes were almost numb with cold, but Blomman was in a good mood now she had figured out how to have warm, dry feet again soon.

The crowd of people seemed to be all heading in the opposite direction as she trudged north along Götgatan. Youngsters kept pushing into her as they walked past and when one young man, who looked to be twice her height, shoved her so forcefully that she almost stumbled into the street, she yelled after him: 'Am I invisible or something? Can't you see me? Bloody oaf!'

On Åsögatan it was quieter, and she only passed a few people on her way before she arrived.

Blomman pushed open the door to the doctor's surgery and went up the stairs. She had made use of the toilets here many times, but on one occasion she had been driven out before she could get to them, and was forced to squat in a nearby doorway.

A small queue had formed at the reception and the woman in white behind the desk seemed to be fully occupied. At one end of the counter was a chair and two baskets; one for new shoe-covers and one for used ones. Blomman sat down and put the blue plastic covers over her shoes. Then she stuffed another pack into her bag, got up, and walked to the toilet with smacking footsteps. No one in the queue gave her so much as a glance, and the receptionist sat and leafed through her papers.

Blomman sat on the toilet seat and took off her shoes and socks. She pulled a thick wad of paper towels out of the dispenser and wiped her foot until it was warm and dry. Then she put on the newly stolen socks, put a shoe-cover over each foot and laced her shoes. It felt great to have warm, dry feet, and the bright blue plastic edges which lay in baggy wrinkles around her ankles looked intriguing, she thought.

When she went out into the street it had stopped snowing, and she stood, hesitating for a moment, before turning right onto Renstiernas Gata. Outside the pharmacy there was a bottle which had contained cherry wine, and she popped it into one of her plastic bags, which she stuffed in her bag. She continued down towards Nytorget where the A Team usually hung out. Not that she in her sober state had any real craving for their rather shameless and drunken company and anyway, they were unlikely to be there in this weather.

Blomman suddenly felt idle and somewhat indecisive after the day's successful tasks. Had it been a couple of weeks earlier, she would now have started looking for somewhere to spend the night, but she was borrowing the tugboat cabin on *Söder Mälarstrand* for a few more weeks, and it had been a very long time since she had had such a luxury.

At the bottle bank on the corner of Skånegatan, she caught sight of Öland. He was standing on tiptoe on an upturned milk crate, his arm deep inside the plastic container as he tried to reach the top layer of bottles. When the discarded bottles began to fill up towards the top, sometimes you could get a whole load of recycled glass, but now it seemed that the bin was probably no more than half full. Öland almost looked as though he was about to disappear down among the bottles as he stood on tiptoe and puffed.

'Hello there, Öland. How's it going?'

Öland extracted his arm from the bin and jumped down from the crate.

'Nothing doing. They're too far down. We'll have to wait a few days. How are you yourself, my lily, my rose?'

'I'm okay,' said Blomman. 'Great, actually.'

It was on the tip of her tongue to tell him about the tugboat, but she stopped herself. Last winter Öland had found a way in to a property on Kocksgatan and had let Blomman share his bedroom in the house's utility room for two whole months before they were discovered. If Öland learned of the cabin, he might insist that she let him stay there as a favour, and there was no question of that. When, for once, she had a home of her own—albeit short-term—she didn't want to share it under any circumstances.

'That's good, baby,' said Öland. 'Fly the flags and sound the trumpets! Great stuff. Got anything to smoke?'

'Nope. And nothing to drink and no dough. So you'll get nothing, Örjan Lage Andersson . Have you ever been to Öland, by the way?'

'Nah. I got the name in the army. There was a guy we called Gotland too. Though he was from there...What are those weird frills on your feet?'

'Oh, my shoes were leaking so I fixed some insulation.'

'Cool,' said Öland, and looked down the park. 'No pals out there today.'

'Nope. They'll all be sitting at home in their castles and drinking champagne.'

Blomman also felt like a cigarette and they decided to go to the alcohol shop on Folkungagatan where, in the long queue which was there every Friday, there was always a chance of scrounging a cigarette. They succeeded almost immediately in cadging some fags from a group of construction workers standing outside the shop, waiting their turn.

After that, Blomman and Öland strolled around Söder for the rest of the afternoon. Blomman gave Öland one of her plastic bags and they shared what they found in the bins and recycling containers between them.

Blomman usually felt at home in Öland's company, but when darkness fell after the brief twilight, she began trying to think of an excuse to part ways without needing to disclose that she had somewhere to go. She was hungry and wanted to go home and had no desire to traipse around with him all night.

The problem was solved at Björns Trädgård. There, Öland met a few friends, equipped with drinks, and Blomman was able to go her own way without any explanation.

It had grown colder and the sky was starry. The slush had frozen to ice and she walked carefully, taking short steps on her worn-out soles.

Below Maria Trappgränd there was an abandoned supermarket trolley. That could come in handy, thought Blomman, so I have something to hold onto on the way home. She put her bag of bottles and glass in the trolley and began to push the rattling carriage in front of her.

After a successful day she would soon be home.

• • ● • •

Netta was woken by an ache in her arm. She was in Olof's bed and in his sleep he had rolled halfway over her so that his hard shoulder blade drilled down into her upper arm.

'Ouch,' said Netta, nudging him while trying to free her arm. 'Move over, you lump.'

'Whaddisit, whaddisit?' said Olof, who turned over and went back to sleep.

Netta looked at the clock. Nearly half past seven, so he wouldn't get many more minutes' sleep.

Although it was Friday, which he usually took off, he had an important meeting at nine and, before they had gone to sleep at four, she had promised to make sure he got there in time.

She sat for a moment on the edge of the bed, aware of the pounding in her head, before she got up, pulled on her dressing gown and went downstairs to the kitchen.

It didn't look too bad. The dinner dishes were stacked on top of the dishwasher and she had at least brought the cups, cognac glasses, and ashtrays from the living room and put them on the kitchen table, among the peanut bowls and glasses.

She washed up one of the glasses and filled it with cold water and two aspirin tablets. As the water settled, she cleared the kitchen table, wiped it down, and started putting things in the dishwasher.

When the tablets had fully dissolved, she drank the liquid in one go, filled it with water and aspirin again, and sat with her head in her hands, waiting for the throbbing headache to subside.

It had started when the neighbours, Sivan and Klutte, had come over with a lot of curious bottles, offering them one of the drinks they had learned to mix in Jamaica. At first, it tasted really good, with rum and fruit juices and ice and berries and God-knows-what, but after the third glass it just felt gooey, and it was decided that Sivan and Klutte would stay for dinner. Then they drank beer and snaps with warm anchovy canapés while they waited for the lamb gratin to cook. And then they drank that new Médoc wine, which Olof had brought home a whole crate of; at least a bottle, she thought. And coffee and cognac, and after Sivan and Klutte had tottered home, Netta and Olof had carried on drinking the cognac and then they had started arguing about something, she couldn't remember what, and then they had made up, but no sex—they hadn't been up to it. No wonder she felt as she did.

The headache began to subside a little and Netta turned on the coffeemaker, squeezed four oranges into two glasses, knocked back one of them and took the other with her, the glass of aspirin in the other hand, as she went upstairs to wake Olof.

It wasn't easy, but in the end he got up, downed both glasses, and went to the bathroom. Meanwhile, Netta sat at the dressing table and began to remove the remains of yesterday's makeup, which in the light of day hardly made her any more attractive.

'Fifty-five years; fuck, it shows,' she said to her reflection. 'Bitch.'

Olof came back and began getting dressed.

'How the hell can I be so stupid, having a load of booze a day before an important meeting.'

'Do those Japanese men have to meet you again today?' said Netta. 'You've had meetings all week. Do they never take a day off in Japan?'

'No, they're always working.'

'You've only got yourself to blame. I, on the other hand, have promised to go to my mother in Äppelviken to see Aunt Sara who's back from Italy. That's at least as tough as a bunch of Japanese businessmen.'

'This suburban social life is starting to get on my nerves,' said Olof as he picked out a tie.

Now Netta remembered what they had argued about. Olof wanted to sell the house and move to the city now that the children had left home, but Netta didn't. Think of the grandchildren, she had said. They need to get out into the countryside. What grandchildren? Olof had asked. Well, we'll have grandchildren one day, Netta had argued and Olof had responded in his dry way: I don't think so. Both Madeleine and Chris are just too selfish to have children. And so the quarrel had started.

But now Netta had neither the energy nor the desire to argue, so she kept quiet while she applied a fresh coat of mascara to her eyelashes.

'I have to hurry now,' said Olof. 'It's almost time for lunch with the Japanese, and then we're going out to look at the new warehouse in Stuvsta all afternoon.'

'So when will you be home?'

'I'll definitely be back by six. At the latest. Let's have something light for dinner today, shall we? And we'll draw all the curtains and lock the doors and let no fucker cross the threshold.'

'Yes, and unplug the phone,' said Netta. 'Lobster. It's cheap now. The fresh American one they cook themselves on Borgmästargatan. I'll get it.'

'Fine,' said Olof. 'And champagne—only champagne. No syrupy cocktails. Put a couple more bottles in the fridge, please.'

He patted Netta on the cheek, which made her eyeliner slip and draw a dash up to her hairline.

'Look what you've done,' she said, but Olof was already on his way down the stairs.

'Good-bye,' he called. The front door slammed shut.

'Bye bye,' said Netta through gritted teeth, rubbing her temples with a cotton swab. 'Men.'

Since she could take the car and stay indoors for most of the day, Netta wore her short coat and, even though it seemed slushy outside, she pulled on her new, tall, mahogany-coloured boots with the high heels; they squeezed her toes a little but looked very chic.

On the way to Äppelviken, she went into the fish shop and bought two huge freshly cooked lobsters that she had wrapped up neatly and put them in the boot of the car.

The afternoon with her mother wasn't as dull as she had feared. Aunt Sara, a sprightly seventy-three-year-old, had met a man in Bologna and she told funny, self-deprecating stories about the two-week romance. And her mother was in a good mood for once and managed not to complain about anything; she handed round sherry and small pastries and even shared a couple of really quite funny stories about the love affairs of her youth.

When Aunt Sara had to go to meet a friend on Kungsholmen at five o'clock, Netta offered her a lift.

She dropped off her aunt at Fridhemsplan and squeezed into the queue towards Vasterbron. It seemed to take an eternity to get over the bridge, but once she was on the other side, she saw that it was only ten past five. Despite the traffic, she should be home before six. And she was excused from cooking today, because they were having lobster.

The queue thinned out and the road looked dry, so she began to speed up as she went down on to Söder Mälarstrand.

Suddenly, as if from nowhere, something appeared in front of her. Something that glistened, and Netta stepped on the brakes, when she felt something hit the car and heard a rattling noise. The traffic light she had just passed had changed to red, so thankfully the road was clear behind her. She came to a stop and pulled up, with the right-hand wheels on the cycle lane, then got out of the car and began to jog back.

As she got closer, she saw what she had hit. There was an overturned shopping trolley on the carriageway, and a bent-over figure seemed to be struggling to turn it upright. Between the trolley and the gutter, some bottles and cans lay scattered. Netta saw that the traffic light was still red and she ran as best she could in her high heels to reach the trolley, tipped it right side up and had just enough time to bring it over to the sidewalk before the cars started coming. She even managed to kick away a few of the bottles lying in the middle of the road.

'How did that happen?' she asked the woman who was still bent over, gathering up bottles and cans and throwing them into the cart. 'You're not hurt, are you? I didn't see you or the trolley. It was suddenly just there.'

The woman put the last bottle in the cart and straightened up. She was wearing a big, bulky man's overcoat, and had a knitted grey cap pulled down to her eyebrows. On her feet, she had running shoes which had probably been white once, and a couple of strange blue plastic bags wrapped around her ankles.

'Well, I'm okay. Just bashed my knee a little when I fell over, I was terrified, but it's not too bad. And the trolley's sorted.'

'I don't understand how I didn't see it,' said Netta.

'I was standing there waiting to cross when, well, it just slipped away from me and began to roll by itself. God, I was scared. I thought the car would skid. But it seems you're a good driver.'

'Oh, Jesus, that could have gone badly. But no harm done, luckily,' said Netta, looking back at her car. She hoped the paint hadn't been scratched, but the bumper had probably taken most of the force.

Then she saw that the woman, who was a head—or rather a high heel—shorter than Netta, was staring at her strangely. She gaped, mouth open so Netta could see that some of her lower teeth were missing. The woman pointed at her and said:

'It's never Netta? Agneta Ljung?'

Netta stared back. How could this person know who she was?

'Ye-es,' she said hesitantly. 'That's me. But how...?'

'Yeah, long time, no see,' said the woman. 'Girls' School. We were in the same class. Don't you remember me? Blomman. Rut Blomberg.'

In Netta's mind, she saw a round, cheerful girl with rosy skin and curly hair and ugly, ill-fitting clothes.

'Blomman,' she said in amazement. 'Is that true? Is it really you?'

She couldn't help sounding slightly incredulous.

'Yes, like I said,' said Blomman. 'Long time, no see. What are we now? Fifty-five, huh? Almost forty years since we finished school. People change over such a long time. Well, not you, of course. Not much. You look quite similar. And the fancy clothes, you were like that back then.'

She looked at Netta with a small smile that made her vaguely recall the girl she once was.

'Come to my place,' said Blomman. 'I live here. On the boat over there.'

'No, I have to go home,' said Netta.

'Just for a little while. I have to look at my knee. See if it's bleeding. Come along for a bit.'

Netta hesitated. What did she have in common with this swamp person, other than the fact that they had gone to the same school about a hundred years ago? But at the same time she was curious about Blomman. And she had never met anyone who lived on a boat.

'Go on,' she said. 'But just five minutes. My husband gets worried if I get home too late. But okay. For a bit.'

Netta didn't know what she had been expecting, but was surprised how pleasant it seemed in the cabin of the tugboat. Almost cosy, though the bedclothes looked extremely tatty: a dirty quilt with several holes from cigarette burns and a scuzzy pillow with no pillowcase. Netta thought of her own scented linen closet.

'I don't have much to offer you' said Blomman. 'Perhaps a cup of tea?'

'No, I don't want anything at all. Let me see your knee.'

Blomman unbuttoned her coat and rolled up her trouser leg. She had two pairs of tracksuit bottoms on, and the outer one at least was worn smooth and blotchy. Her knee was a little swollen and a large blue-brown mark spread out below the kneecap, but the skin wasn't broken. Blomman pulled down the trouser leg again and said:

'Do you have a cig?'

'Sure. We'll have a smoke and then I have to go.'

She gave Blomman a cigarette and lit it for her.

'How did you end up like this? I mean...'

'I know what you mean. Do you remember how I was expelled in the sixth grade because I got pregnant?'

Netta didn't remember. She had left school herself then, to go to sixth form somewhere else. But she said nothing.

'Yeah, to cut a long story short, I had the baby. Svenne did a runner and the kid was adopted. Then I had some tough years, worked a bit here and there, got pregnant again. Obviously, that guy did a runner, too, and the baby was stillborn. Yes, we can skip over all that. I married a guy called Sture who drank, so I started drinking too, to get through it all. He hit me as well, and it took several years before I finished with him. Then things were calm for a while, I worked at the hospital and had a place to live, but I'd acquired a taste for alcohol, as they say, so I lost the job. Started hanging out with drunks, rowdy types, you know, so in the end I was evicted. And that's how it went. I'm just borrowing the boat. In a month or so I'll have to leave here too. That's my life story—the short version. But I feel better now. Don't drink so much. Still, it's natural to long for an orderly life; a house and so on. Sure, I can hardly hope for a job at my age. Do you work, by the way, or are you just married?'

Netta felt like she belonged to a different world when she listened to Blomman's depressing story.

'Yes, I work. In an ad agency. Writing texts and so on. But can't you ask for help? Benefits...' said Netta, breaking off. She realised her knowledge of such things was very limited.

'No, I don't want anything to do with the authorities. Had enough of them. You don't get much help and once you've been evicted, you never get a house again. No, I can manage by myself.'

Netta didn't know what to say. This was a part of life she never even wanted to think about. She just wanted out of this misery. It didn't concern her.

'Well, I have to go now so Olof doesn't worry,' she said, and hoped that Blomman wouldn't ask where she lived or for her phone number.

'Sure, I get it,' said Blomman. 'I'll see you out.'

Netta put her pack of cigarettes on the table.

'Take them. If you forgot to buy some,' she said, and felt stupid.

They went out of the cabin and were hit by an icy wind from Riddarfjärden. It was a starry night, but with no moon and it was dark out here on the quay where the glow of the streetlights did not reach.

Blomman walked down the short iron ladder to the deck and Netta followed close behind.

'Watch your step,' said Blomman. 'It's slippery.'

At that moment, Netta's heel got stuck and she stumbled forward, reached out to grab a railing, but she was groping in thin air and fell against Blomman and Netta heard a splash before she fell face down on the icy steel deck, and it was a long time before she realised that Blomman had fallen overboard.

Netta crawled up onto her knees and now she saw that the rail, which ran along the side of the boat, stopped at the edge of the raised deck, and there was no protection. She held onto one of the posts and leaned forward, but saw only black water which foamed and crashed against the outside of the boat and splashed icy cascades across her face.

In the end, she got up and came over to the quay where the trolley stood with its cargo of bottles and cans. Netta passed by it to get to her car and sat down behind the wheel.

She was shaking all over, she didn't know if it was down to the cold or shock, or both, but she wiped her face with a handkerchief and fixed her hair and sat there until the shaking stopped.

She knew that there was nothing to be done. Or to be said; not even to Olof.

No one would know.

Blomman hadn't been around for forty years—she had suddenly been around for twenty minutes—and now she was gone again.

That's just how it was.

And the only thing Netta could do was drive home to Olof and eat lobster and drink champagne and lie down to sleep between smooth clean sheets, and what had happened wasn't real or even a bad dream.

The Ring

Michael Stanley

I guess some people are just nasty. Take Miss Joubert, for example. Her house is number fifteen in that big fancy complex on Fairfield Street. Rich people live there and they throw out lots of good stuff, so I get there early on Thursdays before the Pickitup people come through to collect. Some people are nice and put the good stuff separately, but most times I just have to dig through the bins to find the plastic and the cardboard and other things that I can sell. That's okay. I shake them off, squash them as flat as I can, and pack them into my trolley. It's a platform on wheels with sacking that can stretch up the sides, and by the time I'm finished with my rounds on a good day, it's almost as tall as me.

But Miss Joubert, she was different. First time I see her, she drives out of the electric gates in her fancy silver BMW and pulls over on the wrong side of the road next to me. I think maybe she has some food she doesn't want anymore. Sometimes people do that—give me half a loaf of old bread or something left over. But not her. She rolls down her window and starts going at me.

'What you doing in my garbage, hey? You leave that alone! It doesn't belong to you.'

I tell her I'm doing recycling, but she cuts me off. 'I left that out for the Pickitup people to take away. Till they do, it's mine. You leave it alone. *Voetsek*!'

I'm offended. I tell her I'm a licenced conveyer of recycling, and once her rubbish is on the street, it belongs to anyone who wants it. The business about the licence I make up, but she doesn't know that. Anyway, she's not impressed. She just swears at me and grabs a spray can from under the driver's seat—a big yellow can of Doom, like I'm an insect or something. I'm taking no chances, so I move away and start on another bin. She shouts at me again, and then drives off, so I go back to her bin. I don't know what all the fuss was about—all I get are some dirty cardboard boxes and some old fruit she threw out. Nothing good.

I see her again the next week, but by then I've found out her name. I asked Freddie—he's the gardener at the complex. He does a great job, place looks like a park. Not one of those Johannesburg city parks with weeds and rubbish, but really, really nice. Okay, he's not the brightest. You have to go slow with him, but he's a great gardener. It's his passion.

'That's Miss Joubert,' he tells me and makes a face. 'I don't like her. Always something wrong, always shouting at me. Says she's going to get me fired cause I'm a *moron*. What's a moron, Mr Malele?'

He always calls me Mr Malele. Nice and respectful of his elders.

'She told me to *voetsek*,' I tell him.

'I can't lose my garden. I just *can't*.' He looks like his mother just died.

'Hey, she can't do nothing to you, Freddie. You're black and disabled. Gold for them. And you do a great job. They'll *never* fire you.'

He nods doubtfully, still looking really unhappy.

Anyway, so when she drives up to me the next week, I'm going to sweet-talk her. Nice and polite. Get her on my side.

'Miss Joubert, ma'am,' I begin. 'I'm so sorry about our little misunderstanding—'

She doesn't even let me finish the sentence. She starts swearing at me and spraying Doom, so I have to run backwards. I trip over some bottles I'd taken from her rubbish, and only save myself by grabbing at a bin.

The next week I don't touch her bin till she's left, but when I dig in it there's a loud snap—gives me a fright, I can tell you—and I jerk my hand out. There's a *mousetrap* in there, brand new. No dead mouse. She put it in to get me, hid it under some newspaper. Like I said, a really nasty person. I got a nice price for that trap, though.

So, I'm nervous, right? Who knows what she's got in there this week? I even use old gardening gloves that I found in number thirteen's bin, but they're not much help. Full of holes and the fingers stick through. Anyway, this time right on top I find a clear plastic bag, and it's got a mask or something in it, all covered with red goo. So, I stand back and take a careful look. Could be black magic. Maybe she's a witch doctor. Maybe it's a curse. Maybe I should just leave her rubbish alone, after all.

Enoch is with me, and he's working the next bin. He's sort of my partner, more like an apprentice. People throw away a lot of good stuff and you have to get in early, so he helps me, and we move through the area much more quickly. And it's good to have two people pulling that trolley into town. Sometimes it's damn heavy up those hills around Melville *koppies*.

'What you found?'

'Nothing. I don't know.' He comes over anyway, takes a look, and jerks back.

'*Eish*,' he says, looking into the bin. 'It's covered in blood.'

'Don't be stupid. She's done that to scare us. Tomato sauce.'

Enoch looks relieved, sticks his finger into the red stuff, and takes a taste.

'Ugh!' He spits. 'Blood, definitely blood.'

Well, maybe it's a pig's head or something she's thrown out. Something really good. So, I pull it out and yank off the plastic bag. It's a head all right, but it's not from a pig. The head belongs to Miss Joubert.

I drop the head right away, and she's looking up at us from the top of the bin.

'We'll have to tell the cops,' Enoch says.

I shake my head. What's he thinking of? Our job is to *avoid* the cops. The cops' job is to make people like us *pay* them to leave us alone. If we tell the cops, it'll be expensive and take lots of time. Sometimes Enoch can be a bit like Freddie.

'No way. We just leave it.'

After a moment, Enoch gets it and nods. 'Put it back in the bag,' he says.

'What for?'

'Cause the Pickitup guys will see it for sure. And they know we go through these bins. And there's fingerprints and stuff.'

I think he's been watching too much *CSI* on TV, but he has a point. I reach into the trolley to get a bag and some newspaper.

'You guys find something?'

I nearly jump out of my skin, but it's just Freddie standing at the complex gate watching us.

'How's it, Freddie? No, nothing special. Just the usual.'

He nods, and gives me the smile. He has a smile to melt hearts, if he only knew it.

Just as I'm about to shove the head in the bag, I see something gold shining in the hair. Shit, it could be real gold. She seemed like a real jewellery sort of woman, what with that BMW and the Fairfield address. I know it's a mistake, but I can't stop myself. I yank it to get it off, and it comes away with some hair still stuck to it. I shove it quickly into my pocket so the others don't see, stuff the bag with the head under some cardboard, and wipe my hands on some newspaper. Waste of good paper, but I throw it on top of the bin, and say bye to Miss Joubert. No one's going to find her head, or Enoch's 'fingerprints and stuff,' in the middle of the rubbish dump, except maybe one of the wild dogs that hang around there. Then we hear the Pickitup truck in the next street, so we leave the rest of the bins in Fairfield unchecked and move on to Johannes Street.

Of course, we know who killed her—that serial killer. The Beheader, the newspapers call him, always leaving a quote from the Koran and a headless body. The cops think he takes the heads as trophies or uses them for black magic. I wonder if they've ever looked in the rubbish? Maybe too simple for them.

Anyway, we do the next street, but we're shaken up and slow. Funny thing. The Pickitup truck doesn't catch up to us. I have a bad feeling about that, and I'm right. Pretty soon we hear the sirens.

•••••

A good thing about the recycling business is that no one knows you. Maybe they see you every week, but most rich people don't take any notice of poor people digging through their garbage. Makes them feel uncomfortable. So even if they give us something, no one asks our names, or where we live, or who we are. We're like the beggars, or the parking guards who 'look after' your car while you're shopping—you just accept that's the way it is in Johannesburg.

That's what I tell Enoch. He's nervous about people knowing we went through that garbage before the Pickitup people got there. I tell him even the people who drove past wouldn't have noticed us, let alone remembered what we look like. But he says he's moving to Cosmos City.

'You mad? Those people aren't rich. They won't throw out good stuff. You'll starve.'

Turns out he has a second cousin there. He says maybe he'll leave Johannesburg altogether. I wish him luck and leave it at that.

When I have a chance, I take a quick look at the ring. It's really big, a heavy gold band. I can't remember her fingers, but I think maybe it wasn't hers. That gives me a funny feeling. Maybe it was the man's ring, and it got tangled in her hair when he cut off her head. Suddenly I'm not sure that selling it would be such a good idea.

That night it's hard to sleep. I share a few *Klippies* and coke with Miriam, but brandy doesn't really relax me. Makes me more alert, gets my mind working, but I eventually doze off.

In the middle of the night I'm thirsty and sweating

from nasty dreams—men after me swinging axes, blood everywhere. I think I'll never get back to sleep because of Miriam's snoring, but I do.

I wake up screaming with my eyes stinging. The dream was so clear I remember it like it was real. It was Miss Joubert, stark naked, holding a can of Doom, and walking towards me. She was saying that I'd stolen her ring and I'd better give it back. I don't know how she talked or how I knew who she was since she had no head. But I did. Then she sprayed me in the face with the Doom.

Miriam sits up and looks at me. 'You and *Klippies* don't mix.'

'What time is it?'

'It's going on five.'

She goes to make the coffee. A good woman, that Miriam.

The next week when I'm back in Fairfield Street, there's a car parked outside the complex. A coloured guy gets out and comes over to me.

'You Malele?' He lights a fag and offers me one. Why not? I thank him, and he lights me up. You never find fags in the rubbish, just *stompies* where you can maybe dig out bits of unburnt tobacco. Maybe ten of them gives you a roll-your-own. So we smoke for a bit, and I wonder what he wants. Like I said, no one stops to talk to recyclers.

Turns out he's a cop—Captain Willemse—but he's not after money, and so right away I know I must be careful. He wants to know about last week.

'No, sir, I saw nothing. We were a bit late starting so we skipped this street and went straight from Kessel to Johannes.'

Why miss out the best street? he wants to know. And who was this 'we'?

I take a long drag while I wonder how I managed to slip up twice in one sentence when I was being careful. I also realise this guy isn't stupid.

I shrug. 'Us recyclers. Sometimes we do that. Work every other street. Others come behind us later. Share, you know?' I can see he doesn't believe me. Shit.

'So you weren't even in Fairfield Street?' He gives me a hard look. 'You heard about the Beheader murder here, didn't you? You know the Pickitup people found the victim's head in the rubbish in this street? They don't know which bin it was in because it fell out of a bag only when they got to the end of the street. You know nothing about that?'

The victim? Hard to think of Miss Joubert as a victim, but I guess that's what she was. I nod firmly. 'Like I told you.'

He gives me another long, hard look. 'So, you won't mind coming down to the Fairlands police station and giving a statement. And we'll take fingerprints. Just to eliminate you.'

Shit. Maybe Cosmos City has possibilities after all.

'Sure,' I say. 'Let me finish my rounds, and I'll come over there.'

But Willemse wasn't born yesterday. 'We'll do it now. Get in the car.' There's an anger in his voice that I don't understand. Like I insulted him. I don't like it one bit.

And I have to get rid of that ring. It seems to be weighing down my pants.

• • ● • •

I asked Freddie to watch my trolley, but that was the day gone. After I'd given the statement, and they'd taken pictures and fingerprints, they let me go but I knew I was in trouble. I was pretty sure that between the plastic bags and the newspaper I'd used to wipe my hands, they were going to match my prints. I wish I'd watched more *CSI*.

Freddie had my trolley safe inside the gate and had even collected some bits of plastic and bottles for me. I'm wondering how Willemse knew me, but Freddie has the answer to that.

'He asked me who looks through the bins, so I told him you and Enoch come every week.'

Not like Freddie to be so chatty. He's *really* shy with strangers. 'You know this guy?'

'He's here sometimes.'

For a moment, I don't get it. 'You mean even before the murder?'

Freddie nods.

'Why?'

'Miss Joubert. He visits there sometimes.'

After a while I close my mouth because it looks funny open, and Freddie's starting to grin. But my mind is really working on this now.

'He was here Wednesday a week ago?'

Freddie thinks for a bit and shakes his head. 'I'm not so good remembering, Mr Malele.'

'He comes during the day or at night?'

Freddie shrugs. 'Sometimes.'

I'm thinking about the ring, and now I'm sure it's a man's ring. And I'm thinking that a wedding ring is tight and doesn't slip off that easily. But maybe a man will take it off if he's visiting a woman. A woman who's not his wife.

'The chairman was just around, Mr Malele. He said I

was doing a really nice job with the garden. He took me round to his own house and I planted some things for him there. He was very happy.' Freddie gives me that special smile of his.

•••••

Right away I call Enoch and tell him the whole story. He's not happy.

'You been following what the news says? The police aren't sure this is the Beheader at all. No Koran verse. They think it could be a copycat.'

This is supposed to make me feel better? Shit.

'I'm thinking about the cop, Enoch. He knows her. Maybe he was with her that night, maybe she was trying to blackmail him. Who knows? She wasn't a nice person.'

Enoch says nothing for so long, I wonder if I've lost the signal. 'Really? A cop? I don't know. But if it's not the Beheader, they need another killer, and your prints and DNA and stuff are all over.' Some more silence. 'I've got family at home in Zululand. I'm going to head down there. Do me a favour. Take my number off your phone.'

That's it. Cuts me off. Doesn't even say good-bye.

I'm left looking at my phone and wondering what I do next.

•••••

I decide I'd better come clean. Keeping out of trouble is one thing, being a murder suspect is something else altogether. And I'm thinking that maybe I'm getting too worked up about the Willemse story. So, he knew Miss Joubert. So, he visited her. Maybe he even slept with her.

Lots of guys cheat on their wives. That doesn't make them murderers, does it? Although I'm guessing Willemse's boss would be pretty unhappy if he knew about it.

So, I go back to Fairlands Police Station, and tell them I want to add to my statement, and they take me in to Willemse. He looks at me like I'm something straight out of one of the bins I go through, but he digs out my statement from his drawer and shoves it over his desk to me.

'Okay, you going to tell me the truth this time?'

But I don't say anything. I'm looking at his hands resting on top of my statement. He's got big hands, big hands and thick fingers. And the ring finger of his left hand has a deep mark running round it, like a ring was there and it was too tight.

'Well?'

'I changed my mind,' I say. 'It's not really that important.' I get up to go, but he's much too quick for me. He looks pretty bulky blocking his office door.

'You're not going anywhere, Malele. Sit down!'

He grabs my arm and yanks me back to his desk. I'm starting to sweat, and I'm not feeling good at all. How am I going to get out of this? But right then I get a bit lucky. The door opens, and a black man in a smart uniform comes in. I wonder if I can sneak out past him, but I don't fancy my chances of getting very far.

'This the suspect?' says the new guy, looking at me. 'I told you I wanted to be in on this one.'

'He just came in voluntarily, sir.'

I'm adding this up very quickly. I'm a suspect, and I was lucky I came in myself or otherwise Willemse would've been out looking for me. I might just've had an accident 'resisting arrest.' Also, Willemse called the new guy 'sir,' so maybe I've got a chance.

'Excuse me, sir,' I say to new guy, 'I do have important information, sir. I'd be happy to make a full statement. To *you*, sir.'

New guy gives me another look and turns back to Willemse. 'Bring him to the interview room. We'll talk to him there.'

Willemse says, 'Yes, Colonel,' but he doesn't look pleased at all. I let out my breath.

It wasn't quite what I wanted. I didn't want to be talking in front of Willemse, but beggars can't be choosers.

So, I tell them what really happened that Thursday morning. Every single thing, except for the ring and Enoch. Why get him into the same mess I'm in?

Willemse glares at me. 'You pig! That's exactly the story you'd give us if you *had* killed her. To explain why your fingerprints are all over everything.'

I wait a few seconds, then I ask him if he lost his wedding ring. He glances at his left hand and tells me to shut up, but the colonel wants to know why I asked.

So, I tell them Freddie's story—he'll also be for it, I guess, and I feel bad about that, but I'm getting desperate now. Willemse tries to interrupt but the colonel shuts him up with one hand wave. When I'm finished, they both look like they're going to explode. I hope I'm far away when it happens. But when the colonel speaks, it's to Willemse and real soft. Like a snake.

'Is this true?'

'Well, yes, sir. I visited the lady a few times, but—'

'And the wedding ring?'

'Yes, I must have lost it. Probably at home somewhere.'

So, I play my last card. I fish the ring out of my pocket and put it on the table. 'I found it.'

The whole thing is almost worth it just to see Willemse's face. Almost.

'Is that it?' the colonel asks Willemse.

Willemse doesn't answer right away. 'It could be. Where the hell did you steal it from you little—?' Again, the colonel shuts him up. He picks up the ring and looks at it carefully. 'The hair's *tied* to it,' he said Shit, I never looked that closely.

'Where did you find this?'

'It was in her hair. It must've got tangled up in it. I thought it was hers, and she didn't need it no more.'

I guess that wasn't the right thing to say. The explosion took place, and I'd been right to hope that I'd be far away, but I wasn't. It was three days before they let me go, and they're still holding charges of stealing evidence and lying to the police over my head. They found a lot of fingerprints in the apartment but not mine, and no one could suggest how I'd get through the security. Then, I had no motive. Break in and kill someone for a ring I didn't even know was there? And Miriam stuck by me. I was with her all that night.

I didn't see Willemse again after that interview with the colonel, but when I leave, another coloured policeman grabs me and pushes me against a wall. Hard.

'Captain Willemse's been suspended you filthy *skelm*, because of you. He's got a wife, and he was with her the whole night. He's worth fifty of you, and a lot of us feel that way. If anything bad happens to the captain, you'd better be watching your back. All the time.'

To drive home the point, he knees me in the balls and leaves me collapsed on the ground. So much for being a good citizen and telling the truth. As I limp off, I console myself by wondering if Mrs Willemse will stick to her story once she hears about where her husband left his wedding ring, and why he took it off in the first place.

•••••

The next Thursday I make a point of chatting to Freddie. I'm guessing he's also had a pretty tough time. All thanks to me.

I find him at the outside tap washing a *panga*, too heavy for a garden tool—more like what you'd use for cutting sugar cane.

'Hello, Freddie. You okay?'

He looks up and nods. 'Hello, Mr Malele. I'm fine. The chairman likes me. And Miss Joubert is gone. My garden is really happy now.' He gives me the big smile.

'Police didn't give you a hard time?'

He shakes his head slowly. 'They had *lots* of questions. About you. About Mr Willemse. I just told them everything true, if I remembered it. And they wanted to know who else I've seen here. I told them about lots of people. Keep them really busy, I guess.' He chuckles. 'They asked me about why my fingerprints were inside Miss Joubert's unit. I told them I help Cynthia—she's Miss Joubert's maid—with windows and stuff when I'm not busy.' He nods a few times. 'That's just what I said. I help with windows.'

I'm thinking about the ring again. Can't seem to get it out of my mind. How Willemse swore he lost it, how Freddie helps Cynthia clean, and how it was *tied* into Miss Joubert's hair.

'Freddie,' I ask before I can stop myself, 'What were you doing that night?'

He frowns, and it's a few moments before he replies.

'They also wanted to know if I let anyone through the gate that night. I told them that I'm not so good at remembering things. But maybe I could remember someone, Mr Malele. Maybe I could remember you.' He's not smiling anymore. 'Got to get back to the tools now. Really important to keep your garden tools clean and sharp, you know that, Mr Malele.'

The *panga*'s all covered in soil. It looks like he's been using it to dig a hole or like it's been buried. What the hell does he need a *panga* for, anyway? He never lets a weed grow to more than a centimetre high.

As he washes it, the water starts to run off a bit pink.

I'm thinking about Freddie and his garden and his *panga*. I'm thinking about Willemse and those coloured policemen and their fists. I'm thinking about Enoch in Zululand, and how I still have his number—I never took it off my phone. I'm thinking how it's nice and warm down there in Zululand. Miriam hates the cold, and the winter's coming on.

The Five-Letter Word

Andrew Taylor

It was the old trick with the weedkiller.

'Hooligans,' went on Mrs Paynton, breathing heavily. 'Teddy Boys. It's all of a piece.'

She had a quiet voice, rather monotonous but not unpleasant, with a touch of Yorkshire in it. Richard Thornhill had to stoop towards her to catch what she was saying.

'This sort of thing never happened before the war. My husband used to say that since the Labour government ruined everything, it's become a case of spare the rod and spoil the child.'

They were standing on the paved area outside the French windows. Chief Inspector Richard Thornhill let his eyes travel down the sunlit lawn, past the circular rose bed to the offending word. The parched brown capitals were set off by the vivid green of the grass. Following a week's drought, it had rained in the night, and the garden looked freshly polished.

The strokes that made the letters were on average three or four inches broad, though the thickness varied.

Whoever had done it had probably used a watering can, and the width of the strokes varied according to the height of its rose from the ground. All in all, though, a neat job.

'That's all very well,' Mrs Paynton said with the air of one reaching her peroration, 'but the rest of us have to live with the consequences. Don't you agree, Mr Thornhill?' She bared her teeth at him in a smile and added, 'Or should I call you Inspector?'

'Whatever you like, Mrs Paynton.'

Sweat trickled down his neck and slipped under his collar. He was wearing a soft shirt, thank God, and open at the neck. Edith had wanted him to change before he went up to Mrs Paynton's, or at least to put on a tie, but she hadn't been in a position to exert too much pressure. It was Sunday morning, and he was off duty. He was doing Edith a favour, and they both knew it.

'Have you any idea who could have been responsible?' he asked.

'It must be Michael,' Mrs Paynton said, wrinkling her nose as if the name were an unpleasant bodily function. 'Who else could it be?'

'I don't know,' Thornhill said, choosing to take the question literally. 'Who's Michael?'

'Mrs Franks's gardener. Well, not what I'd call a gardener.' She waved her gloved hand, dismissing Mike's horticultural skills. 'I don't know if he's actually a Teddy Boy but I wouldn't be at all surprised. He certainly qualifies as a hooligan in my book.'

Mrs Paynton was still in the clothes she had worn to church. She was a sturdy woman and the material of her dress pressed tightly against her, imprisoning her body. She tilted her head up to him. Her forehead was damp with perspiration under the brim of her hat. Her face needed powdering.

'He didn't work for you, then?' Thornhill asked.

'Only for a short while. Mrs Franks mentioned him, you see. He did a few hours a week for her after Mr Franks died—the heavy pruning, the lawn and so on—and she said he was quite good. So when we moved here in March, he turned up on the doorstep one afternoon and asked if I'd like him to carry on. I said yes—after all, it wasn't as if he was a complete stranger, and we needed someone to tide us over.'

'But he wasn't much good?'

'That's one way of putting it. Mrs Franks said he was a good worker, but I'm afraid I can't agree with her. I made the mistake of asking him to do the wisteria on the back wall. Never again. Anyway, he should have done the winter pruning back in January. Of course Mrs Franks is in her seventies now, and I don't think her eyesight's what it was. Nor her memory, come to that, poor lady. And of course it's not that long since her husband died, and that can shake you up terribly. Don't get me wrong' —here Mrs Paynton's gloved hand patted the well-upholstered spot that, roughly speaking, concealed her heart from the vulgar gaze—'I know that from experience. When poor George passed away, I thought I'd never recover. But you simply can't let yourself go when you have a child to consider, can you, particularly when that child has lost her father?'

Thornhill allowed himself to be swept along, an unregarded twig in the current of Mrs Paynton's existence. It would please Edith if he stayed a little longer. When his wife had returned from church this morning, clad in the shining armour of her Sunday best, she told him that she had promised Mrs Paynton he'd come and see her at once. Edith wanted to oblige her new acquaintance.

The Payntons lived near the Jubilee Park at the upper, more expensive end of Victoria Road. The Thornhills lived at the lower end. Edith had mentioned them to her husband on several occasions since they had moved in. She knew for a fact that Mrs Paynton had bought the house outright before they had sold their old house in Bradford. Mother and daughter came to St John's, and Mrs Paynton had made an impressive donation to the spire restoration fund. Mr Paynton, she gathered, had been something very senior in insurance.

That was why Edith had volunteered her husband's services when Mrs Payton mentioned that her lawn had been wilfully damaged while she and her daughter had been away. Edith was not a snob in the old sense of the word but she was a realist. She had a healthy respect for money.

'It's disappointing. I can't pretend it isn't.' Mrs Paynton's hat dipped from side to side as she shook her head in sorrow. 'You expect this sort of thing in a city—it's one of the reasons we moved from Bradford. I thought it would be different in Lydmouth. Such a nice little town.' Her lips formed an inverted U to indicate sadness, a mannerism that might have been charming when she was a girl. 'But this never happened to us in Yorkshire.' She stared at the five-letter word. 'And we had a much larger lawn there.'

Thornhill absorbed what she was saying but, with a skill born of long necessity, his attention was following a parallel and far more interesting track. This weekend was the beginning of his leave. Seven days of sloth. At this very moment, the deck chair was waiting for him under the apple tree in the garden, with his book and the newspaper on the grass beside it. Edith and the girls would be in the kitchen or the scullery, doing the vegetables. The air would be full of the comfortable odours of roasting potatoes and a slowly cooking brisket of beef. Soon Edith would ask him to pour them both a small sherry, a recent innovation of hers.

God, he thought, I'm becoming middle-aged, and I like it.

'Does it happen often here?' Mrs Paynton asked, her voice sharper than before, as if she suspected his attention might be wandering.

'Does what happen?' he said, taken by surprise. He recovered swiftly. 'You mean the weedkiller? No, very rarely, since you ask. A friend in the army told me he'd seen it done in the barracks near Chepstow last summer. Someone didn't like the CO.' He nodded towards the letters and tried the effect of a smile. 'That one was rather worse than this.'

'It's no joking matter, Mr Thornhill. My daughter will be home soon. I really don't want her seeing this. Surely the police can do something?'

'I'm afraid there's not much we can do—not in the short term, at any rate.' Enough was enough, he decided, Edith could expect no more of him. 'Look, this really isn't my field, Mrs Paynton—and in fact I'm on leave. But if you let me use your phone, I can ring the station for you and have them send an officer round. He'll make a note of the details and take it from there.'

'You'll arrest Michael, won't you?'

'Why are you so sure he's responsible?'

Something like a blush appeared under the remaining powder on Mrs Paynton's face, creating a blotchy effect. 'I had to dismiss him a week or so ago. We had words and—and, well, he became rather heated. It was all rather unpleasant.'

'Why did you sack him?'

'His work wasn't up to scratch. I didn't like his manner, either. Very surly.'

'The constable will want to know all about him, I'm sure—his surname, where he lives, and so on.'

'But I've no idea where he lives. I suppose Mrs Franks would know. But she's in Bournemouth now, with her daughter.' Mrs Paynton moistened her lips and glanced at her watch. 'Oh, look at the time. Lunch will be ruined… and Sylvia won't be long now. I really don't want her seeing this. So unpleasant. We could dig it up, I suppose, though that would make a terrible mess of the lawn.'

'Better not,' Thornhill said. 'Let the constable see it as it is. I'm assuming you do want to report it?'

'That's what I'm doing,' she said pettishly. 'To you.'

'You'll need to do it officially, I'm afraid. I'm just advising.' He tried to make a joke of it. 'As you see, I'm not exactly dressed for work. Why not cover it up with some sacks or an old blanket? That would do for the time being.'

'Sacks? I suppose we might have some in there.' She gestured towards the garage, a freestanding building by the fence, set back from the house, with a short concrete drive leading up from the road to its double doors. 'Would you mind? I'm not really dressed for a garage. And it's rather grubby in there. We don't keep a car but the oil from Mr Franks's seems to have got everywhere.'

A thought occurred to him. It was none of his business but he found himself saying, 'Why didn't you notice this before? The letters must have been visible before today.'

'I told you—we've been away. Sylvia's not strong, and she's been off-colour because her dog ran away, so I took her down to a hotel on the Gower. Just for a few days. Nothing like sea air, is there? We only got back last night.'

Mrs Paynton glared at the five-letter word. 'I didn't see it until this morning. Luckily Sylvia's bedroom's at the front of the house. So she hasn't seen it.'

Thornhill glanced at his own watch. It was already half past twelve. If he didn't get a move on, he would be late for lunch.

'Please,' she said, fluttering gloved fingers close to his arm, threatening unwanted intimacy. 'It'll only take a minute. Sylvia will be back from Sunday School at any moment.'

He smiled and said of course he would. It would be churlish to refuse such a small request. Besides, he had young daughters of his own, and he wouldn't like them to come home and find that five-letter word on the lawn.

They walked slowly towards the house—Mrs Paynton wasn't built for haste—to collect the key. On the way they passed the rose bed and she threw it a glance.

'Just look at those weeds. What was Michael doing with his time?'

She collected the key from the kitchen. Thornhill followed her down the path to the garage. Dandelions and groundsel sprouted between the concrete slabs. They could do with some of that weedkiller.

The sun beat down on Thornhill's bare head and on Mrs Paynton's Sunday hat. The hat had a flower attached to its band, which bobbed up and down as she walked. Sherry, he thought, then the ritual of carving, then lunch itself. His mouth filled with saliva at the very thought of it.

Mrs Paynton led him to the garage's back door. She pushed the key into the lock and twisted it. She turned the handle and pulled. Nothing happened. The wood had warped and the door stuck. She tugged harder, but still the door resisted her.

'Let me,' Thornhill said.

At the same moment, Mrs Paynton tried again. The door flew open with such force that it took both of them by surprise. She recoiled and collided with Thornhill. The impact was padded but substantial, like a collision with an armchair. He staggered backwards and almost fell.

The smell swept out to meet them.

You never grow used to it, Thornhill thought, however often it comes your way. You can almost see it, as well as smell and taste it, like a cloud of flies shimmering in the air. More often than not, there are real flies as well. As there were here.

Retching, Mrs Paynton put on a surprising turn of speed and retreated to the relatively pure air near the rose bed. She stood with her back to the garage, her shoulders heaving.

Thornhill filled his lungs and covered his mouth and nose with a handkerchief. He stood in the doorway. Warm, fetid air brushed his cheek.

The garage was a solid affair built of brick, with a pitched roof open to the rafters and a metal window whose glass was opaque with dirt and cobwebs. There was no ventilation other than the open door.

The space around the walls was in the process of silting up with the debris that accumulates over the years in an outbuilding—a wheelbarrow, a lawn mower, a stepladder, a variety of tools and paintbrushes, cans, and packets. In the middle of the floor were rows of greasy planks running parallel to the garage doors. A previous owner had installed an inspection pit so he could tinker with the underside of his car.

Thornhill registered all this in a blink of an eye. The flies were hovering over something in the corner to his left. The wheelbarrow was there, propped against the back wall.

He lifted the barrow aside. There was a bundle of black fur on the floor. The flies swirled above it, making their sinister music.

For a long moment he stared at the small dog. It was a cocker spaniel, a bitch. It was lying on its back, its legs splayed as if waiting for someone to tickle its belly. Around its head was a puddle of vomit. Beside it were an empty bowl and a tin of Chappie lying on its side.

'Oh…' whimpered Mrs Paynton, appearing at his shoulder, with her hand over her mouth. She peered past him. 'It's—it's Flossie.'

He turned and pushed her gently back, into the garden. 'Your dog?'

'Yes. Is she…?'

'I'm afraid she's dead, Mrs Paynton.'

Her eyes widened. 'Here's Sylvia.'

Thornhill's first thought was that this couldn't be Sylvia. Mrs Paynton had talked of her daughter in a way that had led him to expect a fragile little thing wearing long white socks, aged somewhere between his own daughters.

The mention of Sunday School had reinforced this image. At the age of ten, his elder daughter, Elizabeth, had attended the St John's Sunday School, under protest, for a few months. She had made herself so objectionable about the experience that Edith had allowed her to leave.

Even now, Elizabeth was still a child, whatever she

herself might think. But Sylvia Paynton was a young woman. Like her mother, she was well-built, with a square, heavy-featured face. She was dressed conservatively for church and carried a Prayer Book in one hand and her handbag in the other.

'Hello, Mother,' she said as she came up the drive. 'I'm starving!' Her eyes flickered towards Thornhill. 'When's lunch?'

'It'll be a little late, dear,' said Mrs Paynton, advancing towards her child with her hands outstretched. 'I'm afraid something upsetting has happened...Our poor, poor Flossie.'

Sylvia stared blankly at her mother. 'Has she—has she come back?'

'Yes...in a way...I'm afraid she's dead.'

Sylvia's face was the colour of suet. Her eyes slid down to the right. 'But...but I don't understand.'

'Come into the house, darling.'

The girl licked her lips. 'Can't I see her and say goodbye?'

'Not now.' Mrs Paynton gestured at Thornhill. 'This is Inspector Thornhill. You remember nice Mrs Thornhill at church? He's her husband. He says it's better you don't see her, not just now. He needs to check one or two things.'

As she was speaking, she took her daughter by the elbow and urged her towards the back door. Thornhill shut and locked the garage door. He followed them.

At the house, Mrs Paynton glanced back at him. 'Probably best to leave us alone for a moment or two, Inspector. If you don't mind.' She lowered her voice. 'The poor thing is very sensitive. But please don't go.' Her eyes flickered. 'There's still this other matter.'

Thornhill's stomach rumbled. The possibility of his

being home for lunch had receded to the point of invisibility. He stood for a moment on the lawn, staring at the five-letter word, and then went back to the garage.

Once inside, with his handkerchief clamped over his mouth and nose, Thornhill walked slowly around the walls. The blades of the lawnmower were encrusted with dried grass. On the shelf above was an open bag of sodium chlorate. Beyond it was the watering can, still with half an inch of liquid in the bottom. There was a spade leaning on the wall. He crouched to examine it more closely. The iron blade was dark and pitted.

At last he looked directly at the spaniel's body. Her eyes were open. Rats and maggots had found her. One way or another, the dead become a feast for the living.

He touched the tin with his finger so he could look inside. There were maggots in there, too, feeding on what was left of the meat. Dislodging the tin also revealed a few grains of white powder on the floor.

Thornhill looked around the garage again. He let the handkerchief drop and sniffed. The smell made him almost lightheaded. Or was it the hunger? How much smell did one dead dog make?

Desperate for fresh air, he went back outside. Mrs Paynton was by the back door, smoking a cigarette. For a moment she didn't see him. He watched her jabbing the cigarette between her lips again and again, taking fast, jerky puffs, as if she couldn't inhale the tobacco fast enough.

When she saw him, she threw the cigarette away and almost ran towards him. 'I've put her to bed with a couple of aspirin and a hot-water bottle,' she hissed. 'I'll take her up some cocoa in a moment. The poor girl. She was already shattered, after helping with the Mixed Infants at Sunday School. And now this. How she loved that dog.

We both did.'

'Did you ever feed it in the garage?'

'Flossie? No—in the back porch.'

'Someone fed her in the garage. A tin of Chappie.'

She swallowed. 'You don't think…?'

'What?'

'That Michael might have…poisoned her?'

He shrugged. 'When did you last see her?'

'Ten days ago? Two weeks? I reported it to the police a day or two later.'

'May I use your phone?' Thornhill said.

'Of course.' Mrs Paynton took a shuddering breath. 'You mean it was Michael all the time? And he killed her with the same weedkiller he used on the lawn? The wicked, *wicked* man.'

•●⬤●•

The ting of a bicycle bell announced the arrival of reinforcements. PC Porter was at the gate. Thornhill beckoned him into the drive.

Porter propped his bicycle against the side of the house. He was a large young man with a face like a ham.

'Sergeant Kirby's on his way up, sir,' he said. 'And Sergeant Fowles said he'd ring Mrs Thornhill and tell her not to wait lunch.'

Thornhill nodded to the garage. 'There's a dead dog in there. Stinks to high heaven.' He pointed to the five-letter word on the lawn. 'And someone got trigger-happy with the weedkiller over there. Do you have a torch on you, by any chance?'

'No, sir.' Porter patted his tunic pockets. 'I've got some matches.'

'They'll do. Cover your nose and mouth when we go in.'

Thornhill unlocked the door. When they were both inside, he locked it behind them. Porter stared at the dog.

'I want to have a look down there,' Thornhill said, pointing at the planks over the inspection pit. 'Give me the matches, will you?' Then, as it was never wise to take anything for granted with Porter, 'Don't touch anything unless I tell you.'

Whoever had built the pit had done a tidy job. The planks were flush with the surrounding concrete floor and butted neatly against its edges. Near the back door, however, the concrete frame was indented, to simplify the removal of the two end planks.

Thornhill crouched at one end and gestured to Porter to do the same at the other. They lifted out the first two planks.

How much smell did one dead dog make? Was the smell worse now? It was hard to tell.

Thornhill took out a match. Porter's heavy breathing was as loud as the buzzing of the flies. The match scraped along its box. He cupped the flame and lowered it into the cavity below the planks. He opened his hands and the fitful light filled some of the darkness below.

It bounced back from the dull chrome of a handlebar, and briefly illuminated fabric, probably Army surplus khaki. The match burned his fingers and went out. A few sparks fell into the pit.

He lit another match. This time he glimpsed the pale blur of what had once been a face at the far end of the pit. There was a faint, frantic rustling as at least one small creature scurried away from the light.

Thornhill's stomach lurched. Oh, yes, he thought. The dead are a feast for the living.

•••••

It was stifling in here. The station was wrapped in its Sunday calm. The clock on the wall ticked away, relentlessly marking the passage of time towards an unknown destination.

Through the open door of his room, Thornhill stared the length of the CID Office. Vacant chairs waited beside desks heaped with files and family photographs. The ashtrays were clean. The wastepaper baskets were empty. The office looked unreal, which matched the way he was feeling.

His in-tray was full. While he was waiting he should do something useful with the time. But he couldn't be bothered. Perhaps he was sickening with something. That would be all too typical at the beginning of a week's leave.

Thornhill closed his eyes, shutting out the CID Office. He tried to match the evidence so far with the possibilities, to make logical or at least probable connections between them. But heat and hunger turned his mind into a murky liquid where indistinct shapes swam like carp in a pond. Rational thought was out of the question.

The phone jangled on his desk. He seized the receiver. The Bradford CID sergeant he had talked to half an hour earlier had checked the files for the Payntons.

'They were here right enough, sir,' the sergeant said. A match flared at the other end of the line. There was a pause and then: 'I remember hearing about the case. Chichester Gardens. The neighbour complained. Never went to court or anything.'

'What happened?'

Another match. Another pause, filled with a faint popping sound as the man at the other end on the line sucked on his pipe. 'The neighbour claimed that the Paynton girl had been pestering her son—you know, like *that*—wanting to touch his, er, privates, trying to get him to touch hers. He was only about ten, and she was much older, sixteen at least. When he wouldn't do what she wanted, she went berserk, gave him a black eye, and chased him out of the garden. Can you beat it? Kids today…'

'Just happened the once?'

'As far as we know. But Mrs Paynton swore blind it was the other way round, that the boy had been playing Peeping Tom on the girl. What's her name?' A rustle of paper. 'Sylvia. They said the boy had made—and I quote—"a lewd suggestion" to her and called her rude names when she wouldn't do what he wanted.'

'So it was their word against the neighbour's,' Thornhill said, 'but it was the neighbour who complained.'

'Aye. That says something. Even talking to us shows how desperate things had got.' Yet another match, yet another pause. 'A warning shot, maybe? Neither of them really wanted it to come to court. But that's Chichester Gardens for you. Keep themselves to themselves up there. Posh folk. They don't like washing dirty linen in public if they can help it.'

'Thanks. That's very helpful.'

'Have the Payntons been up to something on your patch, sir?'

'You could say that,' Thornhill said. 'By the way, do you happen to know if they had a dog? A cocker spaniel bitch.'

'No. It was the other way round.'

'What do you mean?'

'The dog was the neighbour's. Sylvia made a fuss of it. She asked the boy to bring it round so they could all play together.' There was a strangled sound that might have been a laugh at the other end of the line. 'But Sylvia wanted to play a different sort of game.'

Thornhill thanked him and put down the phone. He glanced at the clock: gone half-past four already. He picked up the phone again and dialled the Deputy Chief Constable's home number. Drake, the DCC, answered on the second ring and, brushing aside Thornhill's apologies, asked why he was ringing up, when he was meant to be on leave.

Thornhill told him. 'A hard one to prove, sir,' he finished. 'I know that. But—'

'Let me get this straight: you think Mrs Paynton sacked the young gardener because the daughter tried to get too friendly with him, and so he pulled that stunt with the sodium chlorate on the lawn as a parting message, and used the same stuff to poison their dog? Then the girl killed him—perhaps slugged him with a spade—because he'd turned her down. Then she hid his body and his bike in the pit.'

'I know it sounds weak, sir, but it sounds like the girl's got form, one way or another. And the mother has too, for covering up what her daughter does.'

'Why would Mrs Paynton call you in?' Drake went on, as relentless as Fate. 'If what you say is right—and it's a big If—surely it would have been better to leave the gardener's body where it was, and fill up the pit.'

'What if the mother didn't know?'

'Know what?'

'About anything, apart from that five-letter word on the lawn. I think she was telling the truth: she saw it only this morning and she told my wife about it at church. She just wanted to make trouble for Michael, the gardener. Otherwise, she wouldn't have let me go inside the garage in the first place. The dead dog really took her by surprise. And she had no idea that Mike's body was in the inspection pit. You see, the smell of the dog covered up his smell.'

'Then why did you look down there?'

Thornhill hesitated. He had a headache. What was instinct? The sum of experience with the preliminary workings rubbed out of your memory? Had there been something about that heavy, suet-faced girl and the way she had looked down when she had asked to see the dog's body, as if she had already known that it was lying on the garage floor? Or perhaps it had been the nature of the smell itself. He said, 'The smell was too bad for just one little body.'

There was a silence at the other end of the line. Then Drake said: 'Why didn't the girl stop her mother from talking to you?'

'Sylvia didn't know about the word. Mrs Paynton had only just seen it on the lawn herself. Then she met my wife at church and acted on impulse.'

'Bitch,' Drake said, taking Thornhill by surprise. 'The gardener got that bit right, at least. Mind you, if what you say is right, I haven't got much sympathy for him.'

'Yes, sir.'

'The poor bloody dog. How the hell do you prove all this?'

'I don't know.' Thornhill paused, dabbing his forehead with his handkerchief. 'Yet. I need to think about that.'

'You think too much for a copper,' Drake said. 'I'll run over there now. Kirby's still at the house?'

'Yes, sir. And a couple of SOCOs. The doc's on his way. I'll meet you there.'

'No, you won't, Richard. I'll talk to you later.'

'But, sir—'

'You're on leave. Go home.'

The normality of it dropped over Thornhill like an old coat.

The smell of the Sunday roast coloured the kitchen. Edith was darning socks, sitting in the chair by the window. Their younger daughter, Susie, was at the table, laboriously colouring in a rainbow with bright waxy crayons that flaked on the page.

Edith looked up, needle in hand, smiling and raising her eyebrows. 'You were a long time.'

There was a question there. He glanced at Susie, then back to Edith. They both knew the answer to it would have to wait.

'You know how these things drag on,' he said, his voice carefully neutral. 'Hard to get away.'

He stared out of the window. Elizabeth, their elder daughter, was under the apple tree. She was sitting in his deckchair with a book on her lap, twisting her hair in the fingers of her left hand. His own book and the newspaper had gone.

'Have you eaten?'

Thornhill became aware of the gaping void inside him. He felt suddenly lightheaded. 'No.'

'I left yours in the oven,' she said. 'It'll have dried out. But I could warm it up again with some gravy.'

'It doesn't matter.' He was empty but he wasn't hungry. Not now.

'Or I could cut you something from the joint. There's quite a lot left.'

'Perhaps later.' His stomach lurched at the memory of what he had seen in the garage.

Edith put down her darning and stood up. 'You must have something. I'll put the kettle on.'

He followed her into the scullery.

Under cover of filling the kettle at the sink, she said, 'You look awful. And you were gone for ages. Was it bad?'

'Bad enough.'

'What was on the lawn?' She put the lid on the kettle. 'A four-letter word or something?'

'No,' he said. 'It had five letters.'

She lit the gas ring. 'It doesn't sound so very bad. Not in the grand scheme of things. So why were you so long?'

The door was open. Thornhill looked down the garden. Elizabeth, their elder daughter, threw her book on the grass with some force, as if it had suddenly offended her. She stood up and, still fiddling with her hair, stalked towards the house. Why? There were too many mysteries in his life.

'It wasn't just the five-letter word,' he said to Edith. 'It was what it meant.'

Afterword

It has been said that anthologies are not profitable enterprises. True or not, No Exit Press and Poisoned Pen Press generously agreed to publish this collection in the UK and U.S. respectively. All the royalties from this publication go to the Royal National Institute of Blind. We are also grateful to the exceptional contributors, and to Martin Edwards, one of the most respected anthology editors—and authors—in the business.

When it came to writing this afterword, I wasn't sure if it should be a brief history of CrimeFest for those who are unaware of what it is, or whether it should be a thank-you to those who have made the convention and this anthology possible. But when I started writing, it quickly became clear that the two are inextricably linked.

CrimeFest came about because of the one-off visit to the UK of the American crime fiction convention Left Coast Crime (LCC) in 2006. During a visit to Janet Rudolph's wonderful Berkeley reading group in California in 2004, one of the attendees mentioned that LCC was looking for people to organise the convention two years on. 'Would Bristol be of interest as a location?' I asked. 'But Bristol isn't on the left coast,' was an initial response. When I pointed out that it was on the left coast of England (and, arguably, Europe) and reminded them of the rich history of British crime fiction, the offer was quickly accepted. Not feeling able to take on the project by myself, I was very lucky that Myles Allfrey said it sounded like something he would be interested in. Even more fortunate was that Donna Moore, whom we invited as the UK Fan Guest of Honour, only agreed to accept if she could help. We asked Donna to do the programming, and Myles and I realise it was one of the best decisions we made. It was a huge relief when the 2006 Bristol Left Coast Crime was declared a great success, and that was supposed to be it. Done. Over. Except…

A few weeks later, Beverley Cousins, then Crime Fiction Editor at Penguin, asked if we had considered continuing the convention, as she could sign up half a dozen or more crime writers for less than the cost of sponsoring one at similar events, and colleagues at other publishers followed suit. At the same time, authors also requested we continue, as it was the only large-scale crime-writing event in the UK where a commercially published writer could have a panel without being invited. (To this day, that still seems to be the case.) Readers also asked if we were going to continue, as it had been the first convention since Dead on Deansgate in the nineties where all participants were able to celebrate crime fiction in a friendly, informal and—most importantly—inclusive atmosphere.

As we had enjoyed organising LCC, the calls to continue easily persuaded us. To avoid confusion with the ongoing U.S. convention, we relaunched the Bristol event as CrimeFest. Bill Selby amended his 2006 Skeleton Bob logo, and agreeing to return were Liz Hatherell, who has been in charge of the registration desk every year (as well as proofing the programmes with Thalia Proctor);

Jennifer Muller, who creates all the programmes; and Sue Trowbridge as the website mistress. And so the core team was formed.

In putting together LCC and CrimeFest, we received help from many people. The advice that LCC central committee members Enid and Tom Schantz, and Bill and Toby Gottfried, had for us was very helpful—Bill and Toby continue to be two of our most loyal attendees. Copied from LCC are trips, an idea from Dana Stabenow and her team for the 2001 Alaska convention, and which Nicky Godfrey-Evans of Tours of Discovery arranges on behalf of CrimeFest. Working with Janet Laurence when she chaired the first years of Dead on Deansgate inspired me to copy her organisational skills for CrimeFest. Basically we borrowed the best from the best.

Along the way there have been many other supporters. Barry Forshaw, Maggie Griffin, Peter Guttridge, and Maxim Jakubowski have advised us on, or helped us secure, some amazing authors. David Headley and Goldsboro Books have supported CrimeFest in many other ways as well, and it is fair to say that David and Edwin Buckhalter's involvement ensured the convention's continued existence. Add to these names the most recent benefactor and long-time delegate Jane Burfield, who also made this anthology possible.

Of course, we wouldn't have made it past year one without the ongoing support of authors and their agents, booksellers, publishers, and, most importantly, readers. The greatest thing about ten years of CrimeFest is the friendships that have been forged. This anthology is a thank you to all those friends.

Adrian Muller
CrimeFest co-host

Biographical Notes

Bill Beverly teaches at Trinity University in Washington, DC. His debut novel, *Dodgers* (No Exit Press), won the Gold Dagger and John Creasey New Blood Dagger from the CWA, the British Book Award, and the Los Angeles Times Book Prize. His dissertation on criminal fugitives became the book *On the Lam: Narratives of Flight in J. Edgar Hoover's America*.

authorbillbeverly.com

Simon Brett has published over a hundred books, many of them crime novels, including the Charles Paris, Fethering, Mrs Pargeter, and Blotto and Twinks series. His extensive comedy writing includes the series *After Henry*, which was successful on both radio and television. In 2014 he received the Crime Writers' Association's highest award, the Diamond Dagger, and in 2016 he was awarded an OBE for services to literature.

simonbrett.com

Lee Child has more than a dozen number-one best sellers under his belt. *Forbes* calls the Jack Reacher series 'The Strongest Brand in Publishing.' Not bad for a guy out of work and on the dole when he first conceived of being a writer. The fictional Reacher is a kind-hearted soul who allows Lee lots of spare time for reading, listening to music, Aston Villa, and the Yankees.

leechild.com

Ann Cleeves is the author of the Vera Stanhope and Shetland series, both of which have been adapted into acclaimed television dramas. She has written thirty-one novels and is translated into as many languages. In 2006 *Raven Black*, was awarded the Duncan Lawrie CWA Gold Dagger for Best Crime Novel, and in 2017, Ann received the Crime Writers' Association's Diamond Dagger.

anncleeves.com

Jeffery Deaver is an international number-one best-selling author who has written thirty-nine novels, three collections of short stories, a nonfiction law book, and is a lyricist of a country-Western album. He's received or been shortlisted for dozens of awards. His *The Bodies Left Behind* was named Novel of the Year by the International Thriller Writers association, and his Lincoln Rhyme thriller, *The Broken Window*, and a stand-alone, *Edge*, were also nominated for that prize.

jefferydeaver.com

Martin Edwards has published eighteen novels, including the Lake District Mysteries, most recently *The Dungeon House*. *The Golden Age of Murder* won the Edgar, Agatha, HRF Keating and Macavity awards. He has edited thirty-seven crime anthologies, is series consultant for the British Library's Crime Classics, and has won the CWA Short Story Dagger, the CWA Margery Allingham Prize, and the

Poirot award. He is president of the Detection Club and Chair of the CWA.

martinedwardsbooks.com

Catherine Edwards was born in Cheshire, and educated locally and at Lincoln College, Oxford, where she read German and Italian. A journalist, writer, and translator, she speaks five languages and lives in Stockholm, where she writes about European news, politics, and culture in her role as Europe editor at *The Local*, an online news network.

Kate Ellis was born and brought up in Liverpool. Described by *The Times* as 'a beguiling author who interweaves past and present,' she is best known for her DI Wesley Peterson series. She has been shortlisted for the CWA Short Story Dagger and for the CWA Dagger in the Library. Her first novel in a new trilogy set in the aftermath of World War I, *A High Mortality of Doves*, was published in 2016.

kateellis.co.uk

Peter Guttridge is a novelist, critic, writing teacher, and chairperson/interviewer at a wide range of literature festivals and events. He is a former director of the Brighton Literature Festival and the current co-director of Books by the Beach, the Scarborough Book Festival. For eleven years he was the *Observer* newspaper's crime fiction critic. He is the award-winning author of twelve novels, two works of nonfiction, and numerous short stories.

peterguttridge.com

Sophie Hannah is an internationally best-selling crime fiction writer. Her crime novels have been translated into thirty-four languages and published in fifty-one countries. In 2014 and 2016, Sophie published *The Monogram Murders* and *Closed Casket*, the first new Hercule Poirot mysteries since Agatha Christie's death, both of which were national and international bestsellers. Sophie is an Honorary Fellow of Lucy Cavendish College, Cambridge. She lives in Cambridge with her husband, two children, and dog.

sophiehannah.com

John Harvey has been a professional writer for more than forty years and his work has been published in over twenty countries. Winner of the CWA Short Story Dagger and the Silver Dagger for Fiction, in 2007 he was awarded the CWA's Diamond Dagger for sustained excellence in crime writing. In addition to his fiction and poetry, he has written for stage, radio, and television. He is the recipient of honorary doctorates from the Universities of Hertfordshire and Nottingham.

mellotone.co.uk

Mick Herron's novels include the Gold and Steel Dagger-winning Slough House series, about a bunch of messed-up spies. His work has been nominated for the Theakston, Macavity, Barry, and Shamus awards, and *Real Tigers* won the 2017 CrimeFest Last Laugh Award. His latest book is *London Rules*. He lives in Oxford and writes full-time.

mickherron.com

Peter James' Roy Grace detective novels have sold over nineteen million copies worldwide, have had twelve consecutive *Sunday Times* number-ones and are published in thirty-seven territories. Peter has won many literary awards, including the publicly voted ITV3 Crime Thriller Awards People's Bestseller Dagger, WH Smith readers' The Best Crime Author of All Time, and the Crime Writers' Association's Diamond Dagger Award.

peterjames.com

Donna Moore is the author of *Go to Helena Handbasket*—a spoof PI novel which won the Lefty Award for humorous crime fiction in 2007—and *Old Dogs*—a caper novel set in Glasgow (nominated for both Last Laugh and Lefty Awards). Her short fiction has been published in various anthologies. She works at Glasgow Women's Library and is currently studying for a PhD in Creative Writing at the University of Stirling.

Caro Ramsay's first novel, *Absolution*, was shortlisted for the CWA New Blood Dagger; her second, *Singing to the Dead*, was long-listed for the Theakston crime novel of the year. The tenth book in the Anderson and Costello series will be published in 2018. She has a diploma in forensic medical science and edited *The Killer Cookbook* for the Million for a Morgue campaign, which led to her having an embalming tank named after her.

www.caroramsay.com

Ian Rankin is the creator of John Rebus and has also written stand-alone novels. He has received four CWA Daggers, including the Diamond Dagger, as well as an Edgar, and awards in Denmark, France, and Germany. He lives in Edinburgh.

ianrankin.net

James Sallis is best known for the Lew Griffin series and *Drive*. He has published seventeen novels, multiple collections of stories and essays, four collections of poetry, three books of musicology, reams of criticism, a landmark biography of Chester Himes, and a translation of Raymond Queneau's novel *Saint Glinglin*. He's received a lifetime achievement award from Bouchercon, the Hammett award for literary excellence in crime writing, and the Grand Prix de Littérature Policière.
jamessallis.com

Zoë Sharp opted out of mainstream education at twelve and wrote her first novel at fifteen. An autodidact with a love of language, house renovation, and improvised weaponry, she writes the award-winning crime thriller series featuring ex-soldier-turned-bodyguard Charlotte 'Charlie' Fox, and various stand-alones, including collaborations with espionage author John Lawton. Lee Child said of Sharp: 'If I were a woman, I'd be Zoë Sharp, and if Jack Reacher were a woman, he'd be Charlie Fox.'
zoesharp.com

Yrsa Sigurðardóttir is an internationally best-selling crime writer from Iceland, published by Hodder and Stoughton in the UK. In 2015 she won the Petrona Award for Best Scandinavian Crime Novel and her novels have twice been selected by the *Sunday Times* as crime novel of the year. Her latest book out in the UK is *The Reckoning*, a novel considered amongst her best work. Yrsa is a civil engineer by trade and still works as such in her native Iceland.

Maj Sjöwall and Per Wahlöö (1926-1975) virtually created the modern detective novel. Their ten police procedurals about Martin Beck and his colleagues were written in the sixties and seventies, and the series amounts to a literary treasure, which has influenced countless contemporary authors.

Michael Stanley is the writing partnership of Michael Sears and Stanley Trollip. Their novels, featuring Detective Kubu, are set in Botswana, a fascinating country with magnificent conservation areas and varied peoples. The mysteries are set against current southern Africa issues, such as the plight of the Bushman peoples, the pervasive power of witch doctors, blood diamonds, the growing Chinese influence, and biopiracy. Their books have been shortlisted for many awards, including the CWA Debut Dagger, the Edgar, and the International Thriller Writers Award.

detectivekubu.com

Andrew Taylor has won the CWA Diamond Dagger, the Historical Dagger (three times), and other awards. His books include the international bestseller, *The American Boy*; the Roth Trilogy (filmed for TV as *Fallen Angel*); the Dougal series and the Lydmouth series; and, most recently, *The Times* number-one bestseller *The Ashes of London* and its sequel *The Fire Court*. He also reviews for the *Spectator* and *The Times*.

andrew-taylor.co.uk